EMPEROR
THE FIELD OF SWORDS

By Conn Iggulden

Emperor: The Gates of Rome
Emperor: The Death of Kings
Emperor: The Field of Swords

EMPEROR
THE FIELD OF SWORDS

Conn Iggulden

HarperCollins*Publishers*

HarperCollins*Publishers*
77–85 Fulham Palace Road,
Hammersmith, London W6 8JB

www.harpercollins.co.uk

Published by HarperCollins*Publishers* 2005
1 3 5 7 9 8 6 4 2

A catalogue record for this book
is available from the British Library

ISBN 0 00 713693 5
ISBN 0 00 719526 5 (trade pbk)

Typeset in Minion with Trajan display by
Palimpsest Book Production Limited, Polmont, Stirlingshire

Printed and bound in Great Britain by
Clays Ltd, St Ives plc

To my daughter Mia, and my wife Ella.

Part of the pleasure of writing a series of four books is being able to thank all those who need thanking before the story ends. Susan Watt is one of those – a great lady whose expertise and energy made the rough run smooth.

In addition, I would like to thank Toni and Italo D'Urso, who let me use the old Amstrad computer in their corridor for years and years without a word of complaint. Eventually, out of good manners, I married their daughter. I owe them.

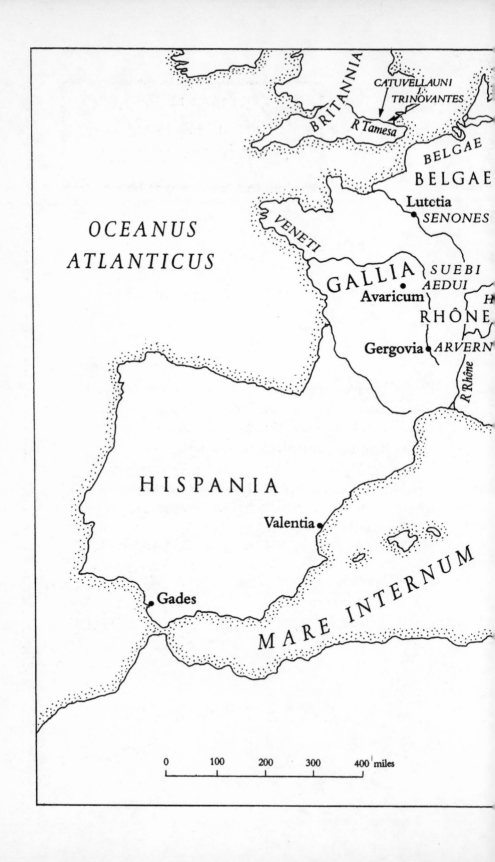

OCEANUS
ATLANTICUS

BRITANNIA

CATUVELLAUNI
TRINOVANTES

R Tamesa

BELGAE

BELGAE

Lutetia
SENONES

VENETI

GALLIA

SUEBI
AEDUI

Avaricum

RHÔNE

Gergovia

ARVERN

H

R Rhône

HISPANIA

Valentia

MARE INTERNUM

Gades

0   100   200   300   400 miles

THE ROMAN WORLD
IN THE TIME
OF JULIUS CAESAR

R Rhine

• Alesia

RHINE

VETII

• Mutina

Ariminum

Corsica

Rome
• Ostia

• Corfinium

SARDINIA

Sardinia

Brundisium

Dyrrhachium
Apolloniae
Oricum

Pharsalus •

Athenae

SICILIA

MARE INTERNUM

Cyrene

PART ONE

CHAPTER ONE

꧁꧂꧁꧂꧁꧂

Julius stood by the open window, gazing out over Spanish hills. The setting sun splashed gold along a distant crest so that it seemed to hang in the air unsupported, a vein of light in the distance. Behind him, the murmur of conversation rose and fell without interrupting his thoughts. He could smell honeysuckle on the breeze and the touch of it in his nostrils made his own rank sweat even more pungent as the delicate fragrance shifted in the air and was gone.

It had been a long day. When he pressed a hand against his eyes, he could feel a surge of exhaustion rise in him like dark water. The voices in the campaign room mingled with the creak of chairs and the rustle of maps. How many hundreds of evenings had he spent on the upper floor of the fort with those men? The routine had become a comfort for them all at the end of a day and even when there was nothing to discuss, they still gathered in the campaign rooms to drink and talk. It kept Rome alive in their minds and at times they could almost forget that they had not seen their home for more than four years.

At first, Julius had embraced the problems of the regions and hardly thought of Rome for months at a time. The days had flown as he rose and slept with the sun and the Tenth made towns in the wilderness. On the coast, Valentia had been transformed with lime and wood and paint until it was almost a new city veneered over the old. They had laid roads to chain the land and bridges that opened the wild hills to settlers. Julius had worked with a frenetic, twitching energy in those first years, using exhaustion like a drug to force away his memories. Then he would sleep and Cornelia would come to him. Those were the nights when he would leave his sweat-soaked bed and ride out to the watch posts, appearing out of the darkness unannounced until the Tenth were as nervous and tired as he was himself.

As if to mock his indifference, his engineers had found gold in two new seams, richer than any they had known before. The yellow metal had its own allure and when Julius had seen the first haul spilled out of a cloth onto his desk, he had looked at it with hatred for what it represented. He had come to Spain with nothing, but the ground gave up its secrets and with the wealth came the tug of the old city and the life he had almost forgotten.

He sighed at the thought. Spain was such a treasure house it would be difficult to leave her, but part of him knew he could not lose himself there for much longer. Life was too precious to be wasted, and too short.

The room was warm with the press of bodies. The maps of the new mines were stretched out on low tables, held by weights. Julius could hear Renius arguing with Brutus and the low cadence of Domitius chuckling. Only the giant Ciro was silent. Yet even those who spoke were marking time until Julius joined them. They were good men. Each one of them had stood with him against enemies and through grief and there were times when Julius could imagine how it might have been to cross the world with them. They were men to walk a finer path than to be forgotten in Spain and Julius could not bear the sympathy he saw in their eyes. He knew he deserved only contempt for having brought them to that place and buried himself in petty work.

If Cornelia had lived, he would have taken her with him to Spain. It would have been a new start, far away from the intrigues of the city. He bowed his head as the evening breeze touched his face. It was an old pain and there were whole days when he did not think of her. Then the guilt would surface and the dreams would be terrible, as if in punishment for the lapse.

'Julius? The guard is at the door for you,' Brutus said, touching him on the shoulder. Julius nodded and turned back to the men in the room, his eyes seeking out the stranger amongst them.

The legionary looked nervous as he glanced around at the map-laden tables and the jugs of wine, clearly awed by the people within.

'Well?' Julius said.

The soldier swallowed as he met the dark eyes of his general. There was no kindness in that hard, fleshless face and the young legionary stammered slightly.

'A young Spanish at the gate, General. He says he's the one we're looking for.'

The conversations in the room died away and the guard wished he were anywhere else but under the scrutiny of those men.

'Have you checked him for weapons?' Julius said.

'Yes, sir.'

'Then bring him to me. I want to speak to the man who has caused me so much trouble.'

5

Julius stood waiting at the top of the stairs as the Spaniard was brought up. His clothes were too small for his gangling limbs and the face was caught in the change between man and boy, though there was no softness in the bony jaw. As their eyes met, the Spaniard hesitated, stumbling.

'What's your name, boy?' Julius said as they came level.

'Adàn,' the Spaniard forced out.

'*You* killed my officer?' Julius said, with a sneer.

The young man froze, then nodded, his expression wavering between fear and determination. He could see the faces turned towards him in the room and his courage seemed to desert him then at the thought of stepping into their midst. He might have held back if the guard hadn't shoved him across the threshold.

'Wait below,' Julius told the legionary, suddenly irritated.

Adàn refused to bow his head in the face of the hostile glares of the Romans, though he could not remember being more frightened in his life. As Julius closed the door behind him, he started silently, cursing his nervousness. Adàn watched as the general sat down facing him and a dull terror overwhelmed him. Should he keep his hands by his sides? All of a sudden, they seemed awkward and he considered folding them or clasping his fingers behind his back. The silence was painful as he waited and still they had their eyes on him. Adàn swallowed with difficulty, determined not to show his fear.

'You knew enough to tell me your name. Can you understand me?' Julius asked.

Adàn worked spit into his dry mouth. 'I can,' he said. At least his voice hadn't quavered like a boy's. He squared his shoulders slightly and glanced at the others, almost recoiling from the naked animosity from one of them, a bear of a man with one arm who seemed to be practically growling with anger.

'You told the guards you were the one we were looking for, the one who killed the soldier,' Julius said.

Adàn's gaze snapped back to him.

'I did it. I killed him,' he replied, the words coming in a rush.

'You tortured him,' Julius added.

Adàn swallowed again. He had imagined this scene as he walked over the dark fields to the fort, but he couldn't summon the defiance he had pictured. He felt as if he was confessing to his father, and it was all he could do not to shuffle his feet in shame, despite his intentions.

'He was trying to rape my mother. I took him into the woods. She tried to stop me, but I would not listen to her,' Adàn said stiffly, trying to remember the words he had practised.

Someone in the room muttered an oath, but Adàn could not tear his eyes away from the general. He felt an obscure relief that he had told them. Now they would kill him and his parents would be released.

Thinking of his mother was a mistake. Tears sprang from nowhere to rim his eyes and he blinked them back furiously. She would want him to be strong in front of these men.

Julius watched him. The young Spaniard was visibly trembling, and with reason. He had only to give the order and Adàn would be taken out into the yard and executed in front of the assembled ranks. It would be the end of it, but a memory stayed his hand.

'Why have you given yourself up, Adàn?'

'My family have been taken in for questioning, General. They are innocent. I am the one you want.'

'You think your death will save them?'

Adàn hesitated. How could he explain that only that thin hope had made him come?

'They have done nothing wrong.'

Julius raised a hand to scratch his eyebrow, then rested his elbow on the arm of the chair as he thought.

'When I was younger than you, Adàn, I stood in front of a

7

Roman named Cornelius Sulla. He had murdered my uncle and broken everything I valued in the world. He told me I would go free if I put aside my wife and shamed her with her father. He *cherished* such little acts of spite.'

For a moment, Julius looked into the unimaginable distance of the past and Adàn felt sweat break out on his forehead. Why was the man talking to him? He had already confessed; there was nothing else. Despite his fear, he felt interest kindle. The Romans seemed to bear only one face in Spain. To hear they had rivalry and enemies within their own ranks was a revelation.

'I hated that man, Adàn,' Julius continued. 'If I had been given a weapon, I would have used it on him even though it meant my own life. I wonder if you understand that sort of hatred.'

'You did not give up your wife?' Adàn asked.

Julius blinked at the sudden question, then smiled bitterly.

'No. I refused and he let me live. The floor at his feet was spattered with the blood of people he had killed and tortured, yet he let me live. I have often wondered why.'

'He did not think you were a threat,' Adàn said, surprised by his own courage to speak so to the general. Julius shook his head in memory.

'I doubt it. I told him I would devote my life to killing him if he set me free.' For a moment, he almost said aloud how his friend had poisoned the Dictator, but that part of the story could never be told, not even to the men in that room.

Julius shrugged. 'He died by someone else's hand, in the end. It is one of the regrets of my life that I could not do it myself and watch the life fade from his eyes.'

Adàn had to look away from the fire he saw in the Roman. He believed him and the thought of this man ordering his own death with such malice made him shudder.

Julius did not speak again for a long time and Adàn felt

weak with the tension, his head jerking upwards as the general broke the silence at last.

'There are murderers in the cells here and in Valentia. One of them will be hanged for your crimes as well as his own. You, I am going to pardon. I will sign my name to it and you will go back to your home with your family and never come to my attention again.'

Renius snorted in amazement. 'I would like a private word, General,' he grated, looking venomously at Adàn. The young Spaniard stood with his mouth open.

'You may not have one, Renius. I have spoken and it will stand,' Julius replied without looking at him. He watched the boy for a moment and felt a weight lift off him. He had made the right decision, he was sure. He had seen himself in the Spaniard's eyes and it was like lifting a veil into his memory. How frightening Sulla had seemed then. To Adàn, Julius would have been another of that cruel type, wrapped in metal armour and harder thoughts. How close he had come to sending Adàn to be impaled, or burnt, or nailed to the gates of the fort, as Sulla had with so many of his enemies. It was an irony that Sulla's old whim had saved Adàn, but Julius had caught himself before he gave the order for death and wondered at what he was becoming. He would not be those men he had hated. Age would not force him into their mould, if he had the strength. He rose from his seat and faced Adàn.

'I do not expect you to waste this chance, Adàn. You will not have another from me.'

Adàn almost burst into tears, emotions roiling and overwhelming him. He had prepared himself for death and having it snatched away and freedom promised was too much for him. On an impulse, he took a step forward and went down on one knee before anyone could react.

Julius stood slowly, looking down at the young man before him.

'We are not the enemy, Adàn. Remember that. I will have a scribe prepare the pardon. Wait below for me,' he said.

Adàn rose and looked into the Roman's dark eyes for a last moment before leaving the room. As the door closed behind him, he sagged against the wall, wiping sweat from his face. He felt dizzy with relief and every breath he pulled in was clear and cold. He could not understand why he had been spared.

The guard in the room below craned his head to stare up at Adàn's slumped figure in the shadows.

'Shall I heat the knives for you then?' the Roman sneered up at him.

'Not today,' Adàn replied, enjoying the look of confusion that passed over the man's face.

Brutus pressed a cup of wine into Julius' hand, pouring expertly from an amphora.

'Are you going to tell us why you let him go?' he said.

Julius lifted the cup to cut off the flow and drank from it before holding it out again. 'Because he was brave,' he said.

Renius rubbed the bristles of his chin with his hand. 'He will be famous in the towns, you realise. He will be the man who faced us and lived. They'll probably make him mayor when old Del Subió dies. The young ones will flock around him and before you know it . . .'

'Enough,' Julius interrupted, his face flushing from the heady wine. 'The sword is not the answer to everything, no matter how you may wish it so. We have to live with them without sending our men out in pairs and watching every alley and track for ambush.' His hands cut shapes in the air as he strained to find words for the thought.

'They must be as Roman as we are, willing to die for our causes and against our enemies. Pompey showed the way with

10

the legions he raised here. I spoke the truth when I said we were not the enemy. Can you understand that?'

'I understand,' Ciro spoke suddenly, his deep voice rumbling out over Renius' reply.

Julius' face lit with the idea. 'There it is. Ciro was not born in Rome, but he came to us freely and is *of* Rome.' He struggled for words, his mind running faster than his tongue. 'Rome is . . . an idea, more than blood. We must make it so that for Adán to cast us off would be like tearing his own heart out. Tonight, he will wonder why he wasn't killed. He will know there can be justice, even after the death of a Roman soldier. He will tell the story and those who doubt will pause. That is enough of a reason.'

'Unless he killed the man for sport,' Renius said, 'and he tells his friends we are weak and stupid.' He didn't trust himself to speak further, but crossed to Brutus and took the amphora from him, holding it in the crook of his elbow to fill his cup. In his anger, some of it splashed onto the floor.

Julius narrowed his eyes slightly at the old gladiator. He took a slow breath to control the temper that swelled in him.

'I will not be Sulla, or Cato. Do you understand *that* at least, Renius? I will not rule with fear and hatred and taste every meal for poison. Do you understand *that*?' His voice had risen as he spoke and Renius turned to face him, realising he had gone too far.

Julius raised a clenched fist, anger radiating off him.

'If I say the word, Ciro will cut out your heart for me, Renius. He was born on a coast of a different land, but he is Roman. He is a soldier of the Tenth and he is mine. I do not hold him with fear, but with love. Do you understand *that*?'

Renius froze. 'I know that, of course, you . . .'

Julius interrupted him with a wave of his hand, feeling a headache spike between his eyes. The fear of a fit in front of them made his anger vanish and he was left feeling empty and tired.

'Leave me, all of you. Fetch Cabera. Forgive my anger, Renius. I need to argue with you just to know my own mind.'

Renius nodded, accepting the apology. He went out with the others, leaving Julius alone in the room. The gathering gloom of the evening had turned almost to night and Julius lit the lamps before standing by the open window, pressing his forehead against the cool stone. The headache throbbed and he groaned softly, rubbing his temples in circular motions as Cabera had taught him.

There was so much work to do and all the time an inner voice whispered at him, mockingly. Was he hiding in these hills? Where once he had dreamed of standing in the senate house, now he drew back from it. Cornelia was dead, Tubruk with her. His daughter was a stranger, living in a house he had visited for only one night in six years. There had been times when he hungered to match his strength and wit against men like Sulla and Pompey, but now the thought of throwing himself back into games of power made him nauseous with hatred. Better, surely better, to make a home in Spain, to find a woman there and never see his home again.

'I cannot go back,' he said aloud, his voice cracking.

Renius found Cabera in the stables, lancing a swelling in the soft flesh of a cavalry hoof. The horses always seemed to understand he was trying to help them and even the most spirited stood still after only a few murmured words and pats.

They were alone and Renius waited until Cabera's needle had released the pus in the hoof, his fingers massaging the soft flesh to help the drain. The horse shuddered as if flies were landing on its skin, but Cabera had never been kicked and the leg was relaxed in his steady hands.

'He wants you,' Renius said.

Cabera looked up at his tone. 'Hand me that pot, will you?'

Renius passed over the cup of sticky tar that would seal the wound. He watched Cabera work in silence and when the wound was coated, Cabera turned to him with his usual humour dampened.

'You're worried about Julius,' the old healer said.

Renius shrugged. 'He's killing himself here. Of course I'm worried. He doesn't sleep, just spends his nights working on his mines and maps. I . . . can't seem to talk to him without it becoming an argument.'

Cabera reached out and gripped the iron muscles of Renius' arm.

'He knows you're here, if he needs you,' he said. 'I'll give him a sleeping draught for tonight. Perhaps you should take one as well. You look exhausted.'

Renius shook his head. 'Just do what you can for him. He deserves better than this.'

Cabera watched the one-armed gladiator stride away into the darkness.

'You are a good man, Renius,' he said, too quietly to be heard.

CHAPTER TWO

⟨⟨⟨⟨⟨

Servilia stood at the rail of the little trade ship, watching the scurrying figures on the docks as they grew closer. There were hundreds of small boats in the waters around the port of Valentia and the merchant captain had twice ordered fishing crews to steer away from his ship as they pressed in. There seemed to be no order to it and Servilia found herself smiling as yet another young Spaniard held up a fish he had caught and shouted prices up at her. She noted how the man balanced as his coracle bucked in the swell. He wore only a narrow cloth around his waist, with a knife dangling from a wide belt on a leather thong. Servilia thought he was beautiful.

The captain waved the boat away and was ignored as the fisherman scented a sale to the woman who laughed down so prettily at him.

'I will buy his catch, Captain,' Servilia said.

The Roman merchant frowned, his heavy eyebrows pulling together.

'They're your coins, but the prices will be better in port,' he said.

She reached out and patted his shoulder and his gruff manner disappeared in confusion.

'Nonetheless, the sun is hot and after so long aboard, I'd love something fresh.'

The captain gave way with little grace, picking up the heavy coil of rope and heaving it over the side. The fisherman tied the end to a net at his feet and then climbed up to the deck, swinging his legs over the rail with easy agility as he reached the top. The young Spaniard was dark and hard from his labours, with white smears of salt on his skin. He bowed deeply in response to her appraisal and began pulling up his net. Servilia watched the play of muscles in his arms and shoulders with the eye of a connoisseur.

'Won't your little boat drift away?' she asked.

The young Spaniard opened his mouth to reply and the captain snorted.

'He'll speak only his own language, I'm afraid. They don't have much in the way of schools until we build them.'

Servilia caught the scornful flash in the young man's eyes as he listened. A narrow rope trailed from the net to his boat and with a flick of his wrist the Spaniard hitched it to the rail, tapping the knot with a finger in answer to Servilia's question.

The net contained a writhing mass of dark blue fish and Servilia shuddered and stepped clear as they flopped and jumped on contact with the deck. The fisherman laughed at her discomfort and pulled a big one up by its tail. It was as long as his arm and still very much alive. Servilia saw its eye move wildly as the fish jerked in his hand. Its blue skin was glossy and perfect and a darker line ran from the tail to the head. She nodded and held up five fingers to an answering beam.

'Will five be enough for the crew, Captain?' she asked.

The Roman grunted his approval and whistled for two of the seamen to take the fish.

'Just a few coppers will do, madam,' he said.

Servilia unclipped a wide band around her wrist, revealing her small coins. She selected a silver denarius and handed it to the young man. He raised his eyebrows and added another of the largest fish from the net before pulling the drawstring tight. He flashed a triumphant expression at the captain and jerked his knot free before climbing the rail and diving into the blue water below. Servilia leaned over to watch him surface and laughed with pleasure as he pulled himself back in, gleaming in the sunlight like his fish. He pulled his net out of the water and waved to her.

'What a wonderful beginning,' she breathed. The captain muttered something unintelligible.

The crewmen who held the fish brought wooden clubs out of a deck locker and, before Servilia realised what they were doing, brought them down on the shining heads with a grim thumping sound. The shining eyes disappeared under the force of the blows, knocked inside the head as blood spattered over the deck. Servilia grimaced as a spot of it touched her arm. The seamen were clearly enjoying themselves, suddenly more vital than they had been at any point in the voyage from Ostia. It was as if they had come alive in the killing and they chuckled and joked with each other as they finished the grisly task.

When the last of the fish were dead, the deck was coated in their blood and tiny silver scales. Servilia watched as the seamen threw a canvas bucket on a line into the sea and sluiced the planks clean.

'The port is tight with ships, madam,' the captain said at her shoulder, squinting against the sun. 'I'll take her in as close as I can, but we'll have to anchor for a few hours until there's a place on the dock.' Servilia turned to look again at Valentia, suddenly longing to be on land again.

'As you say, Captain,' she murmured.

The mountains behind the port seemed to fill the horizon, green and red against the dark blue of the sky. Her son, Brutus, was somewhere over them and seeing him after so long would be wonderful. Strangely, her stomach tightened almost to an ache when she thought of the young man who was his friend. She wondered how the years had changed him and touched her hair unconsciously, smoothing it back where it had fallen in tendrils, made damp by the sea air.

Evening had muted the heat of the sun into grey softness by the time the Roman trade ship was able to ease between the lines of anchored shipping and take her place on the dock. Servilia had brought three of her most beautiful girls with her and they joined her on deck with the crew as they threw ropes to the dockworkers and used the steering oars to bring them safe against the massive wooden beams of the side. It was a delicate manoeuvre and the captain showed his skill in its neatness, as he communicated with the mate at the bow with a series of hand signals and calls.

There was a general air of excitement and the young girls Servilia had brought laughed and joked as the workers on the docks caught sight of them and called ribald comments. Servilia let them preen without a word; all three were the rarity in her business who had not yet lost the love for the work. In fact, Angelina, the youngest, was constantly falling in love with her customers and few months went by without some romantic offering to buy her for marriage. The price always seemed to surprise them and Angelina would sulk for days before someone else took her fancy.

The girls were dressed as modestly as the daughters of any great house. Servilia had taken enormous care with their safety, knowing that even a short sea journey gave a sense of freedom to men that could have caused trouble. Their dresses were cut to obscure the lines of their young bodies, though there were more provocative garments in the trunks Servilia had brought along. If the letters Brutus had sent were correct, there would be a market and the three girls would be the first in the new house she would buy. The sailors who grunted and complained under the heavy trunks would have been shocked at the weight of gold that had been split between them.

Servilia's perusal of the docks was interrupted as Angelina shrieked suddenly. Servilia's sharp glance took in the sailor hurrying away and Angelina's pleased outrage, before she turned back. They had reached land not a moment too soon, she thought.

The captain shouted for the dockworkers to make the ropes fast and the crew cheered the announcement, already anticipating the pleasures of the port. Servilia caught the captain's eye and he crossed the deck to her, suddenly more genial than she had grown to expect.

'We won't break out the cargo until tomorrow morning now,' he said. 'I can recommend a few places if you want to go ashore and there's a cousin of mine who'll rent you as many carts as you want, at a good price.'

'Thank you, Captain. It's been a great pleasure.' Servilia smiled at him, pleased to see a blush start high on his cheeks. Angelina was not the only one with a circle of admirers on the ship, she thought with some pleasure.

The captain cleared his throat and raised his chin to speak again, looking suddenly nervous.

'I will be dining alone later, if you would like to join me. There'll be fresh fruit sent to the ship, so it'll be better than we're used to.'

Servilia laid a hand on his arm and felt the heat of his skin beneath his tunic.

'It will have to be another time, I'm afraid. I'd like to be moving by dawn. Would you be able to have my trunks taken off first? I'll speak to the legion to arrange a guard on it until the carts are loaded.'

The captain nodded, trying to hide his disappointment. His first mate had told him the woman was a whore, but he had the intense impression that offering her money to stay with him would lead to an awful humiliation. For a moment he looked so terribly lonely that Servilia considered letting Angelina raise his spirits. The little blonde loved older men. They were always so desperately grateful, and for such little effort. Looking at him, Servilia guessed he would probably refuse the offer. Men of his years often wanted the company of a mature woman as much as the physical pleasures and Angelina's earthy frankness would only embarrass him.

'Your trunks will be first on the dock, madam. It has been a pleasure,' he said, looking wistfully after her as she went to climb the steps onto the dock. A number of his crew had gathered in case the younger women were unsteady crossing the rail and his eyebrows drew together as he considered them. After a moment of thought, he followed Servilia, knowing instinctively that he should be there to help the men.

Julius was deep in work when the guard knocked on the door to his rooms.

'What is it?'

The legionary looked unusually nervous as he saluted.

'I think you'd better come down to the gate, sir. You should see this.'

Raising his eyebrows, Julius followed the man down the steps and out into the powerful afternoon sun. There was a peculiar tension affecting the soldiers who clustered around the gate, and as they parted for him Julius noticed one or two with the strained faces of men trying not to smile. Their amusement and the heat seemed to feed the prickling anger that had become the foundation of his waking hours.

Beyond the open gate was a string of heavily laden carts, their drivers lightly coated by the dust of the road. A full twenty of the Tenth had taken station to the fore and rear of the odd procession. With narrowed eyes, Julius recognised the officer as one who had been dispatched on port duty the previous day and his temper frayed still further. Like the carts, the legionaries were coated in enough dust to show they had walked every step of the way.

Julius glared at them.

'I do *not* recall giving orders for you to escort trade goods from the coast,' he snapped. 'There had better be an excellent reason for leaving your post and disobeying my orders. I cannot think of one myself, but perhaps you will surprise me.'

The officer paled slightly under the dust.

'The lady, sir . . .' he began.

'What? What lady?' Julius replied, losing patience with the man's hesitation. Another voice sounded then, making him start in recognition.

'I told your men you could not object to them helping an old friend,' Servilia said, stepping down from the riding seat of a cart and walking towards him.

For a moment, Julius could not respond. Her dark hair was wild around her head and his eyes drank in the sight of her. Surrounded by men, she seemed fresh and cool, perfectly aware of the sensation she caused. She walked like a stalking cat, wearing a brown cotton dress that left her arms and neck uncovered. She wore no jewels but a simple chain of gold ending in a pendant that was almost hidden as it disappeared between her breasts.

'Servilia. You should not have presumed on a friendship,' Julius said, stiffly.

She shrugged and smiled as if it were nothing.

20

'I hope you won't punish them, General. The docks can be dangerous without guards, and I had no one else to help me.'

Julius looked coldly at her, before returning his gaze to the officer. The man had followed the exchange and now stood with the glazed expression of one who waited for bad news.

'My orders were clear?' Julius asked him.

'Yes, sir.'

'Then you and your men will take the next two watches. Your rank makes you more responsible than they, does it not?'

'Yes, sir,' the hapless soldier replied.

Julius nodded. 'When you are relieved, you will report to your centurion to be flogged. Tell him twenty strokes on my order and your name to be entered in the lists for disobedience. Now *run* back.'

The officer saluted smartly and spun on his heel. 'Turn about!' he shouted to his twenty. 'Double speed back to the docks.'

With Julius there, no one dared groan, though they would be exhausted before they were halfway back to their original post and the watches to come would see them dropping with tiredness.

Julius stared after them until they were clear of the line of carts, before turning back to Servilia. She stood stiffly, trying to hide her surprise and guilt at what her request had brought about.

'You have come to see your son?' Julius said to her, frowning. 'He is training with the legion and should be back at dusk.' He looked at the line of carts and bellowing oxen, clearly caught between his irritation at the unexpected arrival and the demands of courtesy. After a long silence, he relented.

'You may wait inside for Brutus. I will have someone water your animals and bring you a meal.'

'Thank you for your kindness,' Servilia replied, smiling to cover her confusion. She couldn't begin to understand the differences in the young general. The whole of Rome knew he had lost his wife, but it was like speaking to another man from the one she had known. Dark pouches ringed his eyes, but it was more than simple tiredness. When she had seen him last, he had been ready to take arms against Spartacus and the fires in him were barely controlled. Her heart went out to him for what he had lost.

At that moment, Angelina leapt onto the road from her cart at the back of the line and waved, calling something to Servilia. Both she and Julius stiffened as the girlish voice rang out.

'Who is that?' Julius said, his eyes narrowing against the glare.

'A companion, General. I have three young ladies with me for the trip.'

Something in her tone made Julius glance at her in sudden suspicion.

'Are they . . .'

'Companions, General, yes,' she replied lightly. 'All good girls.' For the right price, they could be superb, she added silently.

'I'll put a guard on their door. The men are not used to . . .' he hesitated. 'It may be necessary to keep a guard. On the door.'

To Servilia's intense pleasure, a slow blush had started on Julius' cheeks. There was still life in him, somewhere deep, she thought. Her nostrils flared slightly with the excitement of a hunt. As Julius marched back between the gates, she watched him and smiled, pressing the fullness of her lower lip between her teeth in amusement. Not too old after all, she told herself, smoothing her tangled hair with a hand.

Brutus stretched his back muscles as he rode the last miles towards the fort. His century of extraordinarii were in formation behind him and he felt a touch of pride as he glanced to each side and saw the neat line of cantering horses. Domitius was in position on his right and Octavian held the line a few places along. They thundered over the plain together, raising a plume of dust that left the taste of bitter earth in their mouths. The air was warm around them and their mood was light. They were all tired, but it was that pleasant lethargy of skilled work, with food and a good night's sleep only a little way ahead.

As the fort came into sight, Brutus called to Domitius over the noise of the horses, 'Let's give them a show. Split and wheel on my signal.'

The guards on the gate would be watching them come in, he knew. Though the extraordinarii had been together for less than two years, Julius had given him what he wanted in the way of men and horses, and he had wanted the best of the Tenth. Man for man, Brutus would have wagered on them against any army in the world. They were the charge-breakers, the first into impossible positions. Every one of them had been picked for his ability with horse and sword and Brutus was proud of them all. He knew the rest of the Tenth considered them more show than substance, but then the legion hadn't seen a battle in their time in Spain. When the extraordinarii had been blooded and shown what they could do, they would justify their expense, he was certain. The armour alone had cost a small fortune: laced bronze and iron strips that allowed them greater movement than the heavier plates of the triarii legionaries. The men of Brutus' extraordinarii had polished the metals to a high sheen and, against the glossy skin of their mounts, they glowed in the dying sun.

Brutus raised his hand and made sharp gestures to each side. He kicked his mount into a gallop as the group slid smoothly apart as if an invisible line had been drawn on the ground. Now the wind pressed against Brutus' face and he laughed with excitement, not needing to look to know the formation was perfect. Specks of white spittle flew back from his horse's mouth and he leaned forward into the saddle-horn, gripping with his legs and feeling as if he was flying.

The fort was growing with astonishing rapidity and, caught up in the moment as he was, Brutus almost left it too late for the signal to re-form the split square. The two groups swerved together only moments before they were changing their holds on the reins to halt, but there were no mistakes. As one man, they dismounted, patting the steaming necks of the stallions and geldings Julius had brought over from Rome. Only cut mounts could be used against enemy cavalry, as intact stallions could be sent berserk by the scent of a mare in season. It was a balancing act between taking the best for the extraordinarii and keeping the bloodlines strong. Even the local Spanish whistled and called when they saw those horses, their love of the breed overcoming the usual reticence they showed to the Roman soldiers.

Brutus was laughing at something Domitius had said when he caught sight of his mother. His eyes widened for a moment before he rushed under the gate arch to embrace her.

'Your letters didn't mention this!' he said, lifting her up to her toes and kissing her on both cheeks.

'I thought you might become overexcited,' Servilia replied. They both laughed and Brutus put her down.

Servilia held him back at arm's length and smiled to see him so full of life. The years in Spain had suited her only son. He had a force for life in him that made other men look up and stand straighter in his presence.

'As handsome as ever, I see,' she said with a twinkle. 'I suppose you have a string of local girls pining after you.'

'I daren't go out without a guard to save me from the poor creatures,' he replied.

Domitius appeared suddenly, moving between them to force an introduction.

'Ah, yes, this is Domitius, who cleans the horses. Have you

met Octavian? He's kin to Julius.' Grinning at Domitius' appalled expression, Brutus had to wave Octavian closer.

Octavian was overcome and attempted a salute that ended in more confusion, making Brutus laugh. He was too familiar with the effect his mother could have to be surprised by it, but he noticed they were quickly becoming the centre of an admiring circle of the extraordinarii as they jostled to see the new arrival in their midst.

Servilia waved to them, enjoying the attention after the dull month at sea.

Young men were so peculiarly vibrant, untouched by the fears of age or death. They stood around her like innocent gods, and lifted her with their confidence.

'Have you seen Julius, Mother? He . . .' Brutus broke off at the sudden hush that fell over the yard. Three young women swept out of an archway and the crowd of soldiers parted before them. They were all beautiful in different ways. The youngest was blonde and slight, her cheeks lit with rising colour as she walked towards Servilia. At her shoulders were two others with features to make grown men weep into their wine.

The spell of their entrance was broken as someone let out a low whistle and the crowd came back to life.

Servilia raised an eyebrow at Angelina as they met. The girl knew exactly what she was doing. Servilia had seen that in her from the beginning. She was the sort of woman men fought each other to protect and her presence in a drinking house was usually enough to start a riot before the evening was over. Servilia had found her serving wine and giving away what men would pay well for. It had not taken much persuasion, considering the sums involved. Servilia kept two-fifths of everything Angelina earned in the house in Rome and still the young blonde was becoming a wealthy woman in her own right. As things stood, she would be looking to start her own establishment in a few years, and she would come to Servilia for the loan.

'We were worried about you, mistress,' Angelina lied cheerfully.

Brutus eyed her with open interest and she returned his gaze without embarrassment. Under the girl's scrutiny, he could hardly confirm the suspicion that had come into his mind. Though he told himself he had come to terms with Servilia's profession, the thought of his men knowing showed him he was not as secure as he'd thought.

'Are you going to introduce us, Mother?' he asked.

Angelina widened her eyes for a split second.

'This is your son? He's just as you said. How wonderful.'

Servilia had never discussed Brutus with Angelina, but was caught between exasperation at the girl's transparency and a shrewder part of her that could smell the money to be made. The crowd had grown, around them. These were not men used to the attentions of young women. She began to suspect that from legion trade alone Valentia was going to be very profitable indeed.

'This is Angelina,' she said.

Brutus bowed and Angelina's eyes sparkled at his courtesy.

'You must join us at the general's table this evening. I'll raid the cellar for wine and we'll wash the dust of the road off you.' He held Angelina's eyes as he spoke and managed to make the proposition sound remarkably sexual. Servilia cleared her throat to interrupt them.

'Lead us in, Brutus.'

The extraordinarii parted again to let them through. The hot meal that awaited them in their barracks did not seem half as tempting as it had on the ride back, without the company of the women as a spice. They stood as if abandoned in the courtyard until the small procession had disappeared inside. The spell was broken then and they broke apart to care for the horses, suddenly brisk in their movements as if they had never been interrupted at all.

Despite Angelina's protests, Servilia left her three companions in the rooms they had been given. Someone had to unpack the trunks and for that first night Servilia wanted her son's full attention. She had not brought them to Valentia to find Brutus a wife from their number, after all.

Julius did not come down with the others, sending a curt apology with his personal guard when Brutus asked if he would join them. Servilia saw the refusal did not surprise any of the men at the table and wondered again at the changes Spain had wrought in them.

In Servilia's honour, the meal was a mixture of local dishes, served in an array of small bowls. The spices and peppers made Octavian cough until he had to be thumped on the back and given wine to clear his throat. He had been in awe of Servilia from the first moment in the courtyard and Brutus teased him subtly, while Servilia pretended not to notice the boy's discomfort.

The room was lit with warm, flickering lamps, and the wine was as good as Brutus had promised. It was a pleasant meal and Servilia found that she was enjoying the banter between the men. Domitius allowed himself to be persuaded into telling one of his stories, though the conclusion was spoiled slightly as Cabera called it out with enthusiasm, then thumped the table in amusement.

'That story was old when I was a boy,' the old man cackled, reaching over to take a portion of fish from a bowl near Octavian. The young man was about to take the same piece and Cabera slapped his fingers to make him drop it, scooping up the rich flesh as it fell. Octavian scowled at him, clearly stifling a response as he remembered the presence of Servilia at the table.

'How did you come to be with the Tenth legion, Domitius?' Servilia asked.

'Brutus arranged it when we were down in the south fighting Spartacus. I'd let him win a couple of practice bouts out of fairness, but on the whole he saw that he could benefit from my training.'

'Lies!' Brutus said, laughing. 'I asked him in passing if he would be willing to transfer to the new legion and he practically bit my arm off in enthusiasm. Julius had to pay a fortune in compensation to the legate. We're all still waiting to see if he'll be worth it.'

Domitius waited patiently until Brutus was drinking from his wine cup.

'I'm the best of my generation, you see,' he told Servilia, watching in amusement as Brutus fought not to choke, turning red in the process.

The sound of footsteps made them all look up and the men rose together to welcome Julius. He took his place at the head of the table and signalled for them to sit. Servants brought fresh dishes and Brutus filled a cup with wine, smiling when he saw Julius raise an eyebrow at the quality.

The conversation began again and as it did Servilia caught Julius' eye and inclined her head slightly. He copied the gesture, accepting her at the table, and she found herself letting out a breath she hadn't realised she was holding.

There was an authority to him that she couldn't recall seeing before. He didn't join in the laughter, merely smiling at the more outrageous chatter. He punished the wine, Servilia noted, drinking as if it was water and with no obvious effect, though a slow flush appeared at his neck that could have been from the evening heat.

The high spirits at the table were quickly restored. The camaraderie between the men was infectious and after a while Servilia was engaged in the stories and humour with the others.

Cabera flirted outrageously with her, winking at inopportune moments and making her snort with amusement. Once as she laughed she caught Julius' eye again and the moment seemed to freeze, hinting at a deeper reality behind the lively façade of the meal.

Julius watched her, constantly surprised at the effect she had wrought on the usually sombre gathering. She laughed without affectation and in those moments he wondered how he could ever have found her less than beautiful. Her skin was dark and freckled from the sun and her nose and chin a little too strong, yet still she had something that set her apart. The calculating part of him saw how she transferred her attention to whoever spoke, flattering them simply by the interest she showed. She was a woman who liked men and they sensed it. Julius shook his head slightly. His reaction to her disturbed him, but she was so different from Cornelia that no comparison occurred to trouble his thoughts.

He had not been in female company for a long time and then only when Brutus managed to get enough drink in him that he didn't care any more. Looking at Servilia reminded him of the world outside his soldiers' rough gatherings. He felt unbalanced with her, out of practice. The thought crossed his mind that he should be careful to keep a distance. A woman of her experience could very well eat him alive.

He shook his head to clear it, irritated with his weakness. The first woman to sit at their table for months and he was reacting with little more sophistication than Octavian, though he hoped his thoughts weren't so obvious. He'd never hear the end of Brutus' mockery if they were. He imagined the amused taunts with a shudder and pushed his wine cup away firmly. No matter what, she was hardly likely to show interest in a friend of her son. It was ridiculous even to entertain the idea.

Octavian interrupted Julius' musings as he reached across the table to offer Servilia the last morsel of a herb dish. The young Roman had grown in strength and skill under the tutelage of Brutus and Domitius. Julius wondered if Octavian would have so much to fear from the apprentices in the city as he'd used to. He doubted it. The boy seemed to thrive in the company of the rough soldiers of the Tenth and even copied the way Brutus walked, to his friend's amusement. He seemed so young, it was strange to think Julius had been married when only a year older.

'I learned a new feint this morning, sir,' Octavian said proudly.

Julius smiled at him. 'You'll have to show it to me,' he said, reaching over to ruffle the boy's hair.

Octavian beamed in response to the small show of affection. 'Will you train with us tomorrow, then?' he asked, readying himself for disappointment.

Julius shook his head. 'I'm going out to the gold mines with Renius for a few days,' he said, 'but perhaps I will when I come back.'

Octavian tried to look pleased, but they could all see he took it as a straight refusal. Julius almost changed his mind, but the dark humours that plagued him eased back into his thoughts. None of them understood his work. They had the light spirits of boys and that carelessness was no longer a luxury he could afford. Forgetting his earlier resolution, Julius reached for his cup and emptied it.

Brutus saw the depression settle on his friend and struggled to find something to divert him.

'The Spanish swordsmith will begin working with our legion men tomorrow. Can't you delay the trip until you've seen what you paid for?'

Julius stared at him, making them all uncomfortable.

'No, the preparations are made,' he said, refilling his cup and cursing softly as he spilled a little of the wine onto the table in the process. Julius frowned at his hands. Was there a tremble there? He couldn't tell. As rather stilted conversation resumed, he watched them all, looking for some sign that they had seen his weakness. Only Cabera met his eyes and the old man's face was full of kindness. Julius drained the cup, suddenly angry with all of them.

Servilia dipped her fingers in the water bowl and wiped her mouth delicately with them, a gesture that held Julius' attention, though she seemed not to notice it.

'I have enjoyed this, very much, but the journey here was tiring,' she said, smiling at them all. 'I will rise early to watch your training, Octavian, if you don't mind?'

'Of course, come and watch,' Brutus said pleasantly. 'I'll get a carriage ready for you in the stables, as well. This is a luxurious post, compared to some. You'll love it here.'

'Find a good horse and I won't need the carriage,' Servilia replied, noting the flicker in Julius' eyes as he digested this piece of information. Men were such strange creatures, but she had yet to find one who didn't enjoy the thought of a beautiful woman on a horse.

'I hope my girls won't be a disruption to you all. I will look for a place in the city tomorrow. Good night, gentlemen. General.'

They rose with her and again she experienced that strange frisson of excitement as Julius' eyes met her own.

Julius stood soon after she had left, swaying slightly.

'I have left my orders in your quarters, Brutus, for the time I am away. Make sure there is a guard on those girls while they are in our care. Good night.' He left without another word, walking with the exaggerated stiffness of a man trying to hide the effects of too much wine in his blood. For a moment there was a pained silence.

'It's good to have a new face here,' Brutus said, carefully avoiding more difficult subjects. 'She'll liven this place up a little. It's been too quiet recently.'

Cabera whistled quietly to himself. 'A woman like that . . . all men are fools around her,' he said softly, his tone making Brutus stare at him in puzzlement. The old man's expression was unreadable as he shook his head slightly and reached for more wine.

'She is very . . . graceful,' Domitius agreed, searching for the final word.

Brutus snorted. 'What did you expect after seeing me with a sword? I'd hardly come from a carthorse, would I?'

'I did think there was a female quality to your stance, yes,' Domitius replied, rubbing his forehead in thought. 'Yes, I see it now. It looks better on her though.'

'It is a manly grace in me, Domitius, *manly*. I'm quite happy to demonstrate it again to you tomorrow.' The old smile had returned to Brutus' face as he narrowed his eyes in mock offence.

'Do I have a manly grace, Domitius?' Octavian asked.

Domitius nodded slowly, his manner easy.

'You do, of course, lad. It is only Brutus who fights like a woman.'

Brutus roared with laughter and threw a plate at Domitius, who ducked it easily. It crashed on the stone floor and they all froze comically before the tension dissolved into humour once again.

'Why does your mother want a house in the city?' Octavian asked.

Brutus looked sharply at him, suddenly sorry to have to puncture his innocence.

'For business, lad. I think my mother's girls will be entertaining the legion before too long.'

Octavian looked around in confusion for a moment, then his face cleared. They were all watching him closely.

'Will they charge full price for someone of my age, do you think?' Octavian said.

Brutus threw another plate in his direction, hitting Cabera.

Lying on the narrow pallet in his rooms above, Julius could hear their laughter and shut his eyes tightly in the darkness.

CHAPTER THREE

꧁꧂

Servilia already loved the little city of Valentia. The streets were clean and busy with people. There was an air of affluence about the place that made her palms itch. Yet despite the signs of wealth, it had a fresh feel to it that her own ancient city had lost centuries before. This was a more innocent town. Even finding the right building had been easier than she'd expected. There were no officials needing a private payment before documents could be signed; it was simply a matter of finding the right place and paying gold to the current owner. It was refreshing after the bureaucracy of Rome and the soldiers Brutus had sent out with her were able to show her three possible locations as soon as she asked. The first two were close to the water and likely to attract more of the dockworkers than she wanted. The third was perfect.

In a quiet street close to the market and away from the waterfront, it was a roomy building with an impressive façade of white lime and hardwood. Servilia was long familiar with the need to present a pleasant face to the world. No doubt there were grimy little houses hidden in the towns where widows and whores earned a little extra on their backs, but the sort of place she wanted would attract dignitaries and officers from the legion, and be correspondingly more expensive.

With so many new houses being built by the Tenth, Servilia had sensed the owner could be pressured and the final price was a bargain, even with the furnishings to come. Some of those would have to be shipped from Rome, though a swift inspection of local seamstresses resulted in a string of smaller payments and deals.

With the house in her possession, she paid for an outgoing merchant to take a list of her requirements back to Rome. At least four more women would be needed and Servilia took great care in choosing their characteristics. It was important to establish a reputation for quality.

After three days, there was little to be done but give the house a name, though that gave Servilia more trouble than she expected. Though there were no clear proscriptions in law, Servilia knew instinctively that it should be something discreet and yet suggestive. Calling it 'The House of Rams' or suchlike would not do at all.

In the end, Angelina surprised her with a suggestion. 'The Golden Hand' was sufficiently erotic without being crude and Servilia had wondered whether Angelina's light colouring had prompted the idea. When she'd acquiesced, Angelina had leapt up and kissed her on both cheeks. The girl could be adorable when she had her own way, there was no doubt about it.

On the third morning after entering the city, Servilia watched a delicately drawn sign lifted onto iron hooks and smiled as a few of the Tenth cheered the sight. They would spread the word that the house was open for business and she expected the first night to be a busy one. After that, the future was assured and she fully expected to be able to pass over control to someone else in a few months. It was tempting to think of a similar establishment in every city of Spain. The finest girls and the feel of Rome. The market was there and the money would pour into her coffers.

Servilia turned to her son's guards and smiled at them.

'I hope you will be able to get passes for tonight?' she said lightly.

They looked at each other, aware that the dock watch had suddenly become a valuable counter in their purses.

'Perhaps your son could intercede for us, madam,' the officer replied.

Servilia frowned at that. Though they had not discussed it openly, she suspected Brutus was more than a little uncomfortable with her business. For that matter, she wondered if Julius had been told about the new house and what he thought of the idea. He might not have heard of her plans away in the south at his mines, though she couldn't see how he could object.

Servilia ran a hand idly along the line of her throat as she thought of him. Today was the day he was due to return. He was probably eating in the barracks at that moment and if she set off without delay, she could be back at the fort before the day was wasted.

'I *will* need permanent guards for the house,' she said as the thought occurred to her. 'If you wish, I will ask the general to post you here,' she told the officer. 'I am a Roman citizen after all.'

The guards looked at each other in wild surmise. Wonderful as the idea seemed, the thought of Caesar hearing their names to guard a whorehouse was enough to cool any man's ardour. Reluctantly, they shook their heads.

'I think he would prefer local men as guards here,' the officer said at last.

Servilia took the reins of her horse from one of the Tenth and leapt into the saddle. The leggings she wore were a little loose on her, but a skirt or *stola* would hardly have been appropriate.

'Mount up, lads. I'll go and ask him and we'll see,' she said, wheeling her horse around and kicking it into a canter. The hooves rattled loudly on the street and the local women raised their eyebrows at this strange Roman lady who rode like a soldier.

Julius was greeting an elderly Spaniard as Servilia rode up to the gates of the fort. During daylight hours the gates were left open and the guards passed them straight through into the yard with only a nod. Her escort from town led their mounts back to food and water, leaving her alone. Being Brutus' mother was proving extremely useful, she realised.

'I would like to have a word with you, General, if I may,' she called, walking her horse over to the pair.

Julius frowned in barely concealed anger.

'This is Mayor Del Subió, Servilia. I'm afraid I have no time to see you this afternoon. Perhaps tomorrow.'

He turned away to guide the older man into the main building and Servilia spoke quickly, acknowledging the mayor with a swift smile.

'I was thinking of riding out to the local towns. Are you able to recommend a route?'

Julius turned to the mayor.

'Please excuse me for a moment,' he said.

Del Subió bowed, glancing at Servilia from under bushy eyebrows. If he had been the Roman general, he would not have left such a beauty to pout alone. Even at his age, Del Subió could appreciate a fine woman and wondered at Caesar's irritation.

Julius walked to Servilia.

'These hills are not completely safe. There are rogues and

travellers who would think nothing of attacking you. If you're lucky they will just steal the horse and let you walk back.'

With the warning delivered, he tried to turn back to the mayor again.

'Perhaps you would like to join me, then, for protection?' Servilia said softly.

He froze, looking into her eyes. His heart thumped in his chest at the thought before he gathered his control. She was not easy to refuse, but his afternoon was filled with work. His eyes raked the yard and caught sight of Octavian coming out of the stables. Julius whistled sharply to catch the boy's attention.

'Octavian. Saddle a horse for yourself. Escort duty.'

Octavian saluted and disappeared back into the darkness of the stable block.

Julius looked at Servilia blankly, as if the exchange was already forgotten.

'Thank you,' she said, but he did not reply as he took Del Subió inside.

When Octavian reappeared, he had already mounted and had to lean low on the saddle to clear the arch of the stables. His grin faded at Servilia's expression as she took a grip on the pommel and threw a leg over her saddle. He had never seen her angry and, if anything, the fury in her eyes made her more beautiful. Without a word to him, she started forward into a gallop through the gates, forcing the guards to step aside or be knocked down. Eyes wide with surprise, Octavian followed her out.

She rode hard for a mile before reining back to a more sedate canter. Octavian closed the gap to ride at her shoulder, unconsciously showing his expertise with the way he matched her pace so exactly. She handled the horse well, he noted, with the skilled eye of the extraordinarii. Small flicks of the reins guided the blowing animal left and right around obstacles and once she urged her mount to jump a fallen tree, rising in the saddle and taking the landing without a tremor.

Octavian was entranced and told himself he wouldn't speak until he found something sufficiently mature and interesting to say. Inspiration didn't come, but she seemed willing to let the silence continue, taking out her anger at Julius' snub in the exertion of the ride. At last she reined in, panting slightly. She let Octavian approach and smiled at him.

'Brutus said you were a relation to Caesar. Tell me about him.'

Octavian smiled back, completely unable to resist her charm or question her reasons.

Julius had dismissed his last supplicant an hour before and stood alone by the window that looked out over the hills. He had signed orders to recruit another thousand for the developing mines, and granted compensation to three men whose lands had been encroached by the new buildings on the coast. How many other meetings had there been? Ten? His hand ached from the letters he had written and he massaged it slightly with the other as he stood waiting. His last scribe had retired a month before and he felt the loss keenly. His armour hung on the wooden tree by his desk and the night air was a relief on the sweat-darkened tunic underneath. He yawned and rubbed his face roughly. It was getting dark, but Octavian and Servilia were still out somewhere. He wondered if she were capable of keeping the boy late to worry him, or whether something had happened. Perhaps one of the horses had become lame and had to be walked back to the fort.

Julius snorted softly to himself. That would be a lesson well learned, if it was so. Away from the roads, the land was rugged and wild. A horse could easily break a leg, especially in the gloom of evening, when pits and animal holes would be hidden in shadow.

It was ridiculous to worry. Twice he lost patience and strode away from the window, but as he thought through the tasks for the next day, he found himself edging back to the view over the hills, looking for them. Away from the breeze, the room could be stifling, he told himself, too weary even to believe his own self-deceptions.

When the sun was little more than a red line against the mountains, he heard the clatter of hooves in the yard and stepped hurriedly back from the window rather than be seen. Who *was* the woman to cause him so much discomfort? He imagined how long it would take for the pair of them to brush and water their horses before coming inside. Would they be joining the officers' table again for a meal? He was hungry, but he didn't want to entertain a guest. He would have food sent up to him, and . . .

A low knocking at his door interrupted his thoughts, making him start. Somehow, he knew it would be her even as he cleared his throat to call, 'Come in.'

Servilia opened the door and walked into the room. Her hair was wild after the ride and a smear of dirt marked her cheek where she had touched it. She smelled of straw and horses and he felt his senses heighten at the sight of her. She was still angry, he saw, summoning the will to resist whatever she had come to demand. It really was too much that she walked in without even an announcement. What was the guard doing below? Was the man asleep? He would hear about it when she had gone, Julius swore to himself.

Without speaking, Servilia walked across the wooden floor to him. Before he could react, she pressed the palm of her hand against his chest, feeling the heart thump under the cloth.

'Still warm, then. I had begun to wonder,' she said softly. Her tone held an intimacy that unsettled him and somehow he couldn't muster the anger he expected. He could feel where her hand had rested, as if she had left a visible sign of her touch. She faced him, standing very close, and he was suddenly aware of the darkness of the room.

'Brutus will be wondering where you are,' he said.

'Yes, he is very protective of me,' she replied. She turned to leave and he almost reached out for her, watching in confusion as she crossed the long room.

'I wouldn't . . . have thought you needed much protecting,' he murmured. He hadn't really meant her to hear it, but he saw her smile before the door closed behind her and he was alone, his thoughts swirling in chaos. He breathed out slowly, shaking his head in amusement at his own reactions. He felt as if he were being stalked, but it wasn't unpleasant. His tiredness seemed to have vanished and he thought he might join the table below for the evening meal after all.

The door opened again and he looked up to see her, still there.

'Will you ride out with me tomorrow?' she asked. 'Octavian said you know the area as well as anyone.'

He nodded slowly, unable to remember what meetings he had planned and not caring, particularly. How long had it been since he'd last had a day away from his work?

'All right, Servilia. Tomorrow morning,' he said.

She grinned then without replying, shutting the door noiselessly behind her. He waited for a moment until he heard her light step going downstairs and relaxed. He was surprised to find he was looking forward to it.

As the light faded, the furnace turned the workshop into a place of fire and shadow. The only light came from the forge and the glow lit the Roman smiths as they waited impatiently to be shown the secret of hard iron. Julius had paid a fortune in gold for them to be taught by a Spanish master, but it was not something to be handed over in a moment, or even a single

40

day. To their exasperation, Cavallo had taken them through the entire process, step by step. At first, they had resisted being treated as apprentices, but then the more experienced of them had seen the Spaniard was exact in every part of his skill and begun to listen. They had cut cypress and alder wood to his order and stacked the logs under clay in a pit as large as a house for the first four days. While it charred, he showed them his ore furnace and lectured them on washing the rough rocks before sealing them with the charcoal to burn clean.

They were all men who loved their craft and by the end of the fifth day they were filled with excited anticipation as Cavallo brought a lump of iron bloom to his furnace and poured it molten into clay racks, finally turning out heavy bars of the metal onto a workbench for them to examine.

'The alder wood burns cooler than most and slows the changes. It makes a harder metal as more of it takes the charcoal, but that is only part of it,' he told them, thrusting one of the bars into the bright yellow heat of his forge. There was barely enough room to heat two pieces at a time, so they clustered around the second, copying every move and instruction he gave them. The cramped workshop could not hold all of them, so they took turns coming in and out of the cooling night air. Only Renius stayed throughout as an observer and he poured with enough sweat to blind him, silently noting each stage of the process.

He too was fascinated. Though he had used swords for all his adult life, he had never watched them being made and it gave him an appreciation for the skills of the dour men who worked earth into shining blades.

Cavallo used a hammer to beat the bar into the shape of a sword, reheating it again and again until the spike looked like a black gladius, crusted with impurities. Part of the skill came in judging the temperature by the colour as it came out of the forge. Each time the sword was at the right heat, Cavallo held

41

it up for them to see the shade of yellow before it faded. He filed and beat the soft metal as his own sweat sizzled on it, falling in fat drops to vanish on contact.

Their own bar was matched to his at every point and as the moon rose, he nodded to the Romans, satisfied. His sons had lit a low pan of charcoal as long as a man and before its metal cover was removed, it glowed as brightly as his forge. While his sword heated again, Cavallo signalled to a row of leather aprons on pegs. They were clumsy things to wear, thick and stiff with age. They covered the whole body from neck to feet, leaving only the arms bare. He smiled as they pulled them on, used by now to following his instructions without question.

'You will need the protection,' he told them as they struggled to move against the constricting coverings. At his signal, his sons used tongs to lift the cover from the charcoal pan and Cavallo pulled the yellow blade from the furnace with a flourish. The Roman smiths crowded closer, knowing they were seeing a stage of the process they did not recognise. Renius had to step back from the sudden wave of heat and craned to watch what was going on.

In the white heat of the charcoal, Cavallo hammered the blade again, sending sparks and whirring pieces of fire into the air. One landed in his hair and he patted the flame out automatically. Over and over he turned the blade, his hammer working it up and down without the force of his first blows. The ringing sound was almost gentle, but they could all see the charcoal sticking to the metal in dark crusts.

'It has to be fast here. It must not cool too far before the quenching. Watch the colour ... now!'

Cavallo's voice had softened, his eyes filled with love for the metal. As the redness darkened, he lifted his tongs and jammed the sword into a bucket of water in a roar of steam that filled the little workshop.

'Then back into the heat. The most important stage. If you

misjudge the colour now, the sword will be brittle and useless. You must learn the shade, or everything I have taught you has been wasted. For me, it is the colour of day-old blood, but you must find your own memory and fix it in your minds.'

The second sword was ready and he repeated the beating in the charcoal bed, once again scattering embers into the air. It was clear enough by then why they wore the leathers. One Roman grunted in pain as a fiery chip settled on his arm before he could pluck it away.

The swords were reheated and shoved into the charcoal four more times before Cavallo finally nodded. They were all sweating and practically blind from the moisture-laden fog in the workshop. Only the blades cut through the steam, the air burning away from their heat in clear trails.

Dawn lit the mountains outside, though they could not see the light. They had all stared into the furnace for so long that wherever they looked was darkness.

Cavallo's sons covered the tray and dragged it back to the wall. As the Romans breathed and wiped sweat from their eyes, Cavallo shut up his forge and removed the bellows from the air-holes, hanging them neatly on hooks ready to be used again. The heat was still oppressive, but there was a sense of it all coming to an end as he faced them, holding a black blade in each hand, his fingers wrapped around a narrow tang that would be encased in a hilt before use.

The blades were matt and rough-looking. Though he had hammered each using only his eye, they were identical in length and width and when they were cool enough to be handed around, the Roman smiths felt the same balance in each. They nodded at the skill, no longer resentful of the time they had spent away from their own forges. Each of them realised they had been given something of value and they smiled like children as they hefted the bare blades.

Renius took his turn with them, though he lacked the experience to be able to judge the weight without a hilt. The blades had been taken from the earth of Spain and he stroked a finger along the rough metal, hoping he would be able to make Julius understand the glory of the moment.

'The charcoal bed gives them the hard skin over a softer core. These blades will not snap in battle, unless you leave impurities within, or quench them at the wrong colour. Let me show you,' Cavallo said, his voice stiff with pride. He took the blades from the Roman smiths and gestured them to stand back. Then he rapped each one hard onto the edge of his forge, causing a deep tone as if a bell sounded the dawn. The swords remained whole and he breathed slowly in satisfaction.

'They will kill men, these ones. They will make an art of death.' He spoke with reverence and they understood him. 'The new day begins, gentlemen. Your charcoal will be ready by noon and you will return to your own forges to make examples of the new swords. I will want to see them, from all of you, in say . . . three days. Leave them without a hilt and I will craft those with you. Now, I am going to bed.'

The grizzled Roman smiths murmured their thanks and trooped out of the workshop, looking back longingly at the blades they had made that night.

CHAPTER FOUR

∽∽∽∽∽

Pompey and Crassus rose from their seats in the shade to acknowledge the crowd. The racegoers of the Circus Maximus cheered their consuls in a wave of sound and excitement that echoed and crashed around the packed seating. Pompey raised a hand to them and Crassus smiled slightly, enjoying the attention. He deserved it, he thought, after the gold it had cost him. Each clay entry token was stamped with the names of the two consuls and, though they were freely given out, Crassus had heard the tokens were as good as currency in the weeks leading up to the event. Many of those who sat waiting for the first race had paid well for the privilege. It never ceased to please him how his people could turn even gifts into an opportunity for profit.

The weather was fine and only the lightest wisps of clouds drifted across the long track as the crowds settled and shouted bets to each other. There was an air of excitement in the benches and Crassus noted how few families there were. It was a sad fact of life that the races were often marred by fights in the cheaper seats, as men argued over losses. Only a month before, the circus had to be cleared by legionaries called in to restore order. Five men had been killed in a minor riot after the favourite had lost in the final race of the day.

Crassus frowned at the thought, hoping it would not happen again. He stretched up in his seat to note the positions of Pompey's soldiers on the gates and main walkways. Enough to intimidate all but the most foolhardy, he hoped. He did not want the memory of his consular year associated with civil unrest. As things stood, his endorsement of the candidates in the coming elections would still be worth a great deal. Even with more than half his term to serve, the factions in the Senate were shifting as those who hoped for the highest posts began to make themselves known. It was the greatest game in Rome and Crassus knew the favours he could gather would be the currency of power for the following year, if not much longer.

Crassus glanced at his co-consul, wondering if Pompey too was planning for the future. Whenever he was tempted to curse the law that restrained them, he took solace from the fact that Pompey was similarly bound. Rome would not allow another Marius to stand as consul over and over. Those wild days had gone with the shade of Sulla and the civil war. Still, there was nothing to prevent Pompey grooming his own favourites to succeed him.

Crassus wished he could shake the sense of inadequacy that assailed him whenever he and Pompey were together. Unlike his own sharp features, Pompey looked as a consul was expected to look, with a broad, strong face, and gently greying hair. Privately, Crassus wondered if the dignified image was helped along with a little white powder at the temples. Even sitting next to him, he couldn't be sure.

As if the gods hadn't given him enough, Pompey seemed to have their blessing with his military enterprises. He had promised the people to rid the seas of pirates and in only a few months the Roman fleet had swept the Mare Internum clean of the scavengers. Trade had boomed as Pompey had promised. No one in the city thanked Crassus for financing the venture, or for bearing the loss of the ships that didn't survive. Instead, he was forced to throw even more gold at the people in case they forgot him, while Pompey could rest easy in their adoration.

Crassus tapped the fingers of one hand on the other as he thought. The citizens of Rome respected only what they could see. If he raised a legion of his own to patrol the streets, they would bless him every time one of his men caught a thief or broke up a fight. Without one, he knew Pompey would never treat him as an equal. It was not a new idea, but he held back from planting a new standard in the Campus Martius. Always, there was the private fear that Pompey was right in his assessment of him. What victories could Crassus claim for Rome? No matter how he clad them in shining armour, a legion had to be well led and while it seemed effortless for Pompey, the thought of risking another humiliation was more than Crassus could bear.

The campaign against Spartacus had been bad enough, he thought miserably. He was sure they still mocked him for building a wall across the toe of Italy. None of the Senate mentioned it in public, but word had filtered back from the soldiers and his spies told him it was still seen as a subject for laughter amongst the chattering masses of the city. Pompey told him there was nothing in it, but then he could afford to be complacent. No matter who was elected at the end of the year, Pompey would still be a force in the Senate. Crassus wished he could be as certain of his own position.

Both men watched as the seven wooden eggs were brought out to the central spine of the track. At the beginning of each lap, one would be removed until the last would signal the frenzy of struggle that marked the end of each contest.

As the ritual before the races approached completion, Crassus motioned behind him and a smartly dressed slave stepped forward to relay his bets. Though Pompey had disdained the opportunity, Crassus had spent a useful hour with the teams and their horses in the dark stables built under the seating. He considered himself a good judge and thought that the team of Spanish whites under Paulus were unstoppable. He hesitated as the slave waited to relay his bet to his masters. The valley between the hills was usually perfect for horses that preferred a soft track, but there had been little rain for nearly a week and he could see spirals of dust on the ground below the consular box. His mouth was similarly dry as he made up his mind. Paulus had been confident and the gods loved a gambler. This was his day, after all.

'Three sesterces on Paulus' team,' he said, after a long pause. The slave nodded, but as he turned, Crassus grabbed his arm in his bony fingers. 'No, two only. The track is quite dry.'

As the man left, Crassus sensed Pompey's grin.

'I really don't know why you bet,' Pompey said. 'You are easily the richest man in Rome, but you wager less valiantly than half the people here. What are two sesterces to you? A cup of wine?'

Crassus sniffed at a subject he had heard before. Pompey enjoyed teasing him, but he would still come begging for gold when he needed to fund his precious legions. That was a secret pleasure for the older man, though he wondered if Pompey ever thought of it. If Crassus had been in that position, it would have been like slow poison, but Pompey never varied his cheerful manner. The man had no understanding of the dignity of wealth, none at all.

'A horse can twist a leg or a driver fall in any race. You expect me to waste gold on simple chance?'

The betting slave returned and handed Crassus a token, which he held tightly. Pompey looked at him with his pale eyes and there was a distaste there which Crassus pretended not to notice.

'Apart from Paulus, who else is running in the first?' Pompey asked the slave.

'Three others, master. A new team from Thrace, Dacius from Mutina and another team shipped over from Spain. They say the horses from Spain went through a storm that unsettled them. Most of the betting money is going on Dacius at the moment.'

Crassus fixed the man with a glare.

'You did not mention this before,' he snapped. 'Paulus brought his horses over from Spain. Did they suffer in the same ship?'

'I do not know, master,' the slave replied, bowing his head.

Crassus reddened as he wondered whether he should withdraw his bet before the race began. No, not in front of Pompey, unless he could find a reason to excuse himself for a few moments.

Pompey smiled at the other consul's discomfort. 'I will trust the people. One hundred gold on Dacius.'

The slave didn't even blink at an amount greater than his own price at sale.

'Certainly, master. I will fetch you the token.' He paused for a moment in silent enquiry, but Crassus only glared at him.

'Quickly, the race is about to start,' Pompey added, sending the slave off at a run. Pompey had seen two flag-bearers approach the long bronze horn at the edge of the track. The crowd cheered as the note sounded and the gates to the stables opened.

First out was the Roman, Dacius, his light chariot pulled by dark geldings. Crassus fidgeted as he noted the arrogant poise and balance of the man as he brought his team around in a smooth turn to line up at the start. The man was short and stocky and the crowd cheered wildly for him. He saluted towards the consular box, and Pompey rose to return the gesture. Crassus copied the action, but Dacius had already turned away to complete his preparation.

'He looks hungry today, Crassus. His horses are fighting the bit,' Pompey told his colleague cheerfully.

Crassus ignored him, watching the next team onto the sand. It was the Thracian entry, marked out in green. The bearded driver was inexperienced and few of the crowd had put money on him. Nevertheless, they cheered dutifully, though many were already craning to see the last two come out of the gloom of the stables.

Paulus flicked the long looping reins over his Spanish horses as they thundered out into the light. Crassus thumped the rail with his fist at the sight of them.

'Dacius will have to work hard to beat these. Look at their condition, Pompey. Glorious.'

Paulus did look confident as he saluted the consuls. Even at a distance, Crassus saw the flash of white teeth against his dark skin and some of his worry eased. The team took its place with the others and the last Spanish competitor rode out to join them.

Crassus had seen nothing wrong with the horses in his first visit, but now he studied them for signs of weakness. Despite his assertions to Pompey, he was suddenly convinced the stallions looked ill at ease compared to the others. Crassus took his seat reluctantly as the horn sounded again and the betting ceased. The slave returned to hand Pompey his token and the consul played idly with it while they waited.

Silence fell across the mass of people. Dacius' team took fright at something and sidestepped into the Thracian, forcing both men to crack their whips over their heads. A good driver could snap the tip of his whip inches away from any one of his horses at full gallop and order was quickly restored. Crassus noted the Thracian's calm and wondered if a chance had been missed. The little man didn't seem at all out of place amongst the more experienced charioteers.

The silence held as the horses pawed and snorted in place for a moment, then the horn was blown a third time, its wail lost in the roar as the teams lunged forward and the race began.

'You have done well, Crassus,' Pompey said, looking over the heads of the crowd. 'I doubt there's a man in Rome who doesn't know your generosity.'

Crassus glanced sharply at him, looking for mockery. Pompey was impassive and didn't seem to feel the gaze.

Below them, the thundering horses reached the first corner. The light chariots scored long sliding arcs in the sand as they were pulled around by the plunging horses. The riders leaned over to balance themselves, held in place by nothing more than their skill and strength. It was an impressive display and Dacius slid neatly between two teams to take an early lead. Crassus frowned at the development.

'Have you decided whom you will support for consul at the end of the year?' he said, forcing a neutral tone.

Pompey smiled. 'It's a little early to be thinking of it, my friend. I am enjoying being consul myself at the moment.'

Crassus snorted at the blatant falsehood. He knew Pompey too well to believe his denials. Under the pressure of his stare, Pompey shrugged.

'I believe Senator Prandus can be persuaded to put his name on the lists,' he said.

Crassus watched the racing teams, considering what he knew of the man.

'There are worse choices,' he said at last. 'Would he accept your . . . guidance?'

Pompey's eyes were bright with excitement as Dacius continued to lead the field. Crassus wondered if he was feigning the interest merely to annoy him.

'Pompey?' he prompted.

51

'He would not be troublesome,' Pompey replied.

Crassus hid his pleasure. Neither Prandus nor his son Suetonius were men of influence in the Senate, but having weak men as consuls would mean he and Pompey could continue to guide the city, merely exchanging the public aspect for the private. Returning to the anonymity of the back benches after leading Rome was an unpleasant prospect for both of them. Crassus wondered if Pompey knew he held debts on the family and would have his own form of control if Prandus was elected.

'I could accept Prandus, if you are sure of him,' he said over the noise of the crowd. Pompey turned an amused expression to him.

'Excellent. Do you know if Cinna will stand?'

Crassus shook his head. 'He's all but retired since the death of his daughter. Have you heard something?'

In his eagerness, Crassus reached out to hold Pompey's arm and Pompey grimaced at the touch. Crassus felt a spike of hatred for the man. What right did he have to assume such airs, when Crassus paid the bills of his great houses?

'I have heard nothing yet, Crassus. If not Cinna, though, we must find another to stand for the second post. Perhaps it is not too soon to begin cultivating a new name.'

As the fourth lap began, Dacius led by a full length, with the Thracian holding position behind him. Paulus was third, with the sea-sick Spanish horses bringing up the rear. The crowd bellowed their approval and every eye was on the teams as they rounded the far corner and galloped through the start for the fifth lap. The wooden egg was removed and the bawling voices were becoming hoarse.

'Have you considered Julius? His term in Spain is almost over,' Crassus said.

Pompey glanced over at him, suddenly wary. He still suspected Crassus of a loyalty to the young Caesar that he did not share. Had the man not waived the debts of the Tenth shortly after Julius took control? Pompey shook his head.

'Not him, Crassus. That dog has teeth. I'm sure you don't want . . . disruption any more than I.'

Dacius had increased his lead and Crassus continued to speak, pleased to be able to ruffle the smooth placidity of his colleague.

'They say Caesar has done very well in Spain. New lands under our control, new cities. I believe there has even been talk of a Triumph for him.'

Pompey looked sharply at Crassus, his brow furrowing.

'I've heard nothing of Triumphs and I have made myself clear. When his posting is over, I will send him somewhere else. Greece, perhaps. Whatever you are planning should be forgotten, Crassus. I witnessed my own men standing in the rain for that one when they saw his oak wreath. My own men, honouring a stranger! You remember Marius well enough. We don't want another one in the city, especially as consul.'

Crassus didn't reply for a long moment and Pompey chose to interpret the silence as assent.

Below them on the track, Dacius came up behind the Spanish team and moved to lap them. The faltering driver swerved violently as Dacius passed him, losing control for a split second. It was long enough. With a crash that could be heard over the appalled howl of the crowd, both teams were fouled and the neat lines of horses became screaming chaos in an instant.

The Thracian heaved his reins over to clear the wreckage. His whip snapped at the inner horses, forcing them to shorten their stride for a turn that nearly had him over. The crowd watched in agony as the little man guided them around, but then they were through and clear and many in the circus rose to their feet to applaud his skill.

Pompey swore under his breath as he saw Dacius lying still on the sand. One of his legs was twisted peculiarly. His knee had clearly been shattered and though he still lived, he would not race again.

'Signal the guards I gave you, Crassus. There will be fighting once they recover from the shock.'

Crassus set his jaw in anger, catching the eye of a centurion and holding up a clenched fist. They moved down amongst the benches and it was not a moment too soon. After the excitement at the destruction of the horses and chariots, the crowd had become aware of their lost bets and howled as one in an orgy of frustration. The final laps went without incident, the Thracian first across the line to general indifference. Fights had already broken out and the legionaries acted swiftly, using the flats of their swords to separate struggling men from each other.

Pompey signalled his personal guard that he was ready to leave and they cleared a path for him. He exchanged a glance with Crassus as he left and saw the man's dislike, for once unmasked. As he reached the street, Pompey was lost in thought, barely hearing the growing disruption behind him.

Julius dismounted at the edge of the village, his horse gently snickering as it cropped at grass between the stones of an ancient road. He and Servilia had ridden far inland and there was no sign of life in the hills around them. It was a beautiful country, with vast swathes of forest and chalky cliffs that dropped into green valleys. The sun had moved past the noon point before they came to this place. They had seen mottled red deer and boars that ran squealing from their horses.

Julius had taken long, looping trails to avoid all signs of people on their ride. He seemed content to be alone with her and Servilia was flattered. At times, it seemed as if they were the only ones alive. The forests were full of shadows and silence and they passed through the gloom almost as ghosts themselves. Then the trees would give way to bright sunlight and a grassy plain and they would gallop recklessly away from the dark until they were panting and laughing together. Servilia could not remember a more perfect day.

The village Julius led her into was a strange place at the foot of a valley. A river ran close by, but as in the forests, there were no voices to break the stillness. The houses were slumping with age and wild ferns and ivy grew out of windows from within. Everywhere there were signs of decay. Doors that had been hung on stiff leather hinges yawned open at them and wild animals scuttled out of their sight as they led their horses along a street towards the centre. The quiet of the empty village made speech difficult, as if it was an intrusion. Servilia was reminded of the echoing vaults of a temple and wondered why Julius had brought her to it.

'Why did they leave?' she asked him.

He shrugged. 'It could be anything: invasion, disease. Perhaps they just wanted to find a new home somewhere else. I spent days here when I first came, but the houses were looted long ago and there's little left to show how they lived. It is a strange place, though I love it. If we ever reach this valley with our bridges and new streets, I will be sad to see it go.'

A faded piece of pottery that could once have been a sign jarred his foot and he knelt to look at it, blowing away the dust. It was blank and so thin that he could snap it in his hands.

'I suppose it looked like Valentia, once. A market and crops to sell, children running around with chickens. Difficult to imagine now.'

Servilia looked around her and tried to conjure up the image of a place full of bustling people. A lizard ran along a wall near her, catching her eye for a second before it vanished under a sagging eave. There was something eerie in walking through such a place, as if at any moment the streets would fill with life and noise again, the interruption to their lives forgotten.

'Why do you come here?' she asked.

He looked sideways at her, smiling strangely. 'I'll show you,' he said, turning a corner into a wider road.

The houses here were little more than heaps of rubble and Servilia could see a square beyond them. The sunlight made the air warm and light as they approached it and Julius quickened his step in anticipation as they reached the open ground.

The heavy stones of the square were cracked and lined with creeping grass and wild flowers, but Julius walked across them without looking, his eyes fastened on a broken pedestal and a statue that lay beside it in pieces. The features were almost completely worn away and the white stone was chipped and battered, yet Julius approached it with reverence. He tied their horses to a sapling that had sprung up through the stone of the square and leaned against the statue, tracing the features with his hand. An arm had gone, but she could see the statue had been a powerful figure once. Servilia saw where words had been cut into the heavy plinth and she traced the strange characters with her finger.

'Who is it?' she whispered.

'One of the local scholars told me it says "Alexander the King".'

Julius' voice was rough with emotion and she felt again the desire to touch him, to share his thoughts. To her astonishment, she saw tears form in his eyes as he gazed at the stone face.

'What is it? I don't understand,' she said, reaching out to him without a thought. His skin felt hot against her hand and he didn't move away.

'Seeing him . . .' he said softly, wiping his eyes. For a moment, he pressed her hand against him with his own before letting it fall. After another long look at the stone figure, he shrugged, having found control once more.

'By the time he was my age, he had conquered the world. They said he was a god. Compared to that, I have wasted my life.'

Servilia sat on the ledge next to him, their thighs touching lightly, though she felt every part of the contact. Julius spoke again after a while, his voice distant with memory.

'When I was a boy, I used to listen to the stories of his battles and his life. He was . . . astonishing. He had the world in his hand when he was little more than a child. I used to imagine myself . . . I used to see his path once.'

Again, Servilia reached up to his face, smoothing the skin. He seemed to feel it for the first time and raised his head to look at her as she spoke.

'It is here for you, if you want it,' she said, unsure as she spoke whether she was offering more than just a hope of glory, or something more personal. He seemed to hear both meanings in her words and took her hand again. This time, his eyes searched hers at the touch, asking a silent question.

'I want it all,' he whispered and she could not have said which of them moved to kiss the other. It simply happened, and they felt the strength of it as they sat at the feet of Alexander.

CHAPTER FIVE

In the days that followed, time seemed to pass more slowly when Servilia could not find an excuse to take the horses out again. The Golden Hand was running well and she had brought two men from Rome large enough to quieten the wildest reveller. Instead of taking pleasure from the success, she found her thoughts constantly drifting back to the strange young man who could be vulnerable and frightening in the same moment. She had forced herself not to ask for him again and then waited for his invitation. When it had come, she had laughed aloud, amused at herself, yet unable to resist the excitement it brought.

She stopped to add another stem to the circlet she was weaving as they walked through a field of swaying corn. Julius paused with her, more relaxed than he had felt for a long time. The depression that had crushed him seemed to vanish in her company and it was strange to think that their first ride into the wilderness had been only a few weeks before. She had seen the parts of his life that mattered most to him and he felt as if he had always known Servilia.

With her, the nightmares he tried to drown like pups in heavy wine had lifted, though he felt them circling still. She was the blessing of Alexander over him, a ward against the shadows that pressed him into despair. He could forget who he had become, dropping the mantle of his authority. An hour or two each day in sunshine that warmed more than his skin.

He looked at her as she straightened, wondering at the force of the feelings she engendered. In one moment she could reveal a knowledge of the city and the senators that would leave him breathless, and in another she could be almost childlike as she laughed or chose another bloom to weave with the rest.

Brutus had encouraged the friendship after that first trip to the village of the broken statue. He saw that Servilia was like a balm to his friend's troubled spirit, beginning to heal wounds that had festered for too long.

'Pompey was wrong to have the slaves crucified,' Julius said, remembering the line of crosses and the weeping, tortured figures on them, waiting for death. The images of the great slave rebellion were still painfully fresh in his mind, even after four years. Crows had gorged until they were too fat to fly and cawed in anger at his men as they kicked out at the staggering birds. Julius shuddered slightly.

'After the beginning, we didn't offer the slaves anything but death. They knew we'd never let them run. They were badly led and Pompey had them tied and nailed all the way up the Via from the south. It was not greatness in him, then, responding to the terror of the mob.'

'You would not have done it?' Servilia asked.

'Spartacus and his gladiators had to die, but there were brave men in the ranks who had faced legions and beaten them. No, I would have formed a new legion and salted it with the hardest bastard centurions from all the others. Six thousand brave men, Servilia, all wasted for his ambition. It would have been a better example than putting them all on crosses, but Pompey can see no further than his petty rules and traditions. He holds his line while the rest of the world moves past him.'

'The people cheered them into the city, Julius. Pompey was the one they really wanted as consul. Crassus took the second seat in his shadow.'

'Better if they had turned the slaves on their own,' Julius muttered. 'They would stand tall then, rather than rushing to kiss the feet of Pompey. Better to grow your crops rather than cry out for men like Pompey to give you food. It's a sickness in us, you know. We always raise unworthy men to rule us.'

He struggled to find words and Servilia stopped, turning to face him. On such a hot day, she had chosen a stola of thin linen and wore her hair bound back with a silver thread, revealing her neck. Every day he spent with her seemed to bring some facet to his attention. He wanted to kiss her throat.

'He destroyed the pirates, Julius. Of all people, you should be pleased at that.'

'Of course I am,' he said bitterly, 'though I wanted the task myself. Pompey doesn't dream, Servilia. There are whole new lands rich with pearls and gold, but he rests and organises games for the people. They starve in the fields while he builds new temples for them to pray for wealth.'

'You would do more?' she asked, taking his arm. The touch was warm and his thoughts fled before the onslaught of a sudden passion that surprised him. He wondered if his thoughts showed, as he stammered a reply.

'I *would* do more. There is gold enough to raise the least of Rome and the chance is there for us, if we can grasp it. There is nothing in the world like our city. They say Egypt is richer, but we are still young enough to fill our hands. Pompey is asleep if he thinks the borders will remain safe with the legions we have. We need to raise more, and pay for them with new lands and gold.'

She let her hand drop, feeling a shiver of desire raise the soft hairs of her skin. There was such a force in him, when it was not shuttered in grief and despair. She saw the darkness cast away with both awe and pleasure. The man who aroused her with a touch was not the one who had met her first at the gates of the fort and she wondered what would come of the reawakening.

When she felt herself longing for him, it had shocked her, almost frightened her. That was not how it was meant to be. The men who loved her never touched more than the skin they craved. They could spend themselves in her without more than a tremble of real response. Yet this strange young man threw her into confusion whenever his blue eyes caught hers. Such strange eyes, with the dark pupil that hurt him in bright light. It seemed to see all her artifice for what it was, breaking through the smoothness of her ways to the privacy of her.

She sighed as they walked on. She was being foolish. This was no time in her life to be moonstruck by a man her son's age. She ran her hand along the line of her bound hair unconsciously. Not that her years showed, at all. She oiled her body every night and ate well and carefully. A man could take her for thirty, she had been told, rather than the year shy of forty to which she admitted. Forty-two. Sometimes she felt older than that, especially in the city, when Crassus came to her. Sometimes she would weep for no reason at all, the mood vanishing as quickly as it had come. She knew the young man at her side could have any of the young girls of the city. He would not want one who carried so many marks on her, that no one else could see.

She crossed her arms, almost crushing the circlet of bound flowers. She didn't doubt she could rouse him to passion if she wanted. He was young and innocent compared to her. It would be easy, and she realised that part of her wanted it, would

61

welcome his hands on her in the long grasses of the meadow. She shook her head slightly. Stupid girl. Should never have kissed him.

She spoke quickly to cover the pause, wondering if he had noticed her distraction, or the flush that had come to her cheeks.

'You haven't seen Rome recently, Julius. There are so many poor now. The slave army left almost no one to work the fields and the beggars are like flies. At least Pompey gives them a taste of glory, even when their bellies are empty. The Senate wouldn't dare to hold him back in anything, in case the mobs rise and consume them all. It was a fragile peace when I left and I doubt anything has improved since then. You couldn't know how close they are to chaos. The Senate lives in fear of another uprising to rival the battles with Spartacus. Everyone who can afford them has guards and the poor kill each other in the streets with nothing done about it. They are not easy times, Julius.'

'Perhaps I should return then. I haven't seen my daughter in four years and Pompey owes me a great deal. Perhaps it is time to call in a few of my debts and make sure I am a part of the work again.'

For a moment, his face lit with a passion that made her heart lift as she saw the image of the man she'd watched at the trial, holding the Senate rapt as he took justice from his enemies. Then, just as quickly, it was gone and he blew air through his lips in exasperation.

'I had a wife to share it with before all this. I had Tubruk, who was more like a father to me than a friend; my home. The future was rushing on me with a kind of . . . joy. Now, I've nothing but new swords and mines and it seems pointless. I would give anything to have Tubruk come back for one hour to share a drink with me, or the chance to see Cornelia just for a while, long enough to say sorry for breaking my promises to her.'

He rubbed his eyes with his hand before walking on. Servilia almost reached for him then, knowing her touch could bring him comfort. She resisted with an enormous effort of will. The touch would lead to more and though she ached to be held herself, she had the strength not to play the game she knew so well, that she had known all her life. A younger woman might have gathered him in without shame at the moment of his weakness, but Servilia knew too much to try. There would be other days.

Then he turned to her and held her tightly enough to hurt, his mouth pressing her lips to open for him. She gave way to it, unable to help herself.

Brutus slid neatly from the saddle as he passed under the gates of the fort. The Tenth had staged complex manoeuvres out in the hills and Octavian had done well, using the force he had been given to flank Domitius in a skilful display. Brutus didn't hesitate as he ran into the buildings. The dark moods that had cast a cloud over them all were already a memory and he knew Julius would be pleased to hear how well his young relative was doing. Octavian had the shoulders to command, as Marius used to say.

The guard at the base of the steps was out of position, standing well back from his post. Brutus heard him shout as he clattered up the stairs, but only grinned.

Julius was lying on a couch with Servilia, their faces flushed in panic at the sudden, noisy arrival of Brutus into the room. Julius leapt naked to his feet and faced his friend in rage.

'Get out!' he roared.

Brutus froze in disbelief, then his face twisted and he spun around, slamming the door shut behind him.

Julius turned slowly to meet Servilia's eyes, already regretting his anger. He pulled his clothes on roughly, sitting back on the long couch. Her perfume was heavy in his nostrils and he knew he smelled of her. As he stood, the warmth of the cloth was left behind and he drew away, thinking of what he had to do.

'I'll go out to him,' she said, standing.

Wrapped in bitterness, Julius barely noticed her nudity. It had been madness to fall asleep where they could be found, but there was no point in regretting what was past. He shook his head as he tied his sandals.

'You have less of an apology to make. Let me find him first,' he said.

Her eyes hardened for a moment. 'You won't apologise . . . for me?' she said, her voice deceptively calm.

Julius stood and faced her. 'Not for a moment of you,' he said, softly.

She came into his arms then and he found there was something indescribably erotic in holding a naked woman while fully clothed. He broke away with a grin despite his worry for Brutus.

'He'll be all right when he's calmed down a little,' he said to reassure her, wishing he believed it. With steady hands, he buckled his gladius to his waist. Servilia looked suddenly afraid.

'I don't want you to fight him, Julius. You must not.'

Julius forced a laugh that seemed to echo in his empty stomach.

'He'd never hurt me,' he said as he left.

Outside the door, Julius' expression settled into a grim mask as he came down the stairs. Domitius and Cabera were there with Ciro, and he imagined their eyes accused him.

'Where is he?' Julius snapped.

'Training yard,' Domitius said. 'I'd leave him for a while if I were you, General. His blood's running hot and it'll do no good to have it out now.'

Julius hesitated, then his old recklessness swept through him. He had brought it about and the price was his to pay.

'Stay here,' he said curtly. 'He's my oldest friend and this is private.'

Brutus stood alone in the empty yard, a gladius by Cavallo glittering in his hand. He nodded as Julius walked towards him and once again Julius almost hesitated at the black glare that followed his every movement. If it came to blood, he could not beat Brutus. Even if he could steal victory, he doubted he could take that life above all others.

Brutus brought the shining blade into first position and Julius emptied his mind with the old discipline Renius had taught. This was an enemy and he could kill him.

Julius unsheathed his sword.

'Did you pay her?' Brutus said softly, breaking his concentration.

Julius fought against the spiky anger that came to him then. They had both learned from the same man and he knew better than to listen. They began to circle each other.

'I think I knew, but I didn't believe it,' Brutus began again. 'I knew you wouldn't shame me with her, so I didn't worry.'

'There is no shame,' Julius replied.

'Yes. There is,' Brutus said and moved.

Of all men, Julius knew his style better than anyone, but he barely managed to parry a blade sent straight at his heart. It was a killing blow and he could not excuse it. Anger rose in him then and he moved a little faster, his step a little firmer on the ground as his senses quickened. So be it.

Julius darted in, ducking under a sweep of silver and forcing Brutus onto his back foot. He pulled his blade to the side to cut, but Brutus skipped away with a sneer, then answered with a rain of blows.

They broke clear, beginning to pant slightly. Julius clenched his left hand into a fist to close a gash across his palm. The blood dripped slowly from it as he moved around, leaving spots like glossy eyes to vanish in the sand.

'I love her,' Julius said. 'I love you. Too much for this.' With a gesture of disgust, he threw his sword away and stood facing his friend.

Brutus brought the point up to his throat and looked into Julius' eyes.

'They all know? Cabera, Domitius, Octavian?'

Julius looked steadily back at him, steeling himself not to flinch.

'Perhaps. We didn't plan it, Brutus. I didn't want you to walk in on us.'

The sword was a still point in a moving world. Julius clenched his jaw, a vast sense of calm settling over him. He relaxed every muscle consciously and stood waiting. He did not want to die, but if it came, he would treat it with contempt.

'This is no small thing, Marcus. Not for me, not for her,' he said.

The sword came down suddenly and the manic light died from Brutus' eyes.

'There is so much between us, Julius, but if you hurt her, I *will* kill you.'

'Go and see her. She's worried about you,' Julius replied, ignoring the threat.

Brutus held his gaze for a long moment more before walking away and leaving him alone in the training yard. Julius watched him go, then opened his hand with a wince. For a moment, anger surged again. He would have hanged any other man who dared to raise a sword against him. There could be no excuse.

Yet they had been boys together and that counted. Perhaps enough to swallow the betrayal of a blade aimed at his heart. Julius narrowed his eyes in thought. It would be harder to trust the man a second time.

The next six weeks were filled with almost unbearable tension. Though Brutus had spoken with his mother and given a tight-lipped blessing to the union, he walked the compound with his anger and loneliness like a cloak around him.

Without a word of explanation, Julius began to drill the Tenth himself again. He took them out alone for days at a time and never spoke except to give his orders. For their part, the legionaries struggled through pain and exhaustion just to receive a nod from him and that seemed to be worth more than effusive praise from anyone else.

When he was in the barracks, Julius wrote letters and orders far into the night, cutting deeply into the reserves of gold he'd built up. He sent riders back to Rome to commission new armour from Alexandria's workshop and caravans of supplies wound their way through the mountains from Spanish cities. New mines had to be cut to supply iron ore for the swords being produced at Cavallo's design. Forests were felled for charcoal and there was never a moment when any one of the five thousand soldiers of the Tenth did not have two or three tasks that needed doing.

His officers were caught between the pain of being excluded and a kind of joy at seeing Julius rediscover the old energy. Long before Julius summoned his subordinates from their posts around the country, they guessed the time in Spain was coming to an end. Hispania was simply too small to contain the general of the Tenth.

Julius chose the most able of the Spanish quaestors to take his place in the interim until Rome appointed another of her sons. He handed over the seal of his office and then threw himself back into working all day and night, sometimes going without sleep for three days in a row before collapsing in exhaustion. After a short rest, he would rise and begin again. Those in the barracks trod carefully around him and waited nervously for the result of all his labour.

Brutus came to him in the early hours of a morning, when the camp was still and silent all around them. He knocked on the door and entered as Julius called out a muttered response.

Julius sat at a desk strewn with maps and clay tablets, with more on the floor at his feet. He stood as he saw Brutus and for a moment, the coldness between them seemed to prohibit speech. The habit of friendship was rusty for both of them.

Brutus swallowed painfully. 'I'm sorry,' he said.

Julius remained silent, watching him. The face he presented was like a stranger's, with nothing of the friendship Brutus missed.

Brutus tried again. 'I was a fool, but you've known me long enough to let it go,' he said. 'I am your friend. Your sword, remember?'

Julius nodded, accepting him. 'I love Servilia,' he said softly. 'I would have told you before anyone else, but it came too quickly between us. There are no games here, but my relationship is private. I will not answer to you for it.'

'When I saw you together, I . . .' Brutus began.

Julius held up a stiff hand.

'No. I don't want to hear that again. It's done.'

'Gods, you won't make this easy for me, will you?' Brutus said, shaking his head.

'It shouldn't be. I care more for you than any man I've ever met, and you struck to kill me in the training yard. That is hard to forgive.'

'What?' Brutus replied quickly. 'I didn't . . .'

'I *know*, Brutus.'

Brutus slumped slightly. Without another word, he pulled up a stool. After a moment, Julius took his own seat.

'Do you want me to keep apologising? I was raging. I thought you were using her like . . . It was a mistake, I'm sorry. What more do you want?'

'I want to know I can trust you. I want all this to be forgotten,' Julius replied.

Brutus stood. 'You can trust me. You know it. I gave up Primigenia for you. Let this go.'

As they looked at each other, a smile crept onto Julius' face.

'Did you notice how I parried the stroke? I wish Renius could have seen that.'

'*Yes*, you were very good,' Brutus replied sarcastically. 'Are you satisfied?'

'I think I could have won,' Julius said cheerfully.

Brutus blinked at him. 'Now that's going too far.'

The tension between them receded to a distant pressure.

'I'm going to take the legion back to Rome,' Julius said in a rush, relieved to have his friend to share his plans once again. He wondered if the weeks after the fight had hurt Brutus half as much as they had hurt him.

'We all know, Julius. The men gossip like a group of old women. Is it to challenge Pompey?' Brutus spoke casually, as if the lives of thousands didn't hang on the answer.

'No, he rules well enough, with Crassus. I will put my name forward to be consul at the elections.' He watched Brutus for a reaction.

'You think you can win?' Brutus replied slowly, thinking it over. 'You'll have only a few months and the people have a short memory.'

'I am the last surviving blood of Marius. I will remind them,' Julius said and Brutus felt the stirring of the old excitement. He reflected on how his friend had experienced almost a rebirth in the last months. The snapping anger had gone and his mother had played her part in it. Even his dear little Angelina was in awe of Servilia and he could begin to understand why.

'It's almost dawn. You should get some sleep,' he said.

'Not yet, there's a lot still to do before we can see Rome again.'

'Then I will stay with you, unless you mind,' Brutus said, stifling another yawn.

Julius smiled at him. 'I don't mind. I need someone to write as I dictate.'

CHAPTER SIX

〰〰〰

Renius stood in the dry riverbed and looked up at the bridge. The structure swarmed with Romans and local men, clambering over a skeleton of wood that shifted and creaked as they moved along the walkways. Two hundred feet from the dry riverbed to the stones of the road above. When it was complete, the dam upriver would be removed and the water would hide the massive feet of the bridge, washing around the shaped edges for long after the builders had gone to dust. Just being in the shadow of it was a strange feeling for the old gladiator. When the waters came, no one would ever stand there again.

He shook his head in silent pride, listening to the orders and calls as the winch teams began to raise another of the blocks that would form the arch. Their voices echoed under the bridge and Renius could see they shared his satisfaction. This bridge would never fall and they knew it.

The road above his head would open up a fertile valley in a direct line to the coast. Towns would be built and the roads extended to meet the needs of the new settlers. They would come for the good ground and for trade and most of all for the clean, sweet water issuing from the underground aqueducts that had taken three years to build.

Renius watched as a team of men threw their strength on the heavy ropes as the archstone was swung over to its position. The pulleys squealed and he saw Ciro was leaning out over the rail to guide the block home. Men at his side slathered brown mortar over the surfaces and then Ciro wrapped his arms around it, chanting with the others in a lulling rhythm to the teams below. Renius held his breath. Though the giant's strength was unmatched among the teams, a slip could easily crush a hand or a shoulder. If the block swung out of position, it was heavy enough to bring the supports crashing down, taking them all with it.

Even so far below, Renius could hear Ciro grunting as he moved the block into place, the mortar squeezing out to fall in wet pats on the riverbed below. Renius shaded his eyes to see if one would come close enough to make him duck away, smiling at their efforts.

He liked the big man. Ciro didn't say a great deal, but he held nothing back when it came to hard work and Renius would have liked him for that alone. It had surprised him at first to find he enjoyed teaching Ciro the skills more experienced legionaries took for granted. A legion could not be stopped by valleys or mountains. Every man on the scaffolding knew that there wasn't a river they couldn't bridge or a road they couldn't cut in all the world. They built Rome wherever they went.

Ciro had been awed by the water and the miles of tunnels they had cut to bring it down from springs high in the mountains. Now the people who settled in the valley would not face disease every summer, with their wells becoming stale and thick. Perhaps then they would think of the men of Rome who had built them.

The peace of Renius' thoughts was interrupted by a single rider in light armour guiding his horse over the bank and down to where he stood. The man was sweating in the heat and craned his neck to look up in instinctive fear as he passed under the arches. A heavy hammer dropped from that height could kill the horse as well as the man on it, but Renius chuckled at his caution.

'You have a message for me?' Renius asked him.

The man trotted into the shadow of the arch and dismounted.

'Yes, sir. The general requests your attendance at the barracks. He said to bring the legionary named Ciro with you, sir.'

'The last arch is nearly finished, lad.'

'He said to come immediately, sir.'

Renius frowned, then squinted up at Ciro high above him. Only a fool would shout orders to a man carrying a stone almost as heavy as he was, but he saw Ciro was standing back, wiping sweat from his brow with a rag. Renius filled his lungs.

'Come down, Ciro. We're wanted.'

Despite the sun, Octavian felt chilled as the breeze whipped past his skin. His fifty were at full gallop down the steepest hill he had ever seen. If he hadn't gone over every foot of it that morning, he would never have dared such a breakneck speed, but the turf was even and none of the experienced riders fell, using the strength of their legs to wedge them in the saddles. Even then, the pommel horns pressed sharply against their groins. Octavian gritted his teeth against the pain as the gallop bruised him unmercifully.

Brutus had chosen the hill with him, to show the reality and power of a charge. He awaited their arrival with a full century of the extraordinarii at the foot of the hill and even at that distance Octavian could see the mounts move skittishly as they instinctively tried to shy away from the thundering fifty coming down.

The noise was incredible, as Octavian shouted for his men to dress the line. The charging rank was becoming a little ragged and he had to roar at his best volume to catch the attention of the wavering riders around him. They showed their skill as the line firmed without slowing and Octavian drew his sword, gripping furiously with his knees. His legs were tortured at such an angle, but he held on.

The ground levelled slightly at the bottom and Octavian barely had time to balance his weight before his fifty were streaming through the wide-spaced ranks that faced them. Faces and horses blurred at appalling speed as they shot through the century and out the other side in what seemed like a single instant of time. Octavian saw an officer looking pale as he flashed past him. If he had held the sword out, the man's head would have flown.

Octavian shouted in excitement as he called for his men to turn and re-form. Some of them laughed in relief as they rejoined Brutus and saw the tense expressions of the men he commanded that day.

'With the right ground, we can be terrifying,' Brutus said, raising his voice for them all to hear. 'I practically lost my bladder there at the end and I *knew* you were just going through us!'

The riders under Octavian cheered the admission, though they didn't believe it. One of them slapped Octavian on the back as Brutus turned to face them, with a leer.

'Now you'll get a taste of it. Form up into wide ranks while I take mine up the hill. Hold them steady as we come through and you'll learn something.'

Octavian swallowed sudden nervousness to grin, still filled with the wild thrill of the charge. Brutus dismounted to lead his horse up the hill and then saw a lone horseman cantering towards them.

'What's this, I wonder?' he murmured.

The soldier dismounted neatly and saluted Brutus.

'General Caesar is asking for Octavian and yourself, sir.'

Brutus nodded, a slow smile beginning.

'Is he now?' He turned to his beloved extraordinarii.

'What if your officers were killed in the first charge? Would there be chaos? Carry on without us. I will expect a full report when you return to barracks.'

Octavian and Brutus fell in behind the messenger as he wheeled his mount. After a while, they tired of the pace he set and galloped past him.

Cabera ran his fingers along a length of blue silk with childish delight. He seemed to be caught between amazement and laughter at the costly furnishings Servilia had shipped in for the Golden Hand, and her patience was wearing thin. He interrupted her again to dart past and handle a delicate piece of statuary.

'So you *see*,' she tried once more, 'I would like to establish a reputation for a clean house and some soldiers use chalk dust to cover the rashes they have ...'

'All this for pleasure!' Cabera interrupted, winking suggestively at her. 'I want to die in a place like this.' As she frowned at him, he approached the edge of a pit of silk cushions, set below the level of the floor. He looked at her for permission and Servilia shook her head firmly.

'Julius said you have a fair knowledge of the diseases of the skin and I would pay well for you to be available to the house.' She was forced to pause again as the old man jumped into the mass of cushions and scrambled around in them, chuckling.

'It isn't difficult work,' Servilia continued doggedly. 'My girls will recognise a problem when they see it, but if there's an argument, I need someone to be able to examine the ... man in question. Just until I can find a more permanent doctor from the town.' She watched astonished as Cabera tumbled around.

'I'll pay five sesterces a month,' she said.

'Fifteen,' Cabera replied, suddenly serious. As she blinked in surprise, he smoothed his old robe down with swift strokes from his fingers.

'I will not go higher than ten, old man. For fifteen, I can have a local doctor living here.'

Cabera snorted. 'They know nothing and you would lose a room. Twelve, but I won't deal with pregnancy. You find someone else for that.'

'I do not run a backstreet whorehouse,' Servilia snapped. 'My girls can watch the moon like any other woman. If they do fall pregnant, I pay them off. Most come back to me after the child is weaned. Ten is my final offer.'

'Examining the rotting parts of soldiers is worth twelve sesterces to anyone,' Cabera told her cheerfully. 'I would also like some of these cushions.'

Servilia gritted her teeth.

'They cost more than your services, old man. Twelve, then, but the cushions stay.'

Cabera clapped his hands in pleasure. 'First month's pay up front and a cup of wine to seal the agreement, I think?' he said.

Servilia opened her mouth to reply and heard a throat delicately cleared behind her. It was Nadia, one of the new ones she had brought to the house, a woman with kohl-rimmed eyes as hard as her body was soft.

'Mistress, there is a messenger from the legion at the door.'

'Bring him to me, Nadia.' Servilia said, forcing a smile. As the woman disappeared, she spun to Cabera.

'Out of there, now. I will not be embarrassed by you.'

Cabera clambered out of the silken pit, his long fingers slipping one of the cushions under his robe as she turned back to greet the messenger.

75

The man was blushing furiously and Servilia could see from Nadia's grin at his shoulder that she had been talking to him.

'Madam, Caesar wants you at the barracks.' His eyes swivelled to Cabera. 'You too, healer. I'm to be your escort. The horses are outside.'

Servilia rubbed the corner of her mouth in thought, ignoring the way the messenger watched her.

'Will my son be there?' she asked.

The messenger nodded. 'Everyone is being called in, madam. I have only Centurion Domitius to find.'

'That's easily done, then. He's upstairs,' she said, watching with interest as the man's blush spread down his neck into his tunic. She could practically feel the heat coming off him.

'I'd leave it a little while, if I were you,' she said.

As they seated themselves in the long room overlooking the yard, every one of them felt hollow twinges of excitement as they caught each other's eyes. Julius dominated the room as he stood by the window, waiting for the last to arrive. The breeze off the hills spun slowly through the room and cooled them, but the tension was almost painful. Octavian laughed nervously as Cabera pulled a silk cushion from under his robe and Renius held his wine cup in too tight a grip.

As the guard closed the door and went down the stairs, Brutus drained his wine and grinned. 'So are you going to tell us why we're here, Julius?'

They all watched the man who faced them. The familiar tiredness had vanished from his features and he stood straight, his armour shining with oil.

'Gentlemen, Servilia. We are finished here. It's time to go home,' he said.

There was a moment of silence and then Servilia jumped in her seat as the others cheered and laughed together.

'I'll drink to that,' Renius said, tilting his cup.

Julius unrolled a map on his desk and they crowded around him as he laid weights at the corners. Servilia felt excluded and then Julius caught her eye and smiled at her. It would be all right.

As Julius discussed the problems of moving five thousand men, she began to calculate. The Golden Hand was barely started and who would run it if she left? Angelina didn't have the iron in her. She'd be running a free house within a year if Servilia left her in charge. Nadia, possibly. A heart of flint and experienced enough, but could she be trusted not to steal half the profits? Hearing her own name snapped her back from her thoughts.

' . . . not by land then, in the time. Servilia gave me the idea when we met the merchant captain she uses. I'll write orders to commandeer every ship on the passage. That is not to be discussed except between ourselves. If they hear we're going to use their ships, they'll put to sea and stay there.'

'Why are you leaving before you're finished here?' Cabera said softly.

The conversation around the table died to nothing and Julius paused with his finger on the map.

'I *am* finished here. This is not where I should be,' he replied. 'You told me that yourself. If I wait out my term, Pompey will send me somewhere else well away from my city and if I refuse, that will be my last posting anywhere. There are no second chances from that man.' Julius tapped his finger on the map over the tiny mark of the city he loved.

'There are elections at the end of the year for two seats as consul. I'm going back to try for one of them.'

Cabera shrugged, still testing. 'And then? Will you fight a war for the city like Sulla?'

Julius became very still for a moment and his eyes pinned Cabera.

'No, old friend,' he said softly. 'Then I will no longer be posted at Pompey's whim. As consul, I will be untouchable. I will be at the heart of things again.'

Cabera wanted to let the moment pass, but his stubbornness forced him to speak.

'But after that? Will you have Brutus drill the Tenth while you write new laws the people will not understand? Will you lose yourself in maps and bridges as you have done here?'

Renius reached out and gripped Cabera by the shoulder to make him stop, but the old man ignored the hand.

'You can do more than that, if you have eyes to see it,' he said, wincing as Renius closed his hand on his thin muscles, hurting him.

'If I am consul,' Julius said slowly, 'I will take what I love to the wildest places I can find. Is that what you want me to say? That Spain is too quiet for me? I know it. I will find my path there, Cabera. The gods listen more closely to those who speak from Rome. They just can't hear me out here.' He smiled to cover his anger and felt Servilia watching him over Octavian's shoulder. Renius dropped his hand from the old man's arm and Cabera scowled at him.

Brutus spoke to smooth the moment over. 'If we start holding ships tonight, how long before we have enough to move the Tenth?'

Julius nodded his head a fraction in thanks. 'A month at most. I have already sent word that we need captains for a large cargo. I think no more than thirty ships will be enough to land at Ostia. The Senate would never let me approach Rome with the whole legion as it is, so I'll need a camp at the coast. I'll take the gold with me on that first trip. We have enough for what I have in mind.'

Servilia watched them argue and wrangle as the sun set behind them. They barely noticed the guard enter the room to light more lamps. After a while, she left to begin her own arrangements, the night air of the yard making her feel alive after the heat of the room.

She could still hear their voices as she walked across the yard and saw the gate sentries stiffen as they saw her.

'Is it true we're going to Rome, madam?' one of them said as she passed him. It came as no surprise to find the man had heard a rumour. Some of her best information in Rome came from the lower ranks.

'It's true,' she said.

The man smiled. 'It's about time,' he said.

When the Tenth moved, they moved quickly. Ten of the largest ships in Valentia port had guards preventing their escape within a day of the meeting in the long room. To the fury of the merchant captains, their precious cargoes were unloaded and left in the warehouses on the docks to make more room for the vast stores of equipment and men that made up a legion.

The gold at the fort was crated and taken out to the ships, with fully armed centuries attending every foot of the journey. The forges of the swordmakers were dismantled and tied on huge wooden pallets that took teams of oxen to lift into the dark holds. The great war ballistae and onagers were reduced to spars and the heavy ships sank lower and lower in the sea as they were filled. They would need the highest tide to sail out of the harbour and Julius set the day exactly one month after he had made the formal announcement. If all went well, they would reach Rome just over a hundred days before the consular elections.

The quaestor Julius had promoted was ambitious and Julius knew he would work like a slave to keep his new post. There would be no loss of discipline in the provinces when the Tenth had gone. The quaestor brought two cohorts to the east under Julius' orders, some of them local men who had joined the

Roman forces years before. It was enough of a force to keep the peace, and Julius took pleasure from the fact that the problem was no longer his.

There were a thousand things to organise before the ships could throw their lines from the dockside and move out to sea. Julius pushed himself to exhaustion, sleeping only one night in two, at best. He met with local leaders from all over the country to explain what was happening and the gifts he left them ensured their aid and blessing.

The quaestor had been quietly amazed when Julius told him how productive the new mines had become during his term. They had toured them together and the man took the opportunity to secure a loan from the coffers of the Tenth to be paid back over five years. No matter who ended up in the position of praetor, the debt would stand. The mines would be developed and no doubt part of the new wealth would be declared. Not before the post was made permanent, Julius thought wryly. It would not do to excite the hunger of men like Crassus in Rome.

As Julius walked out into the courtyard, he had to shade his eyes against the fierce sun. The gates were open and the fort had a vacant feel that reminded him of the village with the statue of Alexander. It was a strange thought, but the new cohorts were expected the following dawn and the fort would come back to life then.

In the glare, he did not see the young man standing by the gate, waiting for him. Julius was crossing to the stables and was jerked out of his reverie as the man spoke. His hand dropped to his gladius in reflex.

'General? Do you have a moment?' the man said.

Julius recognised him and narrowed his eyes. His name was Adàn, he remembered, the one he had spared.

'What is it?' he said impatiently.

Adàn approached him and Julius kept his hand near his hilt.

He didn't doubt he could handle the young Spaniard, but there could be others and he had lived long enough not to drop his guard too easily. His eyes scanned the gate, watching for moving shadows.

'The Mayor, Del Subió, told me you need a scribe, sir. I can read and write Latin.'

Julius looked at him suspiciously. 'Did Del Subió mention the fact that I am about to leave for Rome?' he asked.

Adàn nodded. 'Everyone knows it. I would like to see the city, but I do want the work.'

Julius looked him in the eye, weighing him. He trusted his instincts and he could sense nothing hidden in the man's open face. Perhaps the young Spaniard was telling the truth, though Julius couldn't help but suspect his motives with the legion about to set sail.

'A free trip to Rome, then you disappear in the markets, Adàn?' he said.

The young man shrugged. 'You have my word. I can offer nothing else. I work hard and I want to see more of the world. That is all.'

'Why come to work for me, though? It wasn't long ago you had Roman blood on your hands.'

Adàn coloured, but raised his head, refusing to be cowed. 'You are an honourable man, General. While I would rather Rome did not lay its hand on my people, you made me curious. You would not regret hiring me, I swear it.'

Julius frowned at him. The man seemed unaware of the danger of his words. He remembered the way he had stood before Julius' men in the long room, struggling to control his fear.

'I must be able to trust you, Adàn, and that will come only with time. What you hear from me will be worth money to those who pay for information. Can you be trusted to keep my business secret?'

81

'As you say, you will know in time. My word is good.'

Julius came to a decision and his frown cleared.

'Very well, Adàn. Go up to my rooms and fetch me the papers from the desk. I will dictate a letter to you and judge your hand. Then your time is your own to say goodbye to your family. We leave for Rome in three days.'

CHAPTER SEVEN

❧❧❧❧❧

Brutus vomited helplessly over the side into the heaving sea.

'I'd forgotten about this,' he said miserably.

Ciro could only moan in reply as the last cups of wine they'd taken in Valentia came surging back. The wind gusted and blew some of the foul liquid spattering over both of them. Brutus froze in disgust.

'Move away from me, you ox,' he shouted over the gale. Though his stomach was empty, the painful spasms began again and he winced at the bitterness in his mouth.

The clouds had swept in from the east as the Spanish mountains sank behind them. The ships had scattered before the storm, forced away from each other. Those with oars kept some semblance of control, though the rolling decks had the long blades completely out of the water on one side and then another. The merchants who depended on their sails were trailing sea anchors, great bundles of canvas and spars to slow their progress and give the heavy rudders something to work against. It was little help. The storm brought the darkness early and they lost sight of each other, every ship suddenly alone to fight the waves.

Brutus shivered at the stern as another wild roll brought water over the side in a great rush of whiteness. He gripped the rail hard as it frothed around his knees and then poured away. The oars slapped and skipped over the mountains of dark water and Brutus wondered whether they would strike land in a sudden crash.

The blackness was absolute and even a few paces from him he could barely make out Ciro's bulk. He heard the big man moan softly and Brutus closed his eyes, just wanting it all to stop. He'd been fine until they cleared the coast and the big rolling waves sent them heeling over. Then the sickness had begun with a bout of belching and the sudden urge to head for the rail. He'd known enough to aim out over the stern, though the men below had not had that luxury. Packed tight as they were in the hold, it was a scene from nightmares.

The small part of his mind that could think of anything except his discomfort realised they would have to anchor off Ostia for a day or two before going in, if only to wash the ship down and restore the polish to the Tenth. If they reached port at that moment, the dockworkers would think they were refugees from some terrible battle.

Brutus heard a step behind him. 'Who's that?' he asked, craning his head forward to make out the man's features.

'Julius,' came a cheerful voice. 'I have water for you. It'll give you something to bring up, at least.'

Brutus smiled weakly, accepting the skin and pressing the bronze pipe to his lips. He swilled and spat twice before allowing some of the liquid to trickle down his throat. Ciro took it from him then and gulped noisily.

Brutus knew he should be asking about the men or the course they were cutting to take them between Sardinia and Corsica, but he simply couldn't bring himself to care. His head felt heavy with sickness and he could only manage to wave an apologetic hand to Julius before he was hanging over the rail again. It was almost worse when he wasn't vomiting. Then there was nothing to do but give way to it.

All three of them staggered as the ship rolled at a frightening angle and something fell with a clatter in the hold. Julius lost his footing on the slippery deck and was saved by grabbing Ciro's arm. He pulled in a deep, appreciative breath.

'I have missed this,' he said to them. 'Out of sight of land in the dark.' He leaned closer to Ciro.

'You're on the late watch with me, tomorrow. The stars will take your breath away when the storm blows itself out. The sickness never lasts more than a day, or two at most.'

'I hope so,' Ciro managed doubtfully. As far as he was concerned, Julius was pushing the bounds of friendship by being so obscenely cheerful while they waited for death to take them. He would give a month's pay for just a single hour of calm to settle his stomach. Then he could face anything, he was sure.

Julius worked his way around the rail to speak to the captain. The merchant had settled into surly acceptance of his new role, even going so far as to speak to the soldiers as they packed onto his ship. He'd warned them to have one hand for the ship and the other to save themselves at all times.

'If you go over,' he'd told the legionaries, 'that's the end of you. Even if I turn back, and I won't, a man's head is almost impossible to spot even when the sea is calm. If there's a bit of wind, you might as well suck in a lungful and go under. It'll be faster that way.'

'Are we on course, Captain?' Julius asked as he came up to the dark figure, hunched against the wind in heavy oilcloth.

'We'll know if we hit Sardinia, but I've made the run enough times,' the captain replied. 'The wind is coming from the southeast and we're running across it.'

Julius couldn't see his features in the pitch dark, but the voice didn't seem worried. When the first gales had slapped at the ship, the captain had lashed the steering oars down to a few degrees of arc and taken his post, occasionally shouting orders to the crew as they moved invisibly around the deck.

With the railing at his back, Julius swayed with the roll, enjoying himself immensely. His time on *Accipiter* with Gaditicus as captain seemed a lifetime before, but if he let his mind drift he could almost have been back there, on a different sea in the dark. He wondered if Ciro ever thought of those times. They'd gambled their lives on countless occasions in the hunt for the pirate who had destroyed the little ship.

Julius closed his eyes as he thought of the ones who had died in the chase. Pelitas in particular had been a good man, now long gone. Everything had seemed so simple then, as if his path was waiting for him. Now there were more choices than he wanted. If he found a seat as consul, he could stay in Rome or take his legion to a new land anywhere in the world. Alexander had done it before him. The boy king had taken his armies east into the rising sun, to lands so distant they were little more than legends. Part of Julius wanted the wild freedom he had known in Africa and Greece. No one to persuade or answer to, just a new path to cut.

He smiled in the dark at the thought. Spain was behind them and all his worries and routines and meetings were lifted from his shoulders with the storm.

As he leaned against the rail, a patter of footsteps brought another one out to lose his last meal. Julius heard Adàn's exclamation as he found the way blocked by Ciro and swore in frustration.

'What is this, an elephant? Make room, heavy one!' the young Spaniard snapped and Ciro chuckled weakly, pleased at the chance to share his misery with another.

Rain began to fall in torrents and somewhere ahead, a spike

of lightning made them all jerk round at the sudden brightness.

Unseen, Julius raised his hands in a silent prayer to welcome the storm. Rome was somewhere ahead and he felt more alive than he had for years.

The rain poured from the dark sky over the city. Though Alexandria tried to take comfort from her two guards, she found that she was frightened as night fell early under the clouds. Without the sun, the streets emptied quickly as families barred their doors and lit the evening lamps. The stones of the roads were quickly lost under a slow moving tide of filth that swirled and clutched at her feet. Alexandria almost slipped on a hidden cobble and grimaced at the thought of getting it on her hands.

There were no lights on the streets and every dark figure out in them looked threatening. The gangs of raptores would be looking for easy victims to rape and rob and Alexandria could only hope Teddus and his son would put them off.

'Stay close, miss. Not long now,' Teddus said from ahead of her.

She could barely make out his shape as he limped along, but the sound of his voice helped to steady her fear.

The wind carried the smell of human excrement in a sudden, ripe gust and Alexandria had to swallow quickly as she gagged. It was difficult not to be afraid. Teddus was far from his best years and an old injury to his leg gave him a staggering gait that looked almost comical. His sullen son almost never spoke and she didn't know if she could trust him.

As they moved through the empty street, Alexandria could hear the doors she passed being bolted with grunts as families made themselves secure. The good people of Rome had no protection from the gangs and only those with guards dared the city after dark.

A huddled group appeared at a corner ahead of them, shadows that watched the three figures and made Alexandria shudder. She heard Teddus draw his hunting knife, but they would either have to cross the street or go through the group and she controlled the urge to run. She knew she would die if she broke away from her guards, and only that thought held her steady as they approached the corner. Teddus' son moved to her side, brushing her arm, but bringing no feeling of safety.

'We're nearly home,' Teddus said clearly, more for the benefit of the men at the corner than Alexandria, who knew the streets as well as he did. He sounded unworried, and kept the long blade at his side as they moved past them. It was too dark to see their faces, but Alexandria could smell the dampness of wool and sour garlic. Her heart thudded as a shadow jarred her shoulder, making her stumble. Teddus' son guided her away with his sword hand, showing them the blade as he did. They didn't move and Alexandria could feel the threatening stares as the moment hung in the balance. One slip and they would attack, she was sure, her heart beating at painful speed.

Then they were through and Teddus took her arm in a tight grip, his son on the other side.

'Don't look back at them, miss,' Teddus muttered softly.

She nodded, though she knew he couldn't see her. Were they following, trotting behind them like wild dogs? She ached to look over her shoulder, but Teddus bore her on through the streets, pulling her away. His limp was getting worse and his breath was laboured with pain as they left the corner behind. He never spoke of it, but his right leg had to be rubbed with liniment each night just to hold his weight in the morning.

Above them, the rain pounded on the roofs of houses packed with people who knew better than to be out on the streets after dark. Alexandria risked a glance behind, but could see nothing and wished she hadn't. Anger stirred in her then. The Senate did not have to fear as she did. They never moved without armed guards and the raptores avoided them, recognising the presence of a greater threat than they could deal with. The poor had no such protection and even in the daylight there were thefts and sudden skirmishes in the streets that left one or two dead and the rest walking stiffly away, knowing they would not be caught or even chased.

'We're nearly there, miss,' Teddus said again, this time meaning it.

She heard the relief in his voice and wondered what would have happened if the group had drawn their knives. Would he have died for her, or left her to the mercy of the gang? It was impossible to know, but she calculated the cost of hiring another guard to join them. Who would watch him?

Another two turnings brought them to her own street. The houses were larger than the maze they had walked through, but the slurry of filth was thicker if anything, swollen by the rain. She grimaced as a splash of it reached up under her stola to her knee. Another pair of sandals ruined. The leather would never smell clean again, no matter how often she soaked them.

Grunting slightly in pain, Teddus reached her door first and thumped on it. They waited in silence, the two men glancing up and down the street in case anyone was waiting to rush in after them. That had happened to someone only a few nights before in a street not far away from where she lived. No one had dared to come out to help.

Alexandria could hear footsteps approach from the other side.

'Who's there?' came Atia's voice and Alexandria breathed out slowly in relief at being home. She had known the woman for years and though she lived in the house and cooked for her, Atia was the closest thing she had to family in Rome.

'It's me, Ati,' she said.

Light spilled out as the door opened and they moved in quickly, Teddus waiting until she was off the street before following. He replaced the locking bar carefully and then finally sheathed his knife, the tension easing out of his shoulders.

'Thank you, both of you,' Alexandria said.

The son was silent, but Teddus grunted a reply, patting his hand against the solidity of the door as if for reassurance. 'It's what we're paid for,' he said.

She saw his weak leg was slightly raised as he stood without putting weight on it and her heart went out to him. There were different kinds of courage.

'I'll bring you a hot drink after you've seen to your leg,' she said.

To her surprise, he blushed slightly. 'No need for that, mistress. Me and the boy will look after ourselves. Perhaps later.'

Alexandria nodded, unsure whether she should try again. Teddus seemed uncomfortable with anything approaching an offer of friendship. He appeared to want nothing more from her than regular pay and she had accepted his reserve. Tonight though, she was still shaken and needed people around her.

'You must be hungry and there's cold beef in the kitchen. I'd be pleased if you would eat with us when you're ready.'

Atia shifted her feet and Teddus looked at the floor for a moment, frowning slightly.

'If you're sure, mistress,' he said at last.

Alexandria watched as the two men made their way to their own rooms. She looked at Atia and smiled at the woman's stern expression.

'You are too kind to those two,' Atia said. 'There's little good in either of them, father or son. If you let them have the run of the house, they'll take advantage, I'm sure of it. Servants should not forget their place, nor those who pay them.'

Alexandria chuckled, the fear of the evening beginning to ease. In theory, Atia was a servant herself, though they never mentioned it. Alexandria had known her first when she went looking for clean rooms in the city, and when her jewellery business had grown Atia had come with her to the new house to run it for her. The woman was a tyrant with the other servants, but she made the place feel like a home.

'I'm glad they were with me, Atia. The raptores were out early with the storm and a cup or two of hot wine is fair pay for safety. Come on, I'm starving.'

Atia sniffed rather than reply, but overtook her in the corridor as they walked towards the kitchen.

The senate building was filled with the light of dozens of spluttering lamps around the walls. The echoing hall was warm and dry despite the muted drumming of the rain outside and few of the men present relished the thought of getting wet on the way to their homes. The afternoon had been taken over with the reports on the city budget, with a string of votes to approve vast sums for the legions keeping the Pax Romana in distant lands. The sums were daunting, but the reserves were healthy enough to tide the city over for another year. One or two of the more elderly senators had let the warmth lull them to dozing and only the storm outside held them from making their way to late meals and their own beds.

Senator Prandus stood at the rostrum, his gaze sweeping along the semicircular rows of benches, looking for support. It annoyed him that Pompey sat muttering to a colleague while Prandus announced his candidacy for the seat of consul. It was at Pompey's request that he had agreed to put his name forward and the least the man could do was look attentive.

'If I am elected to the post, I intend to gather the coin makers under a single roof and establish a currency on which the citizens can depend. There are too many coins that only claim to be gold or pure silver and every shop has to have its own scales to weigh the money they are given. A single senate mint will end the confusion and restore trust.'

91

He saw Crassus frown and wondered if he was responsible for some of those false coins that caused so much damage. It would not surprise him.

'If the citizens grant me the right to sit as consul, I will act in the interests of Rome, restoring faith in the authority of the Senate.' He paused again as Pompey looked up and Prandus realised he had made a mistake. Someone chuckled and he felt himself growing flustered.

'. . . *greater* faith in the Senate,' he added. 'Respect for authority and the rule of law. Justice that must be seen to be free of bribery or corruption.' He paused again, his mind going blank.

'It will be an honour to serve. Thank you,' he said, stepping down from the rostrum and taking his seat in the front bench with evident relief. One or two of the men closest to him clapped him on the shoulder and he began to relax. Perhaps the speech hadn't been too bad, after all. He glanced at his son Suetonius to see how he had taken it, but the young man was gazing stonily ahead.

Pompey walked down between the benches and smiled at Senator Prandus as he passed him. Those who had begun whispered conversations fell silent as the consul stepped up to the rostrum. He looked relaxed and confident, Prandus thought with a touch of irritation.

'I thank the candidates for their words,' Pompey said, allowing his eyes to rest on the men in silent recognition before continuing. 'It gives me hope that this great city can still find those willing to devote their lives to her without thought of personal gain or ambition.' He waited through the appreciative chuckle, leaning forward and resting on his arms.

'The election will give my builders a chance to enlarge this place and I am willing to give the use of my new theatre while the work goes on. It should be adequate, I think.' He smiled at them and they responded, knowing the theatre was twice as large as the senate building and at least twice as luxurious. There were no objections.

'As well as those we have heard here, any other candidates must declare before the feast of Volturnalia, ten days from now. Let me know in good time, please. Before we dare the rain, I must announce a public gathering in the forum a week from now. The trial of Hospius will be postponed for a month. Crassus and I will give the consuls' address to the people then. If any of the other candidates would like to add their voices to ours, you should see me before I leave tonight.'

Pompey caught Prandus' eye for a brief moment before moving on. It had all been arranged and Prandus knew his candidacy would be strengthened by association with the more experienced men. He had better practise his speech. For all Pompey's promises, the crowds of Rome could be a difficult audience.

'The day is at an end, senators. Rise for the oath,' Pompey said, his voice raised to be heard over the rain that battered the city.

The storm lasted for three days, sweeping the scattered ships towards their destination. When it had passed, the fleet carrying the Tenth slowly gathered again, each one a hive of activity as they made repairs to sails and oars and heated tar to dribble between the wide planks of the decks where water had leaked through. As Brutus had predicted, Julius signalled the fleet to anchor outside Ostia and the small boats moved between them, carrying supplies and carpenters and making sure that they would stand up under scrutiny. The sun baked the decks dry and the Tenth washed out the holds of the ships, cleaning away the smell of vomit with seawater and white grease.

When the anchors were winched up and scrubbed clean of clay, they moved into the port, with Julius at the bow of the first ship. He stood with one arm wrapped around the high prow, drinking in the sight of his homeland. Looking back over his shoulder showed him the white wings of the oared vessels making an arrowhead behind him, with the sails of the others bringing up the rear. He could not have put his feelings into words if he'd been asked and didn't try to examine them. His headaches had vanished in the fresh sea wind and he had burnt incense in a brazier in thanks to the gods for the safe passage through the storm.

He knew the Tenth could make a permanent camp in the fields beyond the port while he took the road to the city. The men were as excited as the officers at the chance to see families and friends again, but there would be no leave granted until the camp was set up and secure. Five thousand men were too many to descend on his estate. Just feeding such a number caused problems and the prices were better at the docks. Like locusts, the Tenth could eat away the gold he had brought if he let them. At least they would be spending their own pay in the city inns and whorehouses.

The thought of seeing his estate brought a mixture of grief and excitement to him. He would see how his daughter had grown and walk by the river his father had dammed to flow through the estate. Julius' smile faded as he thought of his father. The family tomb was on the road into the city and before anything else, he had to see the graves of those he had left behind.

CHAPTER EIGHT

෴෴෴

Crassus breathed in the steam from the pool as he eased himself in up to his waist. The marble sill was icy against his shoulders as he sat on the inner step and the contrast was exquisite. He felt the knots of tension in his neck and waved a hand to summon a bath slave to massage them away while he talked.

The other men in the pool were all his clients and loyal beyond the monthly stipend they received. Crassus closed his eyes as the slave's hard thumbs began to worry at his muscles and sighed with pleasure before speaking.

'My term as consul has made little mark on the city, gentlemen.' He smiled wryly as the men with him shifted in consternation. Before they could protest, he continued. 'I thought I would have done more in my time. There are too few things I can point to and say "That was mine, alone." It seems renegotiated trade agreements are not what stirs the blood of our citizens.'

His expression became tinged with bitterness as he looked

at them and traced a swirl in the surface of the water with a finger.

'Oh, I gave them bread when they said they had none. But when the loaves were gone, nothing had changed. They have had a few race days from my purse and seen a temple restored in the forum. I wonder, though, if they will remember this year, or ever think of me when I was consul.'

'We are for you,' one of the men said, the sentiment quickly echoed by the others.

Crassus nodded, breathing his cynicism into the steam. 'I have won no wars for them, you see. Instead, they fawn on Pompey and old Crassus is forgotten.'

The clients did not dare to meet each other's faces and see the truth of the words reflected there. Crassus raised his eyes at their embarrassment before going on, his voice firming with purpose.

'I do not want my year to be forgotten, gentlemen. I have bought another day at the racetrack for them, which is a start. I want those who rent from me to be given first choice of tickets, and *try* to get families.' He paused to reach behind his head for a cup of cool water and the slave interrupted his kneading to pass it into the bony fingers. Crassus smiled at the lad before continuing.

'The new sesterces with my head on them are ready. I will need you all to manage the distribution, gentlemen. They are to go only to the poorest of homes and no more than one to each man and woman. You will have to employ guards and take only small amounts with you at a time.'

'May I mention an idea, Consul?' a man asked.

'Of course, Pareus,' Crassus replied, raising an eyebrow.

'Hire men to clean the streets,' he said, the words spilling out too quickly under the consul's gaze. 'Much of the city is stinking and the people would thank you for it.'

Crassus laughed.

'If I do as you say, will they stop throwing their filth on the roads? No, they will say, let fly, for old Crassus will come after us with buckets to clean it up again. No, my friend, if they want clean streets, they should get water and cloths and clean them up themselves. If the stench grows too bad in summer, they may be forced to, and that will teach them to be clean.' Crassus saw the man's disappointment and spoke kindly, 'I admire a man who thinks the best of our people, but there are too many who lack the sense not to foul their own steps. There is no sense in courting the goodwill of such as they.' Crassus chuckled at the thought for a moment, then fell silent.

'On the other hand, if it was popular . . . no. I will not be known as Crassus the cleaner of shit. No.'

'The street gangs, then?' Pareus went on stubbornly. 'They are out of control in some areas. A few hundred men with permission to break the gangs would do more for the city than . . .'

'You want another gang to control the others? And who would keep *them* in control? Would you ask for a still larger group to handle the first?' Crassus tutted to himself, amused by the man's persistence.

'A legion century could . . .' the man stammered.

Crassus sat up, sending a ripple out over the pool. He held up a hand for silence and his clients shifted nervously.

'Yes, Pareus, a legion could do many things, but I do not have one at my call, as you should perhaps have remembered. Would you have me beg more soldiers from Pompey to patrol the poor areas? He asks for fortunes just to have guards at the races and I have had my fill of bolstering his reputation with my gold.' Crassus swung his hand out and knocked the metal cup spinning over the tiles of the bathhouse.

'Enough for now, gentlemen. You have your tasks for the moment and I will have more for you tomorrow. Leave me.'

97

The men climbed out of the pool without a word, hurrying away from their irascible master.

Julius was pleased to leave the noise of the port behind him as he and Octavian took the road to the city. With Brutus overseeing the unloading of men and equipment, the work would be quickly finished. The centurions had been chosen personally and they could be trusted to keep the men on a tight rein until the first groups were allowed to take their leave.

He glanced at Octavian and noted how well he sat his horse. Training with the extraordinarii had schooled his wildness and he rode now as if he had been born in the saddle, not as a street urchin who hadn't seen a horse until he was nine years old.

They walked the mounts on the worn stones of the road into the city, guiding them around the carts and slaves who hurried along it on unknown errands. Grain and wine, precious stones, leather hides, tools of iron and bronze, a thousand other things that were destined for the hungry maw of the city ahead. The drivers flicked their whips with skill over oxen and asses and Julius knew the caravans would extend all the way from the sea to the heart of the markets.

The gentle clopping of the hooves was lulling, but Julius was gripped by a tension that made his shoulders ache. The family tomb was outside the city and he was looking ahead for it, waiting for the first glimpse.

The sun was rising towards the noon point when he felt he was ready and dug his heels into the gelding's flanks. Octavian matched his pace instantly and the two men cantered over the stone, followed by appreciative shouts and whistles from the traders that dwindled behind them.

The tomb was a simple one of dark marble, a rectangular block of heavy stone that crouched at the side of the road with the great gates of the city less than a mile further on. Julius was sweating as he dismounted, leading the horse to the grass between the tombs, made lush by Roman dead.

'This is the one,' Julius whispered, letting the reins fall from his hands. He read the names cut into the dark stone and closed his eyes for a moment as he came to his mother's. Part of him had expected it, but the reality of knowing her ashes were there brought a pain that surprised him, rimming his eyes in tears.

His father's name was still sharp after more than a decade and Julius bowed his head as he touched the characters with the tips of his fingers, tracing the lines.

The third name was still as fresh-cut as the pain he felt to look at it. Cornelia. Hidden from the sun and his embrace. He could not hold her again.

'Do you have the wine, Octavian?' Julius said after a long time. He tried to stand straight, but the hand he laid on the stone seemed to have been fastened there and he could not let them go. He heard Octavian rummage in the bags and felt the cool clay of the amphora that had cost him more than a month's pay for one of his men. There was no better wine than Falernian, but Julius had wanted the finest to honour those he loved the most.

On the top of the tomb, a shallow bowl had been cut into the marble, leading to a hole no larger than a copper coin. As Julius broke the seal on the wine, he wondered if Clodia ever took his daughter out to feed the dead. He didn't think the old woman would have forgotten Cornelia, any more than he could.

The dark wine sloshed into the bowl and Julius could hear it dripping down to fall inside.

'This cup for my father, who made me strong,' he whispered. 'This for my mother, who gave her love. This last for my wife.' He paused, hypnotised by the swirling wine as it vanished into the tomb. 'Cornelia, whom I loved and honour still.'

When at last he returned the amphora to Octavian, his eyes were red with weeping.

'Bind the neck securely, lad. There is another grave to see before we go home to the estate and Tubruk will want more than just a cupful.' Julius forced himself to smile and felt some of his grief lighten in him as he remounted, the gelding's hooves clattering enough to break the stillness of the line of tombs stretching away.

Julius approached his estate with something like fear gnawing at him. It was a place of so many memories and so much pain. The eye of his childhood noted the rough weeds among the straggling crops and saw a subtle air of decay in every over-grown track or poorly repaired wall. The low drone of the hives could be heard and he felt his eyes prickle at the sound.

The white walls around the main buildings caused an ache to start in him. The paint was mottled with bare patches and he felt a stab of guilt at his lack of contact with them. The house had been a part of every wound in memory and not a single letter had come from his hand to his daughter or Clodia. He gripped the reins and slowed his mount, each step bringing more pain.

There was the gatepost where he had watched for his father coming back from the city. Beyond it would be the stables where he had tasted his first kiss and the courtyard where he had almost died at the hand of Renius, years before. Despite its run-down appearance, it was still the same where it counted, an anchor in the changes of his life. Yet he would have given anything for Tubruk to come out to greet him, or for Cornelia to be there.

He paused before the gate and waited in silence, lost in memories that he clutched to him as if they could remain real until the gate opened and everything changed again.

A man he did not know appeared above the wall and Julius smiled as he thought of the steps hidden from view. He knew them as well as anything else in the world. His steps. His home.

'What is your business here?' the man asked, keeping his voice neutral. Though Julius wore the simplest of armour, there was nonetheless an aura of authority in his silent appraisal of the walls and the man sensed it.

'I have come to see Clodia and my daughter,' Julius replied.

The man's eyes widened a fraction in surprise, before he disappeared to signal those within.

The gate swung open slowly and Julius rode through into the courtyard with Octavian behind him. Distantly, he heard someone calling for Clodia, but the moment of memory held for him and he took a deep breath.

His father had died defending that wall. Tubruk had carried him on his shoulders under the gate. Julius shivered slightly, despite the warmth of the sun. There were too many ghosts in that place. He wondered if he would ever be truly comfortable there, with every corner and turn reminding him of his past.

Clodia came out of the buildings in a rush and froze as she saw him. As he dismounted, she went down into a low bow. Age had not been kind to her, he thought, as he took her by the shoulders and raised her into his embrace. She had always been a large, capable woman, but her face was lined by more than time. If Tubruk had lived she would have married him, but that chance for happiness had been stolen away by the same knives that had taken Cornelia.

As she raised her face to him, he saw fresh tears and the sight seemed to pull his private grief closer to the surface. They had shared a loss together and he was unprepared for the rawness of his feelings as the years vanished and they were standing again in the yard while the slave rebellion tore through the south. She had promised to stay and raise his daughter then, the last words they had spoken before he left.

'It's been so long without hearing from you, Julius. I didn't know where to send the news about your mother,' she said. Fresh tears spilled over her cheeks as she spoke and Julius held her tightly.

'I . . . knew it was coming. Was it hard?'

Clodia shook her head, wiping at her eyes.

'She spoke of you at the end and took comfort from Julia. There was no pain for her, none at all.'

'I'm glad,' Julius said softly. His mother had been a distant figure to him for so long that he was surprised at how much he missed the chance to see her and sit on her bed to tell her all the details of Spain and the battles he had seen. How many times had he come to tell her what he had done with his life? Even when her illness had stolen her reason, she seemed to hear him. Now there was no one. No father to run to, no Tubruk to laugh at his mistakes, no one who loved him without limit left in the world. He ached for them all.

'Where is Julia now?' he said, stepping back.

Clodia's face changed slightly as pride and love suffused her features. 'Out riding. She takes her pony into the woods whenever she can. She looks like Cornelia, Julius. The same hair. Sometimes, when she laughs, it's like thirty years have gone and she's there again with me.' She saw the tension in him and misunderstood. 'I never let her ride alone. She has two servants with her, for safety.'

'Will she know me?' Julius asked, suddenly uncomfortable. He glanced at the gates as if speaking of Julia could bring her into sight. He remembered only a little of the daughter he had left in her care. Just a fragile girl he had comforted while her mother was laid out in the darkness. The memory of her tiny hands wrapped around his neck was strangely powerful.

'She will, I'm sure. She's always asking for stories of you and I've told her all I can.' Clodia's gaze strayed past him to Octavian as he stood stiffly by the horses.

'Octavian?' she said, wondering at the changes in him.

Before he could resist, Clodia ran to him and administered a smothering hug. Julius chuckled at his discomfort.

'There's dust in our throats, Clodia. Will you keep us standing out here all day?'

Clodia let Octavian escape her.

'Yes, of course. Give your horses to one of the boys there and I'll see to the kitchen. There's only a few of the slaves and me now. Without the papers in your name, the merchants wouldn't deal with me. Without Tubruk to run the place, it's been . . .'

Julius flushed as the woman came close to tears again. He had not done his duty by her, he realised, wondering at his own blindness. She was making little of hard years and, to his shame, he could have eased the burden. He should have replaced Tubruk before he left and signed the control of funds over to her. Clodia seemed suddenly flustered at the thought of Julius seeing the house she had come to think of as her home and he laid a hand on her arm to ease her.

'I could not have asked for more,' he said.

Some of the tightness in her eased. As the horses were led away to be brushed and fed, Clodia bustled before them into the house and they followed, Julius swallowing dryly as they passed from the courtyard into the rooms of his childhood.

The meal Clodia brought to them was interrupted by a high sweet call outside as a clatter of hooves marked Julia's return. With his mouth filled with bread and honey, Julius leapt to his feet and strode out into the sun. He had thought he would let her come in to him and greet her formally, but the sound of her voice overrode his patience and he couldn't wait.

Though she had seen only ten summers, she was the image of her mother and her dark hair was worn long in a braid down her back. Julius laughed at the sight of the girl as she jumped down from her pony and fussed around him, pulling thorns and snags from his mane with her fingers as a comb.

His daughter started at the sound of the strange voice and looked around to see who dared to chuckle at her in her own home. When her eyes met Julius', she frowned in suspicion. Julius watched her closely as she walked over to him, her head tilted to one side in silent enquiry in a way he remembered Cornelia doing.

She walked with confidence, he noted with pleasure. A mistress of an estate come to meet visitors. She was dressed in a threadbare cream tunic and leggings for riding and with her hair tied back and no sign of breasts under the cloth, she could almost have passed for a boy. He saw a simple silver bangle at her wrist and recognised it as one of his mother's.

Clodia had come out to witness the meeting and smiled at them both with maternal pride.

'This is your father, Julia,' she said. The little girl froze in the act of rubbing dust from her sleeve. She looked up at Julius with a blank expression.

'I remember you,' she said slowly. 'Are you back to stay?'

'For a while,' Julius replied as seriously.

The little girl seemed to digest this and nodded.

'Will you buy me a horse? I'm getting too big for old Gibi and Recidus says I would do well on a mount with a bit of spirit.'

Julius blinked at her and some of the past seemed to melt away in his amusement.

'I will find you a beauty,' he promised, rewarded with a smile that thumped his heart for the woman he had lost.

Alexandria stood back from the heat of the forge, watching as Tabbic removed the cup of molten gold and positioned it over the pouring holes in the clay.

'A steady hand now,' she cautioned unnecessarily, as Tabbic began to rotate the long wooden handle without a tremor. Both of them gave the liquid metal the respect it deserved as it hissed and gurgled into the cast. A single splash would burn flesh to the bone and every part of the process had to be slow and careful. Alexandria nodded in satisfaction as vapour whistled out of the air holes in the clay and the deep gulping sound began to rise in tone until the structure was full. When the gold had cooled, the clay would be painstakingly removed to reveal a mask as perfect as the face of the woman it represented. At a senator's bidding, Alexandria had performed the unpleasant task of taking a cast from his dead wife only hours after her death. Three lesser masks had followed in clay as Alexandria altered the lines of the face to smooth away the ravages of disease. With infinite care, she had rebuilt the nose where sickness had eaten the flesh and at last the man had wept to see the image death had taken from him. In gold, she would be preserved forever young, long after the man who loved her was ashes himself.

Alexandria touched a hand to the clay, feeling the heat constrained within and wondering if a man would ever love her enough to keep her image all his life.

Lost in thought, she did not hear Brutus enter the workshop and only the stillness as he gazed at her made her turn, sensing something she could not have named.

'Break out the good wine and take your clothes off,' he said. His eyes were on her and he didn't even notice Tabbic standing there with his mouth open. 'I'm back, girl. Julius is back and Rome will be turned on its head when we're done.'

CHAPTER NINE

⟡⟡⟡⟡⟡

Brutus patted Alexandria's thigh, enjoying the feel of her as they rode through the dusk out to the estate. After spending the day in bed with her, he felt more relaxed and at ease with the world than he could remember. He wished all his home-comings were of that quality.

Not used to riding, she held him tightly and he could feel the whip of her hair as it struck his bare neck, something he found extraordinarily erotic. She had grown strong while he was away, her body taut with health and strength. Her face too had altered subtly and her forehead was marked with a scar from a splash of hot metal, almost in the shape of a tear.

Her black cloak snapped around him for a moment in the wind and he gripped the edge of it, pulling her in closer. She wrapped her arms around his chest and breathed deeply. The air was warm as the land gave back the heat of the sun and Brutus only wished there was someone there to witness how magnifi-cent they must look as he cut across the fields to the estate.

He saw it from far away, the light of torches blurring together to make the walls a crown of light in the growing darkness. He slowed at the end and for a moment he thought it was Tubruk waiting for him by the open gate.

Julius stayed silent as he watched them slow to a walk, guessing at Brutus' thoughts and understanding them. He put aside his impatience and gave silent thanks for his friend's arrival. It was right that he be there, and they shared a private smile of regret as Brutus turned in the saddle to help Alexandria down and then jumped to the ground beside her.

Julius kissed Alexandria on the cheek. 'I'm honoured to have you at my home. The servants will take you in while I have a word with Brutus,' he said. Her eyes sparkled, he thought, wondering if her mind ever strayed back to one particular evening as his did.

When she had gone inside, Julius took a deep breath and clapped Brutus on the shoulder in affection.

'I can't believe Tubruk isn't here,' Julius said, looking out over the fields.

Brutus glanced at him in silence for a moment, then reached down and picked up a handful of dust.

'Do you remember when he made you hold this?' he said.

Julius nodded, copying the action. Brutus was pleased to see him smile as he let the dust trickle into the breeze.

'Fed with the blood of those who have gone before us,' Julius said.

'And our blood. He was a good man,' Brutus replied, letting his own handful lift away and bringing his hands together in a sharp clap. 'You'll have to find someone else to get the fields ploughed under again. I've never seen the place so ragged. Still, you're back now.'

Julius frowned at him. 'I was going to ask where you had disappeared to, but I see you found something better than seeing to the camp at Ostia.'

Julius could not bring himself to be angry with his friend, though he had intended to make the point very clearly.

'Renius had it all in hand and it's a good thing I did,' Brutus replied. 'Alexandria told me there will be a public debate tomorrow in the forum and I rode straight here to tell you.'

'I know about it. Servilia told me as soon as she heard. Still, I'm glad you came. I would have sent for you even if you hadn't disobeyed my orders.'

Brutus looked at his friend, trying to judge how seriously he was being criticised. The strain and exhaustion of the time in Spain had left Julius' face and he seemed younger than he had for a long time. Brutus waited for a moment.

'Am I forgiven?' he said.

'You are,' Julius replied. 'Now come inside and meet my daughter. There's a room ready for you and I want you with me to plan a campaign. You are the last to come in.'

They walked together through the courtyard, the only sound the snap and flutter of the lamps along the wall. The breeze cut across them for a moment as the gate was shut and Brutus felt the hairs lift on his arms, making him shiver. Julius opened a door into a room of life and chatter and he ducked his head to go in, feeling the first touches of excitement.

Julius had summoned them all, Brutus saw as he looked round the room and greeted his friends. With Alexandria, everyone he cared about was in that one room and they had the bright eyes of joyful conspirators, planning how to rule a city. Servilia, Cabera, Domitius, Ciro, Octavian, all the ones Julius had gathered to his side. The only stranger was the young Spaniard who had come with them as Julius' scribe. Adàn looked from face to face even as Brutus did and when their eyes met, Brutus nodded to him, acknowledging him as Julius would have wanted.

Brutus saw that Alexandria was standing stiffly amongst them and moved to her side instinctively. Julius caught the movement and understood it.

'We need you here, Alexandria. No one else has lived in the city for the last few years and I want that knowledge.'

She blushed prettily as she relaxed and Brutus squeezed her buttock, unseen by the others. His mother looked sharply at him as Alexandria slapped his hand away, but Brutus only smiled at her before looking back at Julius.

'Where is this daughter of yours?' Brutus asked. He was curious to see the girl.

'She'll be out in the stables,' Julius said. 'She rides like a centaur, you know. I'll call her in before she's ready to sleep.' For an instant, pride touched his features as he thought of his daughter and Brutus smiled with him. Then, Julius cleared his throat, looking round at them all.

'Now, I need to decide what I am to do tomorrow morning, when I walk into the forum and declare for the consul's post.'

Everyone tried to speak at once and the knock at the door went unheard for the first few moments. Clodia opened it and her expression brought quiet as they saw her.

'There is . . . I could not stop him,' she began.

Julius took her by the arm. 'Who is it?' he asked.

He froze as he caught sight of the figure behind her and stood back with Clodia to let the door swing open.

Crassus stood there, dressed in a toga of startling white against his dark skin. A gold clasp glittered at his shoulder and Alexandria blinked as she recognised her own work, wondering if it was coincidence or subtle proof of his understanding of the relationships in the room.

'Good evening, Caesar. I believe your post of tribune was never revoked. Should I address you by that title now that you have left the praetorship of Spain behind you?'

Julius bowed his head, struggling to hide the anger he felt at the man's casual entry into his home. His mind spun with sudden thoughts. Were there soldiers outside? If there were, Crassus would find it harder to leave than to enter, he swore silently. Julius released his grip on Clodia's arm and she left the room quickly without looking back. He did not blame her for letting Crassus into his home. Though she had run the house as its mistress, she had been too many years a slave not to be frightened by one of the most powerful men in the Senate. No door could be barred against a consul of Rome.

Crassus saw the tension in the young man he faced and continued. 'Put yourself at ease, Julius. I am a friend to this house, as I was to Marius before you. Did you think you could land a legion on my coastline without word reaching me? I would imagine even Pompey's feeble ring of spies has heard you are back by now.' Crassus caught sight of Servilia in the room and lowered his head slightly in greeting.

'You are welcome here,' Julius said, trying to unbend. He knew he had hesitated too long and suspected the older man had enjoyed every moment of the confusion he had created.

'I am glad,' Crassus replied. 'Well, if someone will fetch another chair, I will join you, with your permission. You will need a strong speech tomorrow if you mean to have a consul's robe next year. Pompey will not be pleased to hear of it, but that is the sweetness to the sauce.'

'Are there no secrets from you?' Julius asked, beginning to recover.

Crassus smiled at him. 'Confirmed by your own mouth! I thought there could be no other reason for you to leave the post as praetor. I trust you appointed a replacement before you sailed for Rome?'

'I did, of course,' Julius replied. To his surprise, he found he was enjoying the exchange.

Crassus took the chair Octavian vacated for him and settled himself, using his long fingers to tweak his toga into neatness. The tension in the room began to ease as they accepted him amongst them.

'I wonder, did you think you would just stride through the

110

forum and ascend the speakers' platform?' Crassus asked.

Julius looked blankly at him. 'Why not? Servilia tells me Prandus will be there to speak. I have as much right as he.'

Crassus smiled, shaking his head. 'I believe you would have done, at that. Better to come at my invitation, Julius. Pompey will not be asking for you to join us, after all. I look forward to seeing his face when you enter your name onto the lists.'

He accepted a cup of wine and sipped at it, wincing slightly.

'You realise Pompey may claim you have abandoned your duty by leaving before your term in Spain was finished?' he said, leaning forward in his seat.

'I am immune from prosecution as tribune,' Julius replied quickly.

'Unless it is a crime of violence, my friend, though I suppose deserting your post is safe enough. Pompey knows your protection, but how will it look to the people? From now until the elections, Julius, you must not only act well, but be seen to act well, or the votes you need will be wasted on another candidate.'

Crassus looked around at the others in the room and smiled as his eyes met Alexandria's. His fingers caressed the gold clasp at his shoulder for an instant and she knew he recognised her and experienced a thrill of danger. For the first time since Brutus had found her in the workshop, she realised that Julius collected as many enemies as he did friends and she was not yet sure which Crassus was.

'What do you gain by helping me?' Julius said suddenly.

'You have a legion I helped to rebuild, Julius, when it was still named Primigenia. I have been . . . persuaded of the need for men in the city. Trained men who cannot be bribed or tempted away by the gangs of raptores.'

'You claim a debt from me?' Julius replied, tensing himself to refuse.

Crassus glanced at Servilia and exchanged a look of understanding that Julius could not fathom.

'No. I waived any debts too long ago to mention. I am asking freely for your help and in return my clients will help to spread your name in the city. You do have only a hundred days, my friend. Even with my aid, that is a short time.'

He saw Julius hesitate and went on: 'I was a friend to your father and Marius. Is it too much to ask for trust from the son?'

Servilia tried to will Julius to look at her. She knew Crassus better than anyone else in the room and hoped Julius would not be fool enough to refuse him. She watched the man she loved with something like pain as she waited for his reply.

'Thank you, Consul,' Julius said formally. 'I do not forget my friends.'

Crassus smiled in genuine pleasure.

'With my wealth . . .' he began.

Julius shook his head. 'I have enough for this, Crassus, though I thank you.'

For the first time, Crassus looked at the young general with the beginning of real respect. He had been right in his judgement, he thought. He could work with him and infuriate Pompey at the same time.

'Shall we toast your candidacy, then?' Crassus asked, raising his cup.

At Julius' nod, the rest of them took wine and held the vessels awkwardly as they waited. For a moment, Julius regretted finishing the Falernian, but thought better of it. Tubruk could raise a cup of it to them, wherever he was.

Julia sat out in the darkness of the stables, enjoying the warm comfort that the horses brought. She walked down the stalls and patted their soft muzzles, speaking softly to each one. She paused at the enormous gelding her father's friend had brought that woman on. It was strange to use the word. Her father.

How many times had Clodia told her about the brave man who had been sent away from the city by a consul's whim? She had made her own pictures of him, telling herself he was held by the bonds of duty and could not return for her. Clodia always said he would come back in the end and everything would be all right, but now that he was there, Julia found him more than a little frightening. As soon as he had put his foot in the dust of the yard, everything had changed and the house had a new master.

He seemed so stern, she thought as she reached up to rub her nose against the gelding's velvet nostrils. The horse whickered gently in reply and pushed at her, blowing warm air against her face. He was not as old as she had expected. She'd imagined him with grey hair at the temples and the quiet dignity of a member of the Senate.

The night air carried a gust of noise from where the new people had gathered. So many of them! The house had never been so full of visitors, she thought, wondering at them. From her perch on the outer wall, she had watched them come in and shaken her head at so many strangers.

They were a different breed to the visitors Clodia invited, especially the old woman with diamonds at her throat. Julia had seen her father kiss her when he thought no one could see and Julia had felt her throat tighten with dislike. She had tried to tell herself it was just a friendship, but there had been something intimate in the way the woman relaxed against him and Julia's cheeks had become hot with embarrassment. Whoever she was, she vowed they would never be friends.

She whiled away a little time imagining the woman trying to win her affection. She would be very cool towards her, Julia thought. Not rude; Clodia had taught her to despise rudeness. Just enough to make the woman feel unwelcome.

A heavy cloak hung on a peg by the gelding's stall and Julia recognised it as the one that had draped the last pair. She remembered the man's laughter as it carried over the fields. He was very handsome, she thought. Shorter than her father, he walked like the man Clodia had employed to teach her to ride, as if he had so much energy that he could only barely stop himself from dancing with the pleasure of it.

Julia thought his companion must love him, from the way she had draped herself against his back. They always seemed to be touching, almost by accident.

She stayed in the stables for a long time, trying to get to the root of what felt different since her father had arrived. She always came there when there was a problem or when she had upset Clodia. Amongst the smell of leather and straw, in the shadows, she had always felt safe. The main house had so many empty rooms that were cold and dark at night. When she crept through them to climb the wall under the moonlight, she could imagine her mother walking there and shiver. It was too easy to think of the men who had killed her, padding up behind until Julia would spin in terror and back away from phantoms she could never see.

A burst of laughter carried to her from the house and she raised her head to listen. The sound faded into a deeper silence and she blinked in the darkness as she realised that having her father's friends here made her feel safe. There would be no assassins creeping over the wall for her tonight, no nightmares.

She patted the gelding's nose and took the cloak from its peg, letting it fall onto the dusty floor in a moment of spite. Her father's friend deserved better than that one, she thought, hugging herself in the gloom.

Pompey paced with his hands clasped tightly behind him. He wore a toga of thick white cloth that left his arms bare and the muscles moved visibly as he worked his fingers against each other. The lamps in his city home had begun to gutter, but he did not call for slaves to refill the reservoirs. The dim light suited the mood of the consul of Rome.

'Only standing in the elections could repair the damage of leaving his post. Nothing else is worth the risk he has taken, Regulus.'

His most senior centurion stood to attention as his general paced the floor. He had been loyal to him for more than twenty years and knew his moods as well as any man.

'I am yours to command, sir,' he said, staring straight ahead.

Pompey looked at him and what he saw seemed to satisfy him.

'You are my right arm, Regulus, I know it. However, I need more than obedience if Caesar is not to inherit the city from my hands. I need ideas. Speak freely and fear nothing.'

Regulus relaxed slightly with the command. 'Have you considered drafting a law to allow you to stand again? He could not take the post if you were the alternative.'

Pompey frowned. If he thought for a moment that such a thing was possible, he would have considered it. The Senate, even the citizens, would revolt against even the suggestion of a return to those old days. The irony of having helped to bring about the very restrictions that now held him was not wasted on him, but such thoughts brought him no closer to a solution.

'It is not possible,' he said through clenched teeth.

'Then we must plan for the future, sir,' Regulus said.

Pompey stopped to look at him with hope in his eyes. 'What do you have in mind?'

Regulus took a deep breath before speaking. 'Let me join his legion. If there is ever a time when you need him to be stopped, you would have a sword close to him.'

Pompey rubbed his face as he considered the offer. Such loyalty, coupled with so violent a man. Though part of him was repelled by the thought of such a dishonourable course, he would be a fool to refuse a weapon for the years to come. Who knew what the future held, for any of them?

'You would have to enlist in the ranks,' Pompey said, slowly.

The centurion breathed hard as he saw his idea was not to be dismissed without a hearing.

'That will be no hardship for me. My promotions came on the battlefield, from your hand. I have been there before.'

'But your scars, they will know you for what you are,' Pompey replied.

'I will say I'm a mercenary. I can play the part easily enough. Let me get close to him, Consul. I am your man.'

Pompey considered, objections coming and going in his thoughts. He sighed. Politics was a practical business, after all.

'It could be years, Regulus. Will you be missed?'

'No, sir. I am alone.'

'Then it is my order to you, Regulus. Go with my blessing.'

Regulus struggled to find words. 'It . . . it is an honour, sir. I will be close to him if you call. I swear it.'

'I know you will, Regulus. I will reward you when . . .'

'It is not necessary, sir,' Regulus said quickly, surprising himself. He would not usually have dared to interrupt the consul, but he wanted to give some sign that the trust was well placed. He was gratified when Pompey smiled.

'If only I had more like you, Regulus. No man is better served than I.'

'Thank you, sir,' Regulus replied, his chest swelling. He knew he faced years of hard discipline and reduced pay, but it worried him not at all.

CHAPTER TEN

Rome was never still, and as dawn came the vast space of the forum had filled with a shifting mass of citizens, constantly changing as currents moved through them. Fathers held children on their shoulders to catch a glimpse of the consuls, just to say they had seen the men who defeated Spartacus and saved the city.

To Julius, the crowd seemed faceless and intimidating. Should he stare into space as he spoke, or fix his gaze on one unfortunate citizen? He wondered if they would even hear him. They were silent for Pompey, but Julius didn't doubt the consul had salted the crowd with his clients. If they shouted and jeered when Julius followed him, it would be a poor start to his candidacy. He went over and over the speech in his mind, praying he wouldn't stumble or lose his place. There could be questions when he was finished, perhaps from men in the pay of the consuls. He could be humiliated. Carefully, Julius rested his damp palms on his knees, letting the cloth soak up the sweat that clung to them.

117

He sat on the raised platform with Crassus and Suetonius' father without looking at either of them. They were listening attentively as Pompey made a witticism and held up his hands to quiet the laughter. There was no hesitation in him, Julius saw. Pompey's skill as an orator could be read in the crowd's reactions. They raised their faces to the consul almost in worship and Julius felt an awful tightness in his gut at the thought of being next to speak.

Pompey's voice became grave as he recounted his service in the consular year and the crowd spattered applause. The military successes were interspersed with promises of free grain and bread, games and commemorative coins. Crassus stiffened slightly at the last. He wondered where Pompey would find the funds to have his face struck in silver. The worst of it was knowing the bribes were unnecessary. Pompey held the crowd, moving them to laughter and stern pride in moments. It was a masterful performance and when it finished, Julius stood and had to force a smile onto his face as Pompey stepped back and gestured to him. Julius gritted his teeth in annoyance at the outstretched hand, as if he was being brought to the front by a fatherly sponsor.

As they passed, Pompey spoke quietly to him. 'No shields in cloaks, Julius? I thought you would have something prepared.'

Julius was forced to smile as if the words were some playful comment rather than a barb. Both of them remembered the trial he had won in that forum, where shields depicting scenes from Marius' life were revealed to the crowd.

Pompey took his seat without another word, appearing calm and interested. Julius stepped close to the rostrum and paused for a moment, looking over the sea of faces. How many had gathered to hear the consuls give their yearly address? Eight thousand, ten? With the rising sun still hidden behind the temples that bordered the great square, the light was grey and cold as his gaze swept over them. Julius took a deep breath, willing his voice to be steady and strong from the first. It was important that they hear every word.

'My name is Gaius Julius Caesar, nephew of Marius, who was consul seven times in Rome. I have written my name in the senate house for the same post. I do it not for the memory of that man, but to continue his work. Do you want to hear me make promises of coins and bread to be handed to you? You are not children to be offered pretty things for your loyalty. A good father does not spoil the child with gifts.'

Julius paused and began to relax. Every eye in the forum was on him and he felt the first touch of confidence since ascending the platform.

'I have known those who break their backs growing wheat for your bread. There are no fortunes in feeding others, but they have pride and they are men. I have known many who fought without complaint for this city. You will see them sometimes on the streets, missing eyes or limbs, passed by the crowds as we look aside, forgetting we can laugh and love only because those soldiers gave so much.

'We have grown this city on the blood and sweat of those who have gone before, but there is still much to do. Did you hear Consul Crassus talk of soldiers to make the streets safe? I give my men to you without regret, but when I take them away to find new lands and riches for Rome, who will keep you safe then, if not yourselves?'

The crowd shifted restlessly and Julius hesitated for a moment. He could see the idea in his head, but he strained for a way to make them understand.

'Aristotle said a statesman is anxious to produce a certain moral character in his citizens, a disposition to virtue. I look for it in you and it is there, ready to be called forth. You are the ones who took to the walls to defend Rome from the slave rebellion. You did not hide from your duty then and you will not now, when I ask it of you.' He went on, louder than before. 'I will set aside funds for any man without work if he cleans the streets and keeps the gangs from terrorizing the weakest of us. Where is the glory of Rome if we live in fear at night? How many of you bar your doors and wait behind them for the first scratching of the murderer or the thief?'

Silently, he thanked Alexandria for what she had told him and saw from the nodding heads that he had struck a chord with many of the crowd.

'Consul Crassus has appointed me aedile, which means I am the one to whom you should complain if there is crime or disorder in the city. Come to me if you are wrongly accused and I will hear your case and defend you myself if I cannot find representation for you. My time and strength are yours now, if you want it. My clients and my men will make the streets safe and I will make the law fair for all. If I am consul, I will be the flood that clears Rome of the filth of centuries, but not alone. I will not *give* you a better city. Together, we will make her new.'

He felt a giddy joy in him as they responded. This was what it was like to be touched by gods. His chest swelled as his voice poured over the crowd and they strove to meet his eye.

'Where is the wealth our legions have brought back to the city? In this forum alone? It is not enough, I think. If I am made consul, I will not shy from the smaller things. The roads are blocked by traffic so that trade is stifled. I will make them move by night and silence the endless shouting of the ox-drivers.' They chuckled at that and Julius smiled back at them. His people.

'Do you think I should not? Should I use my time to build another fine building you will never use?'

Someone shouted 'No!' and Julius grinned at the lone voice, enjoying the ripple of laughter that spread through them.

'To that man who shouted, I say yes! We *should* build great soaring temples and bridges and aqueducts for clean water. If a foreign king comes to Rome, I want him to know we are blessed in all things. I want him to look up – but not tread in anything horrible when he does.'

Julius waited for the laughter to fade before going on. He knew they listened for the simple reason that his voice rang with conviction. He believed what he said and they heard him and were lifted.

'We are a practical people, you and I. We need drains and safety and honest trade and cheap prices for the food to live. But we are also dreamers, *practical* dreamers who will remake the world to endure a thousand years. We build to last. We are the inheritors of Greece. We have strength, but not just that of the body. We invent and perfect until there is nothing so fine as Rome. One street at a time, if need be.'

He took a deep, slow breath and his eyes filled with affection for the people listening.

'I look at you all and I am proud. My blood has helped to make Rome and I do not see it wasted when I look on her people. This is our land. Yet there is a world outside it that has yet to know what we have found. What we have made is great enough to take into the dark places, to spread the rule of law, the honour of our city, until *anywhere* in the world one of us can say "I am a Roman citizen" and be assured of good treatment. If I am made consul, I will work for that day.'

He had finished, though they didn't know it at first. They waited patiently to hear what he would say next and Julius was almost tempted into continuing before an inner voice of caution told him to simply thank them and step down.

The silence broke in a roar of appreciation and Julius flushed with the excitement of it. He was unaware of the men on the platform behind him and could see only the people who had listened, each one hearing him alone and taking in the words. It was better than wine.

Behind his back, Pompey leaned over to Crassus and whispered as he applauded.

'You made him aedile? He is no friend of yours, Crassus. Believe it.'

For the benefit of the crowd, Crassus smiled back at his colleague, his eyes glittering angrily.

'I know how to judge a friend, Pompey.'

Pompey stood then and clapped a hand to Julius' shoulder as he came abreast of him. As the crowd saw the two men smile at each other, they cheered again and Pompey raised his other arm to acknowledge them, as if Julius was his pupil and had done well to please them.

'A wonderful speech, Caesar,' Pompey said. 'You will be like a fresh wind in the Senate if you are successful. Practical dreamers, a wonderful concept.'

Julius clasped the offered hand before turning to call Crassus to the front. The other consul was already moving, too astute to let the opportunity pass without his presence.

The three men stood together while the crowd cheered, and from a distance their smiles looked genuine. Senator Prandus also rose, but no one noticed.

Alexandria turned to Teddus at her side as the crowd cheered the men on the platform.

'Well, what did you think of him?' she said.

The old soldier rubbed the bristles on his chin. He had come because Alexandria had asked him, but he hadn't the slightest interest in the promises of the men who ruled his city and didn't know how to say that without offending his employer.

'He was all right,' he said, after reflection. 'Though I didn't hear him offer to have a coin stamped like the others. Promises are all very well, mistress, but a silver coin buys you a good meal and a jug.'

Alexandria frowned for a moment, then snapped open the heavy bangle she wore on her wrist, sliding a denarius out in her hand. She gave it to Teddus and he accepted it, raising his eyebrows.

'What's that for?' he said.

'You spend it,' she replied. 'When it's gone and you're hungry again, Caesar will still be there.'

Teddus nodded as if he understood her, carefully tucking the coin into the hidden pocket of his tunic. He glanced around to see if anyone had noted where he kept his money, but the crowd seemed focused on the raised stage. Still, it paid to be careful in Rome.

Servilia watched the man she loved as Pompey clapped an arm on his shoulders. The consul could scent a changing wind as fast as any of the other men in the Senate, though she wondered if Pompey knew Julius would not allow even the semblance of control from the outgoing consuls.

There were times when she hated the shallow games they all played. Even giving Julius and Prandus the chance to speak at the formal consuls' address was part of it. She knew of two more candidates on the senate list and there were still a few days to go before the lists were closed. None of those had been allowed to cheapen the consuls' address with their tin promises.

The crowd would remember only three men and Julius was one of them. She let out a breath of tension. Unlike most of those in the forum, she had not been able to relax and enjoy the speeches. While Julius stood to face them, her heart had pounded in fear and pride. He hadn't slipped. The memory of the man she had found in Spain was simply that now. Julius had recaptured the old magic and it touched even her as she listened and saw his bright eyes sweep over her without stopping. He was so young; could the crowd see that? For all their skill and wit, Pompey and Crassus were fading powers compared to him, and he was hers.

A man stepped a little too closely to her as he wound his way through the crowd and Servilia caught a glimpse of a hard, scarred face, damp with sweat. Before she could react, a strong hand fastened on the man's arm, making him cry out.

'Be on your way,' Brutus said softly.

The man yanked hard to free himself and retreated, though he paused to spit when he was safely out of range. Servilia turned to her son and he smiled at her, the incident forgotten.

'I think you have backed the right horse, Mother,' he said, looking up at Julius. 'Can't you feel it? Everything is in place for him.'

Servilia chuckled, caught by his enthusiasm. Without his armour, her son looked more boyish than usual and she reached up to ruffle his hair affectionately.

'One speech doesn't make a consul, you know. The work starts today.' She followed his gaze up to where Julius was turning away at last to make his way into the crowd, taking outstretched hands and responding to the citizens as they called to him. Even at a distance, she could see his joy.

'But it is a good start,' she said.

Suetonius walked with his friends through empty streets away from the forum. The stalls and houses were shut and barred and they could still hear the muted sound of the crowd behind the rows of houses.

Suetonius didn't speak for a long time, his face stiff with bitterness. Every cheer from the tradesmen had eaten at him until he couldn't stand it any longer. Julius, always Julius. No matter what happened, the man seemed to have more luck than any three others. A few words to a crowd and they fawned on him, sickeningly, while Suetonius' father was humiliated. It was appalling to see them swayed by tricks and words while a good Roman went unnoticed. He had been so proud when his father allowed his name to be entered for consul. Rome deserved a man of his dignity and his honour, not a Caesar, out for nothing more than his own glory.

Suetonius clenched his fists, almost growling at what he had witnessed. The two friends with him exchanged nervous glances.

'He's going to win, isn't he?' Suetonius said without looking at them.

Bibilus nodded, a pace behind his friend, then realised the gesture couldn't be seen.

'Perhaps. Pompey and Crassus seem to think so, at least. Your father could still take the second post.'

He wondered whether Suetonius was going to march them all the way back to the estate outside Rome. Good horses and comfortable rooms awaited them in the other direction as Suetonius stalked along, blind with his hatred. Bibilus hated to walk when horses were available. He hated riding as well, but it was easier on his legs and he sweated less.

'He deserts his post in Spain and strolls in to announce he will try for consul and they simply accept it! I do wonder what bribes have changed hands to make this happen. He is capable of it, believe me. I know him well. The man has no honour. I remember that from the ships and Greece. That *bastard*, come back to haunt me. You would think he'd leave politics to better men after his wife died, wouldn't you? He should have learned the dangers then. I tell you, Cato may have made enemies, but he was twice the man Caesar is. Your father knew that, Bibilus.'

Bibilus looked nervously around to see if anyone was within earshot. With Suetonius in this mood, there was no telling what he would say. Bibilus enjoyed his friend's bitterness when they were in private rooms. He was quite in awe of the level of anger Suetonius seemed able to produce. In a public street, though, he felt his perspiration making his armpits slap wetly. Suetonius still marched as if the rising sun was nothing more than a vision, and the heat was growing.

Suetonius slipped on a loose stone and swore. Always Caesar to torment him. Whenever he was in the city, the fortunes of his family suffered. He knew Caesar had spread the slurs about him that had kept him from command in a legion. He had seen the covered smiles and whispers and known the source.

When he had seen the assassins creeping towards Caesar's home, he had experienced a moment of true pleasure. He could have raised an alarm, sent riders to warn them. He could have stopped it, but he had walked away, saying nothing. They had torn Caesar's wife apart. Suetonius remembered how he had laughed when his father told him the awful news. The old man had such an expression of gravity that Suetonius had not been able to help himself. His father's amazement seemed to fuel it until his eyes were pouring tears.

Perhaps his father would understand a little better now he had seen Caesar's flattery and promises for himself. The thought sat strangely in his mind, that he might be able to speak to his father again, with something shared between them. Suetonius couldn't recall the last time he had said more than a few curt words to his son and that coldness too was Caesar's doing. His father had given back the land they had won so cleverly while Julius was away. Given back the plot where Suetonius was to have built his house. He still remembered his father's eyes when he protested. There was no love, just a cool appraisal that found him always wanting.

Suetonius raised his head and relaxed his tight hands. He would see his father and commiserate with him. Perhaps he wouldn't flinch when Suetonius looked him in the eye, as if he was sickened by what he saw there. Perhaps he wouldn't look so *disappointed* in his son.

Bibilus had seen the change in his friend's gait and took the opportunity.

'It's getting hot, Suetonius. We should be heading back to the inn.'

Suetonius stopped and turned to his friend.

'How wealthy are you, Bibilus?' he asked suddenly.

Bibilus rubbed his hands nervously, as he always did when the subject of money came up between them. He had inherited a sum large enough never to have to work, but talking about it made him hot with embarrassment. He wished Suetonius didn't find the subject so fascinating.

'I have enough, you know. Not like Crassus, obviously, but enough,' he said warily. Was he after another loan? Bibilus hoped not. Somehow the only time Suetonius promised repayment was at the moment of asking. When he had the money, it was never mentioned again. When Bibilus summoned enough courage to bring up the outstanding sums, Suetonius became irritable and usually ended up storming off, until Bibilus had to apologise.

'Enough to stand for consul, Bibilus? There's still another day or two before the senate list is closed to new names.'

Bibilus blinked in confusion and horror at the idea.

'No, Suetonius, definitely not. I will not, even for you. I *like* my life and position in the Senate as it is. I wouldn't want to be consul even if they offered it to me.'

Suetonius stepped closer to him and took hold of his damp toga, his face filled with distaste.

'Do you want to see Caesar as consul? Do you even remember the civil war? Do you remember Marius and the damage he did? If you stand, you could split the vote for Caesar and let one of the others in with my father. If you are a friend to me, you won't hesitate.'

'I am of course, but it won't work!' Bibilus said, trying to pull away from the anger. The thought that Suetonius would smell his sweat was humiliating, but the grip was hard on his toga, exposing the white skin of his sagging chest.

'Even if I stand and gather a few votes, I could take them from your father as easily as Caesar, don't you see? Why don't you stand yourself, if that's what you want? I'll give you campaign funds, I swear it.'

'Have you lost your mind, telling me to stand against my own father? No, Bibilus. You may not be much of a friend, or much of anything, but there's no one else on the list of any note. If we do nothing, my father will be destroyed by Caesar. I know how he panders to the mob, how they love him. How many would honour my father with Caesar parading himself like a glittering whore? You come from an old family and you have the money to raise your name before the election.' His eyes brightened with malice as he considered the idea.

'My father has not been away from Rome for years, remember, and he has support in the richer centuries, who vote first. You saw the speeches. Caesar appeals to the shiftless poor. If a majority is reached early, half of Rome may not be called to vote. It can be done.'

'I don't think –' Bibilus stammered.

'You *must*, Bibi, for me. Just a few of the early centuries at the vote would be enough and then he will be shamed into leaving Rome. If you see my father's vote is suffering, you can withdraw. Nothing could be simpler, unless you would prefer to let Caesar be consul without a fight?'

Bibilus tried again. 'I don't have the funds to pay for . . .'

'Your father left you a fortune, Bibi; did you think I didn't know that? Do you think he would want to see Cato's old enemy as consul? No, those petty loans you have given me in the past are nothing more than a few days' living for you.' Suetonius seemed to sense the incongruity of holding his friend so tightly even as he tried to persuade him. He let go and straightened Bibilus' toga with a few twitches of his fingers.

'That's better. Now will you do this for me, Bibilus? You know how important it is to me. Who knows, you might enjoy being consul with my father, if it comes to that. More importantly, Caesar must not be allowed to slide his way into power in this city.'

'No. Do you hear? I will not!' Bibilus said, wheezing slightly in fear.

Suetonius narrowed his eyes and gripped Bibilus by the arm, pulling him away from their companions. When he could not be overheard, Suetonius leaned in close to the sweating face of the young Roman.

'Do you remember what you told me last year? What I saw when I came to your house? I know why your father despised you, Bibilus, why he sent you away to your fine house and retired from the Senate. Perhaps that was why his heart gave out, who knows? How long do you think you would survive if your tastes became public knowledge?'

Bibilus looked ill, his face twisting.

'It was an accident, that girl. She had a flux . . .'

'Can you stand the light of day on you, Bibilus?' Suetonius said, pressing still closer. 'I've seen the results of your . . . enthusiasm. I could bring a case myself against you and the penalties are unpleasant, though not more than you deserve. How many little girls and boys have passed through your hands in the last few years, Bibilus? How many of the Senate are fathers, do you think?'

Bibilus' wet mouth shook in frustration. 'You have no right to threaten me! My slaves are my own property. No one would listen to you.'

Suetonius showed his teeth, his face ugly with triumph. 'Pompey lost a daughter, Bibi. *He'd* listen. He'd make sure you suffered for your pleasures, don't you think? I'm sure he would not turn me away if I went to him.'

Bibilus slumped, his eyes filling with tears.

'Please . . .' he whispered.

Suetonius patted him on the shoulder. 'There is no need to mention it again, Bibi. Friends do not desert each other,' he said, rubbing the damp flesh comfortingly.

*　　*　　*

'One hundred days, Servilia,' Julius said as he took her in his arms on the steps of the Senate. 'I have men searching the law cases to come. I'll choose the best of them to make my name and the tribes will come to listen. Gods, there's so much to do! I need you to contact everyone with debts to my family. I need runners, organisers, anyone who can argue for me on the streets from dawn to dusk. Brutus must use the Tenth to bring the gangs to heel. It's my responsibility now, thanks to Crassus. The old man is a genius, I swear it. In one stroke, I have the power I need to prove I can make the streets safe. It's all come so quickly, I almost don't . . .'

Servilia pressed her fingers onto his lips to stop the torrent of words. She laughed as he continued to talk, mouthing muffled ideas as they struck him. She kissed him then and for a second he continued to talk as their lips touched, until she slapped him lightly on the cheek with her free hand.

He broke away, laughing.

'I have to meet the Senate and I can't be late for them. Start the work, Servilia. I'll meet you here at noon.'

She watched him as he ran up the steps and disappeared into the gloom within, and then walked down to where her guards waited, her step light.

As Julius reached the door to the outer chamber, he found Crassus waiting for him. The older man looked strangely nervous and beads of sweat ran into the lines of his face.

'I must speak to you before you go in, Julius,' Crassus said. 'Not inside, where there are ears to hear us.'

'What is it?' Julius asked, feeling a sudden weight descend on him as he registered the consul's nervousness.

'I have not been entirely honest with you, my friend,' Crassus replied.

*   *   *

They could both hear the droning voices of the senators behind them as the two men sat on the wide steps, facing the forum.

Julius shook his head in disbelief.

'I would not have believed you capable of this, Crassus.'

'I am *not* capable of it,' Crassus snapped. 'I am telling you now, before the conspirators move against Pompey.'

'You should have stopped it when they came to you. You could have gone straight to the Senate and denounced this Catiline before he had anything more than ideas. Now you tell me he has gathered an army? It is a little late to claim the clean robe for you, Crassus, no matter how you protest.'

'If I had refused, they would have killed me and, yes, when they promised me the rule of Rome, I was tempted by it. There, you have heard me say it. Should I have given them to Pompey to parade as another victory before the people? To see him made Dictator for Life like Sulla before him? I was tempted, Julius, and I let it go too long unreported, but I am changing that now. I know their plans and where they have gathered. With your legion, we can destroy them before any harm is done.'

'Is that why you made me aedile?' Julius asked.

Crassus shrugged. 'Of course. Now it is your responsibility to stop them. It will make a fine pillar for your campaign for the people to see *nobilitas* like Catiline held responsible for crimes as any other citizen would be. They will see you as one above the petty bonds of class and tribe.'

Julius looked at the consul pityingly. 'And if I had not returned from Spain?'

'Then I would have found another way to beat them before the end.'

'Would you?' Julius pressed him softly.

Crassus turned to glare at the young man at his side.

'Do not doubt it. However, now *you* are here. I can give the leaders to you and the Tenth will destroy the rabble they have gathered. They were only a danger when no one knew. Without that surprise, you will scatter them and the consulship will be yours. I trust you will not forget your friends then.'

Julius rose quickly, looking down at the consul. Had he heard the entire truth of it, or just the parts Crassus wanted him to hear? Perhaps the men he betrayed were guilty of nothing more than being enemies to Crassus. It would not do to send the Tenth into the homes of powerful men on the strength of a conversation Crassus could deny. The consul was capable of it, Julius was sure.

'I will think what to do, Crassus. I will not be your sword to strike at enemies.'

Crassus rose to face him, his eyes glinting with suppressed anger.

'Politics is *bloody*, Julius. Better to learn that now than too late. I waited too long to deal with them. Be sure you don't make the same mistake.'

The two men entered the senate building together, but apart.

CHAPTER ELEVEN

The house Servilia had found for the campaign was three floors high and filled with people. Most importantly, it was central in the Esquiline valley, a busy part of the city that kept Julius in contact with those who needed to see him. From before dawn until the sun fell, his clients rushed in and out of the open doors, carrying errands and orders as Julius began to organise his strategy. The Tenth deployed in groups at night and after three vicious fights with the gangs of raptores, they had cleared eleven streets in the poorest areas and were spreading out. Julius knew only a fool would believe the gangs were beaten, but they didn't dare to gather in the areas he had chosen and in time the people would realise they were under the protection of the legion and walk with confidence.

He had accepted three cases in the forum court and won the first, with the next only three days away. The crowds had come to see the young orator and cheered the decision in his favour, though the crime was relatively mild. Julius still hoped, against reason, that he would be asked to try a murderer, or some other offence that would bring the people in their thousands to hear him speak.

He hadn't seen Alexandria for nearly two weeks after she accepted the commission to armour the fighters for a great sword tourney outside the city. When Julius was exhausted by the work, he refreshed himself by riding out to the Campus Martius to see the arena being constructed. Brutus and Domitius had sent word to every Roman town and city within five hundred miles to ensure the best quality of challenger. Even so, both men expected to be in the final and Brutus was convinced he would win, going so far as to put most of a year's salary on his success.

When Julius walked to the forum, or rode out to the ring being constructed, he made a point of travelling without guards, convinced the people must see his confidence in them. Brutus had argued against the decision, then given way with suspicious ease. Julius guessed his friend had men shadow their general whenever he moved around the city, ready to defend him. He didn't mind such a tactic as long as it was hidden. The appearance was far more important than the reality.

As promised, Julius had argued in the Senate to order trade traffic to enter and leave Rome only at night, keeping the streets clear for citizens. His soldiers were on every corner to enforce the quiet after dark and after a few bouts of shouting with incensed merchants, the change had come easily enough. As aedile, the responsibility for city order was his and with Crassus openly supporting him there had been few restrictions imposed by the other members of the Senate.

Julius pressed the weariness from his eyes with his knuckles until he could see flashing lights. His clients and his soldiers were working hard for him. The campaign was going well and he could have been content if it hadn't been for the problem Crassus had dropped in his lap.

The consul pressed him daily to move against those he had

named as traitors. While Julius delayed, he was tormented by the thought that they could strike and the city would plunge into a chaos he could have prevented. He had spies watching their houses and it was clear enough that they met in private rooms and bath-houses where no listening ear could intrude. Still Julius did not act. To believe there was a plot of the magnitude Crassus had described seemed impossible when he looked out on the quiet streets around the campaign house. Yet he had seen war touch Rome before and that was enough for him to send Brutus to scout where Crassus had pointed them.

This was the burden of the responsibility he had craved, Julius could acknowledge wryly to himself. Though he could wish for someone else to risk their career and life, the decision had been left in his hands. He did not underestimate the stakes. With nothing but a few names, Julius could not accuse senators of treason without putting his own neck on the line. If he failed to make a case, the Senate would turn against him without a moment's regret. Worse, the people might fear a return to the days of Sulla, where no one knew who next would be dragged out of their homes for treason. Rome could be damaged more by error than if he had done nothing, and that pressure was almost too much to bear.

Alone for a few precious moments, Julius thumped his fist on the table, shaking it. How could he trust Crassus after such a revelation? As consul, he should have denounced Catiline's conspiracy the moment he stepped into the senate building. Of all the men in Rome, he had failed in his most basic duty and, despite his protestations of innocence, Julius found it hard to forgive him that weakness. Not since Sulla had an armed force threatened to enter the city and the memory of that night still caused Julius to shudder. He had seen Marius brought down by soldiers in dark cloaks, swarming over him like the ants of Africa. Crassus should have known better than to listen to men like Catiline, no matter what they promised him.

Julius was startled from his thoughts by a commotion down-stairs. His hand dropped to the gladius laid on the table before he recognised Brutus' voice and relaxed. That was what Crassus had brought about, a return to the fear he had felt when Cato threatened him and every man had to be considered an enemy. Anger swelled as he understood how Crassus had manipulated him, yet he knew the old man would have what he wanted. The conspirators had to be reined in before they acted. Could they be threatened, he wondered. A century of the Tenth sent with his best officers to their homes, perhaps. If the men realised their plans were known, the conspiracy could be allowed to die stillborn.

Brutus knocked and entered and Julius knew it was bad news as he saw his expression.

'I had my men scout the villages Crassus warned you about. I think he's telling the truth,' Brutus said without preamble. There was none of his usual lightness of manner.

'How many swords do they have?' Julius asked.

'Eight thousand, maybe more, though they're spread out. Every town up there is full of men, far too many to support. No legion marks or banners, just an awful lot of blades too close to Rome for comfort. If my lads hadn't been looking for signs, they might have missed them completely. I think the threat is real, Julius.'

'Then I must move,' Julius said. 'It's gone too far to warn them off. Take men to the houses we've been watching. Go to Catiline's home yourself. Arrest the conspirators and bring them to the senate meeting this afternoon. I'll take the floor there and tell our senators how close they came to destruction.' He rose and buckled his sword onto his belt. 'Be careful, Brutus. They must have supporters in the city for this to work. Crassus said they would start fires in the poor areas as the signal, so we must have men on the streets, ready for them. Who knows how many are involved?'

'The Tenth will be spread thinly if we try to cover the whole city, Julius. I can't keep order and take the field against the mercenaries at the same time.'

'I will convince Pompey to use his men on the streets. He'll see the need. After you have brought the men to the Senate, give me an hour to put the case and then march. If I'm not there to lead, go alone against them.'

Brutus paused for a moment, understanding what he was being asked to do.

'If I take the field without a senate order, that could be the end of me, whether we bring victory or not,' he said softly. 'Are you sure you can trust Crassus not to betray you in this?'

Julius hesitated. It would be enough to finish them all if Crassus refused to repeat his accusations in the senate house. The old man was subtle enough to have created the conspiracy simply to remove a few of his opponents. Crassus could be rid of his competitors, while remaining unstained by all of it.

Still, what choice did he have? He could not allow a rebellion to begin while he had the chance to stop it.

'I can't trust him, no, but no matter who is responsible for that gathering of soldiers, I cannot allow a threat to Rome. Arrest the men he has named before any more harm is done by waiting. I'll take the responsibility if I can get to you. If I am not there, it's your decision. Wait as long as you can.'

Brutus led twenty of his best with Domitius to take Catiline at his own home. To his fury, they were delayed crucial moments as they broke through his outer gate. By the time they reached the private rooms, Catiline was warming his hands at a brazier filled with burning papers. The man seemed calm as he greeted the soldiers. His face was almost sculpted out of hard planes and the breadth of his shoulders showed he was one who took

137

care of his strength. Unusually for a senator, he wore a gladius at his side in an ornate scabbard.

Rushing in, Brutus threw a jug of wine on the flames. As the wet smoke hissed out, he rammed his hand into the sodden ashes, but there was nothing left.

'Your master has overstepped the mark, gentlemen,' Catiline remarked.

'My orders are to take you to the Curia, Senator, to answer charges of treason,' Domitius told him.

Catiline let his right hand rest on the pommel of the gladius and both Brutus and Domitius stiffened.

'If you touch that sword again, you will die right now,' Brutus warned him softly and Catiline's eyes opened wide under the heavy lids as he assessed the danger facing him.

'What is your name?' he asked.

'Marcus Brutus of the Tenth.'

'Well, Brutus, Consul Crassus is a good friend of mine and when I am free, I will discuss this with you in more detail. Now do as you have been told and take me to the Senate.'

Domitius put out a hand to hold the senator's arm and Catiline knocked it aside, his temper showing through the false calm.

'Do not *dare* to put hands on me! I am a senator of Rome. When this is over, do not think I will forget the insults to my person. Your master will not always be able to protect you from the law.'

Catiline swept out past them, his expression murderous. The soldiers of the Tenth formed up around him, exchanging worried glances. Domitius said nothing more as they reached the street, though he hoped for all their sakes that the other groups had found some proof with which to accuse the men. Without it, Julius could well have created his own destruction.

The road outside was heaving with the morning crowds and Brutus had to use the flat of his sword to clear the way for them. The press was too great for the citizens to move away easily and progress was slow. Brutus swore under his breath as they reached the first corner and didn't sense the change in the crowd until it was almost too late.

The children and women had vanished and the soldiers of the Tenth were surrounded by hard-looking men. Brutus glanced back at Catiline. The senator's face had lit with triumph. Brutus felt himself shoved and hemmed in and, in a sickening flash of understanding, knew Catiline had been prepared for them.

'Defend yourselves!' Brutus roared. Even as he gave the order, he saw swords torn free from under cloaks and tunics as the crowd came alive with violence. Catiline's men had been hidden among the passers-by, waiting to free their leader. The street seethed with swords and screams as the first soldiers of the Tenth were caught unawares and cut down.

Brutus saw Catiline being drawn clear by his supporters and tried to grab him. It was impossible. Even as Brutus stretched out his arm, someone cut at it and he defended himself furiously. Pressed by bodies, he felt close to panic. Then he saw Domitius had cleared a bloody space in the street and moved to his side.

The soldiers of the Tenth held their nerve, cutting Catiline's supporters down with the grim efficiency of their training. There were no weak men amongst them, but each was faced with two or three swords swinging wildly. For all the attackers' lack of skill, they fought with fanatical energy and even the legionary armour could turn only a few of the blows.

Brutus grabbed a man by the throat with his left hand and jerked him into the path of two more, killing them with neat strokes as they struggled against each other. He felt his pounding heart settle then, giving him the chance to glance around him. He leaned back from a gladius aimed to cut through his sword arm and sent a riposte into the throat of the wielder. Throat and groin, the quickest deaths.

Brutus staggered as something hit him low in the back and he felt one of the straps give on his chestplate, shifting the weight. He spun with the sword at a sharp angle to cut into another man's collarbone and drop him into the mess of filth and flesh at their feet. Blood spattered across him and he blinked quickly, looking for Catiline. The senator had gone.

'Clear this damned street, Tenth!' he shouted and his men responded, cutting their way through. The heavy gladius blades chopped into the enemy, cutting limbs free as easily as a butcher's cleaver. With some of Catiline's men retreating with the senator, the numbers were thinning and the legionaries were able to isolate those remaining, ramming their blades over and over into the bodies to repay the insult of the attack in the only coin it deserved.

When it was done, the legionaries stood panting, their armour covered in dark blood that dripped slowly from the polished metal. One or two of them walked carefully to each of Catiline's men and thrust their swords in one last time to be sure.

Brutus wiped his gladius on a man he had killed and sheathed it carefully after checking the edge. There were no flaws on Cavallo's work.

Of the original twenty, only eleven of them stood, with two more dying. Without having to be ordered, Brutus saw his men lift their comrades up from the street and support them, exchanging a last few words as their lives bled away.

Brutus tried to concentrate. Catiline's men had been ready to steal him back from the Tenth. He could already be on the way to join the rebels, or they to him.

Brutus knew he had to make a decision quickly. His men watched him in silence, waiting for the word.

'Domitius, leave our wounded in the care of the nearest houses. Before you catch us up, take a message to Julius at the Senate. We can't wait for him now. The rest of you, run with me.'

Without another word, Brutus broke into a fast jog, his men falling in behind him as quickly as they were able.

The senate house was in chaos, as three hundred senators fought to shout over the others. The protests were loudest in the centre of the floor as four of the men Julius had arrested were chained there, demanding proof of the accusations against them. The men had been resigned at first, but when they realised Catiline would not be dragged in to join them, their confidence quickly returned.

Pompey waited impatiently for silence and finally was forced to add his own voice to the din, bellowing over them.

'Take your seats and be still!' he roared at the men, glaring around. Those nearest to him sat quickly enough and the ripple that followed restored some semblance of order.

Pompey waited until the noise had sunk to whispers. He gripped the rostrum tightly, but before he could begin to address the unruly Senate, one of the four accused lifted his chains up in appeal.

'Consul, I demand our release. We have been dragged from our homes on . . .'

'Be silent, or I will have you gagged with iron,' Pompey replied. He spoke quietly, but this time, his voice carried to the furthest reaches of the house. 'You will have a chance to answer the charges Caesar has brought against you.' He took a deep breath.

'Senators, these men are accused of a plot to create riots in the city leading to full-scale rebellion and an overturn of the power of this body, culminating in the murder of our officials. Those of you crying so loudly for justice would do well to consider the seriousness of these offences. Be silent for Caesar, who accuses them.'

As Julius walked towards the rostrum, he felt sweat break

out on his skin. Where was Catiline? There had been enough time for Brutus to bring him with the others, but now Julius felt each step as a slow march to destruction. He had nothing except Crassus' word with which to attack the men or to assuage his own doubts.

He faced the ranks of his colleagues, noting the rebellious expressions of many of them. Suetonius sat almost opposite with Bibilus. The two of them were practically quivering with interest at the proceedings. Cinna was there, his expression unreadable as he nodded to Julius. Since the death of his daughter, he had rarely been seen in the Senate. There could be no friendship between them, but Julius did not judge him an enemy. He wished he could be as sure about the other men of the Senate.

Julius took a calming breath as he arranged his thoughts. If he was wrong about any of it, it was all over for him. If Crassus had placed him at this point intending to leave him for the wolves, he faced disgrace and possibly even banishment.

Julius met Crassus' eyes, looking for a sign of triumph. The old man touched himself lightly on the chest and Julius gave no sign he had seen.

'I accuse these men and one other, by the name of Lucius Sergius Catiline, of treason against the city and her Senate,' Julius began, the words echoing in the dead silence. The breath seemed to shudder out of him. There was no going back.

'I can confirm that an army has been assembled in towns north of the city, eight to ten thousand strong. With Catiline as their leader, they were to attack on the signal of fires set on the hills of Rome, coupled with general unrest. This was to have been fomented by supporters within the city.'

Every eye turned on the four men who were chained at their feet. They stood together defiantly, glaring back. One of them shook his head as if in disbelief at Julius' words.

Before Julius could continue, a messenger in senate livery

ran to his side and handed up a wax tablet. Julius read it quickly, frowning.

'I have further news that the leader of these men has escaped those I sent to arrest him. I ask now for a senate order to take the Tenth north against the brigands they have assembled. I must not delay here.'

A senator stood slowly from the seated ranks. 'What proof do you offer us?'

'My word and that of Crassus,' Julius replied quickly, ignoring his own doubts. 'It is the nature of a conspiracy not to leave too many traces, Senator. Catiline escaped by killing nine of my men. He approached Consul Crassus with these four before you, offering the death of Pompey and a new order in Rome. More will have to wait until I have dealt with the threat to the city.'

Crassus stood then and Julius met his eyes, still unsure whether he could trust him. The consul looked down at the chained conspirators in front of him and his expression showed a deep anger.

'I name Catiline as traitor.'

Julius felt a great wave of relief as Crassus spoke. Whatever the old man was doing, at least he was not the one to fall. Crassus glanced over at him before continuing and Julius wondered how much the man understood of his thoughts.

'As consul, I give my consent for the Tenth to leave Rome and take the field. Pompey?'

Pompey rose, his glance snapping to each man in turn. He too could feel there was more to the story than he was being told, but after a long pause, he nodded.

'Go then. I will trust the need is as great as I am told, Julius. My own legion will guard against a rebellion in the city. However, these men you call conspirators will not be sentenced until you return and I am satisfied the issue is clear. I will question them myself.'

A storm of whispering broke out on the benches at this terse exchange and the three men took silent stock of each other's positions. There was no give in any of them.

Crassus broke first and called for a scribe to write the order, handing it into Julius' hands as he came down from the rostrum.

'Do your duty and you will be safe,' he murmured.

Julius stared at him for a moment before hurrying out into the forum.

CHAPTER TWELVE

෬෨෬෨෬

Brutus rode with his extraordinarii at the head of the Tenth, covering many times the distance of the marching ranks as they scouted ahead and to the sides of the column. Of necessity, they were north and west of the city as the bulk of the legion had to be summoned from the camp near the coast and make their way across country to meet the single century Brutus had brought from the old Primigenia barracks.

When they had joined, some of the nerves that had affected Brutus vanished in the excitement of leading the legion against an enemy for the first time. Though he hoped to see Julius coming up behind them, another part of him wanted to be left alone to lead them in battle. His extraordinarii wheeled at his order as if they had fought together for years. Brutus revelled in the sight and felt more than a little reluctance at the thought of giving it up to anyone.

Renius had stayed at the coast with five centuries to protect the equipment and gold from Spain. It had to be done, but Brutus begrudged every man lost while the numbers of the enemy were unknown. As he cast a professional eye back down the column, he felt a thrill of pride at the men who marched for him. They had started with nothing more than a gold eagle and a memory of Marius, but were once again a legion, and they were his.

He cast an eye up to the position of the sun and remembered the maps his scouts had drawn. Catiline's forces were more than a day's march away from the city and he would have to decide whether to make a fortified camp, or to march through the night. The Tenth were undoubtedly as fresh as they could ever hope to be, long recovered from the sea journey that had brought them home. As well as that, a rebellious thought reminded him that Julius would be able to catch them if they camped and the command would shift to him once more. The broken ground would be treacherous in the dark, but Brutus resolved to drive his men on until they met the enemy.

The region of Etruria, of which Rome formed the southernmost point, was a land of hills and ravines, difficult to cross. The Tenth were forced to spread into wider lines to negotiate their way around ancient tors and valleys and Brutus was pleased to see the formations change with speed and discipline.

Octavian galloped across his line of vision, turning his gelding in a flashy display of skill as he came abreast.

'How much further?' he called over the jingle and tramp of the ranks.

'Another thirty miles to the villages we scouted,' Brutus replied, smiling. He could see the excitement he felt mirrored in Octavian's face. The boy had never known a battle and for him, the march was untempered by thoughts of death and pain. Brutus should have been immune, but the Tenth shone in the sun and the boy he had once been revelled in command.

'Take a century to scout the back trail,' Brutus ordered, ignoring the look of disappointment that flashed across the younger man's face. It was hard on him, but Brutus knew better than to allow Octavian the first charge before he had learned a little more of the reality of battle.

He watched as Octavian gathered riders and moved in perfect formation to the rear of the column. Brutus nodded in satisfaction, taking pleasure from the chance to think as a general.

He remembered how, years before, he had handed Primigenia over to Julius and a bitter regret stole over him before he crushed it. The command he exercised was only a proxy until Julius arrived, but he knew the moments of this march would stay in his memory for a long time.

One of the scouts came in fast, the horse skidding in the loose earth as the rider yanked on the reins. The man's face was pale with excitement.

'The enemy is in sight, sir. They are marching towards Rome.'

'How many?' Brutus snapped, his heart racing.

'Two legions of irregulars, sir, in open squares. No cavalry that I could see.'

A shout went up from behind and Brutus turned in his saddle with a feeling almost of dread. Behind the column, two riders galloped towards them. He knew then that Domitius had done his duty and brought Julius to the Tenth. He clenched his jaw against the anger that swamped him.

He turned to the scout and hesitated. Should he wait for Julius to arrive and take command? No, he would not. The order was his to give and he took a cool breath.

'Pass the word. Advance and engage the enemy. Have the cornicens sound maniple orders. Velites on point to meet them. Extraordinarii to the flanks. We'll break these bastards on the first charge.'

The scout saluted before galloping away and Brutus felt empty as he watched the dust cloud that promised blood and battle. Julius would take them in now.

*　　*　　*

As they sighted the legion coming at them, the ranks of merce-naries wavered and slowed. The Tenth were sliding over the land towards them like some great silvered beast and the ground shivered delicately with the cadence of their march. A host of flags had been raised into the wind and the wail of the corni-cens could be heard thinly against the breeze.

Four thousand of those who had come for Catiline's gold were from Gaul and their leader turned to the Roman, resting a powerful hand on his shoulder.

'You said the way to the city would be undefended,' he growled.

Catiline shook the hand free.

'We have the numbers to take them, Glavis,' he snapped. 'You knew it would be bloody work.'

The Gaul nodded, squinting through the dust to the Roman ranks. His teeth showed through his beard as he pulled a heavy sword from a scabbard across his back, grunting as he took the weight. All around him, his men followed the gesture, until a host of blades were raised above their heads to meet the charge.

'Just this little legion then, and one more in the city. We'll eat them,' Glavis promised, tilting back his head to roar. The Gauls around him responded and the front ranks separated and moved faster, sprinting across the broken ground.

Catiline drew his own gladius and wiped sweat from his eyes. His heart pounded with unaccustomed fear and he wondered if the Gaul had seen it. He shook his head in bitterness and cursed Crassus for his lies. There may have been a chance to take Rome in confusion and panic and the dark, but a legion in the field?

'We have the numbers,' he whispered to himself, swallowing hard. Ahead of him, he saw a flowing mass of horses overtake the ranks. The ground shook with the weight of the charge and Catiline suddenly believed he was going to die. In that moment, his fear vanished and his feet were light as he ran.

*   *   *

Julius took command without hesitation as he rode his lath-
ered mount up to Brutus. He handed over the wax tablet signed
by the consuls.

'Now we are legitimate. You have given the battle orders?'

'I have,' Brutus replied. He tried to hide the coldness he felt,
but Julius was looking away from him, judging the line of
approach to the rebel forces.

'The extraordinarii are ready on the flanks,' Brutus said. 'I
would like to join them there.'

Julius nodded. 'I want these mercenaries broken quickly. Take
the right and lead them in on my signal. Two short notes from
the horns. Listen well for it.'

Brutus saluted and moved away, relinquishing his command
without a backward glance. His extraordinarii had taken station
in ranks. They let his horse through to the front as they saw
him join them and a few cheerful voices called out a welcome.
Brutus frowned at that, hoping they were not too confident.
As with Octavian, there was a difference between smashing
target shields to pieces and sending spears into living men.

'Hold your line,' Brutus bellowed over their heads, glaring
at them.

They quietened then, though the excitement was palpable.
The horses whinnied and pulled to be allowed to run, but were
reined in with tight hands. The men were nervous, Brutus could
see. Many of them checked their spears over and over, loosening them in the long leather holders that hung down by the
horses' sides.

They could see the faces of the rebels now, a mass of shouting,
running men who held swords high over their shoulders for
one smashing blow. The blades caught the sun.

The centuries of the Tenth tightened their formations, each
man ready with his drawn gladius, his shield protecting the
man on his left. There were no gaps in their lines as they trotted
forward. Then the cornicens blew three short blasts and the

Tenth broke into a run, holding silence until the last moment when they roared as one and heaved their spears into the air.

The heavy iron points punched men from their feet along the enemy line and Brutus had the extraordinarii launch a fraction behind, their more accurate strikes aimed at anyone trying to rally the enemy. Before the armies met in earnest, hundreds had died without a Roman life taken. The extraordinarii circled on the wings and Julius could see the riders bring their shields around automatically to cover their backs as they wheeled. It was a superb display of skill and training and Julius exulted at the sight of it as the main lines crashed together.

Glavis spent his first mighty blow on a shield, smashing it through. As he tried to recover, a sword entered his stomach. He winced in expectation of the pain to come, dragging his blade up again. As he tried for a second blow, another Roman crashed his shield into him and he fell sideways, the sword knocked from numb fingers. Glavis panicked then as he looked up and saw the forest of legs and swords beginning to pass over him. They kicked and stamped at him and in seconds his body had been stabbed four more times. The blood poured out of him and he spat wearily, tasting it in his throat. He struggled to rise, but they kept pounding at his body. No one could have marked the exact instant of his death. He didn't have time to see the front line of his Gauls collapse as they found they could not break the fighting rhythm of the Tenth.

As Glavis was seen to fall, the Gauls wavered and that was the moment Julius had waited to see. He shouted to his signaller and two short notes rang out.

Brutus heard and felt his heart leap in his chest. Despite the advantage of numbers, the mercenaries were breaking against the Roman charge. Some of them were already streaming away, dropping their swords. Brutus grinned as he raised his fist in the air, sweeping it down towards the enemy. Their spear holders were empty and now they would prove their true worth. The extraordinarii responded as if they had fought together all their lives, wheeling away to give themselves room and then hitting the enemy like a knife into their ranks, tearing them. Each rider guided his mount with one hand on the reins and his long *spatha* sword cutting heads from those that faced them. The horses were heavy enough to smash men from their feet and nothing could stand against the sheer weight of them as they plunged into the lines, deeper and deeper, breaking the rebels apart.

The front rank of the Tenth moved quickly over their enemies, each man using his blade and shield in the knowledge that he was protected by his brother on the right. They were unstoppable and after the first ranks went down they picked up speed, heaving and grunting with the strain as arms began to tire.

Julius called the maniple orders and his centurions roared them out. The velites moved back on light feet and let the triarii come forward in their heavier armour.

The rebels broke then as the fresh soldiers came at them. Hundreds threw down their weapons and hundreds more sprinted away, ignoring the calls of their leaders.

For those that surrendered too early, there could be no mercy. The Roman line could not afford to let them through the advance and they were killed with the rest.

The extraordinarii flowed around the rebels, a black mass of snorting horses and shouting riders, splashed red with blood and wild enough for nightmares. They hemmed them in and, as if there had been a general signal, thousands of men dropped their swords and raised empty hands, panting.

Julius hesitated as he saw the end. If he did not have the cornicens sound the disengage, his Tenth would continue until the last of the rebels were dead. Part of him was tempted to let that happen. What would he do with so many prisoners? Thousands of them had been left alive and they could not be allowed to go back to their lands and homes. He waited, sensing the eyes of his centurions on him as they waited for the signal to stop the killing. It was butchery by then and already those closest to the Roman ranks were beginning to reach for their weapons again, rather than die unarmed. Julius swore softly to himself, chopping a hand down. The cornicens saw the motion and blew a falling tone. And it was finished.

Those left alive had been disarmed as quickly as the Tenth could spread amongst them. In small groups, they searched the mercenaries, a single Roman removing blades while the others watched in grim concentration, ready to punish any sudden movement.

The mercenary officers had been called out of the ranks to stand in front of Julius. They watched him in silent resignation, a strange group, dressed in rough cloth and mismatched armour.

A breeze blew coldly through the battlefield as the sun sank towards the horizon. Julius looked at the kneeling prisoners arranged in a semblance of ranks, with corpses breaking the neat lines. Catiline's body had been found and dragged to the front. Julius had looked down at the pierced and bloody thing that had been a senator. There would be no answers from him.

Though Julius thought he knew the truth of the failed rebellion, he suspected Crassus would remain untouched by his part in it. Perhaps some secrets were better kept from the public gaze. It could not hurt to have the richest man in Rome in his debt.

He glanced over as Octavian slapped his mount's neck, practically glowing with the fading thrill of speed and fear. The extraordinarii had been blooded at last. Horses and men were spattered with gore and earth thrown up in the charge. Brutus stood amongst them, exchanging quiet words of praise while he waited for Julius to end it. It was not an order he would have enjoyed, Brutus admitted to himself, but Rome would not allow a show of mercy.

Julius signalled to the men of the Tenth to herd the officers closer to him. The optios thumped their staffs into the mercenaries, knocking one of them sprawling. The man cried out in anger and would have thrown himself at them if another hadn't reached out to hold him. Julius listened as they argued, but the language was unknown to him.

'Is there a commander amongst you?' he asked them at last.

The leaders looked at each other and then one stood forward.

'Glavis was, for those of us from Gaul,' the man said. He jerked a thumb back at the piles of bodies that littered the ground. 'He's back there, somewhere.'

The man returned Julius' cold appraisal before looking away. He gazed over the battlefield with a sad expression before his eyes snapped back.

'You have our weapons, Roman. We're no threat to you any more. Let us go.'

Julius shook his head slowly. 'You were never a threat to us,' he said, noting the spark of fire that shone in the man's eyes before it was hidden. He raised his voice to carry to all of them.

'You have a choice, gentlemen. Either you die at my word . . .' He hesitated. Pompey would go berserk when he heard. 'Or you take an oath as legionaries for me, under my orders.'

The babble of noise that followed was not restricted to the mercenaries. The soldiers of the Tenth gaped at what they were hearing.

'You will be paid on the first day of each month. Seventy-five silver coins to each man, though part of that will be kept back.'

'How much of it?' someone called.

Julius turned in the direction of the voice.

'Enough for salt, food, weapons, armour, and a tithe to the

widows and orphans. Forty-two denarii will be left for each man to spend as he sees fit.' A thought struck him then and made him hesitate. The pay for so many men would amount to thousands of coins. It would take huge wealth to keep two legions, and even the gold he had brought back from Spain would quickly dwindle under such a demand. How had Catiline found the money? He thrust the sudden suspicions aside to continue.

'I will seed your ranks with my officers and train you to fight as well as the men who made you look like children today. You will have good swords and armour and your pay will come on time. That or you die now. Go amongst your men and tell them. Warn them that if they are thinking of slipping away, I will hunt them down and hang them. Those who choose to live will be marched back to Rome, but not as prisoners. The training will be hard, but they have courage enough to make a beginning. Anything else can be taught.'

'Will you give us back our weapons?' the voice came from the officers.

'Don't be a fool,' Julius said. 'Now move! One way or another, this will be over by sunset.'

Unable to meet his glare, the mercenaries moved off, heading back to their brothers kneeling in the mud. The legionaries let them pass through, exchanging glances of amazement.

While they waited, Brutus walked over to stand at Julius' side.

'The Senate will not be pleased, Julius. You don't need any more enemies.'

'I am in the field,' Julius replied. 'Whether they like it or not, in the field I speak for the city. I *am* Rome, here, and the decision is mine.'

'But we had orders to destroy them,' Brutus said quietly enough not to be overheard.

Julius shrugged. 'It may come to that yet, my friend, but you should be hoping they will take the oath.'

'Why should I be hoping that?' Brutus asked suspiciously.

Julius smiled at him, reaching out to clap him on the shoulder.

'Because they will be your legion.'

Brutus held himself very still, taking it in.

'They broke against us, Julius. Mars himself couldn't make a legion out of this lot.'

'You did it once, with Primigenia. You will do it with these. Tell them they *survived* a charge by the best legion ever to come out of Rome, under a general blessed. Raise their heads for them, Brutus, and they will follow you.'

'They will be mine alone?' Brutus asked.

Julius looked into his eyes then. 'If you will still be my sword, I swear I will not interfere, though the overall command must be mine when we fight together. Aside from that, if you walk my path, it will be by your own choice – as it has always been.'

One by one, the mercenary officers were gathering again. As they met, they nodded sharply to each other, visibly relaxing. Julius knew he had them before their spokesman walked towards him.

'It wasn't much of a choice,' the man said.

'There are no ... dissenters?' Julius said softly. The Gaul shook his head.

'Good. Then have them stand. When every man has taken the oath, we will light torches and march through the night back to Rome. There is a barracks there for you and a hot meal.' Julius turned to Brutus.

'Send out the freshest riders carrying messages for the Senate. They won't know whether we're the enemy or not and I don't want to set off the very rebellion we have fought to prevent.'

'We *are* the enemy,' Brutus muttered.

'No longer, Brutus. Not one of them will take a step before he is bound by oath. After that, they will be ours, whether they know it or not.'

* * *

As Julius rode up to the city with a picked guard of the extra-ordinarii, he saw the gates had been closed against them. The first grey light of dawn was already showing on the horizon and he felt a gritty tiredness in his joints. There was still more to be done before he could sleep.

'Open the gate!' he shouted as he reined in, looking up at the shadowed mass of timber and iron that blocked his way.

A legionary wearing Pompey's armour appeared on the wall, looking down at them. After a glance at the small group of riders, he peered out along the road, satisfying himself that there was no hidden force waiting to storm into the city.

'Not till dawn, sir,' he called down, recognising Julius' armour. 'Pompey's orders.'

Julius swore under his breath. 'Throw me a rope then. I have business with the consul and it won't wait.'

The soldier disappeared, presumably to see his superior officer. The extraordinarii stirred restlessly.

'We were told to escort you to the senate house, General,' one of them ventured.

Julius turned in his saddle to look at the man.

'If Pompey has sealed the city, his legion will be out in force. I'll be in no danger.'

'Yes, sir,' the rider replied, discipline preventing him contesting the order.

On the walls, an officer appeared in full armour, his helmet plume moving slightly in the night breeze.

'Aedile Caesar? I'll send a rope down to you if you give me your word to come alone. The consuls made no allowance for you to return this early.'

'You have my oath,' Julius replied, watching as the man signalled and heavy coils came thumping down to the ground at the foot of the gate. He saw archers covering him from the gate towers and nodded to himself. Pompey was no one's fool.

As he dismounted and took hold of the rope, Julius looked back at the extraordinarii.

'Return to the old Primigenia barracks with the others. Brutus is in command until my return.'

Without another word, he began to climb hand over hand.

CHAPTER THIRTEEN

∽∾∽∾∽

A light rain began to fall as Julius walked through the empty city. With dawn on the horizon, the streets should have been filled with workers, servants and slaves, bustling along on a thousand errands. The cries of vendors should have been heard, coupled with the din of a thousand trades. Instead, it was eerily quiet.

Julius hunched his shoulders against the rain, hearing his own footsteps echo back from the houses on either side. He saw faces at the high windows of the tenements, but no one called down to him and he hurried on towards the forum.

Pompey's men stood at every corner in small groups, ready to enforce the curfew. One of them gripped his hilt as he caught sight of the lonely figure. Julius threw back his riding cloak to reveal the armour underneath and they let him pass. The whole city was nervous and Julius felt a prickling anger at the part Crassus had played in it.

He strode quickly along the Alta Semita, following the

158

Quirinal hill down into the forum. The great flat crossing stones kept him clear of the sluggish filth of the roadbed below his feet. The rain had begun to wash the city clean, but it would take more than a brief shower to finish the task.

In all his life, he had never seen the vast space of the forum so empty. A wind that had been blocked by the rows of houses hit him as he passed into it, making his cloak snap out behind. There were soldiers at the entrances to the temples and the senate house itself, but no lights showed within. The temple priests had lit flickering torches for those who prayed inside, but Julius had no business with them. As he passed the temple to Minerva, he muttered under his breath to her, that he might have the wisdom to see his way through the tangle Crassus had made.

The iron studs of his sandals clacked on the flagstones of the great space as he approached the senate building. Two legionaries held station there, absolutely still despite the rain and wind that bit at their exposed skin. As Julius set his foot on the first step, both men drew their swords and Julius frowned at them. They were both young. More experienced men would not have drawn with so little provocation.

'By order of Consul Pompey, no one may enter until the Senate is called again,' one of them said to Julius, filled with the importance of his duty.

'I need to see the consuls before that meeting,' Julius replied. 'Where are they?'

The two soldiers glanced at each other for a moment, trying to decide whether it would be right for them to volunteer the information. Soaked to the skin by then, Julius felt his temper rising.

'I was told to report as soon as I returned to Rome. I am here. Where is your commander?'

'The prison house, sir,' the soldier answered. He opened his mouth to continue, then thought better of it, resuming his position as before and sheathing his gladius. Once again they were like twin statues in the rain.

There were dark clouds over the city by then and the wind was growing in strength, beginning to howl as it rushed across the empty forum. Julius resisted the urge to run for cover and stalked over to the prison that adjoined the senate house. It was a small building, with only two cells below ground. Those who were to be executed were held there on the night before their death. There were no other prisons in the city: execution and banishment prevented the need to build them. The very fact that Pompey was there told Julius what he would find and he prepared to face it without flinching.

Another pair of Pompey's men guarded the outer door. As Julius approached, they nodded to him as if he were expected and threw open the locking bars.

The armour he wore was marked with the insignia of the Tenth and he was not questioned until he reached the steps leading down to the cells. Three men moved subtly apart as he announced himself and another went down the steps behind them. Julius waited patiently as he heard his name spoken somewhere below and Pompey's answering rumble. The men who watched him were stiff with tension and so he leaned against the wall in the most relaxed fashion he could, brushing some of the surface water from his armour and squeezing it from his hair. The actions helped him to relax under their silent stares and he was able to smile as Pompey came up with the soldier.

'That is Caesar,' Pompey confirmed. His eyes were hard and there was no answering smile. At the confirmation from their general, the men in the room took their hands from their sword hilts and moved away, leaving the entrance to the steps open.

'Is there still a threat to the city?' Pompey asked.

'It is ended,' Julius replied. 'Catiline did not survive the battle.'

Pompey swore softly. 'That is unfortunate. Come down with me, Caesar. You should be part of this,' Pompey said.

As he spoke, he wiped sweat from his hairline and Julius saw a smear of blood on his hand. He followed Pompey down the steps with his heart thumping in anticipation.

Crassus was there in the cells. The blood seemed to have drained from his face, so that under the lamplight he looked like a figure of wax. He looked up as Julius entered the low room and his eyes glittered unhealthily. There was a sickly smell in the air and Julius tried not to look at the figures bound to chairs in the centre of it. There were four of them and the smell of fresh blood was one he knew well.

'Catiline? Did you bring him back?' Crassus asked, putting a hand on Julius' arm.

'He was killed in the first charge, Consul,' Julius replied, watching the man's eyes. He saw the fear go out of them as he had expected. Catiline's secrets had died with him.

Pompey grunted, motioning to the torturers who stood by the broken bodies of the conspirators.

'A pity. These creatures named him as their leader, but they know nothing of the details I wanted. They would have told us by now.'

Julius looked at the men and repressed a shudder at what had been done to them. Pompey had been thorough and he too doubted the men could have held anything back. Three of them lay as still as the dead, but the last rolled his head towards them with a sudden jerk. One of his eyes had been pierced and wept a shining stream of liquid down his cheek, but the other peered around aimlessly, lighting up as he saw Julius.

'You! I accuse you!' he spat, then cackled weakly, dribbling blood over his chin.

Julius fought against a rising gorge as he caught sight of white shards on the stone floor. Some of them still had the roots attached.

'He has lost his mind,' he said softly and, to his relief, Pompey nodded.

'Yes, though he held out the longest. They will live long enough to be executed and that will be the end of it. I must thank you both for bringing this to the Senate in time. It was a noble deed and worthy of your ranks.' Pompey looked at the man who would stand for the position of consul in only two months.

'When my curfew is over, I suppose the people will rejoice at being saved from bloody insurrection. They will elect you, don't you think? How can they not?'

His eyes belied the light tone and Julius did not look at him as he felt the man's gaze. He felt shamed by all of it.

'Perhaps they will,' Crassus said softly. 'We three will have to work together for Rome. A triumvirate will bring its own problems, I am sure. Perhaps we should . . .'

'Another time, Crassus,' Pompey snapped. 'Not now, with the stink of this place in my lungs. We still have a senate meeting at sunrise and I want to visit the bath-house before that.'

'Dawn is here now,' Julius said.

Pompey swore softly, using a rag to wipe his hands clean. 'It's always night down in this place. I am finished with these.'

He gave orders to the torturers to have the men cleaned and made presentable before turning back to Crassus. As Julius watched, dark sponges were dipped in buckets and the worst of the blood began to be sluiced away, running in stone gutters along the floor between his legs.

'I will set the execution for noon,' Pompey promised, leading them up the stairs to the cool rooms above.

The grey light had taken on a reddish tint as Julius and Crassus stepped out into the forum. The rain pounded on the stones, rebounding in thousands of tiny spatters that drummed in the emptiness. Though Julius called his name, Crassus walked

162

quickly away into the downpour. No doubt a bath and a change of clothes would remove some of the sickly pallor from his skin, Julius thought. He hurried to catch up with the consul.

'Something occurred to me when I was destroying the rebels gathered in your name,' Julius called, his voice echoing.

The consul stopped dead at that, looking around. There was no one close.

'In *my* name, Julius? Catiline led them. Did his followers not murder your soldiers in the street?'

'Perhaps, but the house you showed me was a modest one, Crassus. Where would Catiline have gathered enough gold to pay ten thousand men? Very few in this city could have paid for such an army, don't you think? I wonder what would happen if I sent men to investigate his accounts. Would I find a traitor with huge reserves of hidden wealth, or should I look for another, a paymaster?'

Crassus could know nothing of the burnt papers Brutus had found at the house and the spark of worry Julius saw was all he needed to confirm his suspicions.

'It strikes me that such a large force of mercenaries, coupled with riots and fires in the city could well have worked with only Pompey's legion to guard Rome. It was not an empty offer they made you, Crassus, do you realise? The city could well have been yours. I am *surprised* you were not tempted. You would have been left standing on the heap of corpses, and Rome might have been ready for Dictatorship.'

As Crassus began to reply, Julius' expression changed and his mocking tone became hard.

'But without warning, another legion is brought home from Spain and then . . .? Then you must have been in a very difficult position. The forces are set, the conspiracy is in place, but Rome is guarded by ten thousand and victory is no longer guaranteed. A gambling man might have risked it, but not you. You are a man who knows when the game is over. I wonder when you decided it was better to betray Catiline than see it through? Was it when you came to my home and planned my campaign with me?'

Crassus put a hand on Julius' shoulder.

'I have said I am a friend to your house, Julius, and so I will ignore your words – for your own good, I will.' He paused for an instant. 'The conspirators are dead and Rome is safe. An excellent outcome, in fact. Let that be enough for you. There is nothing else that should trouble your thoughts. Let it go.'

Ducking his head against the rain, Crassus walked away, leaving Julius staring after him.

CHAPTER FOURTEEN

Cold grey clouds hung low in the sky over the vast crowd waiting in the Campus Martius. The ground was sodden underfoot, but thousands had left their houses and work to walk to the great field and witness the executions. Pompey's soldiers waited in perfect, shining ranks, showing no sign of the labour that had gone into constructing the prisoners' platform, or laying out a host of wooden benches for the Senate. Even the ground had been covered with dry rushes that crackled underfoot.

Children were held aloft by their parents to get a glimpse of the four men waiting miserably on the wooden platform and the crowd talked quietly amongst themselves, feeling something of the solemnity of the moment.

As noon had approached, the Senate had left their deliberations in the Curia and walked together to the Campus. Soldiers of the Tenth had joined Pompey's men in closing the city, pressing wax seals against the gates and raising the flag on the

Janiculum hill. With the Senate absent, the city was kept in a state of armed siege until their return. Many of the senators glanced idly at the distant flag on the hill to the west. It would remain as long as the city was safe and even the execution of traitors would be halted if the flag was pulled down to warn of an enemy approach.

Julius stood with the damp folds of his best cloak wrapped tightly around him. Even with the tunic and heavy toga underneath it, he shivered as he watched the miserable men his actions had brought to that place of death.

The prisoners had no protection from the biting wind. Only two could stand and they were hunched in pain, their chained hands pressed in mute misery against the wounds of the night. Perhaps because death was so close, those two gulped at the cold air, filling their lungs and ignoring the sting of their exposed skin.

The tallest of the pair had long dark hair that whipped and veiled his face. His eyes were swollen, but Julius could see a glint almost hidden by the bruised flesh, the feverish brightness of a trapped animal.

The one who had raved at Julius in the prison house was sobbing, his head wrapped in a cloth. A dark coin of blood had appeared in the material, marking the place his eye had been. Julius shuddered at the memory and took a tighter grip on his cloak, feeling the icy metal of one of Alexandria's clasps touch his neck. He glanced at Pompey and Crassus, standing on the bed of rushes laid over the mud. The two consuls were talking quietly and the crowd waited for them, their eyes bright with anticipation.

Finally, the two men stood apart. Pompey caught the eye of a magistrate from the city and the crowd shuffled and chattered as the man ascended the platform and faced them.

'These four have been found guilty of treason against the city. By order of consuls Crassus and Pompey and by order of

166

the Senate, they will be executed. Their bodies will be cut apart and their flesh scattered for the fowls of the air. Their heads will be placed on four gates as a warning to those who threaten Rome. This is the will of our consuls, who speak as Rome.'

The executioner was a master butcher by trade, a powerfully built man with close-cropped grey hair. He wore a toga of rough brown wool, belted to hold in his swelling waist. He did not rush, enjoying the gaze of the crowd as it focused on him. The silver coins he would receive for the work were nothing to the satisfaction he took from it.

Julius watched as the man made a show of checking his knife, running a stone down its length one last time. It was a vicious-looking blade, a narrow cleaver as long as his forearm with the tang set in a sturdy wooden handle. The spine was almost a finger wide. A child laughed nervously and was shushed by her parents. The long-haired prisoner began to pray aloud, his eyes glassy. Perhaps it was his noise, or just a sense of showmanship, but the butcher came to him first, laying the cleaver alongside his neck.

The man flinched and his voice grew sharper, the air hissing in and out of his lungs in sharp jerks. His hands shook and his pale skin was wax-white. The crowd watched fascinated as the butcher took a handful of his hair in his hand and bent the head slowly to one side, exposing the clean line of the neck.

The man's voice was deep and low. 'No, no ... no,' he muttered, the crowd straining to hear his last words.

There was no fanfare or warning. The butcher adjusted his grip in the man's hair and began to cut slowly into the flesh. Blood sprayed out, drenching them both, and the condemned man raised his hands to scrabble weakly at the blade as it ate at him, back and forth with terrible precision. He made a soft sound, an ugly cry that lasted only a moment. His legs collapsed, but the butcher was strong and held him up until his cleaver scraped against bone. He pulled it back then and with two quick chops he was through and the head tore clear, the body falling loose. Muscles still fluttered in the cheeks and the eyes remained open in a parody of life.

In the crowd, hands covered mouths in shuddering pleasure as the body slipped bonelessly from the platform onto the rushes below. They stood on tiptoes and jostled for a view as the butcher held the head to show them, blood running down his arm and staining his toga almost black. The jaw flopped open with the movement, revealing the teeth and tongue.

One of the other prisoners vomited over himself then cried out. As if at a signal, the other two joined him, wailing and pleading. The crowd were roused by the noise, jeering them and laughing wildly with the break in tension. The butcher shoved the head into a cloth bag and turned slowly to reach down to the man nearest him. He closed his heavy fist on an ear and dragged the screaming figure to his feet.

Julius looked away until it was finished. As he did so, he saw Crassus turn his head, but ignored the gaze. The crowd cheered each head as it was held up to them and Julius watched them curiously. He wondered if the events Crassus paid for gripped them half as much as this day's entertainment.

They were his people, this crowd stretching darkly over the wet ground of the Campus Martius. The nominal masters of the city, sated with vicarious terror and cleansed by it. As it ended, he saw the faces ease as if some great weight had been lifted. Husbands and wives joked together, relaxing, and he knew there would be little work in the city that day. They would pass through the great gates and head for wineshops and inns to discuss what they had seen. The problems of their own lives would become less important for a few hours. The city would slip into the evening with none of the usual rush and hurry of the streets. They would sleep well and wake refreshed.

The lines of Pompey's men opened to let the Senate through. Julius rose with the others and made his way back to the gates, watching as the seals were cracked and a bar of light appeared between them. He had two cases to prepare for the forum court and his sword tournament was only days away, but like the crowd of citizens, he felt strangely at peace when he thought of the work to come. There could be no striving on such a day and the damp air tasted clean and fresh in his lungs.

That evening, Julius stood and rapped his knuckles on the long table in the campaign house. The noise fell as quickly as good red wine would allow and he waited, looking around at those who had come with him in the race for consul. Every person at the table had risked a great deal in their public support of him. If he lost, they would all be made to suffer in some way. Alexandria could find her clients disappearing with a single word from Pompey, her business ruined. If Julius were allowed to take the Tenth to some distant post, those who went with him would be giving up their careers, forgotten men who would be lucky to see the city again before retirement.

As they fell silent, Julius looked down at Octavian, the only one at the table bound to him by blood. Seeing the hero-worship in the young man was painful when Julius thought of all the grey years that would follow his failure and banishment. Would Octavian look back on the campaign with bitterness then?

'We have come so very far,' he said to them. 'Some of you have been with me almost from the beginning. I can't even remember a time when Renius wasn't there, or Cabera. My father would be proud to see his boy with such friends.'

'Will he mention me, do you think?' Brutus said to Alexandria.

Julius smiled gently. He had been going to raise a simple toast to those who had entered the sword tournament, but the executions that morning had stayed with him through the day, casting a grey spell over his mood.

'I wish there were others at this table,' Julius said. 'Marius for one. When I look back, the good memories are lost in the rest, but I have known great men.' He felt his heart thumping in his chest as the words came.

'I have never known a straight path in my life. I stood at Marius' side as we rode through Rome throwing coins to the crowds. The air was full of petals and cheering and I heard the slave whose task it was whisper in his ear, "Remember you are mortal."' Julius sighed as he saw again the colours and excitement of that day.

'I have been so close to death that even Cabera gave me up. I've lost friends and lost hope and I've seen kings fall and Cato cut his own throat in the forum. I have been so drenched in death I thought I would never laugh or care for anyone again.'

They stared at him over the dishes that littered the long table, but his gaze was far away and he did not see the effect of his words.

'I saw Tubruk die and Cornelia's body so white she did not look real until I touched her.' His voice faded to a whisper and Brutus glanced at his mother. She had paled, pressing a hand against her mouth as Julius spoke.

'I tell you, I would not wish what I have seen on anyone,' Julius murmured. He seemed to come back to them, aware of the chill in the room.

'I am here, though, still. I honour the dead, but I will use my time. Rome has only seen the beginning of my struggle. I have known despair and it holds no fear for me now. This is my city, my summer. I have given my youth to her and I would throw the years at her again if I had the chance.'

He raised his cup to the stunned table.

'When I look at you all, I cannot imagine a force in the world that can stop us,' he said. 'Drink to friendship and love, for the rest is just tin.'

They stood slowly, raised their cups and drank the blood-red wine.

170

CHAPTER FIFTEEN

ᕫᕬᕫᕬᕫ

The sight of twenty thousand citizens of Rome standing in their seats was a memory to cherish, Julius thought, his gaze sweeping over them. Every place had been filled for each day of the sword tournament and the clay tokens that gave entrance to the Thirty-twos were still changing hands for larger and larger sums each morning. Julius had been surprised at first to see callers on the four gates of the circus ring, offering to buy the tokens from the crowd as they streamed in. There were few takers once the early rounds were over.

The consular box was cool in the shade from a cream linen awning suspended between slender columns. It commanded the best view of the ring and not one of the men Julius had invited had refused the offer. All the candidates had arrived with their families and Julius had been amused to see the conflict in Suetonius and his father as they accepted his generosity.

The heat had built all morning and by noon the sand would

be baked enough to sting bare flesh. Many of the crowd had brought water and wine with them, but still Julius thought he would have a fair return on the drinks and food his clients were selling for him. Cushions cost only a few coppers to hire for the day and the stocks vanished quickly.

Pompey had responded to the invitation with grace and as he and Crassus took their seats the crowd had stood out of respect until the blaring horns announced the first bouts.

Renius too was there and Julius had posted runners near him in case there was trouble at the barracks. He didn't have it in him to deny the old gladiator his place, but with Brutus still in the last thirty-two with Octavian and Domitius, he hoped his mercenary recruits would behave themselves. With that in mind, he had been forced to deny most of the Tenth the chance to see the combats, though he changed the guards three times a day to share the experience among as many as possible. As an exercise of his new authority, Brutus had added ten of the most promising of the new men to the muster of guards. Julius thought it was too early, but he had not imposed his will, knowing how important it was for them to see their general excel. Though the men looked uncomfortable in their legionary kit, they seemed docile enough.

The betting was as fierce as always. His people loved to gamble and Julius guessed fortunes would be won and lost before the final bouts were played out. Even Crassus had placed a handful of silver on Brutus at Julius' word. As far as Julius knew, Brutus himself had bet everything he owned on winning the final. If he won, he would be less dependent on Julius and creditors for supplies. His friend had reached the Thirty-twos without upset, but the standard was high and bad luck could spoil the best chance.

Below the consular box, the last fighters stepped from their barracks onto the roasting sand. The silver armour glowed almost white and the crowd gasped at the sight of them, already cheering for their favourites. Alexandria had excelled herself with the high sheen of the metal they wore. Julius was sure the quality of the finalists was in part due to the promise that they would be allowed to keep the armour after the bouts were over. In sheer weight, each set would buy a man a small farm if he sold it and with the fame of the contest spread far, they could bring more than that. Julius tried not to think how much they had cost him. The whole of Rome had talked about his generosity and they did look fine in the sun.

A few of the fighters showed bruises from the early rounds. It had been a civilised few days, with only four men dead and those from accidental strikes in the heat of a contest. First blood ended each bout, with no other limit except exhaustion. The longest before the finals had lasted the best part of an hour and both men had barely been able to stand when it was settled with a clumsy cut across the back of a leg. The crowd had cheered the loser as loudly as the man who went on to the finals.

The first rounds had been a riot of skill and strength, with more than a hundred pairs on the sand at the same time. In its way, seeing so many swords flashing was as exciting as the individual bouts of the last thirty-two, though the true connoisseurs preferred the single contests, where they could concentrate on styles and skill.

The range was staggering and Julius had made notes on a number of men to recruit for the new legion at the barracks. Already he had bought the services of three good swordsmen. Of necessity, he had been forced to hire those who fought in the Roman style, but it pained him to overlook some of the others. The call for fighters had spread much further than his messengers and there were men there from all over Roman lands and even further. Africans mixed with men the colour of mahogany from India and Egypt. One man, Sung, had the slanted eyes of races so far to the east they were almost mythical. Julius had been forced to assign guards to stop the crowds trying to touch him in the streets. The gods alone knew what he was doing so far from his home, but the long sword Sung carried was wielded with a skill that had brought him into the last rounds with the shortest bouts of all the men there. Julius watched him as he saluted the consuls with the others and determined to make the man an offer if he reached the Eights, Roman style or not.

At this late stage, the names of the men on the sand were announced to the crowd, each stepping forward to be cheered by the people of Rome. Brutus and Octavian stood together with Domitius, their armour glowing in the sun. Julius smiled at the pleasure he saw in their expressions. No matter who won the victor's sword, they would never forget the experience.

The three Romans raised their blades to the crowd and then to the consuls. The crowd roared, a wall of sound that was astonishing, almost painful. The day had begun. The announcer stepped up to the brass tubes that magnified his voice and bellowed the names of the first bout.

Domitius was to face a northerner who had travelled home with his legion commander's permission to attend the tournament. He was a big man with powerful forearms and a narrow, supple waist. As the others left the sand, he eyed Domitius warily, watching as Domitius began his stretching exercises. Even from a distance, Julius could see no sign of tension on Domitius' face. He felt his heart beat faster with growing excitement and the others in the box sensed it too. Pompey stood and clapped a hand on his shoulder.

'Should I bet on your man, Julius? Will he make the Sixteens?'

Julius turned and saw the glint in the consul's eyes. A line of shining perspiration had appeared on Pompey's forehead and his eyes were bright with anticipation. Julius nodded.

'Domitius is the second best swordsman I have ever seen. Summon the betting slaves and we will throw a fortune on

174

him,' he said. They grinned like boys together and it was difficult to remember this man was not a friend.

The slave came in at their call, ready for them. Pompey raised his eyes in exasperation as Crassus counted out three silver coins to hand to the boy.

'Just once, Crassus. Just once, I would like to see you bet enough for it to hurt you. There is no joy in small coins. It must sting a little.'

Crassus frowned, glancing at Julius. A dark flush spread into his cheeks as he put his coins away.

'Very well. Boy, give me your betting slate.'

The slave produced a wooden square covered in a thin skin of wax and Crassus pressed his ring into it, writing his name and figures without showing them to the others. As he passed it back, Pompey reached out and twitched it away, whistling softly to himself. The slave waited patiently.

'A fortune indeed, Crassus. You amaze me. One gold piece is more than I have ever seen you bet on anything.'

Crassus snorted and looked away at the two fighters, watching them walk to their positions and wait for the horn to be blown.

'I'll put a hundred on your man, Julius. Will you match me?' Pompey asked.

'A thousand for me. I know my man,' Julius replied.

Pompey's face hardened at the challenge. 'Then I shall match you, Julius.'

The two men wrote the sums and their names on the wax square.

Renius cleared his throat. 'Five gold on Domitius for me,' he said gruffly.

Of all of them, he was the only one to actually produce the coins, holding them out stiffly until the slave took them from his hands. The old gladiator watched until the gleam disappeared into a cloth bag, then sat back, sweating. Suetonius had been about to hand over his own bet, but returned to his father for funds after seeing that. Ten gold pieces were produced from them and the slate was passed around one more time, with even Bibilus risking a few silvers from his purse.

The slave scurried back to his master and Julius stood to signal the cornicens. The crowd became quiet as they saw him stand and he wondered how many of them would remember his name at the elections. He savoured the stillness for an instant, then brought his hand chopping down. The sharp wail of the horns rang out over the sand.

Domitius had watched as many of the early bouts as he could when he was not fighting himself. He had made notes on those he thought would win through to the later rounds, and of the last thirty-two only half of them were truly dangerous. The northerner he faced was skilled enough to have reached this stage, but he panicked when he was crowded and Domitius intended to crowd him from the very first moment.

He felt the man's eyes on him as Domitius stretched his back and legs and kept his face as peaceful and unhurried as he possibly could. He had fought in enough tournaments to know that many bouts were won not with the sword but in the moments before it. His old trainer had had a habit of sitting with his legs split and flat on the ground in utter stillness before his opponents. While they lunged and jumped to loosen their muscles, that man had been like a rock and nothing unnerved them as much as that. When finally he had risen like smoke to face them, the battle was already half won. Domitius had understood the lesson and he allowed none of his tiredness to show in his movements. In truth, his right knee felt stiff and painful where it had been jolted in an earlier bout, but he did not wince, moving slowly and fluidly through his exercises, mesmerising in their smoothness. He felt a great calm descend on him and offered up a silent prayer for his old teacher.

Holding his sword low and away from his body, Domitius came to his mark and stood motionless. His opponent rolled his shoulders in a nervous action, flicking his head from side to side. When their eyes met, the northerner glared at him, unwilling to be the first to look away. Domitius stood like a statue, the sharply defined muscles of his shoulders shining with sweat. The silver armour protected the chests of the fighters, but Domitius could shave a lock of hair from a man running past him and he felt strong.

The horns snapped him out of his stillness and he lunged before the sound had fully registered with the other man. The northerner's footwork had brought him to the finals and before the blade could cut, he had shifted out of range. Domitius could hear his breathing and focused on it as the man counter-attacked. The northerner used his breath to increase the force of the blow, grunting with each strike. Domitius let him relax into a rhythm, backing up a dozen steps against the rush, watching for further weaknesses.

On the last step, Domitius felt a spike of pain as his weight came on his right leg, as if a needle had been jammed into his kneecap. It buckled, destroying his balance and he was hard-pressed as the northerner sensed the weakness. Domitius tried to put it out of his mind, but dared not trust the leg. He pressed forward in shuffling steps until their sweat mingled as it spattered. The northerner backed away and then further as he tried to gain space, but Domitius stayed with him, breaking the rhythm of blows with a short punch as their blades locked.

The northerner swayed away from the blow and they broke apart, beginning to circle each other. Domitius listened to his breath and waited for the tiny sip of air that came before each attack. He dared not look at his knee, but every step brought a fresh protest.

The northerner tried to wear him down with a flurry of strikes but Domitius blocked them, reading his man's breath and waiting for the right moment. The sun was high above them and the sweat poured into their eyes, stinging. The northerner drew in a gasp and Domitius lunged. Even before the touch, he knew the stroke was perfect, slicing open a flap of skin on the man's skull. A sliver of ear fell to the ground as blood poured out and the northerner roared, cutting wildly back as Domitius tried to pull away.

Domitius' knee buckled, shooting agony up into his groin. The northerner hesitated, his eyes clearing as he felt the growing pain of his wound. Blood poured from him. Domitius watched him closely, trying to ignore the pain in his knee.

The northerner touched the hot wetness on his neck, staring at his bloody fingers. Grim resignation came into his face then and he nodded to Domitius, both men walking back to their marks.

'You should bind that knee of yours, my friend. The others will have noted it,' the northerner said softly, gesturing to where the rest of the finalists watched from the shadowed awnings of their enclosure. Domitius shrugged. He tested the joint and winced, stifling a cry.

Understanding, the northerner shook his head as they saluted the crowd and the consuls. Domitius tried not to show the sudden fear that had come to him. The joint felt strange and he prayed it was only a sprain or a partial dislocation that could be shoved back into place. The alternative was unbearable for a man who had nothing else in his life but his sword and the Tenth. As the two men walked back across the baking sand, Domitius struggled not to limp, gritting his teeth against the pain. Another pair in silver armour came out into the sun for the next bout and Domitius could feel their confidence as they looked at him and smiled.

*   *   *

178

Julius watched his friend disappear into the shade and winced in sympathy.

'Excuse me, gentlemen. I would like to go down and see their wounds are well treated,' he said.

Pompey clapped him on the back in response, too hoarse from shouting to reply. Crassus called for cooling drinks for all of them and the mood was infectiously light as they settled back in their seats for the next contest. Food would be brought to them in their seats as they watched and each man there felt the thrill of blood and talent. Suetonius was demonstrating a feint to his father and the older man smiled with him, joining in the excitement.

Renius stood as Julius reached his seat at the edge of the box. He fell in behind without a word and they walked from the heat into the cool of the path under the seating without exchanging a word.

It was a different world below the crowds, the roaring muted and somehow distant. The sunlight came through chinks in the great timbers and lay on the ground in mottled bars, shifting as people moved above. The ground there was the soft earth of the Campus Martius, without the layer of sand that had been brought from the coast.

'Will he fight again?' Julius asked.

Renius shrugged. 'Cabera will help him. The old man has power.'

Julius did not reply, remembering how Cabera had touched his hands to Tubruk as he lay, his body pierced over and over in the attack on the estate that had killed Cornelia. Cabera refused to talk about his healing, but Julius remembered that he had once told him it was a matter of paths. If the path was ended, there was nothing he could do, but with some, like Renius, he had stolen back a little time.

Julius cast a sideways glance at the old gladiator. As the years passed, the brief energy of youth was giving way to age. The

179

face was again showing the craggy, bitter features of an old man and Julius still didn't know why he had been saved from death. Cabera believed the gods watched them all with jealous love and Julius envied him his conviction. When he prayed, it was like shouting into a void with no response, until he despaired.

Above, the crowd stood to cheer a blow, changing the pattern of light on the dusty ground. Julius passed between the last two pillars of wood into the open area beyond and gasped at the heated air that seemed too thick to breathe.

He looked out onto the sand, squinting against the glare to see two figures rushing at each other as if it were a dance. Their swords caught the light in bright flashes and the crowd stayed on their feet stamping in time. Julius blinked as a trickle of dust touched his skin from above. He glanced up at the heavy bolts that held the seating, feeling the tremble in the wood as he pressed his hand against it. He hoped it would hold.

Cabera was wrapping a thin cloth around Domitius' knee and Brutus was kneeling by them with Octavian, oblivious to the fight on the sand. They looked up as Julius joined them and Domitius waved a hand, smiling feebly.

'I can feel the rest of them watching me. Vultures, every one of them,' he said, gasping as Cabera pulled the cloth tighter.

'How bad is it?' Julius asked.

Domitius didn't answer, but there was a fear in his eyes that shook them all.

'I don't know,' Cabera snapped at the silent pressure. 'The kneecap is cracked and I don't know how it held him this long. He should not have been able to walk and the joint may be . . . who knows. I will do my best.'

'He needs it, Cabera,' Julius said softly.

The old healer snorted under his breath. 'What does it matter if he fights once more out there. It is not . . .'

'No, not for that. He's one of us. He has a path to follow,' Julius said more urgently. If he had to, he would beg the old man.

Cabera stiffened and sat back on his heels. 'You don't know what you are asking, my friend. Whatever I have is not to be used on every scrape or broken bone.' He looked up at Julius and seemed to slump with weariness. 'Would you have me lose it for a whim? The trance is . . . agony, I cannot tell you. And each time, I do not know if the pain is wasted or whether there are gods who move my hands.'

They were all silent as Julius held his gaze, willing him to try. Another of the Thirty-twos cleared his throat as he approached them and Julius turned to the man, recognising him as one of those he had noted for skill. His face was the colour of old teak and, of all of them, he did not wear the armour he had been given, preferring the freedom of a simple robe. The man bowed.

'My name is Salomin,' he said, pausing as if the name might be recognised. When it was not, he shrugged. 'You fought well,' he said. 'Are you able to continue?'

Domitius forced a smile. 'I will rest it for a while, then I'll see.'

'You must use cold cloths against the swelling, my friend. As cold as you can find in this heat. I hope you will be ready if we should be called together. I would not like to fight an injured man.'

'I would,' Domitius replied.

Salomin blinked in confusion as Brutus chuckled, wondering what joke was being made. He bowed to them and walked away and Domitius looked down at his knee stretched out in front of him.

'I'm finished if I can't march,' he said, his voice almost a whisper.

Cabera used his fingers to massage fluids away from the joint, his expression hard. The silence stretched interminably and a bead of sweat ran down from the old man's hairline to the tip of his nose, where it shivered, ignored.

None of them heard Brutus called the first time. The man who was to fight him strode past them out into the sun without a backward glance, but Salomin came close and nudged the Roman out of his concentration.

'It is your turn,' Salomin said, his large eyes dark even against his skin.

'I'll finish this one quickly,' Brutus replied, unsheathing his sword and stalking out after his opponent.

Salomin shook his head in amazement, shielding his eyes as he edged to the shadowline to watch the bout.

Julius sensed Cabera would not be moved while he stood there staring at him and took the opportunity to leave Domitius alone with him.

'Give them room, Octavian,' he said, motioning to Renius to follow.

Octavian took the hint, moving away, his face creased with worry. He too shaded his face to squint out to where Brutus was waiting impatiently for the horns to sound.

Under the seats, Julius heard the sharp wail of the cornicens and broke into a run. Before he and Renius had moved more than a few paces, the crowd's cheering was suddenly cut off into an eerie silence. Julius broke into a sprint, arriving panting back at the consular box.

They too were frozen in surprise as Julius entered. Brutus was already walking stiffly back to the fighters' area, leaving a figure sprawled on the sand behind him.

'What happened?' Julius demanded.

Pompey shook his head in amazement. 'So fast, Julius. I've never seen anything like it.'

Of all of them, only Crassus seemed unmoved. 'Your man stood still and ducked away from two blows without moving his feet, then he knocked his opponent out with a punch and cut his leg while he lay on the ground. Is it a win, then? It doesn't seem a fair blow.'

Mindful of another large bet on Brutus, Pompey was quick to speak.

'Brutus drew first blood, even if his man was unconscious. It will count.'

The crowd's silence had broken as the same question was asked all over the benches. Many of the faces looked to the consular box for guidance and Julius sent a runner to the cornicens to confirm Brutus' win.

There were grumblings then from those who had bet against the young Roman, but the majority of the crowd seemed content with the decision. Julius saw them act out the blow to each other, laughing all the while. Two soldiers from the Tenth woke the fallen fighter with a slap on his cheeks and helped him from the sand. As his wits returned, he began to struggle in their grip, shouting angrily at the result. They were unmoved by his protests as they vanished from sight into the shadowed awnings.

The afternoon wore on with the remaining battles of the thirty-two. Octavian made it through his bout with a cut to his opponent's thigh as he stepped along the outside of a blow. The crowd suffered under the sun, unwilling to miss a moment.

The sixteen victors were brought out once more in their armour for the crowd to show their appreciation. The torch-light session would begin at sunset to whittle them down for the final day, giving the victors a chance to heal and recover overnight. Coins littered the sand around their feet as they raised their swords, and flowers that had been hoarded since morning were thrown down in splashes of colour. Julius watched closely as Domitius was called and his heart lifted as he saw him walk as smoothly and surely as he had ever done. There was no need for words, but he saw Renius' knuckles whiten on the railing as they looked over the sand and cheered as wildly as the crowd.

183

CHAPTER SIXTEEN

ᘓᕤᘓᕤᘓᕤ

Servilia joined them in the box for the final day. She wore a loose-fitting sheath of white silk, open at the neck. Julius was amused at the way the other men seemed hypnotised by the deep cleavage that was revealed as she stood to cheer the men of the Tenth who had made it to the last sixteen.

Octavian took a cut to his cheek in the last match of the Sixteens. He lost to Salomin, who went triumphantly on to the Eights with Domitius, Brutus and five others Julius did not know except for his notes. When there were strangers in the ring, Julius dictated letters to Adàn in quick succession, only falling silent when a fight reached a climax and the young Spaniard could not tear his eyes away from the men on the sand. Adàn was fascinated by the spectacle and awed by the sheer numbers of people present. The increasing sums wagered by Pompey and Julius made him shake his head in silent amazement, though he did his best to seem as casual as the other occupants of the box.

The first session of the day had been long and hot, with the pace of the battles slowing. Each man still in the lists was a master and there were no quick victories. The mood of the crowd had changed too, keeping up a constant discussion of technique and style as they watched and cheered the better strokes.

Salomin was hard-pressed as he fought to reach the last four for the evening climax. Despite the pressure of work, Julius broke off his dictation to watch the man after Adàn had twice lost the thread of the dictation. Choosing to fight without the silver armour marked Salomin apart and he was already a favourite of the crowd. His style showed the wisdom of the choice. The little man fought like an acrobat, never still. He tumbled and rolled in a fluid series of strikes that made his opponents look clumsy.

Yet the man Salomin fought for the Fours was no novice to be startled into overreaching himself. Renius nodded approval at footwork that was good enough to keep the spinning Salomin from finding a gap in his defence.

'Salomin will exhaust himself, surely,' Crassus said.

None of the others answered, entranced by the spectacle. Salomin's sword was inches longer than the gladius the others used and had a frightening reach at the end of a lunge.

It was the extra length that tipped the contest, after the sun had moved a half-span across the sky in the afternoon heat. Both men poured with sweat and Salomin was a little off in a straight blow that he had disguised with his body. The other man never saw it as it entered his throat and he collapsed, pumping blood onto the sand.

As close as they were, Julius could see Salomin had not intended a mortal stroke. The little man stood appalled, his hands trembling as he stood over his fallen opponent. He knelt by the body and bowed his head.

The crowd came onto their feet to shout for him and after

185

a long time their noise seemed to reach through his reverie. Salomin looked angrily at the baying citizens. Without raising his sword in the customary salute, the small man ran a finger and thumb down his blade to clean it and stalked back to the shaded enclosure.

'*Not* one of us,' Pompey pronounced with amusement. He had won another of the large bets and nothing could shake his good humour, though a few of the crowd began to jeer as they realised there would be no salute to the consuls. The body was dragged away and another battle was called quickly before the crowd could become restless.

'He's earned his place in the Fours, though,' Julius said.

Domitius had struggled through the Eights, but he too would be one of the last two pairs to fight in the contest. There was only one place still to be decided and Brutus would fight for it. By then, the crowd had watched them all for days and the whole of Rome followed their progress, runners taking news out to those who could not get seats. With the election less than a month away, Julius was already being treated as if he had gained a seat as consul. Pompey had mellowed noticeably towards him and Julius had refused meetings with both men to discuss the future. He did not want to tempt fate until his people had voted, though in quiet moments he daydreamed of addressing the Senate as one of the leaders of Rome.

Bibilus had attended the last day and Julius glanced at the young man, wondering at his motivation for staying in the race for consul. Many of the initial candidates had dropped out as the election neared, having gained a temporary status over their colleagues. Bibilus, it seemed, was there to stay. Despite his apparent tenacity, Bibilus spoke poorly and an attempt to defend a man charged with theft had ended in farce. Still, his clients roamed the city with his name on their lips and the young of Rome seemed to have adopted him as a mascot. The old money in Rome might well prefer one of their own against Julius and he could not be ruled out.

Julius fretted at the costs of the campaign as he waited for Brutus to be called for his bout. More than a thousand men collected their pay from the house at the bottom of the Esquiline hill each morning. What good they could actually achieve in a secret ballot, Julius wasn't sure, but he had accepted Servilia's argument that he must be seen to have supporters. It was a dangerous game, as too much support might mean many of Rome staying at home for the vote, content in the knowledge that their candidate could not lose. It was a fault of the system that had the free men of Rome voting in centuries. If only a few of the named group were present, they could carry the vote for all of them. Bibilus could benefit from such misplaced confidence, or Senator Prandus, who seemed to have as many men in his employ as Julius.

Still, his part in defeating Catiline was becoming well known and even his enemies must concede that the sword tourney was a success. In addition, Julius had won enough on his men to clear a few of the campaign debts. Adàn kept the accounts and each day the Spanish gold dwindled, forcing him to run lines of credit. At times, the figures owed worried him, but if he were made consul, none of it would matter.

'My son!' Servilia said suddenly, as Brutus came out onto the sand with Aulus, a slim fighter from the slopes of Vesuvius in the south.

Both men looked splendid in the silver armour and Julius smiled down at Brutus as he saluted the consuls' box, winking at his mother before turning and jerking his sword up for the crowd. They bellowed their approval and the two men walked lightly to their marks in the centre. Renius snorted softly under his breath, but Julius could see the tension in him as he leaned forward, drinking it in.

Julius hoped Brutus could bear a loss as easily as he bore

his wins. Just reaching the last eight was an achievement with which to regale the grandchildren, but Brutus had said from the beginning that he would be in the final. Even he had stopped short of swearing he would win it, but his confidence was clear enough.

'Put everything on him, Pompey. I will take your bets myself,' Julius said, caught up in the excitement.

Pompey hesitated only a moment. 'The betting men share your confidence, Julius. If you will give me decent odds, I may take you up on the offer.'

'One coin for your fifty on Brutus. Five coins to your one on Aulus,' Julius said quickly. Pompey smiled.

'You are so convinced Marcus Brutus will win? You tempt me to this Aulus with such a return. Five thousand gold against your man, at that rate. Will you take it?'

Julius looked out onto the sand, his good mood suddenly wavering. It was the last match of the Eights and Salomin and Domitius had already gone through. Surely there could be no other fighter with skill enough to beat his oldest friend?

'I'll take it, Pompey. My word on it,' he said, feeling fresh sweat break out on his skin. Adàn was clearly appalled and Julius did not look at him. He held a calm expression as he tried to remember how much his reserves had shrunk after the new armour for the mercenaries and the wages for his clients each week. If Brutus lost, twenty-five thousand in gold was enough to break him, but there was always the thought that as consul, his credit would be good. The moneylenders would queue for him, then.

'This Aulus. Is he skilful?' Servilia asked to break the silence that had sprung up in the box.

Bibilus had changed his seat to be close to her and he answered with what he thought was a winning smile.

'They all are at this stage, madam. Both have won seven battles to reach this point, though I am sure your son will prevail. He is the crowd's favourite and they say that can lift a man wonderfully.'

'Thank you,' Servilia replied, favouring him with a smile.

Bibilus blushed and wound his fingers into knots. Julius watched him with something less than affection, wondering whether the manner concealed a sharper mind, or if Bibilus was really the hopeless fool he seemed to be.

The horns sounded and the first clash of blades had them all against the rail, jostling for space without thought for rank. Servilia breathed quickly and her nervousness showed enough for Julius to touch her arm. She didn't seem to feel it.

On the sand, the swords flickered, the two men moving around each other at a speed that mocked the heat. They circled quickly, breaking step to reverse with a skill that was beautiful to watch. Aulus had a similar build to Brutus' taut frame and the two men seemed well matched. Adàn counted the number of blows under his breath, almost unconsciously, clenching his fists with the excitement. His notes and letters were forgotten on the chair behind him.

Brutus struck armour three times in quick succession. Aulus allowed the blows through his defence to give him the chance to counter and only Brutus' footwork saved him each time after the ring of metal. Both men poured with sweat, their hair black and sopping with it. They broke apart in a strained pause and Julius could hear Brutus' voice over the sand. No one in the box could make out the words, but Julius knew they would be barbs to spoil Aulus with anger.

Aulus laughed at the attempt and they joined again, standing frighteningly close as their swords spun and flashed, the hilts and blades knocking and sliding in a flurry that was too fast for Adàn to count. The young Spaniard's mouth opened in amazement at the level of skill and the whole crowd fell silent. In the awful tension, many of them held their breath, waiting for the first splash of blood to spring from the battling pair.

'There!' Servilia cried at a stripe that had appeared on Aulus' right thigh. 'Do you see it? Look, there!' She pointed wildly, even as the swordplay reached a manic intensity on the sand. Whether Brutus knew or not, it was clear that Aulus had no idea he had been wounded and Brutus could not disengage at such close range without risking a fatal cut. They remained locked in the rhythms while sweat spattered off them.

At Julius' signal, the cornicens blew a warning note across the arena. It was dangerous to jar their concentration in such a fashion, but both men stepped back at once, panting in great heaves. Aulus touched a hand to his thigh and held up the reddened palm to Brutus. Neither could speak and Brutus pressed his hands onto his knees to suck in great lungfuls over the pounding of his heart that seemed to throb at every part of him. He spat out a sinewy mouthful of saliva and had to spit again to clear the long strand that reached down to the ground. As their pulses ceased hammering, the two men could hear the crowd cheering and they embraced briefly before raising their blades once again in salute.

Servilia hugged herself, laughing aloud with the thrill of it.

'He has made the last four, then? My darling son. He was astonishing, was he not?'

'He has a chance to win it now and bring honour to Rome,' Pompey replied with a sour glance at Julius. 'Two Romans in the last two pairs. The gods alone know where the other two come from. That Salomin is as dark as a pit and the other with the slanted eyes, who knows? Let us hope it is enough to have a Roman take that sword of yours, Julius. It would be a shame to see a pagan win it after all this.'

Julius shrugged. 'In the hands of the gods.'

He waited for the consul to bring up the bet that stood between them and Pompey sensed his thoughts, frowning.

'I will have a man bring it to you, Julius. No need to stand there like a pregnant hen.'

190

Julius nodded instantly. Despite the friendly appearances, every scrap of conversation in the box was like a bloodless duel as they manoeuvred for advantage. He looked forward to the final session that evening, if only to see the end of it.

'Of course, Consul. I will be at the house on Esquiline until the last bouts tonight.'

Pompey frowned. He had not expected to have to produce such a large sum so quickly, but now the occupants of the box were watching him closely and Crassus had a nasty little smile ghosting around his lips. Pompey seethed inwardly. He would have to collect his winnings to pay it, all his earlier success wiped out. Only Crassus would have that sort of gold to hand. No doubt the vulture was thinking smugly of the solitary coin he had won on Brutus.

'Excellent,' Pompey said, unwilling to give a definite commitment. Even with his winnings, it would leave him short, but he would see Rome burn before turning to Crassus for another loan.

'Until then, gentlemen, Servilia,' Pompey said, smiling tightly. He signalled his guards and left the box stiff-backed.

Julius watched him go before grinning with pleasure. Five thousand! In a single bet, his campaign was solvent once again.

'I love this city,' he said aloud.

Suetonius stood with his father to leave and though courtesy forced the young man to mumble a platitude as he passed, there was no pleasure in his thin face. Bibilus rose with them, looking nervously at his friend as he too murmured his thanks and fell in behind.

Servilia stayed, her eyes reflecting something of the same excitement she saw in Julius. The crowd were streaming away to find food and the soldiers of the Tenth were in full view as she kissed him hungrily.

'If you had your men adjust the awning and stand back, we would have privacy to be as naughty as children, Julius.'

'You are too old to be naughty, my beautiful lover,' Julius replied, opening his arms to embrace her. She stiffened then, a flush of anger making her cheeks glow.

Her eyes flashed as she spoke and Julius was appalled at the sudden change in her.

'Another time then,' she snapped, sweeping past him.

'Servilia!' he called after her, but she did not turn back and he was left alone in the empty box, furious with himself for the slip.

CHAPTER SEVENTEEN

꧁꧂

In the coolness of the evening, Julius paced the box waiting for Servilia to arrive. Pompey's man had sent a trunk of coins to him only minutes before he left for the final bouts and Julius had been forced to delay while he summoned enough of the Tenth to guard such a fortune. Even with men he trusted, he worried at the thought of so much wealth sitting openly.

All the others had arrived long before him and Pompey smiled mirthlessly at his worried expression as Julius came running up the steps to take his seat. Where was Servilia? She had not joined him at the campaign house, but surely she would not miss her son's final contests? Julius could not remain seated for more than a moment, and paced up and down the edge of the box, fretting.

The sand ring was lit with flickering torches and the evening had brought a gentle breeze to ease the heat of the day. The seats were packed with citizens and every member of the Senate was in attendance. There would be no work in the city until the tournament was over and the tension seemed to have spilled over the meanest streets. The people gathered in a formless crowd on the Campus Martius, as they would again in the election to come.

Servilia's arrival coincided with the first blast from the cornicens, summoning the final four to the sand. Julius looked questioningly at her as they settled, but she did not meet his eyes and looked colder than he had ever seen her.

'I'm sorry,' he whispered, bending his head towards her. She gave no sign she had heard and he sat back, irritated. He vowed he would not try again.

The crowd stood to cheer their favourites and the betting slaves hovered. Pompey ignored them, Julius saw, taking a vicious pleasure in the change in attitude he had brought about. He glanced at Servilia to see if she had noticed and his resolve vanished at the cold mask she turned to him. He leaned close again.

'Do I mean so little to you?' he whispered too loudly, so that Bibilus and Adàn jerked in their seats and then tried to pretend they hadn't heard. She did not reply and Julius set his jaw in anger, staring out over the dark sand.

The final competitors walked slowly out under the light of the torches. The crowd stood for them and the sound was crushing as they roared together, twenty thousand throats joined as one. Brutus walked at Domitius' side, trying to speak over the noise. Salomin followed and behind him the final fighter trotted out, hardly acknowledged by the crowd. Somehow, Sung's style and victories had not caught their imagination. He showed no emotion and his salutes were perfunctory. He was taller and more massive than Salomin and his flat face and shaved head gave him a forbidding aspect as he strode behind the others, almost as if he were stalking them. Sung carried the longest blade in the last four. Doubtless it gave him an advantage, though any of the competitors could have used a blade of similar dimensions if they chose. Julius knew Brutus had considered it, having some experience with the spatha sword, but in the end the familiarity of the gladius had won him.

Julius watched the four men closely, looking for stiffness or a favoured limb. Salomin particularly seemed to be suffering and he walked with his head down close to his chest. They all carried bruises and the exhaustion of the days before. To some extent, the final winner might be decided not by skill, but stamina. He wondered how the pairs would be split and hoped Brutus would fight Domitius, to force a Roman into the final. The political part of him was well aware that the crowd would lose interest if the last bout saw Salomin and Sung alone on the sand. It would be a terrific anticlimax to the week and his heart sank as he heard the pairs called: Brutus would fight Salomin; Domitius, Sung. The bets began to fly again in a cacophony of calls and nervous laughter. The tension hung over them and Julius felt sweat break out again in his armpits, despite the breeze that crossed the sand.

The four men watched closely as a steward tossed a coin into the air. Sung nodded at the result and Domitius made some aside to him that could not be heard over the noise of the crowd. There was a professional respect between the four men that was clear in every movement. They had seen each other win over and over and laboured under no illusions as to the harshness of the struggle to come.

Calling encouragement over his shoulder to Domitius, Brutus walked with Salomin back to the enclosure. He noted the new stiffness in Salomin's movements and wondered if he had torn a muscle. Such a little thing could mean the difference between reaching the final and walking away with nothing. Brutus studied him closely, wondering if the little man was acting for his benefit. It wouldn't have surprised him. At that stage, they were all willing to try anything for the slightest advantage.

The crowd fell silent so quickly that it was spoiled by nervous laughter. The cornicens were ready in their places, glancing upwards to see if Julius was still in his seat.

Julius waited patiently as Domitius began his stretching exercises. Sung ignored the Roman he was to fight, instead staring at the crowd until some of them noticed it and began to point and glare in return. It was all part of the excitement of the last night and Julius could see hundreds of young children by their parents, thrilled to be kept from their beds by the last night.

Domitius ended his slow movements with a lunge onto his right knee and Julius saw a smile crease the dark face as it held without pain. He thanked the gods for Cabera, though he felt guilt for having asked him. The old healer had fallen to the ground after the healing and was as grey and ill-looking as Julius had ever known him. When it was over, Julius swore to himself, he would give the old man whatever reward he wanted. The thought of being without him was something on which he did not dare dwell for long, but who knew how old Cabera was?

Julius brought down his hand and the horns blew. It was clear from the first moment that Sung intended to make use of the advantage his long sword gave him. His wrists must have been like iron to hold it so far from his body and take the weight of Domitius' blade, Julius realised. Yet his powerful legs seemed anchored in the sand and the long silver length of metal kept Domitius away as they feinted and struck. Each man knew the style of the other almost as well as his own after so much study and the result was stalemate. Domitius did not dare to step inside the long reach of Sung's blade, yet when he was pressed there was no gap in his defence.

Renius thumped his fist onto the railing at a good stroke, cheering in hacking barks as Domitius forced Sung onto his back foot for a moment, spoiling his balance. The long blade whipped round and Domitius ducked under it, darting in at last. His lunge was perfect, but Sung moved smoothly to one side, letting it slide past his armoured chest, then bringing his hilt down into Domitius' cheek.

It was a glancing blow, but much of the crowd winced to see it. Julius shook his head in wonderment at the level of skill, though to the untrained eye, it could have seemed a messy fight. There were none of the perfect attacks and counters they had seen when better men fought novices in the early rounds. Here, each sudden parry and riposte was spoiled almost as soon as it had begun and the result was a flurry of ugly blows with not a drop of blood spilt between them.

Domitius pulled away first. His cheekbone was swollen from where the hilt had caught him and he raised his palm to it. Sung waited patiently with his blade ready while Domitius showed him the unmarked hand. The skin had not split and they leapt in again with greater ferocity.

Only the pounding of his pulse made Julius realise he was holding his breath. They could not hold such a pace for long, he was certain, and at any moment he expected one of them to cut.

They broke apart again and circled almost at a run, setting up and breaking rhythms as fast as the other man saw them. Twice Domitius almost lured Sung into a false step as he changed direction and the second time led to a blow that should have cut Sung's arm from his body if he had not flung it back and taken the impact on his armour.

The exhaustion of the previous days was beginning to show in both men, perhaps more so in Domitius, who was panting visibly. Julius knew the battle he watched was fought as much in their minds as with their blades and could not guess whether it was another ruse, or whether Domitius was really suffering. His strength seemed to come in spurts and the speed of his arm varied as it grew heavy.

Sung too was unsure and twice let opportunities go by where he might have taken advantage of a late parry. He tilted his head to one side as if in judgement and again he held the Roman away with a dazzling series of sweeps with the point.

A blisteringly fast reverse almost won the match, as Domitius slapped his hand into the flat of his blade and changed direction so quickly that Sung threw himself flat on his back. Renius cried out in excitement. There were few with the knowledge to see the collapse was deliberate and controlled. There was no faster way of avoiding a stroke, but the crowd cheered as if their favourite had won and howled as they saw Sung skitter like a crab away from Domitius' stabs until, miraculously, he was on his feet again.

Perhaps it was the frustration of coming so close, but Domitius checked his rush a fraction too late and Sung's point whipped up, biting into flesh at the bottom edge of Domitius' armour. Both men froze then and those with keen eyes in the crowd wailed in frustration, even as their neighbours craned to see who had won.

Blood dribbled down Domitius' leg and Julius could see him mouthing a torrent of curses before he gathered his control and returned to the first mark. Sung's face never changed, but when both men faced each other, he bowed for the first time in the contest. To the pleasure of the crowd, Domitius returned the gesture and grinned openly through his exhaustion as they saluted the crowd together.

Renius turned to Julius, his eyes bright.

'With your permission, sir. If I had Domitius, my training of the new men would go much better. He is a thinking fighter and they would respond to him.'

Julius could feel every ear in the box pricking up at this mention of his ragged new legion.

'If he and Brutus agree, I will send him to you. I promised my best centurions and optios for the task. He shall go with them.'

'We need smiths and tanners as much —' Renius began, halting as Julius shook his head.

Servilia stood as Brutus and Salomin walked out onto the sand. She shuddered unconsciously as she watched her son, tightening her hand into a fist. There was something terribly forbidding about the torch-lit ring.

Julius wanted to reach out to her, but controlled the impulse, aware of every aspect of her movement close by his shoulder. He could smell her scent in the night air and it tormented him. His anger and confusion almost spoiled the moment when he put his signet ring against a bet of five thousand gold on Brutus. Pompey's expression was a delight and he felt his mood lift, despite Servilia's stiffness. Adàn too stifled a look of horror and Julius winked at him. They had gone over the reserves together and the simple fact was that the Spanish gold he had brought back was very nearly gone. If he lost the five thousand, they would be forced to rely on credit until the campaign was over. Julius chose not to tell the young Spaniard about the black pearl he had bought for Servilia. He felt the weight of it in a pouch against his chest, and was so pleased with it that he wanted to hand it over regardless of her mood. The price made him shrink slightly as he considered the armour and supplies he could have bought in its stead. Sixty thousand gold coins. He had been mad. Certainly, it was far too extravagant to put in his accounts. The merchant had sworn on his mother's blood not to reveal the sum, which meant it might be at least a few days before the huge sale was known to every inn and whorehouse in Rome. Julius could feel the weight of it pull at his toga, and occasionally he would reach almost unconsciously to feel the curve of the pearl under the cloth.

Salomin too had watched every battle fought by Brutus, including the one where he had knocked a man senseless, then taken first blood with an almost contemptuous slice of the leg. If he had been at his best, he would still have preferred to be drawn against Domitius, or the lazy Chinese, Sung. He had watched the young Roman fight without the slightest pause for thought or tactics, as if his body and muscles were trained to act without conscious direction. As he faced him over the sand, Salomin swallowed dryly, willing himself to focus. Despair filled him as he loosened his shoulder muscles and felt the scabs and bruises break open on his back. The sweat poured from his brow as he stood waiting for the horns to sound.

The soldiers had come for him that afternoon as he ate and rested at a modest rooming house near the outer wall of the city. He did not know why they had dragged him out into the street and held him to be whipped until their sticks broke. He had rubbed goose grease into each of the cuts and tried to remain supple, but whatever chance he may have had was gone and only his pride made him take his place. He mumbled a short prayer in the language of his own city and felt it calm him.

As the horns sounded, he reacted instinctively, trying to slide away. His back wrenched in agony and tears filled his eyes, making stars of the torches. He brought up his blade blindly and Brutus swayed away from it. Salomin cried out with pain and frustration as his rigid muscles tore. He tried another blow and missed cleanly. The sweat ran in great drops from his face as he stood, willing himself on.

Brutus stepped away, puzzled and frowning. He pointed to Salomin's arm. For a moment, Salomin did not dare look, but when he felt the sting, his eyes darted to a shallow cut in his skin and he nodded in resignation.

'Not my worst cut, today, my friend. I hope you were innocent of the others,' Salomin said softly.

Brutus looked blank as he raised his sword to the crowd, suddenly aware of the cramped way the usually lithe little man was standing. His face cleared in a flash of horrified under-standing.

'Who was it?'

Salomin shrugged. 'Who can tell one Roman from another? They were soldiers. It is done.'

Brutus paled in rage, his eyes snapping up in suspicion to where Julius was cheering him. He strode from the sand, deaf to the cheers in his name.

With a break of two hours before the final, the sand was raked clean while many of the citizens left to eat and wash, talking excitedly amongst themselves. The box emptied quickly and Julius noticed that Senator Prandus left before his son, who walked into the crowd with Bibilus, barely acknowledging his father as they passed.

Julius heard Brutus approach as the shifting crowd near the box recognised their champion and cheered with fresh enthu-siasm. Though he shook with emotion, Brutus kept enough of his sense to sheathe his blade before approaching the guards around the box. Their duty would have forced them to chal-lenge, regardless of his new status.

Julius and Servilia went quickly to him and Julius' congrat-ulations died in his throat as he saw his friend's expression. He was white with rage.

'Did you have Salomin beaten?' Brutus snapped as he came up. 'He could barely stand. Did you do it?'

'I . . .' Julius began, appalled. He was interrupted by the sudden snap to attention of Pompey's soldiers as the curtain was swept aside and the consul stepped out.

Trembling with suppressed emotion, Brutus saluted and stood stiffly to attention while Pompey looked him over.

'I gave that order. Whether you profited from it or not is of no interest to me. A foreigner who does not salute can expect no better and deserves worse. If he had not been amongst the last four, I would have had him swinging in the breeze by now.'

201

He returned their astonished gazes levelly.

'Even a foreigner can be taught respect, I believe. Now, Brutus, go and rest for the final.'

Dismissed, Brutus could do no more than shoot a glance of apology at his friend and mother.

'Perhaps it might have been better to wait until the tournament was over,' Julius said after Brutus had gone. Something about Pompey's reptilian gaze made him careful in his choice of words. The man's arrogance was greater than he had ever realised.

'Or just forget it altogether, perhaps?' Pompey replied. 'A consul *is* Rome, Caesar. He must not be mocked or treated lightly. Perhaps you will understand that in time, if the citizens give you the chance to stand where I stand today.'

Julius opened his mouth to ask if Pompey had bet on Brutus and closed it just in time before he destroyed himself. He recalled that Pompey had not: his twisted sense of honour would have prevented taking a profit from his punishment.

Suddenly tired and sick of it all, Julius nodded as if he understood, holding the curtain open so that Servilia and Pompey could pass through it. She did not look at him even then and he sighed bitterly to himself as he followed them. He knew she would expect him to come to her in private and though it galled him, there was little choice. His hand strayed to the pearl's bulge and he tapped it thoughtfully.

Still panting from his ride, Julius took a deep breath before knocking on the door. The tavern keeper had confirmed Servilia had come back to her room and Julius could hear the splash of water inside as she bathed before the last bout. Despite his agitation, Julius could not help but feel the first silken touches of arousal as he heard footsteps approach, but the voice that called was that of the slave girl who filled the baths of customers.

'Julius,' he replied to the query. Perhaps his titles might have made the girl move a little faster, but there were ears along the little corridor and there was something faintly ludicrous in addressing a closed door like a lovesick boy. He cracked his knuckles as he waited. At least the tavern was close enough to the city walls for him to make it back in time. His horse was munching hay in the small stable and he only needed a minute to give Servilia the pearl, bear her delighted embraces and gallop back to the Campus with her for the last bout at midnight.

The slave girl opened the door at last, bowing to him. Julius could see amusement in her eyes as she edged past into the corridor, but he forgot her as soon as the door closed behind him.

Servilia was dressed in a simple white robe, with her hair tied into a coil on her neck. Part of him wondered how she had found time to apply paint and oils to her face, but he rushed forward to her.

'I do not care about the years between us. Did they matter in Spain?' he demanded. Before he could touch her, she held up a hand, her back stiff as a queen.

'You understand nothing, Julius, and that is the simple truth.'

He tried to protest, but she spoke loudly over him, her eyes flashing.

'I knew it was impossible in Spain, but everything was different there. I can't explain ... it was as if Rome was too far away and you were all that mattered. When I am here, I feel the years, the decades, Julius. *Decades* between us. My forty-third birthday passed yesterday. When you are in your forties, I will be an old woman with grey hair. I have them now, but covered in the best dyes from Egypt. Let me go, Julius. We can have no more time together.'

'I don't care, Servilia!' Julius snapped. 'You are still beautiful ...'

Servilia laughed unpleasantly. '*Still* beautiful, Julius? Yes, it

203

is a wonder I have kept my looks, though you know nothing of the work it takes me to present a smooth face to the world.'

For a moment, her eyes crumpled and she struggled against tears. When she spoke again, her voice was filled with an infinite weariness.

'I will not let you watch me grow old, Julius. Not *you*. Go back to your friends, before I call the tavern guards to throw you out. Leave me to finish dressing.'

Julius opened his hand and showed her the pearl. He knew it was the wrong thing to do, but he had planned the gesture all the way from the Campus and now it was if his arm moved without conscious will. She shook her head in disbelief at him.

'Should I throw myself into your arms now, Julius? Should I weep and say I'm sorry I ever thought you were a boy?'

With jerky spite, she snatched at the pearl and threw it straight at him, striking him in the forehead and making him flinch. He heard it roll into the recesses of the room and the sound seemed to go on endlessly.

She spoke slowly, as if to one lacking in wits. 'Now get out.'

As the door closed behind him, she rubbed angrily at her eyes and stood to search the corners of the room for the pearl. When her fingers closed over it, she held it up to the lamplight and for a moment her expression softened. Despite its beauty, it was cold and hard in her hand, as she pretended to be.

Servilia stroked the pearl with the pads of her long fingers, thinking of him. He had not yet lived thirty years and though he didn't seem to think of it, he would want a wife to give him sons. Tears glittered on her eyelashes as she thought of her drying womb. No blood for three months and no life stirring within her. For a while, she had dared to hope for a child, but when another period was missed, she knew she was past the last age of youth. There would be no son from her and it was better to send him away before his thoughts turned to children she could not give him. Better than waiting for him to cast her off. He wore his strength so easily and well that she knew he would never understand her fear. She took a deep breath to calm herself. He would recover, the young always did.

When Brutus and Sung emerged at midnight, the torches had been refilled with oil and the ring glowed in the darkness of the Campus. The betting slaves had been discreetly withdrawn and no more money was being taken. Many of the citizens had been drinking steadily through the afternoon in preparation for the climax and Julius sent runners to summon more of the Tenth in case of a riot at the end. Despite the weariness that assailed his spirit, Julius felt the thrill of pride as he watched Brutus raise one of Cavallo's swords for the last time. The gesture had a personal, painful meaning for all of them who understood it.

Without thinking, Julius reached out his hand to take Servilia's and then let it drop.

Her mood would change if Brutus won, he was almost certain.

The moon had risen, a pale crescent that hung above the ring of torches. Though it was late, the news of the finalists had passed quickly across the city and all of Rome was awake and waiting for the result. If he won, Brutus would be famous and the wry thought occurred to Julius that if his friend stood for consul, he would almost certainly win the seat.

As the cornicens blew their horns, Sung attacked without warning, trying for a win in the first instant. His blade blurred as it whipped out at Brutus' legs and the young Roman batted it aside with a ring of metal. He did not counter and for a moment Sung was left off balance. The sharp slits of his eyes remained impassive as Sung shrugged and moved in again, his long sword cutting a curve in the air.

Once again, Brutus knocked the blade away and the sound of metal was like a bell that rang out over the silent crowd.

They watched in fascination at this last battle that was so different from those that had gone before.

Julius could see the mottle of anger still on Brutus' face and neck and wondered whether he would kill Sung or be killed himself as his mind dwelled on the false win against Salomin.

The bout developed into a series of dashes and clangs, but Brutus had not moved a step from his mark. Where Sung's blade would reach him, it was blocked with a short jab of the gladius. Where the blow was a feint, Brutus ignored it, even when the metal passed close enough for him to hear it cut the air. Sung was breathing heavily as the crowd began to raise their voices with each of his attacks, falling silent for the blow and then letting out a hissing gasp that seemed like mockery. They thought Brutus was teaching the man a lesson about Rome.

As Julius watched, he knew Brutus was wrestling with himself alone. He wanted to win almost to desperation, but the shame of Salomin's treatment ate at him and he merely held Sung while he thought it through. Julius realised he was witnessing the display of a perfect swordsman. It was a staggering truth, but the boy he had known had become a master, greater than Renius or any other.

Sung knew it, as sweat stung his eyes, and still the Roman stood before him. Sung's face filled with rage and frustration. He had begun to grunt with every blow and without making a conscious choice, he was no longer striking to take first blood, but to kill.

Julius couldn't bear to watch it. He leaned out over the railing and bellowed across the sand to his friend: 'Win, Brutus! For us, win!'

His people roared as they heard him. Brutus turned Sung's blade on his own, trapping it long enough to hammer his elbow into the man's mouth. Blood spilled visibly over Sung's pale skin and Sung stepped back, stunned. Julius saw Brutus raise his hand and speak to the man and then Sung shook his head and darted in again.

Brutus came alive then and it was like watching a cat startled into a leap. He let the long blade slide along his ribs to get inside the guard and rammed his gladius down into Sung's neck with every ounce of his anger. The blade vanished under the silver armour and Brutus walked away across the sand without looking back.

Sung looked after him, his face twisted. His left hand plucked at the blade as he tried to shout, but his lungs were ribbons of flesh inside him and only a hoarse croaking could be heard in the deathly silence.

The crowd began to jeer and Julius felt ashamed of them. He stood and bellowed for quiet, enough to silence those who could hear. The rest followed into a tense stillness as the people of Rome waited for Sung to fall.

Sung spat angrily onto the sand, all colour seeping out of his face. Even at a distance, they could hear each heaving breath torn out. Slowly, with infinite care, he unbuckled his armour and let it fall. The cloth underneath was drenched and black in the torchlight and Sung looked at it in amazement, his dark gaze flickering up at the rows of Romans watching him.

'Come on, you bastard,' Renius whispered to himself. 'Show them how to die.'

With the precision of agony, Sung sheathed his long sword and then his legs betrayed him and he dropped to his knees. Still, he looked around at them all and the hard breaths were like screams, each one shorter than the last. Then he fell and the crowd released their breath, sitting like statues of gods in judgement.

Pompey mopped at his brow, shaking his head.

'You must congratulate your man, Caesar. I have never seen better,' he said.

Julius turned cold eyes on him and Pompey nodded as if to himself, calling for his guards to escort him back to the city walls.

CHAPTER EIGHTEEN

᠗᠗᠗᠗᠗

Bibilus glared in silence as Suetonius paced up and down the long room where he met visitors. Like every part of the house, it was decorated to Bibilus' taste and even as he watched Suetonius, he took comfort from the simple colours of the couches and gold-capped columns. Somehow, the stark cleanliness never failed to calm him and on entering any room in the villa, he would know if anything was out of place at a glance. The black marble floor was so highly polished that every step Suetonius took was matched by a coloured shadow under his feet, as if he walked on water. They were alone, with even the slaves dismissed. The fire had died long before and the air was cold enough to frost their breath. Bibilus would have liked to call for wine heated with a burning iron, or some food, but he dared not interrupt his friend.

He began to count the turns as Suetonius strode, the tension showing in his tight shoulders and the white-knuckled grip of his hands at his back. Bibilus bore the nightly use of his home with resentment, but Suetonius had a hold over him and he felt bound to listen, even as he grew to despise the man.

Suetonius' hard voice snapped the silence without warning, as if the anger could no longer be held within. 'I swear if I could reach him, I would have him killed, Bibi. By Jupiter's head, I swear it!'

'Don't say it,' Bibilus stammered, shocked. Even in his own house, some words should never be spoken.

Suetonius broke his stride as if he had been challenged and Bibilus shrank back into his padded couch. Drops of white spittle had gathered at the corners of Suetonius' mouth and Bibilus stared at them, unable to look away.

'You don't know him, Bibilus. You haven't seen how he plays the part of a noble Roman, like his uncle before him. As if his family were anything more than merchants! He flatters those he needs, puffing them up in his wake like cock birds. Oh, I'll give him that! He is a master at finding those to love him. All built on lies, Bibilus. I have seen it.' He glared at his friend as if waiting to be contradicted.

'His vanity shines out until I can't believe I am the only one who notices, yet they fall into line for him and call him the young lion of Rome.'

Suetonius spat on the polished floor and Bibilus looked at the wet lump of phlegm with distress. Suetonius sneered, his bitterness making an ugly mask of his features.

'It's all a game to them – Pompey and Crassus. I saw it when we came back from Greece together. The city was poor, the slaves were on the edge of the greatest rebellion in our history and they put Caesar up as a tribune. I should have known then I would never see justice. What had he done to deserve it, after all? I was there when we fought Mithridates, Bibi. Caesar was no more the leader than I was, though he played at it. Mithridates practically gave us the victory, but I never saw Julius fight. Did I mention that? I never saw him even draw his sword to help us when the blood was flying.'

Bibilus sighed. He had heard it all before, too many times to count. The rage had seemed justified to him once, but every time he heard the tale of grievances, Caesar became more and more the villain Suetonius wanted him to be.

'And Spain? Oh, Bibi, I know all about Spain. He goes there with nothing and returns with enough gold to run for consul, but do they challenge him? Is he broken by the courts? I wrote to the man who took his place there and questioned the figures he gave the Senate. I did their work for them, Bibi, those old fools.'

'What did he say?' Bibilus asked, looking up from his hands. This was a new part of the rant and it interested him. He watched as Suetonius searched for words and hoped he would not spit again.

'Nothing! I wrote again and again and finally the man sent me a curt little note, a warning not to interfere with the government of Rome. A threat, Bibilus, a *nasty* little threat. I knew then that he was one of Caesar's men. No doubt his hands are as dirty as the man before him. He covers himself well, does Julius, but I'll trap him.'

Tired and hungry, Bibilus could not resist a little barb. 'If he becomes consul, he will be immune from prosecution, Suetonius, even for capital crimes. You will not be able to touch him then.'

Suetonius sneered and hesitated before speaking. He remembered watching the dark men heading down to Caesar's estate to murder Cornelia and her servants. Sometimes, he thought that memory was all that prevented him from going insane. The gods had not protected Julius that day. Julius had been sent to Spain with rumours of disgrace, while his beautiful wife had her throat cut. Suetonius thought he had finally conquered his anger then. The death of Cornelia was like a boil bursting in him, with all the poison flowing away.

Suetonius sighed for the loss of that peace. Julius had abused his term in Spain, raping the country of gold. He should have been stoned in the streets, but he had come back and spoken his lies to the simple crowds and won them over. His tournament had spread his name over the city.

'Is there surprise when his friend wins the sword tournament, Bibi? No, they just cheer in their empty-headed way, though anyone with eyes could see that Salomin could barely walk to his mark. That was the true Caesar, the one I know. Right there in front of thousands and they would not see it. Where was his precious honour then?' Suetonius began to pace again, every step clattering against his mirrored image. 'He must not be consul, Bibilus. I will do what I have to, but he must not. You are not my only hope, my friend. You may yet take enough of the century votes to break him, but I will find another way if that is not enough.'

'If you are caught doing something, I . . .' Bibilus began.

Suetonius waved him to silence.

'Do your own work, Bibilus, while I do mine. Wave to crowds, attend the courts, make your speeches.'

'And if that is not enough?' he asked, fearing the answer.

'Do not disappoint me, Bibilus. You will see it through to the end unless your withdrawal would help my father. Is that too much to ask of you? It is nothing.'

'But what if . . .'

'I am tired of your objections, my friend,' Suetonius said softly. 'If you like, I can go to Pompey now and show him why you are not fit to stand for Rome. Would you like that, Bibi? Would you like him to know your secrets?'

'Don't,' Bibilus said, tears pricking his eyes. At times like that, he felt nothing but hatred for the man before him. Suetonius made everything sound sordid.

Suetonius approached and cupped his hand under the flesh of his chin.

'Even small dogs can bite, can't they, Bibilus? Would you betray me, I wonder? Yes, of course you would, if I gave you the chance. But you would fall with me, and harder. You know that, don't you?'

Suetonius gripped a jowl between two fingers and twisted. Bibilus shivered with the pain.

'You really are a *dirty* bastard, Bibilus. I need you, though, and that binds us better than friendship, better than blood. Don't forget it, Bibi. You could not stand torture and Pompey is known to be thorough.'

With a jerk, Bibilus pulled away, his soft white hands pressed against his bruised throat.

'Call your pretty children and have them light the fire again. It's cold in here,' Suetonius said, his eyes glittering.

In the dining room of the campaign house, Brutus stood at the head of the table and held up his cup as he looked at his friends. They rose to honour him and some of the bitterness he felt over Salomin eased in their company. Julius met his eyes and Brutus forced a smile, ashamed that he had ever believed his friend responsible for the beating.

'What shall we drink to?' Brutus said.

Alexandria cleared her throat and they looked to her.

'We will need more than one toast, but the first should be to Marcus Brutus, first sword in Rome.'

They smiled and echoed the words and Brutus could hear Renius' bass voice growl above the rest. The old gladiator had spoken to him for a long time after winning the tournament and, as it was him, Brutus had listened.

Brutus raised his cup as their eyes met, making it a private thanks. Renius grinned in response and Brutus felt his mood lighten.

'Then the next must be to my beautiful goldsmith,' he said, 'who loves a good swordsman, in more ways than one.'

Alexandria blushed at the laughter that followed and Brutus leered into her cleavage.

'You are drunk, you lecher,' she replied, her eyes bright with amusement.

Julius called for the cups to be refilled.

'To those we love who are not here,' he said and something in his tone made them all pause. Cabera lay upstairs with the best physicians in Rome at his side, not one of them with half his skill. Though he had healed Domitius, the old man had collapsed immediately afterwards and his illness cast a pall over the rest of them.

They echoed the toast, falling silent as they remembered those they had lost. As well as the old healer, Julius thought of Servilia, and his gaze strayed to the empty chair set aside for her. He rubbed his forehead in memory of where the pearl had struck him.

'Are we going to stand all night?' Domitius asked. 'Octavian should be in bed by now.'

Octavian tilted his cup back, emptying it. 'I was told I could stay up late if I'm good,' he replied cheerfully.

Julius looked affectionately at his young relative as they sat. He was growing into a fine man, though his manners were a little rough. Even Brutus had remarked on the number of times Octavian had been seen at Servilia's house and apparently he was becoming something of a favourite with the girls there. Julius watched as Octavian laughed at something Renius had said and hoped the extraordinary confidence of his youth would not be too harshly taken from him. Yet if the young man was never truly tested, he would be a shell. There were many things Julius would change from his own past, but without them, he knew he would still be the angry, proud little boy that Renius had trained. It was a terrible thing to consider, but he hoped that Octavian would know at least some pain, to take him into manhood. It was the only way he knew and while Julius could forget his triumphs, his failures had shaped him.

213

The food came on Julius' own silver plates, fashioned in Spain. They were all hungry and for a long time no one spoke to interrupt the soft sound of chewing mouths.

Brutus leaned back in his chair and covered a belch with his hand.

'So are you going to be consul, Julius?' he asked.

'If they vote in sufficient numbers,' Julius replied.

'Alexandria is making you a consul's clasp for your cloak. It's very fine,' Brutus continued.

Alexandria rested her head on a hand. 'A surprise, remember Brutus? I said it was to be a surprise. What did that mean to you, exactly?'

Brutus reached out and squeezed her hand. 'Sorry. It *is* fine, though, Julius.'

'I hope I have the chance to wear it. Thank you, Alexandria,' Julius replied. 'I just wish I could be as sure of victory as Brutus.'

'Why wouldn't you be? You lost one case in the forum that no one could have won. You won three that you should have lost. Your clients are out every night for you and the reports are good.'

Julius nodded, thinking of the debts he had amassed to achieve it. The gold he had won from Pompey had vanished over a few short days of the campaign. Despite the extravagant reputation he had earned, he regretted some of the wilder expenses, the pearl particularly. Even worse was the way the moneylenders assumed a familiarity with him as the debts increased. It was as if they felt they owned a part of him and he longed for the day when he would be free of their grasping hands.

Flushed with the wine, Brutus stood once more. 'We should have another toast,' he said. 'To victory, but victory with honour.'

They all came to their feet and raised their cups. Julius wished his father could see them.

CHAPTER NINETEEN

～～～～～

There was a great solemnity about the vast crowd that had come out of the city to vote. Julius watched with pride as they divided into the election centuries and took the wax tablets to the diribitores to be stored in baskets for the count. The city loomed on the horizon, while to the west, the distant flag on the Janiculum hill was held high to signal the city was safe and sealed while the vote went on.

Sleep had been impossible the night before and when the augurs were ready to go out and consecrate the ground, Julius was there with them at the gate, nervous and strangely light-headed as he watched them prepare their knives and lead a great white bullock away from the city. Its slumped body lay near where he stood in silence, trying to gauge the mood of the crowd. Many of them nodded and smiled to him as they passed their votes into the wicker baskets, but Julius took little pleasure in it. Only the votes of their centuries would count and with the richer classes voting first, Prandus had already secured seven against four for Bibilus. Not a single one of the first eleven centuries had declared for Julius and he felt sweat running from his armpits under the toga as the day's heat began to mount.

He had always known the richest freemen would be the hardest votes to gain, but seeing the reality of each missed vote was a bitter experience. The consuls and candidates stood at his side in a dignified group, but Pompey could not hide his amusement and chatted with a slave at his elbow as he held out his cup for a cool drink.

Julius tried hard to keep a pleasant expression on his face. Even after all his preparation, the early votes might influence the later centuries and the result could be a landslide, with no room for him. For the first time since returning to the city, he wondered what he would do if he lost.

If he stayed in a city run by Bibilus and Prandus, it would be the end of him, he was sure. Pompey would find a way to destroy him, if Suetonius did not. Just to survive the year, he would be forced to beg for a posting in some dismal hole on the edges of Roman influence. Julius shook his head unconsciously, his thoughts touching on worse and worse possibilities as the votes were called out. Supporters of Prandus and Bibilus cheered each success and Julius was forced to smile his congratulation, though it was like acid in him.

He told himself there was nothing he could do and found a momentary calm in that. The men of Rome voted in small wooden cubicles and passed their tablets to the diribitores face down to hide the marks they had made. There could be no coercion at this stage and all the bribes and games came to nothing as the citizens stood alone and pressed the wax twice against the names they favoured. Even so, the waiting crowd heard each result and soon they would vote with the mass of men before them. In many elections, Julius had seen the poorer classes sent back to Rome as soon as a majority was called. He prayed that would not be the case this day.

'. . . Caesar,' the magistrate cried and Julius jerked his head up to hear. It was the end of the first class and he had taken a vote from the tail. Now those with less property and wealth would have their turn. Even as he smiled, he fretted to himself, trying not to show it. He had most of his support among the poorest, who saw him as a man who had dragged himself up to the position; yet without more votes from the wealthy, his people wouldn't even have the chance to mark the wax in his name.

The results of the second class were more even and Julius stood a little straighter as he heard his tally rise with the others. Prandus had seventeen to Bibilus' fourteen and five more centuries had declared for Julius, raising his hopes. He was not the only one to suffer, he saw. Suetonius' father had gone pale with the extraordinary tension and Julius guessed he wanted the seat as badly as he did himself. Bibilus too was nervous, his eyes sliding over to Suetonius at intervals, almost as if he were pleading.

Over the next hour, the lead changed three times and at the end, the total for Suetonius' father had him third and falling further behind. Julius watched as Suetonius strode to Bibilus' side. The fat Roman shrank away, but Suetonius grabbed his arm and whispered harshly into his ear. His anger made it perfectly audible to all of them and Bibilus blushed crimson.

'Withdraw, Bibi. You must withdraw now!' Suetonius snarled at him, ignoring Pompey's glance.

Bibilus nodded nervously, like a spasm, but Pompey laid his massive hand on Bibilus' shoulders as if Suetonius was not there, forcing the young Roman to step away in haste rather than touch the consul.

'I hope you are not thinking of leaving the lists, Bibilus,' Pompey said.

Bibilus made a sound that could have been a reply, but Pompey went on over it.

'You have made a fair showing amongst the first classes, and may do better still before the end. See it through and who knows? Even if you are not successful, there is always a place for the old families in the Senate.'

Bibilus plastered a sick smile onto his face and Pompey patted his arm as he let him go. Suetonius turned away rather than try again and watched coldly as Bibilus took another three votes.

By noon, every result was greeted with cheers as the wine sellers sold their wares to the crowd. Julius felt able to unbend enough to drink a cup, but could not taste it. He exchanged inanities with Bibilus, but Senator Prandus remained aloof and only nodded stiffly when Julius congratulated him on his showing. Suetonius had nothing like his father's skill at hiding his emotions and Julius felt his eyes on him constantly, wearing his nerves.

As the sun passed its zenith, Pompey called for awnings to shade them. A hundred centuries had voted and Julius was second and seventeen votes clear of Prandus. As things stood, Bibilus and Julius would take the seats, and the crowd began to show their interest more openly, cheering and jostling each other to observe the candidates. Julius watched as Suetonius drew a large red cloth from his toga and mopped his brow with it. It was a strangely flamboyant gesture and Julius smiled grimly, glancing to the west, where the Janiculum flag could be seen.

The Janiculum hill commanded a full view of the city and the land around it. A huge mast rose from a stone base at the highest point and the men who watched for invasion never shifted their gaze. It was usually an easy duty, more suited to the ancient days when the city was in constant danger from outlying tribes and armies. This year, the Catiline conspiracy had brought home the continued need for the duty and those who had won the task by lot were alert and watchful. There were six of them, four boys and two veterans from Pompey's legion. They discussed the candidates as they ate a cold lunch, thoroughly enjoying the break from their normal duties. At sunset, they would complete their day with a note from a long horn and the solemn lowering of the flag.

They did not see the men creeping up the hill behind them until a pebble clicked against a rock and went skipping down the steep side below the crest. The boys turned to see what animal had disturbed them and one cried out in warning at the sight of armed men scrambling up. There were seven of them; big, scarred raptores who showed their teeth as they caught sight of the small number of defenders.

Pompey's men jumped to their feet, scattering food and knocking over a clay jug of water that darkened the dusty ground. Even as their blades came free, they were surrounded, but they knew their duty and the first of the raptores was punched flat as he came too close. The others surged in, snarling, and then another voice snapped through the air.

'Hold! Who moves, dies,' Brutus shouted. He was running towards them with a full twenty soldiers at his heels. Even if he had been alone, it could have been enough. There were few in Rome who would not have recognised the silver armour he wore, or the gold-hilted sword he had won.

The raptores froze. They were thieves and killers and nothing in their experience had prepared them to face the soldiers of their own city. It took only an instant for them to abandon the attempt on the flag and leap away in all directions down the steep slopes. A couple of them lost their footing and rolled, dropping their weapons in the panic. By the time Brutus arrived at the flag mast, he was panting lightly and Pompey's men saluted him, their faces flushed.

'It would be a shame to have the election stopped by a few

thieves, wouldn't it?' Brutus said, looking down at the dwindling figures.

'I'm sure Briny and I could have held them, sir,' one of Pompey's men replied, 'but these boys are good lads and no doubt we would have lost one or two.' The man paused as it occurred to him he was being less than gracious about the rescue. 'We were glad to see you, sir. Are you letting them go?'

The legionary moved to the edge with Brutus, watching the progress of the raptores below. Brutus shook his head.

'I have a few riders at the bottom. They won't reach the city.'

'Thank you, sir,' the soldier replied, smiling grimly. 'They don't deserve to.'

'Can you see which one of the candidates is losing at the moment?' Brutus asked, narrowing his eyes at the dark mass of citizens in the distance. He could make out where Julius was standing and saw a speck of red appear on one of the men at his side. He nodded to himself in satisfaction. Julius had guessed right.

Pompey's soldier shrugged. 'We can't see much from here, sir. Do you think that red cloth was their signal?'

Brutus chuckled. 'We'll never be able to prove it, you know. It's tempting to try to turn those thieves with a little gold, sending them against their master. More satisfying than just leaving their bodies out here, don't you think?'

The soldier smiled stiffly. He knew his general was no friend of the man who stood at his shoulder, but the silver armour put him in awe. He could tell his children that he had talked to the greatest swordsman of Rome.

'Better by far, sir,' he said, 'if they'll do it.'

'Oh, I think they will. My riders can be very persuasive,' Brutus replied, looking at the flag snapping in the breeze above his head.

*   *   *

Suetonius glanced as casually as he could at the Janiculum flag. It was still flying! He bit his lower lip in irritation, wondering if he should take the red cloth from his toga one more time. Were they asleep? Or had they just taken his money and were sitting in some tavern drinking themselves blind? He thought he could make out figures moving on the dark crest and wondered if the men he had hired were unable to see his signal. He looked around guiltily and reached inside the soft cloth of his robe once more. At that moment, he saw Julius was smiling at him, the amused gaze seeming to know every thought in his head. Suetonius let his hand fall away to his side and stood stiffly, painfully aware of the flush that had started on his neck and cheeks.

Octavian lay in the long grass with his horse beside him, its great chest heaving in long, slow breaths. They had trained the mounts for months to be able to hold the unnatural position and now the extraordinarii only had to lay a hand on the soft muzzles to keep them still. They watched as the raptores came slipping and leaping down the Janiculum and Octavian grinned. Julius had been right that someone might try to lower the flag if the election turned against them. Though it was a simple ploy, the effects would have been devastating. The citizens of Rome would have streamed back to the city and the results up to that point declared void. Perhaps another month would pass before they assembled again and many things could change in that time.

Octavian waited until the running men were close, then gave a low whistle, swinging his leg into the saddle as his horse rose. The rest of his twenty leapt up smoothly with him, gaining their saddles before their mounts were fully upright.

To the fleeing thieves, it seemed as if fully armed cavalry sprang out of the ground at them. The seven men panicked completely, either throwing themselves flat or raising their hands in instant surrender. Octavian drew his sword, holding their eyes. Their leader watched him in resignation, turning his head to spit into the long grass.

'Come on, then. Get it over with,' he said.

Despite his apparent fatalism, the thief was fully aware of the positions of the riders and only relaxed when every avenue of retreat had been blocked. He had heard a man could outrun a horse over a short distance, but looking at the glossy mounts of the extraordinarii, it didn't seem likely.

When the last few blades had been taken from the men, Octavian unstrapped his helmet from the saddle and put it on. The plume waved gently in the breeze, adding to his height and giving him a forbidding aspect. He thought it was well worth the portion of his pay that had gone to buy it. Certainly, the raptores all looked to him now, waiting grimly for the order to cut them down.

'I don't expect charges could ever be brought against your master,' Octavian said.

The leader spat again. 'Don't know any master, soldier, except maybe silver,' he said, his face suddenly cunning as he sensed something was up.

'It would be a shame if he escaped without even a good beating, don't you think?' Octavian asked innocently.

The raptores nodded, even the slowest beginning to realise the order to kill wasn't going to come.

'I can find him again, if you let us go,' their leader said, trying not to hope. There was something terrifying about horses to a man who had grown up in the city. He had never quite understood how big they were before and shuddered as one snorted behind him.

Octavian tossed a small pouch into the air and the man caught it, feeling the weight automatically before making it disappear inside his tunic.

'Do a professional job,' Octavian said, backing his horse to leave a gap for the men to pass. A couple of them tried to salute as they walked through the riders and began to make their way back to the city. None of them dared look back.

Before the last centuries had voted, Julius knew he and Bibilus had won seats as consuls for the year to come. He was reminded of the motions of bees as senators clustered around both of them and he grinned at Bibilus' bemused expression.

Julius had his shoulder gripped and his hand taken by scores of men he barely knew and before he had fully understood the change in his status, he was fielding questions and requests for his time and even being told of opportunities to invest. In their role as the formal 'Comitia Centuriata', the citizens of Rome had created two new bodies for the city to suck dry and Julius felt overwhelmed and irritated by the attention. Where had these smiling supporters been when he was campaigning?

In comparison to the shallow heartiness of the Senate, having Pompey and Crassus congratulate him was a genuine pleasure, particularly as he knew Pompey would rather have eaten glass than say the words. Julius shook the offered hand without a sign of relish, his mind already on the future. No matter who the people had elected to lead the Senate, the outgoing consuls were still a force in the city. Only a fool would scorn them at the moment of triumph.

The magistrate climbed onto a small platform to dismiss the last centuries. They bowed their heads as he bellowed a prayer of thanks at them, finishing with the traditional order, 'Discedite!'

The citizens did as they were told and scattered, laughing and joking as they began the walk back to the sealed city.

Suetonius and his father had paid their respects and Julius had spoken warmly to them, knowing it was a chance to mend the bridges broken in the campaign and the past. He could afford the gesture and Prandus seemed to accept his good wishes, bowing slightly to the consul elect of Rome. His son Suetonius had looked straight through him, his face blank with defeat.

Pompey's men had brought horses and Julius looked up as reins were passed into his hand. From the back of a grey gelding, Pompey looked down at him, his expression unreadable.

'It will be hours before the Senate sit again to confirm the postings, Julius. If you ride with us now, we will have the Curia to ourselves.'

Crassus leaned down on his horse's neck to speak more privately. 'Will you trust me one more time?'

Julius looked up at both men, sensing the subtle tension in them as they waited for his response. He didn't hesitate, swinging himself up into the saddle and raising an arm to those in the crowd who were watching the exchange. They cheered him as he wheeled and set off across the vast field with the two other men, a century of Pompey's cavalry falling in behind as their escort. The crowd parted before them and their shadows stretched behind.

CHAPTER TWENTY

⁐⁐⁐⁐⁐

Without the voting centuries, the city was strangely empty as the three men rode through the streets. Julius was reminded of the night of the storm when he had gone down into the cells of the prison house and seen the tortured figures of Catiline's men. He glanced at Crassus as they dismounted before the senate house and the old man raised his eyebrows, guessing at the reason for the attention.

Julius had never before entered the senate house without it being filled with men on the benches. It echoed extraordinarily, reflecting each footstep as they took seats together near the rostrum. The door had been left open and the sun shone in as a bar of gold, making the marble walls feel light and airy. Julius leaned back against the hard wooden bench with a sense of vast satisfaction. His election was just beginning to sink in and he could barely resist grinning to himself at the thought.

'Crassus and I thought we might all benefit from a private

conversation before the Senate sits,' Pompey began. He stood and began to pace as he spoke. 'Leaving aside the flowery words for the public, we three have little friendship between us. There is respect, I hope, but no great liking.' He paused and Crassus shrugged. Julius said nothing.

'If we do not come to some arrangement for next year,' Pompey went on, 'I expect it to be a wasted time for the city. You saw the influence Suetonius has over Bibilus. The whole Senate has heard his bleating complaints about you over the years. Together, they will delay or frustrate anything you propose until nothing can be done. It would not be good for Rome.'

Julius looked up at the man, remembering when he had first met him, in that very hall. Pompey was a superb tactician on the field and in the Senate, but both he and Crassus were facing the loss of the power and respect they enjoyed. That was the real reason for the private meeting, rather than any concern for the best use of Julius' consular year. A deal was certainly possible, if he could find terms that would satisfy them all.

'I have already given the matter some thought,' Julius said.

Suetonius rode back to the stables of the inn near the gates where he had taken a room for the day of the election. His father had hardly spoken to him and only nodded when Suetonius had offered his condolences for the loss. Senator Prandus had eaten quickly and in silence before making his way up to the room above, leaving his son to drown his own frustration in cheap wine.

The door to the tavern opened and Suetonius looked up, hoping it was Bibilus come to join him. No doubt his friend was back at his palatial home in the centre of the city, being massaged by attractive slaves without a care in the world. Suetonius had not yet begun to consider the implications of

Bibilus as consul. His first, panicky thought was that the consular immunity would remove the hold he had over the man, but he dismissed that as soon as he thought of it. Immune or not, Bibilus would be terrified of his habits becoming generally known in the city. Perhaps there could even be benefits to having his fat friend leading the Senate. It was not what he had planned, but having a consul at his bidding could be interesting. Suetonius resolved blearily to visit his home and remind Bibilus of their relationship.

The man who entered was a stranger and Suetonius ignored him after the first glance. He was too drunk to be startled when the man cleared his throat and spoke.

'Sir, the stable boy says there is a problem with your horse. He thinks it has taken a thorn in the hoof.'

'I'll have him flogged if it has,' Suetonius snapped, rising too quickly. He barely noticed the steadying hand on his shoulder as he was guided out of the inn into the darkness.

The night air did something to remove the fog of wine from his thoughts and he pulled away from the arm that held him as he entered the low stables. There were men there, too many to be looking after the horses. They grinned at him as a cold panic settled his heaving blood.

'What do you want? Who are you?' Suetonius blustered.

The leader of the raptores stepped out from the shadows and Suetonius fell back at the man's expression.

'Just a job to me, this, though I always give value if I can,' he said, strolling towards the young Roman.

Suetonius was held tightly by both arms even as he began to struggle and a hand was clamped over his mouth.

The leader flexed his hands menacingly.

'Snuff the lamps, lads. I don't need light for this,' he said and in the sudden darkness there came the thud of heavy blows.

*   *   *

Julius wished he had slept the night before. His weariness weighed on him but now, of all times, he needed to be sharp to deal with the two men.

'Together, you still command enough support in the Senate to force anything through.'

'Unless there is a consular veto,' Pompey replied immediately.

Julius shrugged. 'Do not consider it. I will deal with Bibilus when the time comes.'

Pompey blinked at him as Julius continued.

'Without that block, your factions in the Senate are enough. The question is merely what I must give you to ensure your support.'

'I don't think . . .' Crassus began stiffly, but Pompey held up a hand.

'Let him speak, Crassus. You and I have discussed this enough without a solution. I want to hear what he has in mind.'

Julius chuckled at their eagerness. 'Crassus wants trade. Together, Pompey, we could grant him an absolute monopoly throughout Roman lands. A licence for two years, say. He would have a stranglehold on every coin in the dominions and yet, I do not doubt, the total wealth will increase under his hand. If I know Crassus, the treasury of Rome will be swollen to bursting in less than a year.'

Crassus smiled at the compliment, but he did not seem especially moved. Julius had hoped the old man would be tempted by the licence alone, but the deal had to leave them all satisfied or it would be broken at the first test.

'But perhaps that is not enough?' Julius said, watching them both carefully.

Pompey's eyes glittered with interest and Crassus was deep in thought. The idea of a total grip on trade was wonderfully intoxicating to him and he knew better than Julius what he could achieve with that power. His competitors would be beggared at a single stroke, their houses and slaves put up for auction. In only a short time, he could treble his land holdings and own a merchant fleet as great as any the world had seen. He would be able to ignore the losses of distant storms and send his ships out to far countries, Egypt, India, places without names, even. None of this showed in his expression. Crassus frowned carefully to show the young man he still needed to be persuaded, while his mind reeled at the thought of the fleet he would gather.

'What about your own concessions, Julius?' Pompey said impatiently.

'I want six months in Senate, working with you in mutual support. The promises I made to the people of Rome were not empty. I want to pass new laws and ordinances. Some will upset the more traditional members of the Senate and I must have your votes with me to ride over their objections. The people have elected me; let us not be held back by Bibilus or a pack of toothless old men.'

'I cannot see what advantage there is to me in such an arrangement,' Pompey prompted.

Julius raised his eyebrows. 'Apart from the good of Rome, of course.' He smiled to ease the barb as Pompey coloured, knowing he could still lose it all with a false step.

'Your own desires are simple enough, my friend,' Julius said. 'You want Dictatorship, though you may resist the name. Crassus and I will endorse any motion or vote you put to the Senate. Anything. Between us, we could have the Senate at our feet.'

'That is no small thing,' Pompey said quietly. What Julius was proposing completely undermined the purpose of having two consuls as a check on each other, but Pompey couldn't find it in himself to mention it.

Julius nodded. 'I would not if I thought you were a lesser man, Pompey. We have disagreed in the past, but I have never questioned your love of this city, and who knows you better than I? We destroyed Cato together, remember? Rome will not suffer under you.'

The flattery was perhaps a little obvious, though Julius found to his surprise that he believed at least part of it. Pompey was a solid leader and would defend Roman interests with determination and strength, even if he would never extend them.

'I do not trust you, Caesar,' Pompey said bluntly. 'All these promises could come to nothing unless we are more firmly bound.' He cleared his throat. 'I need a token of goodwill from you, a proof of your support that is more than air.'

'Tell me what you want,' Julius said, shrugging.

'How old is your daughter?' Pompey asked. His face was deadly serious and Julius understood his meaning immediately.

'Ten this year,' he replied. 'Too young for you, Pompey.'

'She will not always be. Bind your blood to me and I will accept your promises. My own wife is in the grave more than three years and a man is not meant to be alone. When she is fourteen, send her to me and I will marry her.'

Julius rubbed his eyes. So much depended on reaching an agreement with the two old wolves. If his daughter had been one of his soldiers, he knew he would sacrifice her without a moment's thought for such stakes.

'Sixteen. She will be your bride at sixteen,' he said at last.

Pompey beamed at him and nodded, stretching out his hand. Julius felt cold as he took it. He had them both, if he could supply the final pieces, but still the problem of Crassus worried at his thoughts. In the silent Curia, Julius could hear the echoes of Pompey's soldiers as they marched in the forum and listening to them gave him the answer.

'A legion also, Crassus,' Julius said, thinking quickly. 'A new eagle in the Campus Martius, raised in your name. Men I would train and mingle with my best officers for half a year.

We will send to the country for them, to the tens of thousands of simple men who have never had the chance to fight for Rome. They would become yours, Crassus, and I can tell you there is no greater bond or joy than forming them into a legion. I will make them for you, but you will wear the general's plume.'

Crassus looked up sharply at both men, considering the offer. He had longed for a command ever since the disaster against Spartacus, held from it by the nagging doubt that he could not lead as easily as Pompey and Caesar. Listening to Julius made it seem possible, but he tried to speak, to explain his doubts.

Julius laid a hand on his arm.

'I have taken men from Africa and Greece and made them soldiers, Crassus. I will do more with those of Roman blood. Catiline saw a weakness we must remove if Rome is to thrive with your trade, don't you think? The city needs good men on the walls above all else.'

Crassus flushed. 'I may ... not be the man to lead them, Caesar,' he said through clenched teeth.

Julius could imagine what it had cost him to make the admission in front of Pompey, but he snorted in reply, 'Neither was I until Marius and Renius and, yes, Pompey showed me how, by example and by training. No man leaps full-grown into that role, Crassus. I will be with you in the first steps and Pompey will always be there. He knows Rome needs a second legion for protection. I doubt he would want anything less in a city that answers to him.'

Both of them looked to Pompey and he answered immediately.

'Whatever you need, Crassus. There is truth in what he says.' Before they could do more than smile, Pompey went on, 'You paint a pretty picture for us, Julius. Crassus with his trade, I with a bride and the city I love. But you have not told us the price for this generosity. Say it now.'

Crassus interrupted, 'I will accept these terms, with two additions. A licence for five years not two, and my eldest son Publius is to be taken into the Tenth as an officer, a centurion. I am an old man, Julius. My son will lead this new legion after me.'

'I can agree to that,' Julius said.

Pompey cleared his throat impatiently. 'But what do *you* want, Caesar?'

Julius rubbed his eyes again. He had not considered binding his family to Pompey's line, but his daughter would rise in one stroke to the highest social rank in Rome. It was a fair bargain. They were both too old in politics to refuse such an arrangement and what he offered was a world better than the misery of losing their power and influence, even in part. Julius knew the addictive nature of command. There was no greater satisfaction than to lead. When he looked up at them, his eyes were bright and sharp.

'When my six months are up in the city and the laws I want have been added to the rolls, then it is simple. I want to take my two legions out to new lands. I will give my proxy to Pompey and I want you both to sign orders giving me complete freedom to levy soldiers, strike bargains and make laws in the name of Rome. I will not report back unless I see fit. I will answer to no man but myself.'

'Will that be legal?' Crassus asked.

Pompey nodded. 'If I have the consul's proxy, it will. There is some precedent.' Pompey frowned in thought. 'Where will you take these legions, to do this?' he asked.

Julius grinned, carried away by his own enthusiasm. How he had argued with his friends over the destination! Yet in the end, there had been only one choice. Alexander had gone east and that path was well trodden. He would go west.

'I want the wild land, gentlemen,' he said. 'I want Gaul.'

*   *   *

In full armour, Julius strode through the night, heading towards Bibilus' home. Pompey and Crassus believed he knew some way to muzzle his co-consul, but the truth was he had no clear idea of how to prevent Bibilus and Suetonius making a mockery of all their plans.

Julius clenched his fists as he walked. He had given up his daughter and pledged time and money and power to Pompey and Crassus. In return, he would have a freedom greater than any Roman general in the city's history. Scipio Africanus had not had the range of powers Julius would have in Gaul. Even Marius had answered to the Senate. Julius knew he would not let such a thing fall from his hands because of one man, no matter what he had to do.

The crowds parted for him as he swept through. Those who recognised him fell silent. The new consul's expression forbade any attempt to greet or congratulate him and more than a few wondered what news could have so angered a man on the very day of his election.

Julius left them murmuring in his wake as he approached the great gates and columns of Bibilus' house. His resolve hardened as he raised his fist to hammer on the oak door. He would not be denied this last step.

The slave that answered the summons was a youth whose face was heavily painted, giving him a lascivious expression even as he recognised the visitor and his eyes opened in surprise.

'I am a consul of Rome. You know the law?'

The slave nodded, terrified.

'Then bar no door to me. Touch my sleeve and you will die. I have come to see your master. Lead me in.'

'C-Consul . . .'

The young man tried to drop to one knee and Julius snapped at him.

'Now!'

The painted boy needed no other urging. He turned and

almost ran from Julius, leaving the door to the street swinging behind them.

Julius marched behind, passing through rooms where a dozen similarly painted children watched, frozen as he passed. One or two of them cried out in amazement and Julius glared at them. Were there no adults in this place? The way they were dressed reminded him more of Servilia's whores than ...

He almost lost the boy slave around a corner as the thought came to him. Then he hurried and the slave increased his speed through antechambers and corridors until they burst together into a lighted room.

'Master!' the young man cried out. 'Consul Caesar is here!'

Julius paused, panting slightly with the anger that coursed through his veins. Bibilus was there in the room and Suetonius stood bent over him, whispering into his ear. More of the pretty slaves were standing at the edges and two naked boys lolled at the feet of the two men. Julius saw their faces were flushed with wine and their eyes were older than their flesh. He shuddered as he turned his face to Suetonius.

'Get out,' he said.

Suetonius had risen slowly as if in a trance at Julius' entrance. He was ugly with malice as he struggled with conflicting emotions. A consul could not be touched, could not be held. Even Suetonius' position in the Senate would not save him after an insult.

Casually, Julius dropped his hand to his sword. He knew Bibilus would be weaker without his friend. Julius had known that even when he had not had a lever to twist into the fat man's innards. Now he had found one.

As Suetonius looked to Bibilus for a reprieve, he found nothing but terror in the consul's fleshy face. Suetonius heard Julius march across the marble floor and still he delayed, waiting for the single word that would allow him to stay.

Bibilus watched like a child with a snake as Julius came close to Suetonius and leaned in towards him. Suetonius shrank back.

'Get out,' Julius repeated softly and Suetonius fled.

As Julius turned to Bibilus, the consul found a stammering voice.

'This is my h-home . . .' he attempted.

Julius roared at him, a crash of sound that sent Bibilus scrambling backwards on his couch.

'You filth! You dare to talk to me with these children sitting at your feet! If I killed you now, it would be a blessing for Rome. No, better, I should cut off the last thing that makes you a man. I will do it, now.'

Drawing his sword, Julius advanced on the couch and Bibilus screamed, clawing at the cloth to try to get away. He wept heavy tears as Julius held the gleaming blade next to his groin.

Bibilus froze. 'Please,' he whimpered.

Julius twisted the blade, worrying it deeper into the folds of cloth. Bibilus pressed himself against the back of the couch, but could retreat no further.

'Please, whatever you want . . .' he began a series of choking sobs that added shining mucus to his tears until his face was barely human.

Julius knew the fates had given everything into his hands. The coldest part of him rejoiced in Bibilus revealing such a weakness. A few choice threats and the man would never dare show his face in the Senate again. Yet even as Julius began to speak, one of the children shifted and Julius glanced at him. The boy was not looking at Julius, but at his master, craning to get a better view. There was hatred there, horrifying in such a young face. The boy's ribs could be clearly seen and his neck bore a purple bruise. Julius realised his daughter was the same age. He turned his anger on Bibilus.

'Sell your slaves. Sell them where they will not be hurt and send me the addresses, that I may check each one. You will live alone, if I let you live at all.'

Bibilus nodded, his jowls quivering.

'Yes, yes, I will . . . don't *cut* me.' He broke down again into a stream of miserable sound and Julius struck him twice across the face, rocking his head back. A thin stream of blood dribbled down across his lips and he shook visibly.

'If I see you in the Senate, your immunity will not protect you, I swear by all the gods. I will see to it that you are taken somewhere quiet and burnt and broken over days. You will beg for an end to it.'

'But I am consul!' Bibilus choked.

Julius leaned in with the sword tip, making him gasp.

'Only in name. I will not have a man like you in my senate house. Never in this life. Your time there is over.'

'Can he hurt me now?' the slave boy asked suddenly.

Julius looked at him and saw that he had risen to his feet. He shook his head.

'Then give me a knife. *I'll* cut him,' the boy said.

Julius looked into his eyes and saw nothing but resolve.

'You'll be killed if you do,' Julius said softly.

The boy shrugged. 'Worth it,' he said. 'Give me a blade and I'll do it.'

Bibilus opened his mouth and Julius twisted the gladius viciously.

'You be quiet. There are men talking here. You've no part in it.' He turned back to the slave and saw the way he stood a little straighter at the words.

'I won't stop you, lad, if you want it, but he's more use to me alive than dead. At least for now.' A corpse would mean another election and a new adversary who might not have Bibilus' weaknesses. Yet Julius did not send the boy away.

'You want him alive?' the child said.

Julius returned the gaze for a long moment before nodding.

'All right, but I want to leave here tonight.'

'I can find you a place, lad. You have my gratitude.'

'Not just me. All of us. No more nights here.'

Julius looked at him in surprise. 'All of you?'

'All of us,' the slave said, holding his eyes without the slightest tremor. Julius looked away first.

'Very well, boy. Gather them at the front door. Leave me alone with Bibilus for a little while longer and I'll come to you.'

'Thank you, sir,' the boy said. In a few moments, all the children in the room had vanished with him and the only sound was Bibilus' tortured breathing.

'How d-did you find out?' Bibilus whispered.

'Until I saw them, I did not know you for what you are. Even if I had not, you are greasy with guilt.' Julius growled, 'Remember, I will know if you bring more children into your home. If I hear of a single boy or girl coming through your doors, I will know and I will not hold back from you. Do you understand me? The Senate is mine, now. Completely.'

At the last word, Julius jerked his blade and Bibilus screamed, releasing his bladder in terror. Moaning, he clutched at the spreading stain of urine tinged with blood. Julius sheathed the sword and headed back to the front, where more than thirty of the slaves had gathered.

Each one of the refugees held a few items of clothing bundled in their arms. Their eyes were large and fearful in the light of the lamps and the silence was almost painful as they all turned to look at him.

'All right. Tonight you'll stay in my own home,' Julius said. 'I'll find you families who have lost a child and who will love you.' The happiness in their expressions shamed him worse than knives. He had not come to the house for them.

CHAPTER TWENTY-ONE

❦❦❦❦❦

The summer had come and gone with its long, busy days, but winter was still far off as Julius mounted his horse at the Quirinal gate, ready to join the legions in the Campus. He looked around him as he took the reins, trying to fix this last picture of the city in his mind. Who knew how long it would have to sustain him in distant Gaul? Those travellers and merchants who had been to the small Roman camp at the far foot of the Alps said it was a bitter place, colder than any they had known. Julius had punished his lines of credit for furs and provisions for ten thousand soldiers. Eventually, he knew there would have to be a reckoning, but he did not allow the thought of debt to spoil the final moments in his city.

The Quirinal gate was open and Julius could see the Campus Martius through it, with his soldiers waiting patiently in shining squares. Julius doubted there was a legion anywhere to equal the Tenth and Brutus had worked hard to make something greater out of the men he had conscripted. Not one of them had been allowed leave in almost a year and they had used their time well. Julius was pleased with the name Brutus had chosen for them. The Third Gallica would be hardened in the land for which they had been named.

Brutus and Octavian mounted up beside him, while Domitius checked his saddle straps for tightness one last time. Julius smiled to himself at their silver armour. All three men had earned the right to wear it, but they made an unusual sight in the streets by the gate and already there was a crowd of urchins come to point and gawk at them. As well they might. Every part of their armour shone as brightly as polish and cloths could make them and Julius felt a thrill at riding for Rome with these men.

If Salomin had come with them, it would have been perfect, Julius thought. It was just one more nagging regret in a sea of them that he had not been able to persuade the little fighter to make the trip to Gaul. Salomin had spoken for a long time about Roman honour and Julius had listened. It was all he could offer after Pompey's shameful treatment of him, but he had not pressed him after the first refusal.

The months in Senate had exceeded Julius' hopes and the triumvirate was holding better than he had any right to expect. Crassus had begun his domination of trade and his great fleet already rivalled anything Carthage had ever put to sea. His fledgling legion had been hammered into some sort of shape by the best officers in the Tenth and Pompey would continue that work when they were gone. The three men had developed a grudging respect for each other in their months together and Julius did not regret the bargain he had struck with them.

After the night of the election, Bibilus had not been seen in the senate house for a single meeting. Rumours of a long-term illness had spread through the city but Julius maintained his silence about what had happened. He had kept his promises to the children, sending them to be raised in loving families far in the north. His private shame at profiting from their distress had prompted him to buy them free, though it bled his funds even whiter on top of everything else. Strangely, that simple act had given him more satisfaction than almost anything else in his months as consul.

'Brutus!' a voice called, shattering the moment.

Julius turned his horse in a tight circle and Brutus laughed aloud at the sight of Alexandria struggling through the crowds to the gate. As she reached him, she stood on tiptoe to be kissed, but Brutus reached down and heaved her into the saddle. Julius looked away, not that they would have noticed. It was difficult not to think of Servilia as he saw their happiness together.

When Alexandria was lowered to the road, Julius noticed she carried a cloth package. He raised his eyebrows as she held it out for him, blushing with embarrassment from the embrace he had witnessed. Julius took the bundle and unwrapped it slowly, his eyes widening as he revealed a helmet worked with extraordinary skill. It was polished iron and shining with oil, but the strangest thing was the full face of it, shaped to resemble his own features.

Reverently, Julius lifted it above his head and then lowered it, pressing the hinged face back until it clicked. It fitted like a second skin. The eyes were large enough to see out easily and he knew from the reactions of his companions that it achieved the effect Alexandria had wanted.

'It has a cold expression,' Octavian murmured, gazing at him.

Brutus nodded and Alexandria reached up to Julius' saddle to speak privately to him.

'I thought it would protect your head better than the one you usually wear. There is a slide on the top for a plume, if you want one. There is nothing like it in Rome.'

Julius looked out through the iron mask at her, wishing for

one painful moment that she was his and not his friend's.

'It is perfect,' he said. 'Thank you.' He reached down and hugged her, smelling the rich scent she used. An impulse struck him then and he removed the helmet as she stood back, his face flushed with more than just the heat. The legion would wait a little longer, after all. Perhaps there was still time to visit Servilia before he left.

'Alexandria, I must ask you to excuse us,' Julius said. 'Gentlemen? I have an errand to run in the city before we join the men.'

Domitius vaulted into his saddle as an answer and the other two formed up. Alexandria blew a kiss to Brutus as Julius dug his heels into the horse's flanks and they trotted down the road, the crowd scattering before them.

As they neared Servilia's house, Brutus lost some of the glow Alexandria had imparted. If anything, he was relieved that the relationship between Julius and his mother had ended. But now, seeing his friend's eager expression, he groaned inwardly. He should have known Julius wouldn't give up so easily.

'Are you sure?' Brutus asked him as they dismounted at the door and passed the horses into the hands of her slaves.

'I am,' Julius replied, striding in.

As consul, he could go where he pleased in the city, but all four of them were known to the house in various fashions and Octavian and Domitius paused in an outer chamber to say their own goodbyes to their favourites while they had the chance. Brutus threw himself onto a long couch and settled down to wait. He alone of them had never visited the house for anything except to see his mother. There was something vaguely incestuous about the idea and he ignored the interest of the girls she kept there. Anyway, there was Alexandria, he told himself virtuously.

Julius strode through the corridors to Servilia's private rooms. What would he say to her? They had not spoken in

months, but there was a magic to leaving, a lack of conse-
quence that might help them find some sort of friendship, at
least.

His spirits lifted as he saw her. She wore a dark blue wrap
that left her shoulders bare and he smiled as he saw his black
pearl set in gold against the first gentle swell of her breasts.
Alexandria deserved her reputation, he thought.

'I'm leaving, Servilia,' he said, walking towards her. 'For
Gaul. I was at the gate when I thought of you.'

He thought he saw a smile touch her mouth as he reached
her and took heart from it. She had never looked so beautiful
as she did then, and he knew he would have no difficulty
remembering her face on the long march ahead. He took her
hands in his and pressed them, looking into her eyes.

'Why don't you come?' he said. 'I could have the best carriage
in Rome brought to the column. There's a Roman settlement
in the south of Gaul and you could be with me.'

'To save you finding your own whores, Julius?' she said
softly. 'Are you worried what you'll do without a woman so far
from home?'

He gaped at her, seeing a cold hardness that was almost
frightening in its intensity.

'I don't understand you,' he said.

She pulled her hands back from him and he swayed. He was
close enough to smell her perfume and it was maddening. Not
to be able to touch her after every inch had been his. He felt
anger surge in him.

'You are cruel, Servilia,' he muttered and she laughed at him.

'Do you know how many jilted lovers I have seen shouting
in this house? Consuls as well, Julius, or do you think they are
too mighty for such a display? Whatever it is you wanted from
me, it is not here. Do you understand?'

Somewhere behind her, Julius heard a man's voice call out.
He tensed.

'Crassus? Is he here?'

Servilia took a step forward, pushing her hand against his chest. Her teeth bared as she spoke and her voice had lost all of the softness he loved.

'It is no business of yours whom I see, Julius.'

Julius lost his temper, his hands clenching in impotent rage. In his passion, he thought of snatching the pearl from her neck and she moved back from him as if she sensed it.

'You'll be his whore now? He's closer to your age, at least,' Julius said.

She slapped him hard and he rocked her head back with a blow of his own, following instantly from hers so that the sounds came almost together.

Servilia raked her other hand at his eyes, scoring his cheek with her nails and Julius snarled at her, stepping in to attack. He was blind with fury as she fell back at last from him and then the anger left him empty and panting, his face bitter. A drop of blood fell from his chin where she had marked him. His gaze followed it.

'So this is who you are, Julius,' she said, standing stiffly before him.

He saw her mouth already beginning to swell and shame overwhelmed him.

She sneered. 'I wonder what my son will say when you see him next.' Her eyes glittered with malice and Julius shook his head.

'I would have given you everything, Servilia. Anything you wanted,' he said softly. She walked away from him then, leaving him alone.

Brutus was standing as Julius came back through the outer rooms of the house. Octavian and Domitius were with him and Julius knew from their expressions that they had heard.

Brutus was pale, his eyes dead and Julius felt an involuntary shudder of fear as he looked at his friend.

'You hit her, Julius?' Brutus said.

Julius touched his bloody cheek. 'I will not explain myself to you, even to you,' he replied, beginning to walk past the three men.

Brutus dropped his hand to the gold hilt he had won and Domitius and Octavian touched their own, moving to stand between him and Julius.

'Don't,' Domitius snapped. 'Take a *step* back!'

Brutus broke off his gaze from Julius to the men facing him with such menace.

'Do you really think you could stop me?' he said.

Domitius returned his glare.

'If I have to. Do you think drawing your sword will change anything? What goes on between them is no more your business than it is mine. Let it go.'

Brutus took his hand away from his sword. He opened his mouth to speak and then walked past them all out to the horses, leaping into the saddle and kicking his mount into a canter back towards the gates.

Domitius wiped sweat from his forehead with his hand. He glanced at Octavian and saw the worry there as the young man was caught between forces he could not stand.

'He'll calm down, Octavian, depend on it.'

'The march will sweat it out of him,' Julius said, looking after his friend. He hoped it was true. He touched his cheek again and winced.

'Not the best omen,' he murmured to himself. 'Let's go, gentlemen. I have seen enough of this city to last me for a long time. Once we step across the gate line, we are free of all of it.'

'I hope so,' Domitius replied, but Julius did not hear him.

*　　*　　*

As they trotted towards the Quirinal gate, Brutus was there in its shadow. Julius saw his eyes were bloodshot holes in a murderous expression and he reined in by him.

'I made a mistake going back to her, Brutus,' Julius said, watching him closely. He loved his friend more than anyone in the world, but if his hand moved for the hilt of his gladius, Julius was ready to kick his horse straight at him to spoil an attack. Every muscle of his legs was tense for the action as Brutus looked up.

'The legions are ready to march. It's time,' he said. His eyes were cold and Julius let out a slow breath, words dying in his throat.

'Then lead us out,' he said softly.

Brutus nodded. Without a word, he rode under the gate and out onto the Campus, without looking back. Julius pressed his heels into his horse to follow him.

'Consul!' a shout came from the crowd.

Julius groaned aloud. Was there no end to it? The gate's shadow was so close, beckoning him. With a grim expression, he watched a group of men run up to the horses. Herminius the moneylender was at their head and as Julius recognised him, he eyed the gate with real longing.

'Sir, I'm glad I caught you. You cannot be meaning to leave the city without making good on your loans, I am sure?' Herminius said, panting from his exertions.

'Come over here,' Julius said, beckoning to the man. He walked his horse under the shadow of the gate and onto the Campus and Herminius came with him, uncomprehending.

Julius looked down at the man.

'Do you see that line, where the gate has left a ridge in the stone?' he asked.

Herminius nodded blankly and Julius smiled.

'Good. Then I can tell you I have spent every last copper coin I could borrow or beg to fit my men for Gaul. The provisions alone and the oxen and asses to carry them cost a small fortune. Salt, leather, iron pigs, gold for bribes, horses, spears, saddles, tents, tools, the list is endless.'

'Sir? Are you saying . . .' Herminius began, comprehension dawning.

'I am saying the moment I crossed that line, my debts were left behind me. My word is good, Herminius. I will pay you when I return, on my honour. But for today, you will not get a coin from me.'

Herminius stiffened in impotent anger. He glanced at the silver armour of the men mounted at Julius' side. Then he sighed and attempted a smile.

'I will look forward to your return, Consul.'

'Of course you will, Herminius,' Julius replied, inclining his head in ironic salute.

When the moneylender had gone, Julius looked back through the gate for the last time. The problems of the city were no longer his, at least for a time.

'Now,' he said, turning to Domitius and Octavian, 'we go north.'

PART TWO

Gaul

CHAPTER TWENTY-TWO

'So why do you stay with him?' Cabera asked. The silver-armoured warrior at his shoulder showed only flashes of the boy he had been and few others in the camp would have dared to ask Brutus such a question.

They watched as Julius climbed oak steps to the archers' wall at the top of the barrier they had built. He was too far away to make out details, though Brutus could see the sun catch the breastplate he wore. Eventually Brutus looked away, then glanced at Cabera sharply as if he had remembered his presence.

'Look at him,' he replied. 'Less than two years ago he left Spain with nothing and now he is a consul with a blank mandate from the Senate. Who else could have brought me to this place with my own legion to command? Who else would you have me follow?'

His voice was bitter and Cabera feared for the two men he had known as boys. He had heard the details of Julius' parting from Servilia, though her son had never spoken of it. He longed

249

to ask Brutus, if only to judge the damage it had caused.

'He is your oldest friend,' Cabera said and Brutus seemed to stir himself at the words.

'And I am his sword. When I look calmly at what he has done, it staggers me, Cabera. Are they fools in Rome not to see his ambition? Julius told me of the bargain he made with them and I still can't believe it. Does Pompey think he had the best of it, I wonder? The man may have the city, but he sits like a tenant waiting for the owner to come home. The people know it. You saw the crowds that came out to the Campus to see us off. Pompey must be a fool if he thinks Julius will be satisfied with anything less than a crown.'

He broke off then, looking around automatically to see if anyone was within hearing. The two men leaned against the fortification that had taken months to build. Twenty miles of wall and earth and never less than the height of three tall men. It towered over the river Rhone and dominated its course around the northern border of the Roman province. It was as solid a barrier as the Alps to the east.

Enough stone and iron had been gathered on the wall to sink any army that tried to cross the river. The legions were confident as they maintained their watch, though not a man there believed Julius would be satisfied with a defence, not with the document he had brought.

Julius had shown it to the praetor of the tiny Roman province that crouched at the foot of the Alps and the man had paled as he read, touching a reverent finger to the seal of the Senate. He had never seen such a vaguely worded command and could only bow his head as he considered the implications. Pompey and Crassus had not quibbled over the details; indeed, Brutus knew Julius had dictated the letter to Adàn and then sent it to them for their seals and the Senate vote. It was brief and complete in the powers it gave Julius in Gaul and every legionary with him knew it.

Cabera rubbed the loose muscles on the side of his face and Brutus looked at him in sympathy. After healing Domitius, the old man had suffered a weakness that left his face slack on one side and half his body almost useless. He would never draw a bow again and on the march across the Alps he had been carried in a litter by the men of the Tenth. He had never complained. Brutus thought that only the old man's intense curiosity kept him alive. He simply would not die while there were things to see and Gaul was as wild and strange to him as to any of the others.

'Are you in pain?' Brutus asked.

Cabera shrugged as best as he was able and dropped his hand from his face. One eyelid drooped as he returned the look and occasionally he would dab at the left corner of his mouth to clean it of spittle before it could fall. The gesture had become a part of his life.

'I am never better, beloved general of Rome, whom I knew as a snot-faced little boy. Never better, though I would like to see the view from the top and may need someone to carry me up. My weakness is upon me and the climb calls for a pair of strong legs.'

Brutus stood. 'I was going to go myself, now that the Helvetii are gathering on the far bank. When they hear Julius will not let them through our little province, there may be an interesting scene. Up, old man. Gods, you are no weight at all.'

Cabera suffered himself to be lifted onto Brutus' back, the general's powerful arms holding his legs tight while he kept his own grip with his right arm. The other dangled uselessly.

'It is the quality of the burden you must consider, Brutus, not the weight,' he said and though the words were blurred by his illness, Brutus understood and smiled.

Julius stood at the top of the rampart, looking across the fast-running water of the Rhone, churned white in places by the force of the spring flood. On the other side of the wide river, the horizon was filled with people: men, women and children. Some sat and dangled their feet in the water as if they were contemplating nothing more serious than an idle afternoon. The children and the elderly were dressed in simple clothes, belted or drawn with cord. Amongst them, he saw hair of yellow and red as well as the more common brown. They drove oxen and asses along with them, carrying the vast amount of food and supplies needed to keep an army of that size on the march. Julius understood their difficulties, considering the problems he had found in feeding the legions under his own command. With so many hungry mouths, it simply was not possible to stay in one place for long and every living thing would be stripped out of the lands they passed through, depleting the stocks for generations. The Helvetii left poverty in their wake.

Their soldiers stood out, wearing some sort of dark leather armour. They moved amongst the crowd, calling to those who stepped too close to the river. Julius watched as one drew a blade and used the flat to clear a space for the boat they were bringing through. It was a chaotic scene and Julius could hear the notes of a tune carry over the cool air, the musician hidden from view in the mass.

The Helvetii lowered the boat with a rhythmic chanting and held it steady in the shallows while a team of rowers took their places. Even with three men to a side, Julius saw they would have to work hard against a current that threatened to sweep them downriver. The idea of an invasion to follow it was ludicrous and there was no tension amongst the Romans who watched them.

Even a rough estimate by centuries was impossible. Julius had been told the Helvetii had burnt their land behind them to come south and he didn't doubt it. Every one of the vast tribe had left their homes and unless they could be stopped, their path lay right through the narrow Roman province at the base of the Alps.

'I have never seen such a migration,' Julius said, almost to himself.

The Roman officer at his side glanced at him as he spoke. He had welcomed the legions Julius brought with him, especially the veterans of the Tenth. Some of those in the trading outpost had resented the shift in authority that Caesar had brought, but for others it was like a sudden immersion in the energy of their old city. When they talked amongst themselves, it was with restrained glee and a new confidence in their dealings. No more would they have to suffer the scorn of Gaulish merchants and know they were tolerated but never accepted. With only one legion, the outpost was barely acknowledged by Rome and without the trade in wine, the province might have been abandoned completely. Those who still dreamed of promotion and a career welcomed Caesar with open arms and none more so than their commander, Mark Antony.

When Julius had presented him with the orders from the Senate, the general could not help the slow grin that spread across his face.

'At last we will see action, then,' he had said to Julius. 'I have written so many letters and I was beginning to lose hope.'

Julius had been prepared for dismay, even the threat of disobedience. He had come into the Roman town with a face like thunder to impose his will, but at this response, the tension had vanished and he had laughed aloud at Mark Antony's honest pleasure. They weighed each other up and both men found something to like. Julius had listened in fascination to the general's summary of the region and the uneasy truce with local tribes. Mark Antony held nothing back of the problems they faced, but he spoke with a deep insight and Julius had included him immediately in his councils.

If the others resented the sudden rise of the new man, it did not show. Mark Antony had been in the province for four years and painted a detailed picture of the web of alliances and feuds that were the mire of trade and the bane of efficient administration.

'It is not so much a migration as a march of conquest, sir,' Mark Antony said. 'Any smaller tribe will lose its women, its grain, everything.' He was in awe of the man Rome had sent, but he had been told to speak freely and he enjoyed the new status it had given him, especially amongst his own men.

'Then they cannot be turned?' Julius asked, watching the shifting mass on the far shore.

Mark Antony looked down from the rampart to where the legions were arrayed in full battle order. A pleasurable shudder touched him at the thought of the strength represented in those squares. As well as the ten thousand men Julius had brought, another three legions had been summoned from the north of Italy. As nothing else could, it demonstrated the new power Julius had been granted that he had only to send riders carrying copies of his orders for them to return with fifteen thousand soldiers at a forced march over the Alps.

'If they are turned, they will starve to death this winter, sir. My scouts reported four hundred villages in flames, with all their winter grain. They know they cannot go back and they will fight all the harder as a result.'

Brutus reached the platform behind them, letting Cabera down onto it so that he could grip the wooden railing with his good arm and watch the proceedings. Brutus saluted as he approached Julius, more than usually conscious of the appearance of discipline in front of the newcomer. He could not be said to like Mark Antony, exactly. Something about the way he seemed so completely in accord with Julius' aims and ambitions struck a false note with Brutus, though he had said nothing rather than have it interpreted as jealousy. In fact, he felt a

254

touch of that very emotion at seeing the two men talking as easily as old friends while they watched the army of the Helvetii on the far bank. Brutus frowned as Mark Antony made a humorous comment about the vast host and both he and Julius appeared to be trying to outdo the other in studied casualness.

It did not help that Mark Antony was such a big, hearty man, the sort that amused Julius on the rare occasion that he found them. Brutus knew Julius enjoyed nothing as much as the booming laugh and courage of men like his uncle Marius, and Mark Antony seemed to fit that type as if he had known the man personally. He stood a head taller than Julius and his nose shouted to the world that he was a man of ancient Roman blood. It dominated his face under heavy brows and unless he was laughing, in repose he looked naturally stern and dignified. At the slightest prompt, he would mention his family line and Mark Antony seemed to believe he was of noble blood simply by the number of ancestors he could name.

No doubt Sulla would have loved the man, Brutus thought irritably. Mark Antony was full of the things that could be achieved now Julius had arrived, yet somehow he had not managed to do any of them on his own. Brutus wondered if the noble Roman realised what Julius would have achieved in his place, one legion or not.

Putting these thoughts aside, Brutus leaned on the railing himself and looked out as the boat approached the Roman side and the oarsmen leapt out into the shallow water to drag it clear of the river. They stood in the very shadow of the wall the Romans had built to stop them. Even with their numbers, Brutus didn't think they would try to break the Roman line.

'They must see we could sink every boat with spears and stones before they can land. It would be suicide to attack,' Julius said.

'And if they go in peace?' Mark Antony asked, without taking his eyes from the messengers that stood aside from their oarsmen below.

Julius shrugged. 'Then I will have demonstrated Roman authority over them. One way or another, I will have my foothold in this country.'

Brutus and Cabera both turned to look at the man they knew and saw a savage pleasure in his face as he stood tall on the rampart to hear the words of the Helvetii.

They had seen a similar expression when Mark Antony had addressed the first council of generals months before.

'I am glad you are here, gentlemen,' Mark Antony had said. 'We are about to be overrun.'

Julius had wanted a wild land to win, Brutus thought to himself. The Helvetii were only one of the tribes in that region, never mind the entire country that Julius dreamed of taking for Rome. Yet the dark moods of Spain could never be imagined in the man who stood with them on the ramparts. They could all feel it and Cabera closed his eyes as his senses were cast loose against his will into the tumbling roads of the future.

The old man slumped and would have fallen had Brutus not caught him. No one else moved as the messengers spoke and Julius turned to his interpreter to hear the words in halting Latin. Out of sight of the riders, he grinned to himself, then stood to face them, both hands on the wide railing.

'No,' he called down. 'You shall not pass.'

Julius looked at Mark Antony.

'If they march west around the Rhone before striking south, which tribes lie in their path?'

'The Aedui are directly west of us, so they would suffer most, though the Ambarri and Allobroges . . .' Mark Antony began.

'Which of those is the richest?' Julius interrupted.

Mark Antony hesitated. 'The Aedui are reputed to have vast herds of cattle and . . .'

'Summon their leader to me with the fastest riders and guarantees of safety,' Julius said, looking back over the railing. Below, the boat was already pulling for the far shore, still close enough for him to see the anger of the men in it.

Two nights later, the small fort was quiet, though Julius could hear the tramp of feet as the watch changed on the walls. New barracks had been built for the soldiers he had brought from Rome, but the three legions from Ariminum still slept in their tents in fortified camps. Julius didn't intend building anything more permanent for them. He hoped it would not be necessary.

He waited impatiently as his words were relayed to the chief of the Aedui through the interpreter Mark Antony had supplied. The man seemed to ramble on far longer than Julius thought was justified, but he had decided not to tell them Adàn could speak their language, preferring to keep that advantage secret. His Spanish scribe had been startled when they had first heard the words of the Gauls. His people spoke a variation of the same tongue, enough for him to understand most of the conversations. Julius wondered if they had been one nation at some time in the far past, some nomadic tribe from distant lands who had settled Gaul and Spain while Rome was still a small village amongst seven hills.

Adàn attended every meeting after that, masking his listening with laborious copying out of Julius' dictated notes and letters. When they were alone, Julius would question him closely and his memory was usually faultless.

Julius glanced at the studious young Spaniard as the interpreter repeated the danger of the Helvetii in what must have been endless detail. The leader of the Aedui was typical of his race, a dark-haired man with black eyes and a hard, fleshless face, partly hidden by a growth of beard that shone with oil. The Aedui claimed to have no king, but Mhorbaine was their chief magistrate, elected rather than born.

Julius tapped the fingers of one hand on the other as Mhorbaine answered and the interpreter paused to consider his translation.

'The Aedui are willing to accept your aid in repelling the Helvetii from their borders,' the interpreter said at last.

Julius barked a laugh that made Mhorbaine jump.

'"Are willing"?' he said with amusement. 'Tell him I will save his people from destruction if they pay in grain and meat. My men have to be fed. Thirty thousand men need more than two hundred cattle slaughtered each day, as a minimum. I will accept the equivalent in game or mutton, as well as grain, bread, oil, fish and spices. Without supplies, I do not move.'

The negotiation began in earnest then, delayed at every stage by the slow translation. Julius ached to throw the interpreter out and have Adàn's quick wits in his place, but held his patience as the hours stretched on and the moon rose orange over the mountains behind them. Mhorbaine too seemed to be losing his patience, and when they were all waiting for the interpreter to complete another hesitant phrase, the Gaul chopped his hand in the air, speaking in clear Latin, with an accent of Rome.

'Enough of this fool. I understand you well enough without him.'

Julius broke into laughter at the revelation. 'He murders my language, I know that. Who taught you the words of Rome?'

Mhorbaine shrugged. 'Mark Antony sent men to all the tribes when he first came. Most of them were killed and sent back to him, but I kept mine. This miserable creature learned from the same man, though badly. He has no ear for languages, but he was all I had to offer.'

The negotiations went faster after that and Julius was amused by the Gaul's attempt to conceal his knowledge. He wondered if Mhorbaine guessed at Adàn's function at the meeting. It was probable. The Aedui leader was sharply intelligent and Julius could feel the man's cool assessment of him right to the end.

When it was finished, Julius stood to clasp Mhorbaine by the shoulder. There was muscle there, underneath the woollen cloth. The man was more a battle-leader than a magistrate, at least as Julius understood the role. He ushered Mhorbaine out to the horses and went back in to where Adàn stood to meet him.

'Well?' Julius said. 'Did I miss anything useful before Mhorbaine lost his patience?'

Adàn smiled at his amusement. 'Mhorbaine asked the interpreter if you had the strength to turn the Helvetii and he said he thought it likely. That's all you did not hear. They have no choice if they do not wish to see their herds swallowed by the Helvetii.'

'Perfect. I am transformed from a foreign invader every bit as dangerous as the Helvetii, to a Roman answering a call for help from a beleaguered tribe. Put that in the reports back to the city. I want my people to think well of what we do here.'

'Is that important?' Adàn asked.

Julius snorted. 'You have no idea how important. The citizens do not want to know how countries are won. They prefer to think of foreign armies surrendering to our moral superiority rather than our strength. I am forced to tread carefully here, even with my orders from the Senate. If the powers shift in Rome, I can still be recalled and there will always be enemies who would delight in seeing me disgraced. Send the reports with enough coin to have them read on every street and in the forum. Let the people know how we are progressing in their name.'

Julius paused, his amusement fading as he thought of the problems he faced.

'Now all we have to do is defeat the largest army I have ever seen and there really will be good news to send back to Rome,' he said. 'Summon Brutus, Mark Antony, Octavian, Domitius, all of my council. Renius too, his advice is always sound. Tell Brutus to send out his scouts. I want to know where the Helvetii are and how they are organised. Quickly, lad. We have a battle to plan and I want to be on the march by dawn.'

CHAPTER TWENTY-THREE

Julius lay on his stomach to watch the Helvetii move across the plain. Even as he concentrated, some part of him noted the lush greenness of the land. It made the soil of Rome look poor in comparison. Instead of the barren mountains of the south he knew, where farmers scratched a living, he saw vast rolling plains of good earth and hungered for it with all the primitive desire of a man who had worked his own crops. Gaul could feed an empire.

The light was beginning to fade and he clenched his fist in excitement as he heard the notes of wailing horns carried to him on the breeze. The great column was halting for the night. One of his scouts came to a skidding stop by him, panting as he too stretched out.

'It looks like all of them, sir. I couldn't see any sort of rearguard or reserve. They're moving fast, but they must rest tonight, or they'll start leaving bodies on the plain.'

'They're stopping now,' Julius said. 'Can you see how the soldiers are settling into groups around the core? Greek spear phalanx, it looks like. I wonder if they came to it on their own, or if their ancestors ever passed through that land. If I have the chance, I'll ask one of them.'

He scanned the plain, considering his alternatives. A mile behind him in the woods, he had thirty thousand legionaries ready to descend on the Helvetii, but after forcing a march of almost forty miles to intercept the tribe, the men were exhausted. Julius felt frustration that he had been unable to bring the great war ballistae and scorpion bows that formed such a part of the legions' power. The plain would have been perfect for them, but until he cut roads through the land, they stayed in pieces on the carts he'd brought from Rome.

'I've never seen so many warriors,' the scout whispered, awed by the army they faced. The Helvetii were too far away to hear, but the sheer size of the migration was oppressive and Julius pitched his voice as low to reply.

'I'd guess eighty thousand, but I can't be sure amongst the followers,' he replied.

It was too many to send the legions in a straight attack, even if they were not worn down by the march.

'Bring Brutus to me,' he ordered.

It was not long before he heard running footsteps and Brutus was there with him, crouching in the damp leaves.

The Helvetii had marched through a wide valley that led into the lands of the Aedui. They had forced a hard pace to skirt the river and Julius was impressed at their stamina and organisation as the night camp began to form on the plain. If they struck any deeper into Aedui lands, they would be into heavy forest and the legions' advantages would be lost. These were not the wide-spaced woods he knew from Rome, but dense undergrowth that would trap horses and make any sort of organised fighting impossible. Sheer numbers would carry the day then, and the Helvetii had a host of warriors, with nowhere to go but onward.

The tribe had burnt the first village they came to on the border of the Aedui and the scouts reported no one left alive. Women and animals had been taken into the column and the rest butchered. Village by village, they would cross the land like locusts unless Julius could catch them on the plain. He thanked his gods that they were not pushing on through the night. No doubt their numbers made them overconfident, though even with his legions ready, it was difficult to see how to attack so many and win.

Julius turned to Brutus.

'You see that hill to the west?' He pointed to a solid crag of layered green and grey in the dim distance. Brutus nodded. 'It's a strong position. Take the Tenth and Third to the crest, ready for dawn. The Helvetii will see the threat and they cannot leave you there to harry them. Take the archers from Ariminum, but keep them far back from the front. The bowmen will be better used on your hill than on the plain.'

He smiled grimly and clapped Brutus on the shoulder with his hand.

'These tribesmen have never fought legions, Brutus. They will see a mere ten thousand facing them as the sun comes up. You will educate them.'

Brutus looked at him. The sun was already setting and its light was reflected in Julius' fierce gaze.

'It will be dark before I reach it,' Brutus replied. It was the closest he would come to questioning an order with the scouts listening all around them.

Julius seemed not to notice his reservations, continuing quickly, 'You must have silence as you move up. When they see you and charge, I will hit them from the rear. Go quickly.'

Brutus slithered back until he was clear and could run for his men.

'On your feet, lads,' he said as he came to the first ranks of the Tenth. 'You won't get much sleep tonight.'

*　　*　　*

262

As dawn approached, Julius was back looking over the plain. The sun came up behind him and there was a grey light long before it rose over the mountains. The Helvetii began to move into their marching order and Julius watched as the warriors bullied the other castes onto their feet. Those with swords and spears had status, Julius could see. They did not carry supplies themselves, remaining free to fight and run. Julius watched for the moment when they would see the legions arrayed on the hill and the time seemed to stretch endlessly.

Behind him, Mark Antony waited with his legion and three others, cold and grim without breakfast or fires to warm them. It hardly seemed enough to tackle such a vast army, but Julius could think of nothing else to alter the balance.

A horse galloped up from behind and Julius turned in fury to wave the man down before he was seen. He rose to a crouch as he saw the scout's pale features and when the man slid from his saddle, he could not speak at first for panting.

'Sir, there is an enemy force on the hill to the west! A large number of them.'

Julius looked back at the Helvetii in the dim light. They were getting ready to decamp, with no sign of panic or distress. Had they spotted his scouts and prepared a flanking position? His respect for the tribe increased a notch. And where was Brutus? The two forces clearly hadn't met in the darkness or the sound of battle would have been heard for miles. Had he climbed the wrong hill in the night? Julius swore aloud, furious with the setback. He had no way of communicating with his missing legions and until they showed themselves, he dared not attack.

'I'll have his balls,' he promised, then turned to the men at his side.

'No horns or signals. Just fall back. Pass the word to regroup at the stream.'

As they moved away, Julius heard the tinny blaring of horns as the Helvetii began to move on. The frustration was appalling and the thought of having to take them in the thick forests was nothing like the crushing victory he had hoped for.

Brutus waited for the sun to banish the dark shadows on the hill. He had the Tenth arranged before his Third Gallica, depending on their greater experience to stand anything the Helvetii could send against them. In addition, a part of his own legion were from Gaul. Julius had said a legion could be raised in less than a year. Living, working and fighting together bound men stronger than anything, but there was always the nagging suspicion of what could happen if those men were ordered to fight their own people. When Brutus had asked them about the Helvetii, they had only shrugged at him, as if there could be no conflict. None of them were from that tribe and those that had come to Rome for gold seemed to claim no special loyalty to those they had left behind. They had been the sort of mercenaries who lived for nothing except pay and found companionship only amongst their own kind. Brutus knew the regular silver and food of the legions would be a dream for some of them, but still he had placed the Tenth to take the first charge.

Though he was unutterably weary after the climb, he had to admit Julius had an eye for good land. If anything, Brutus regretted leaving the extraordinarii back in the camp, but he could not have known the ascent would be easy, with only a few sprains and one broken arm from a bad fall in the darkness. Three men had lost their swords and now carried daggers, but they had crested the hill before dawn and gone over to the far slope without losing a single man. The legionary with the broken arm had strapped it to his chest and would fight left-handed. He had scorned being sent back and pointed to Ciro in the front rank of the Tenth, saying that the big man could throw his spears for him.

In the first glimmers of grey light, Brutus sent whispered orders to dress the formation that stretched across the slopes. Even the veterans of the Tenth looked a little ragged after finding their positions in darkness and his own legion needed the staffs of their optios to create order. They loosened the ties on their spears as he watched and with four to a man, Brutus knew they would destroy any charge sent against them. The Helvetii carried oval shields, but the heavy spears would pin them to the ground, shields and all.

The sun rose behind the mountains as the Helvetii marched unaware towards their position. Brutus felt the old excitement build as he waited for their soldiers to see the Tenth and Third looking down at them. He grinned in anticipation of the first rays of light and when it came, he laughed aloud at the sight. The sun spread a beam across them from the peaks. Ten thousand helmets and sets of armour went from dull grey to gold in a few minutes. The yellow horsehair plumes of the centurions seemed to glow and the column of the Helvetii staggered below on the plain as men pointed and shouted a warning.

For the tribe, it was as if the legion had appeared out of nothing and yet they were not without courage. As soon as the initial shock had faded, they saw the small army that clung to the slopes and almost as one they roared defiance, filling the valley.

'There must be half a million of them. I swear by Mars, there must,' Brutus whispered.

He saw the fighting phalanxes swarm to the front, bristling with spears as they began to accelerate over the ground between the armies. Their front ranks carried wide shields to batter the enemy, but the formations would never survive the broken ridges of the hill. They raced across the shifting scree like wolves and Brutus shook his head in amazement at the numbers coming towards him.

'Archers – range!' Brutus cried, watching as four arrows flew high and marked the outermost limit of their shots. He had only three hundred from the Ariminum legions and didn't know how skilled they were. Against unprotected men, their fire could be devastating, but he doubted they would be more than an irritation to the Helvetii under their shields.

'Ready spears!' he bellowed.

The Tenth gathered their four, checking the points one last time. They would not aim them, but launch the heavy iron-headed weapons high into the air, so that they would be dropping almost vertically at the moment of impact. It called for skill, but it was their trade and they were experts.

'Range!' Brutus shouted.

He watched as Ciro tied a red cloth around the butt of one of his spears and heaved it into flight with a grunt. None of them could match the big man's distance and as it slammed quivering into the turf, Brutus had his outermost point marked, fifty paces short of the arrows further down the rocky slope. When the Helvetii charge crossed those lines, they would be running through a hail of missiles. As they pushed past Ciro's spear, forty thousand more would be launched in less than ten heartbeats.

The Helvetii howled as they began to pound up the slope and a dawn breeze skimmed the hillside, blowing dust off the plains.

'Archers!' Brutus called and, ten ranks back, the lines of bowmen fired with smooth skill until their quivers were empty. Brutus watched the flight of arrows as they fell into the yelling men below, still out of range of the more deadly spears. Many of the shafts were deflected as the tribesmen raised their shields and ran on, leaving only a few bodies behind them. First blood had been taken. Brutus hoped Julius was ready.

Julius was in the saddle when he heard the tribe roar. He jerked his horse round viciously, looking for the scout who had brought him the news.

'Where is the man who told me the enemy were on the hill?' he shouted, his stomach suddenly dropping away in a hollow feeling.

The call went round and the man came trotting up on his horse. He was very young and pink around the cheeks in the morning cold. Julius glared at him in terrible suspicion.

'The enemy you reported. Tell me what you saw,' Julius said.

The young scout stammered nervously under the stare of his general. 'There were thousands up on the hill, sir. In the dark, I could not be sure of numbers, but there were many of them, sir. An ambush.'

Julius closed his eyes for a moment.

'Arrest that man and hold him for punishment. Those were our legions, you *stupid* bastard.'

Julius wheeled his horse, thinking furiously. They had not travelled more than a few miles from the plain. It might not be too late. He untied his helmet from the saddle horn and pulled it roughly over his face, turning the metal features to face the gathered men.

'The Tenth and Third Gallica are without support. We will march at our fastest pace to attack the Helvetii. Straight in, gentlemen. Straight in, now.'

Brutus waited as the Helvetii streamed past the ranging spear until it could not be seen. If he gave the order too early, the Third behind him could throw short. Too late and the crushing damage of seeing an attack destroyed would be wasted as the front ranks were passed over.

'Spears!' Brutus cried at his best volume, launching his own into the air.

Ten thousand arms jerked forward and then they were reaching for the second at their feet. Before the first wave landed, Brutus knew the Tenth would have two more in the air. The

Third were slower, but only by a little, inspired by the example of the veterans and the nervous fear of the attack.

He had judged it perfectly and the different ranks of the Tenth and Third sent spears in a carpet of whistling iron onto the enemy. Not just the front rank, but most of the first ten went from running warriors to broken corpses in moments. Hundreds died from the first wave, and the men who survived could see the black launch of the second coming at them, even as they urged each other on.

There was no way to avoid the death from the air. The spears moved in flight to fall in groups or widely apart. One man could be struck with a cluster of them, or a whole charging line destroyed bar one, miraculously untouched. Though the Helvetii ducked under their shields, the heavy iron heads punched through wood and bone into the soft ground beneath. Brutus saw many tribesmen struggle to free their shields, sometimes pinned to others through the overlapping edges. Many of them still lived, but could not rise as their blood poured from them.

Brutus watched as the attack stuttered to a stop. The third strike did less destruction and they pulled back from the last, running wildly from the men on the hill. The Tenth cheered as the Gauls turned and Brutus looked east for Julius. If he sent in his legions at that moment, they could very well panic the Helvetii into a rout. There was no sign of him.

The Helvetii re-formed at the edge of the range and began to advance once more over the bodies of their finest.

'These men have never fought a legion of Rome!' Brutus called to the men around him.

Some of them smiled, but their eyes were on the advancing hordes that made the broken bodies vanish as they climbed the hill again. A few of the legion spears were tugged from corpses and thrown up at the Tenth, but against the rise of the land, they fell short.

'Ready swords!' Brutus ordered and for the first time both legions drew their blades and held them high for the sun to catch. Brutus looked around him and raised his head proudly. Let them climb, he thought.

As they began to pant and blow, the phalanx formations broke apart as the Helvetii neared the Roman lines. The Tenth waited patiently for them, each man standing amongst friends he had known for years. There was no fear in the Roman lines. They stood in perfect formation with the cornicens ready to rotate the front ranks as they tired. They carried swords of hard iron and all along the faces of his men Brutus could see eager anticipation. Some of the legionaries even beckoned to the warriors, urging them on. In a flash of insight, Brutus saw them as the Helvetii did, a wall of men and shields without gaps.

The first of the Helvetii met the Tenth and were cut down with efficient ferocity. The hard Roman blades chopped into them all along the line, cutting arms and heads free in single blows. The long spears of the Helvetii could not pierce the Roman shields and Brutus exulted at the toll.

He stood in the third rank of the right and raised his head from the fascination of the carnage to view the position. There was a mass of men struggling to support their comrades and even more were streaming around the hill to flank them. He felt fresh sweat break out on his skin as he looked for Julius once again. The sun was in his eyes at that angle, but he squinted against the glare to the tree line.

'Come on, come *on*,' he said aloud.

Though it would be some time before the Helvetii could surround his men, if they reached the crest behind him the Tenth and Third would have no line of retreat. He groaned aloud in frustration as he saw the small number the Helvetii had left to guard the women and children. An attack at the rear would cause instant panic amongst the warriors.

The sheer numbers of the charge began to cut gaps in the front rank of the Tenth. The velites were fast and lightly armoured and though they could fight for two hours without a rest, Brutus thought of sending the heavy men in to keep them fresh for the retreat he may have to order. If Julius did not come quickly, Brutus knew he would have to take the legions back to the crest of the hill, fighting every inch of the way. It would be worse when they were followed down naked to the blades of the tribe behind.

Brutus looked over the heads of his men, his heart pounding with anger. If he survived the retreat, he swore Julius would pay for the destruction of the Tenth. He knew almost all of them after the years in Spain and every death was like a blow.

Suddenly, in the distance, he saw the silvered lines of Julius' legions surging onto the plain and he shouted with pleasure and relief. The Helvetii of the column blew horns in warning and Brutus saw their phalanx reserves go out to meet the new threat. More horns sounded on the hill as the tribe halted and looked back at the plain. Brutus roared at them in incoherent triumph as they began to fall back from the Tenth, a gap opening between the armies. There would be no flanking movement then, with every warrior desperate to protect his spoils and his people.

'Tenth and Third!' Brutus shouted, over and over to his left and right. They were ready for his orders and he raised his arm to sweep down towards the plain.

'Close formation! Archers gather shafts as you find them! Charge Tenth! Charge Third!'

Ten thousand men moved as one at his word and Brutus thought his chest would burst with pride.

The Helvetii had no cavalry and Julius sent the extraordinarii out to hammer their lines as they tried desperately to re-form to repel the new attack. As Julius marched with Mark Antony, he watched Octavian guide the lines of horsemen along an oblique angle to the Helvetii phalanxes. At full gallop, each man reached down to the long tube of leather at his leg and drew a thin javelin, releasing it with crushing accuracy. The Helvetii roared and brandished their shields, but Octavian would not close with them until the last spears had gone. By the time Julius reached the rear of the column, the reserves were in chaos and it was no difficulty to clear the last of them.

At his order, the cornicens sounded the command to double their speed and twenty thousand legionaries broke into the dog trot that could carry them for miles, straight at the enemy. The vast column of the Helvetii followers watched them in silence as they streamed by without even a call. There was no danger from them and Julius thought furiously how he should make the best use of the position.

The warriors who had attacked the hill were in full panicked flight back to the column by then and Julius smiled as he saw the shining squares of the Tenth and Third coming behind them, their tight formations making them look like silver plates in the dawn sun. The hill was littered with bodies and Julius saw the Helvetii had lost all direction, their phalanxes forgotten. Their fear was weakening them and Julius wanted it to increase. He considered calling the extraordinarii back to harass the column, but at that moment Octavian signalled a charge and the mass of horses formed into a great wedge that hammered into the running warriors. Julius waited until the extraordinarii had disengaged and were wheeling to go in again before he sent the signal to hold their position.

'Ready spears!' Julius called. He hefted his own in his hand, feeling the solid weight of the wooden stock. Already, he could see the faces of the warriors running at him. There would barely be time for more than one throw before the armies met.

'Spears!' he shouted, heaving his own into the air.

271

The ranks around him blackened the sky with iron and the front lines of the Helvetii were battered down. Before they could recover, the first legions met their charge and smashed through.

The centurions behind kept up the barrage as each group came into range and Julius roared as they went unstoppably deep into the mass of tribesmen. There were so many of them! His legionaries crushed anything that stood in their path and the advance was so fast that Julius felt a stab of worry that he was inviting a flanking manoeuvre. The cornicens blew his warning to widen the line and behind him the Ariminum legions spread out to envelop the enemy. The extraordinarii moved out with them, waiting to attack.

A splash of blood caught Julius in the mouth as he slowed and he spat quickly, rubbing his hand across his face. He called for second spears to be thrown in waves of ten ranks at a time, not even seeing where the iron spikes landed. It was a dangerous practice, as nothing damaged morale more than the weapons falling short into the Roman lines, but Julius needed every advantage to reduce the huge force of the tribe.

The Helvetii fought with desperate ferocity, trying to get back to their main column, now unprotected behind the Roman legions. Those who were not in the front lines milled like bees at the edges, spreading further out onto the plain. Julius countered with a wider and then wider front, until he had his four legions in a line only six deep, sweeping all before them.

For a time, Julius could not see much of the battle. He fought as a foot soldier with the others and wished he had stayed on some high outcrop to direct the fighting.

Brutus spread the Tenth and Third wide to cut off a retreat and both legions hacked their way through while the sun rose and baked them. Boys ran amongst the ranks with leather bags of water for those who had drunk the ration they carried and still they fought on.

Julius ordered the last two spears his men carried to be

thrown blind. On the flat ground, many of them were sent back as fast as they were thrown, but the soft iron heads had bent on impact and they flew poorly, with little strength. Julius saw a man only feet from him reach up to bat one away as it spun at him and Julius heard his arm crack. He began to realise the Helvetii would fight to the last man and summoned the most senior of the Ariminum generals to him.

General Bericus arrived looking calm and fresh, as if they were engaged in nothing more difficult than a training manoeuvre.

'General,' Julius said, 'I want you to take a thousand men and attack the column behind us.'

Bericus stood slightly stiffer at the order. 'Sir, I do not believe them to be a threat. I saw only women and children as we passed.'

Julius nodded, wondering if he would regret having such a decent man leading his soldiers.

'Those are my orders, General. However, you have my permission to make as much noise as you can during the disengage.'

For a moment, Bericus looked blank, then his lips twitched in understanding.

'We'll shout like maniacs, sir,' he said, saluting.

Julius watched him go and called a messenger to him.

'Tell the extraordinarii they are free to attack as they see fit,' he said.

As soon as Bericus reached his lines, Julius saw them shift as the commands were passed down the chain of authority. In only a short while, two cohorts had detached from the battle and their places in the lines were filled. Julius heard them roar as they turned and began a deliberate march back to attack the column. Bericus had taken horns with him and the cornicens kept up a constant racket until there was not a man on the plain who was not aware of the threat they posed.

273

At first, the warriors of the Helvetii fought with renewed energy, but the extraordinarii had resumed their scything strikes on the wing and Roman discipline held the wild charges of the tribesmen. Suddenly they were despairing, dreading the sight of the legion lines cutting into the naked column.

A distant cheer went up and Julius craned to see the cause. He ordered the maniples to rotate the velites back to the front and went with them, gasping with weariness. How long had they been fighting? The sun seemed to have frozen overhead.

The cheering intensified on the left wing, but though it brought him hope, Julius found himself faced with two men who were using their shields to batter the Roman line. He had a glimpse of a mouth ringed in white spittle before he lunged forward and felt his gladius sink into flesh. The first fell screaming and Mark Antony cut his throat as they marched over him. The second was knocked from his feet by a legionary and Julius heard his ribs crack as the soldier dropped his weight onto a knee, caving in the chest. As the legionary stood, the Helvetii threw down their weapons in a great crash that stunned the ears and stood, panting and dazed. Julius ordered the halt with grim pleasure and looked back over the plain to the mass of bodies left behind them. There was more flesh than grass and only the two Roman cohorts moved over the red ground.

A great low wail went up from the column of followers as they saw the surrender and again Julius heard cheering, recognising it now as the voices of the Tenth and Third. Julius took the bronze horn from the nearest cornicen and blew a falling note to stop Bericus before he could begin his attack. They halted in perfect formation as the sound carried to them and Julius smiled. Whatever else went against him, he could not complain at the quality of the legions he commanded.

Julius paused then, removing his helmet and turning his face into the breeze. He sent the call for centurions and optios to gather the men back into their units. It had to be done quickly and sometimes brutally, if the surrender was to hold. Army tradition held that the slave price of captured enemy soldiers would be shared between the legions, which tended to prevent massacres of those who surrendered. Yet in the battle rage, Julius knew many of his legionaries would think nothing of cutting down an unarmed foe, especially if that man had just wounded them. Julius had the cornicens sound the halt over and over until it penetrated and some semblance of order began to come back to the plain.

Spears and swords were collected and removed from the battlefield, guarded by the extraordinarii as they reassembled. The Helvetii warriors were made to kneel and had their arms tied behind them. Those who asked were given water by the same boys who served the legions and Julius began to gather them into lines of prisoners, moving amongst his men, congratulating where it was due and simply being seen.

The legionaries walked with stiff pride as they surveyed the numbers of prisoners and dead. They knew they had beaten a far larger force and Julius was pleased to see one of his men calling a water boy over to a bound warrior, holding the bronze pipe to his lips for him.

As Julius passed through them, assessing the losses, the Romans stared in the hope of catching his eye and when they were successful they nodded as respectfully as children.

Brutus came cantering up on a horse he had found, its rider amongst the dead.

'What a victory, Julius!' he called, leaping from the saddle.

The soldiers around him gestured and whispered to each other as they recognised his silver armour and Julius grinned at the awe in their faces. He had thought wearing the silver into battle was dangerous, given that the metal was so much softer than good iron, but Brutus had kept it, saying it raised the men's spirits to fight with the best of a generation.

Julius chuckled at the memory.

'I was pleased to see you on the plain. I can't tell you,' Brutus said.

Julius looked sharply at him, sensing the question. A smile played about his lips as he called for the scout to be summoned and Brutus raised his eyebrows when he saw the miserable Roman with his hands tied as tightly as the prisoners. The young man had been forced to march with the legions, an optio's staff thudding into his back every time he slowed. Julius was pleased he had survived and with the glow of victory on him, he decided against having the man whipped as he almost certainly deserved.

'Untie him,' Julius said to the scout's optio, who did so with a swift jerk of a knife. The scout looked as if he was close to tears as he struggled to stand to attention before his general and the winner of the sword tournament in Rome.

'This young gentleman brought me a report that the enemy had taken the hill I ordered you to climb. In the darkness, he mistook two good Roman legions for a mass of tribesmen.'

Brutus broke into a guffaw of delighted amusement.

'You didn't fall back? Julius, that is . . .' he broke off to laugh and Julius turned a mock severe expression on the desolate young scout.

'Have you any idea how difficult it is to build a reputation as a tactical genius if I am seen retreating from my own men?' he asked.

'I am sorry, sir. I thought I heard Gaulish voices,' the scout stammered. He was flushed with confusion.

'Yes, that would have been my lot,' Brutus said, cheerfully. 'That is why you carry a password, son. You should have called before haring home.'

The young scout began to smile in response and Brutus' expression changed instantly.

'Of course, if you'd delayed the attack much longer, I would be taking a skinning knife to you.'

The sickly grin died on the scout's face.

'Three months' pay docked and you scout on foot until your optio is certain you can be trusted with a horse,' Julius added.

The young man breathed out in relief, not daring to look at Brutus as he saluted and left. Julius turned to Brutus and they shared a smile.

'It was a good plan,' Brutus said.

Julius nodded, calling for a horse. As he mounted, he looked over the battlefield, seeing the beginnings of order return as Roman wounds were stitched and splinted and bodies readied for funeral pyres. He would have the worst of the wounded taken back to the Roman province for treatment. The armour of those who had died would be sold off for replacements. The gaps left by dead officers would be filled by promotions from the ranks, signed by his hand. The world was turning the right way up and the heat of the day was beginning to fade.

CHAPTER TWENTY-FOUR

Julius sat on a folding stool in the great tent of the Helvetii king and drank from a golden cup. The mood was light amongst the men he had summoned. The Ariminum generals in particular had been drinking heavily from the king's private stores and Julius had not stopped them. They had earned the right to rest, though the work ahead was still daunting. Julius had not appreciated at first how large a task it would be simply to catalogue the baggage, and the night was loud with the sound of soldiers counting and piling the Helvetii possessions. He had sent Publius Crassus with four cohorts to begin retrieving spears and weapons from the battlefield. It was not a glorious task, but the son of the former consul had gathered his men quickly and without fuss, showing something of his father's ability for organisation.

By the time the sun was edging towards the far west, the spear shafts of the Tenth and Third had been returned to them. Many of the heavy iron heads were twisted into uselessness, but Crassus had filled Helvetii carts with them, ready to be repaired or melted down by the legion smiths. By a twist of fate, one of the cohorts had been commanded by Germinius Cato, promoted after Spain. Julius wondered if the two men ever considered the enmity of their fathers behind their polite salutes.

'Enough grain and dried meat to feed us for months, if it doesn't spoil,' Domitius said with satisfaction. 'The weapons alone are worth a small fortune, Julius. Some of the swords are good iron, and even the bronze ones have hilts worth keeping.'

'Any coin?' Julius asked, eyeing the cup in his hand.

Renius opened a sack at his feet and brought out a few rough-looking discs.

'What passes for it here,' he said. 'A silver and copper mix. Hardly worth anything, though there are chests of them.' Julius took one and held it up to the lamp. The circle of tarnished metal had a piece cut out of it, reaching right to the middle.

'A strange thing. Looks like a bird on the face, though with that slice out of it, I can't be sure.'

The night breeze came into the tent with Brutus and Mark Antony.

'Are you calling the council, Julius?' Brutus asked. Julius nodded and Brutus put his head back out of the flap, shouting for Ciro and Octavian to join them.

'Are the prisoners secure?' Renius asked Brutus.

Mark Antony answered. 'The men are tied, but we don't have nearly enough soldiers to stop the rest of them from leaving in the night if they want to.' He noticed the sack of coins and picked one up.

'Hand stamped?' Julius asked as he saw his interest.

Mark Antony nodded.

'This one is, though the larger towns can produce coins as good as anything you'll see in Rome. Their metalwork is often very beautiful.' He dropped the coin back into Renius' outstretched palm. 'Not these, though. Quite inferior.'

Julius indicated stools for the two men and they accepted the dark wine in the cups from the king's private hoard.

Mark Antony tilted his up and gasped with satisfaction.

'The wine, however, is not inferior at all. Have you thought what you will do with the rest of the Helvetii? I have a couple of suggestions, if you will allow me.'

Renius cleared his throat. 'Like it or not, we're responsible for them now. The Aedui will kill them all if they go south without their warriors.'

'That is the problem,' Julius said, rubbing tiredness from his eyes. 'Or rather this is.' He hefted a heavy roll of skin parchment and showed them the leading edge, marked with tiny characters.

'Adàn says it is a list of their people. It took him hours just to get an estimate.'

'How many?' Mark Antony asked. They all looked to Julius, waiting.

'Ninety thousand men of fighting age, three times that amount in women, children and the elderly.'

The numbers awed them all. Octavian spoke first, his eyes wide.

'And how many men did we capture?'

'Perhaps twenty thousand,' Julius replied. He kept his face still as the rest of them broke into amazed laughter, clapping each other on the back. Octavian whistled.

'Seventy thousand dead. We killed a city.'

His words sobered the others as they thought of the mounds of dead on the plain and on the hill.

'And our own dead?' Renius asked.

Julius recited the figures without a pause.

'Eight hundred legionaries with twenty-four officers amongst them. Perhaps the same again in wounded. Many of those will fight again once we've stitched them.'

Renius shook his head in amazement. 'It is a good price.'

'May it always be so,' Julius said, raising the king's cup. The others drank with him.

'But we still have quarter of a million people on our hands,' Mark Antony pointed out. 'And we are exposed on this plain, with the Aedui coming up fast to share in the plunder. Do not doubt it, gentlemen. By noon tomorrow, there will be another army claiming a part of the riches of the Helvetii.'

'Ours, by right, such as they are,' Renius replied. 'I haven't seen much in the way of actual riches apart from these cups.'

'No, there may be something in cutting them a share,' Julius said thoughtfully. 'They lost a village and the battle took place on their land. We need allies amongst these people and Mhorbaine has influence.' He turned to Bericus, still in his blood-spattered armour.

'General, have your men take a tenth part of everything we have found here. Keep it safe under guard for the Aedui.'

Bericus rose and saluted. Like the others, he was pale with weariness, but he left the tent quickly and they all heard his voice growing in strength as it snapped out orders in the darkness.

'So what are you going to do with the prisoners?' Brutus asked.

'Rome needs slaves,' Julius replied. 'Though the price will plunge, we must have funds for this campaign. At the moment, coins like this one are the only wealth we have. There is no silver to pay the Tenth and Third and six legions eat their way through a fortune each month. Our soldiers know the slave price of captured soldiers comes to them and many are already discussing their new wealth.'

Mark Antony looked a little stiff at hearing this. His own legion received their pay directly from Rome and he had assumed it was the same for the others.

'I did not realise . . .' he began, then paused. 'May I speak?'

Julius nodded. Mark Antony held out his own cup to Brutus, who ignored him.

'If you sell the tribe back in Rome, the lands of the Helvetii will remain empty, right up to the Rhine. There are Germanic tribes there who would be only too willing to cross and occupy undefended land. The Gauls revere strong warriors, but they have nothing good to say about the men across the river. You would not want them on the borders of the Roman province.'

'We could take that land ourselves,' Brutus broke in. Mark Antony shook his head.

'If we left a few legions there to guard the Rhine banks, we would lose half our force for no good end. The land is worthless ash at present. Food would have to be brought in until the fields could be cleared and resown and then who would work them? Our legionaries? No, it is far better to send the Helvetii back to their own country. Let them guard the north for us. They have more to lose, after all.'

'Would they not be overrun by these savage tribes you mentioned?' Julius asked.

'They have twenty thousand warriors left to them. No small number and more importantly, they will fight to the death to repel any new invader. They have seen what legions can do and if they can't migrate south, they must stay and fight for their fields and homes. More wine, here, Brutus.'

Brutus looked at Mark Antony with dislike as the man held out his cup again, apparently unaware of the first refusal.

'Very well,' Julius said. 'Though the men won't be pleased, we will leave the Helvetii enough food to go home, taking the rest for ourselves. I will arm one in ten so that they may protect their people. Everything else comes back with us, bar the share for the Aedui. Thank you, Mark Antony. It is good advice.'

Julius looked around at the men in the tent.

'I will tell Rome what we achieved here. My scribe is copying the reports as we speak. Now, I hope you are not tired, because

I want that column moving home by first light.' There was a barely audible groan from them and Julius smiled.

'We will stay to hand over their portion to the Aedui and then an easy march back to the province, arriving the day after tomorrow.' He yawned, setting off one or two of the others. 'Then we can sleep.' He rose to his feet and they stood with him. 'Come on, the night is short enough in summer.'

The following day gave Julius a more than grudging respect for the organisational skills of the Helvetii. Just getting so many people ready to move was difficult enough, but weighing out enough food to keep them alive for the march home took many hours. The Tenth were given the task and soon long lines stretched out to the soldiers with their measuring cups and sacks, doling out the supplies to each surviving member of the tribe.

The Helvetii were still stunned by their sudden reversal of fortunes. Those of the Aedui they had taken as prisoners had to be forcibly separated after two stabbings in the morning. The Aedui women had taken revenge on their captors with a viciousness that appalled even hardened soldiers. Julius ordered two of them hanged and there were no more such incidents.

The army of the Aedui appeared out of the tree line before noon, when Julius was wondering if they were ever going to get the huge column moving. Seeing them in the distance, Julius sent a scout out to them with a one-word message: 'Wait.' He knew the chaos could only be increased with several thousand angry fighters itching to attack a beaten enemy. To help their patience, after an hour Julius followed the message with a train of oxen, bearing Helvetii weapons and valuables. The prisoners he had liberated were sent with them and Julius was pleased to have them off his hands. He had been generous with the Aedui, though Mark Antony told him they would assume he

283

kept the best pieces for himself, no matter what he sent them. In fact, he had kept back the gold cups, splitting them between the generals of his legions.

As noon passed and the Helvetii were still on the plain, Julius became red-faced and irritated with the delays. Part of it was down to the inescapable fact that the leaders of the tribe had all been killed in the fighting, leaving a headless mass of people who milled about until he was tempted to have the optios use their staffs on them to start them on their way.

At last, Julius ordered swords to be returned to two thousand of the warriors. With weapons in their hands, the men stood a little more proudly and lost the forlorn look of prisoners and slaves. Those men bullied the column into something like order and then, with a single horn blowing against the breeze, the Helvetii moved off. Julius watched them go with relief and, as Mark Antony had predicted, the moment it was clear they were heading north the Aedui started streaming onto the plain, calling and shouting after them.

Julius had his cornicens summon the six legions to block the path of Mhorbaine's warriors, and as they approached he wondered if they would stop or whether another battle would end the day. In the mood he was in, he almost welcomed it.

The lines of the Aedui halted a quarter of a mile away on the plain. They had crossed the site of the battle and tens of thousands of unburied bodies that were already beginning to stink. There could be no greater way of demonstrating the power of the legions facing them than walking over a field of the dead they had left behind. They would spread the word.

He watched as Mhorbaine rode out with two followers carrying high pennants that fluttered on the breeze. Julius waited for them, his impatience disappearing as the Helvetii began to dwindle behind. Many of his men threw glances at the receding column, feeling the soldier's natural dislike at being trapped between large groups, but Julius showed nothing of this, his weariness giving him an empty calm, as if all his emotion had been drained away with the column.

Mhorbaine dismounted and opened his arms in a wide embrace. Gently, Julius deflected him and Mhorbaine covered his confusion with a laugh.

'I have never seen so many of my enemies dead on the ground, Caesar. It is astonishing. Your word was good to me and the gifts you sent make it sweeter, knowing the source. I have brought cattle for a great feast, enough to fill your men until they are near bursting. Will you break bread with me?'

'No,' Julius replied, to the man's obvious astonishment. 'Not here. The bodies bring disease if they are left. They are on your land and they should be buried, or burnt. I am returning to the province.'

Mhorbaine looked angry for a moment at the refusal.

'You think I should spend a day digging holes for Helvetii corpses? Let them rot as a warning. As a stranger here, you may not know the custom to hold a feast after a battle. The gods of the earth must be shown the living have respect for the dead. We must send those we kill on the path, or they cannot leave.'

Julius rubbed his eyes. When had he last slept? He struggled to find words to appease the man.

'I will return to the foot of the mountains with my men. It would be an honour to have you join me there. We will feast then and toast the dead.' He saw Mhorbaine look speculatively at the retreating column and continued, his voice hardening. 'The Helvetii who live are under my protection until they return to their lands. Do you understand?'

The Gaul looked doubtfully at the Roman. He had assumed the column was under guard and being taken into slavery. The idea of simply letting them go was difficult for him to take in.

'Under your protection?' he repeated slowly.

'Believe me when I say that whoever attacks them will be my enemy,' Julius replied.

After a pause, Mhorbaine shrugged, running a hand over his beard.

'Very well, Caesar. I will ride ahead with my personal guard and be there to meet you as you come in.'

Julius clapped him on the shoulder, turning away. He saw Mhorbaine was watching in fascination as Julius nodded to the cornicens. The notes blared out across the plain and six legions turned on the spot. The soft earth trembled and Julius grinned as they marched away in perfect lines, leaving Mhorbaine and the Aedui behind. As they entered the tree line at the edge of the plain, Julius called Brutus to him.

'Pass the word. I will not be beaten home. We march through the night and will feast when we get there.' Julius knew the men would accept the challenge, no matter how exhausted they were. He sent the Tenth to the front to set the pace.

As dawn came, the six legions crossed the last crest before the Roman settlement at the foot of the Alps. The men had jogged and marched for more than forty miles and Julius was just about finished. He had marched every step of the way with his men, knowing his example would force them to keep going. Such small things mattered to those he led. In spite of their blisters, the men gave a ragged cheer at the sight of the sprawling buildings, moving easily into the faster pace for the last time.

'Tell the men they have eight hours of sleep and a feast to bulge their bellies when they wake. If they're as hungry as I am, they won't want to wait, so have cold meat and bread served to them to take the edge off. I am proud of them all,' Julius said to his scouts, sending them away to the other generals. He wondered idly whether his legions would have proved a match for the armies of Sparta, or Alexander. He would have been surprised if they hadn't been able to run the legs off them, at least.

By the time Mhorbaine reached the same crest with fifty of his best fighters, the sun was above the horizon and Julius was sound asleep. Mhorbaine reined in there, looking at the changes the Romans had wrought. The dark wall they had built curved north into the distance, a slash in the fertile landscape. Everywhere else he could see was being transformed into squares of buildings, tents and dirt roads. Mhorbaine had crossed the legion trail a few miles before, but he was still astonished to see the reality. Somehow, he had been left behind in the darkness. He leaned on his saddle-horns and looked back at the massive figure of his champion, Artorath.

'What a strange people they are,' he said.

Instead of replying, Artorath squinted behind them.

'Riders coming,' he said. 'Not ours.'

Mhorbaine turned his horse and looked back down the gently sloping hill. After a while, he nodded.

'The other leaders are gathering to see this new man in our land. They will not be pleased that he beat the Helvetii before they could get here.'

Holding flags of truce high above their heads, groups of riders approached. It looked as if every tribe for two hundred miles had sent their representatives to the Roman settlement.

Mhorbaine looked down at the vast encampment with its orderly lines and fortifications.

'If we are canny, there is a great advantage here for the taking,' he said aloud. 'Trade in food, for one, but those pretty legions are not a standing army. From what I've seen so far, this Caesar is hungry for war. If he is, the Aedui have other enemies for him to fight.'

'Your schemes will get us all killed, I think,' Artorath rumbled.

Mhorbaine raised his eyebrows at the man who sat a heavy stallion as if it was a pony. Artorath was the biggest man he had ever known, though sometimes he despaired of finding an intelligence to match his strength.

'Do you think bodyguards should talk to their masters in that way?' Mhorbaine said.

Artorath turned his blue eyes to meet him and shrugged. 'I was speaking then as your brother, Mhor. You saw what they did to the Helvetii. Riding a bear would be easier than using your silver tongue on these new men. At least when you jump off the bear, you can still run for it.'

'There are times when I can't believe we share the same father,' Mhorbaine retorted.

Artorath chuckled. 'He wanted a big woman for his second son, he said. Killed three men to take her from the Arverni.'

'To make an ox like you, yes. But not a leader, little brother, remember that. A leader needs to be able to protect his people with more than just unpleasantly bulbous muscles.'

Artorath snorted as Mhorbaine continued, 'We need them, Artorath. The Aedui will prosper with an alliance and that is the reality, whether you like it or not.'

'If you use snakes to catch rats, Mhor . . .'

Mhorbaine sighed. 'Just once, I would like to talk to you without having animal wisdom thrown in my face. It does not make you sound intelligent, you know. A child could put things more clearly, I swear it.'

Artorath glowered at him, remaining silent. Mhorbaine nodded in relief.

'Thank you, brother. I think, for the rest of the day, you should consider yourself my bodyguard first and my brother second. Now are you coming with me?'

His men were given tents while they waited for Julius to wake. Mhorbaine sent riders back to hurry on the herd he had brought for the feast and before noon had fully passed the slaughter of the animals had begun, with Mhorbaine and Artorath taking a personal hand in the preparation and spicing of the meat.

As the other leaders began to arrive, Mhorbaine greeted them with intense inner amusement, thoroughly enjoying their surprise at seeing him red to the elbows and issuing orders to boys and men as the bellowing cattle were killed and cut into a feast for thirty thousand. The sizzle of beef filled the air as a hundred fire pits were fed and heavy iron spits erected. Drowsy legionaries were rousted out of their warm blankets to help with the work, rewarded with a taste as they licked burnt fingers.

When Mark Antony woke, he had slaves bring buckets of river water for him to wash and shave, refusing to be hurried. If Julius was prepared to sleep through the biggest gathering of tribal leaders in living memory, then he was certainly not going out to them with two days of stubble on his face. As each hour passed, Mark Antony was forced to wake more and more of the soldiers, ignoring the swearing that came from the tents as his messages broke through the numbness of their exhaustion. The promise of hot food did wonders for their tempers and hunger silenced the complaints as they followed Mark Antony's example and washed before dressing in their best uniforms.

There were many small villages in the Roman province and Mark Antony sent riders out to them for oil, fish sauce, herbs and fruit. He thanked his gods the trees were heavy with unpicked apples and oranges, no matter how green. After drinking water for so long, the bitter juice was better than wine after it had been pressed out into jugs for the men.

Julius was one of the last to wake, sticky with the heat. He had slept in the solid buildings of the original settlement, now much extended. Whoever designed them had shared the Roman taste for cleanliness and Julius was able to sluice himself with cold water in the bathing room, then lie on a hard pallet to have olive oil scraped on and off his skin, leaving him clean and refreshed. The muscles that ached in his back finally eased as he sat to be shaved and he wondered whether the daily massage kept him supple. Before he dressed, he looked down at himself, checking his bruises. His stomach in particular was tender, and marked as if he had taken a heavy impact. Strange that he did not remember it. He dressed slowly, enjoying the coolness of clean linen against his skin after the smell of his own sweat on the march. His hair snagged in the fine teeth of the comb and when he tugged, he was appalled to see the mass of strands that came away. There was no mirror in the bathing rooms and Julius tried to remember the last time he had seen an image of himself. Was he losing his hair? It was a horrible idea.

Brutus entered with Domitius and Octavian, all three men wearing the silver armour they had won in the tournament, polished to a high sheen.

'The tribes have sent their representatives to see you, Julius,' Brutus said, flushed with excitement. 'There must be thirty different groups on our land, all under flags of truce and trying to hide how interested they are in our numbers and strategy.'

'Excellent,' Julius replied, responding to their enthusiasm. 'Have tables put up for them in the dining hall. We should be able to get them all in, if they don't mind the crush.'

'All done,' Domitius said. 'Everyone is waiting for you to join them, but Mark Antony is frantic. He says they won't move until you invite them to your table and we wouldn't let him wake you.'

Julius chuckled.

'Then let us walk out to them.'

CHAPTER TWENTY-FIVE

The air in the dining hall was thick with the heat of bodies as Julius took his seat at the long table. Though linen covered its length, Julius could not resist running a hand underneath to feel the rough new wood. It had not been there when he'd arrived that morning and he smiled to himself at the energy of Mark Antony and the legion carpenters.

He asked Mhorbaine to sit on his right hand and the Gaul took his place with obvious pleasure. Julius liked the man and wondered how many of the others would be friends or enemies in the years to come.

The men at his table were a mixed group, though all of them shared features as if their ancestors had sprung from the same tribe. They had hard faces, as if carved from pine. Many were bearded, though there was no style that dominated the gathering, and Julius saw as many moustaches and shaved skulls as there were beards and long braids dyed red at the roots. In the same way, there was no pattern to their clothes or armour.

Some wore silver and gold brooches that he knew would fascinate Alexandria, while others were bare of any ornament. Julius saw Brutus eyeing an ornate clasp on Mhorbaine's cloak and decided to bargain for a few fine pieces to give to her when they next saw Rome. He sighed at the thought, wondering when he would sit with his own people at a long table and hear their beautiful language rather than the throaty expectoration of the Gauls.

When they were all seated, Julius motioned for Adàn to stand at his side and rose to address the chieftains. For such an important meeting, he'd banished the elderly interpreter back to his tribe.

'You are welcome in my land,' Julius said, waiting for Adàn to echo the words in their own language. 'I believe you know I prevented the Helvetii cutting through my province and that of the Aedui. I did this at Mhorbaine's request and I use it to show my good faith to you.'

While Adàn translated, Julius watched their responses. It was an odd advantage to be removed from them by that one step. The pauses gave him the chance to marshal his arguments and see how they went across while the eyes of the Gauls were on Adàn.

'The people of Rome do not live in constant fear of enemy attack,' he continued. 'They have roads, trade, theatres, bathing houses, cheap food for their families. They have clean water and laws that protect them.'

He saw from the expressions around the table that he was on the wrong track with his description. These were not men to care about the luxuries given to those they ruled.

'More importantly,' Julius went on quickly, as Adàn struggled over a word, 'the leaders of Rome have vast lands and homes ten times the size of this small fort. They have slaves to tend their needs and the finest wines and horses in the world.'

A better reaction.

'Those of you who become my allies will come to know all of that. I intend to bring the roads of Rome further into Gaul and trade with the furthest recesses of the land. I will bring the biggest market in the world here for your goods.'

One or two of the men smiled and nodded, but then a young warrior stood and all the Gauls looked to him, becoming still. Julius could feel Brutus bristle on his left. There was nothing unusual in the figure who faced Julius twenty feet away. The Gaul wore his beard short and his blond hair tied back in a club on his neck. Like many of the others, he was a short, powerful figure dressed in wool and worn leather. Yet, despite his youth, the Gaul looked arrogantly around at the gathered representatives of the tribes. His face was badly scarred and cold blue eyes seemed to mock them all.

'And if we refuse your empty promises?' the man said.

As Adàn translated, Mhorbaine stood at Julius' side.

'Sit down, Cingeto. You want another enemy to add to your list? When did your father's people last know peace?'

Mhorbaine spoke in his own language and the young Gaul responded far too quickly for Adàn to follow. The two men roared at each other across the table and Julius swore he would learn their language. He knew Brutus was already studying it and he would join his daily lesson.

Without warning, the yellow-haired warrior stormed away from the table, slamming the door open to the outside. Mhorbaine watched him go with narrowed eyes.

'Cingeto's people would rather fight than eat,' Mhorbaine said. 'The Arverni have always been that way, but do not let it trouble you. His elder brother, Madoc, has less of a temper and it is he who will wear his father's crown.'

The exchange had clearly worried Mhorbaine, but he forced a smile onto his face as he looked at Julius.

'You must ignore the rudeness of the boy. Not everyone feels as Cingeto does.'

Julius called for the plates of beef and mutton to be brought in from the fire pits, glistening with oil and herbs. He tried to hide his surprise as they were followed with heaped platters of fresh bread, sliced fruit and roasted game birds. Mark Antony had been busier than he realised.

The awkward pause after Cingeto's departure disappeared in the clatter of plates. The chieftains fell to with a will, each man bringing out his own knife to slice and spear the hot food. Finger bowls of fresh water were used to dilute the wine, to the surprise of the servants, who quickly refilled them. Julius understood that the chieftains did not want to lose their wits in drunkenness and on reflection, he tipped his own water bowl into his wine cup as well. Brutus and Octavian followed his example with a private grin between them.

A sudden crash from outside the hall brought two of the guests half to their feet. Julius rose with them, but Mhorbaine remained in his seat, frowning.

'That will be Artorath, my guard. He will have found some men to wrestle by now.' Another crash and grunt punctuated his words and he sighed.

'The big man?' Julius asked, amused.

Mhorbaine nodded. 'He becomes bored too easily, but what can you do with family? My father raided the Arverni for his mother when he was really too old for such activities. Cingeto's people do not forgive, though they take their own wives in the same way when they can.'

'The women must be very unhappy with such an arrangement,' Julius said slowly, trying to understand.

Mhorbaine laughed aloud. 'They are if we take the wrong one in the dark. You'll never hear the end of it, then. No, Julius, when the tribes meet at the Beltane festival for barter and trade, there are a lot of matches made. You might even enjoy seeing it one year. The women make their wishes clear to the young warriors and it's a grand adventure trying to steal them away from their people. I remember my wife fought me like a wolf, but she never called for help.'

'Why not?' Julius asked.

'She might have been rescued! She was very taken with my beard, I think. Mind you, she pulled a handful of it out while I tried to get her over my shoulders. I had a bald patch for a while, right on the chin.'

Julius poured wine for the Gaul and watched as Mhorbaine topped it up with water.

'I've never seen a finger bowl used like this before,' Mhorbaine said. 'Good idea, though, when the wine is so sharp.'

Artorath dropped his weight, shifting his centre of balance. Domitius collapsed over him and found himself being lifted into the air. There was a brief sensation of terrifying flight and then the ground connected and Domitius had the wind knocked out of him. He lay groaning while Artorath chuckled.

'You're strong for such a little fellow,' he said, though he knew by then that not one of the Romans could understand real words. They did not seem particularly bright to the big Gaul. At first, when he had held up a coin and mimed holds for them, they seemed to think he was insane. Then one of them had come too close and Artorath had flipped him onto his back with a grunt. Their faces had lit up at that and they dug in their pouches for coins to match his own.

Domitius was his fifth opponent for the evening and though Artorath still went through the routine of biting the silver coins he was given, he thought he could well have enough for a new horse by the time Mhorbaine had finished charming the Roman leader.

Artorath had noticed Ciro standing apart from the others. Their eyes had met only once, but Artorath knew he had him.

He relished the challenge and took pleasure from throwing Domitius as close to Ciro's feet as he could.

'Any more?' Artorath boomed at them, pointing to each one and waggling his bushy eyebrows as if he spoke to children. Domitius had pulled himself upright by then and had a mischievous grin on his face. He held up a flat palm in an unmistakable gesture.

'Wait here, elephant. I know the man for you,' Domitius said slowly.

Artorath shrugged. As Domitius jogged away into the main buildings, Artorath looked questioningly at Ciro, beckoning him forward and waving a coin in the air with the other hand. To his pleasure, Ciro nodded and began to remove his armour until he stood wearing only a breechcloth and sandals.

Artorath had drawn a ring in the ground with a stick and he pointed for Ciro to step over the line. He loved to fight big men. Small ones were used to looking up at their opponents, but warriors of Ciro's size had probably never met a man who towered over them as Artorath did. It gave him a great advantage, though the crowd never knew it.

Ciro began to stretch his back and legs and Artorath gave him room, moving swiftly into his own loosening routine. After five bouts, he hardly needed it, but he enjoyed showing off to a crowd and the Roman soldiers were already three deep around the little space. Artorath spun and leapt, enjoying himself immensely.

'Do they say big men are slow where you come from, little soldiers?' he taunted their blank faces. The evening was cool and he felt invincible.

As Ciro stepped into the ring, a voice called out and many of the soldiers grinned in anticipation as Brutus came running back with Domitius.

'Hold, Ciro. Brutus wants a turn before you beat the big ox,' Domitius said, panting.

Brutus came to a halt as he caught sight of Artorath. The man was enormous and more heavily muscled than anyone he had ever seen. It was not simply a question of strength, he saw. Artorath's skull was half as large again as Ciro's and every other bone was thicker than a normal man's.

'You have to be joking,' Brutus said. 'He must be seven feet tall! You go ahead, Ciro. Don't wait for me.'

'I fought him,' Domitius said. 'Nearly had him over as well.'

'I don't believe you,' Brutus said flatly. 'Where are your marks? One punch from those big fists would put your nose through the back of your head.'

'Ah, but he isn't punching. It's like Greek wrestling, if you've ever seen it. He uses his feet to trip you, but the rest is holds and balance. Very skilful, but as I said, I almost had him.'

Ciro still waited patiently and Artorath only raised an eyebrow in Brutus' direction, completely oblivious to the conversation going on around him.

'I can beat him,' Ciro said, in the pause.

Brutus looked dubiously at Artorath. 'How? He's like a mountain.'

Ciro shrugged. 'My father was a big man. He taught me a few throws. It is not Greek wrestling that he is doing. My father learned it from an Egyptian. Let me show you.'

'He's yours, then,' Brutus said, clearly relieved.

Artorath looked at him as he spoke and Brutus waved a hand to Ciro, stepping back.

Once again, Ciro stepped over the line and this time he moved forward in a quick lunge. Artorath matched him and the two men met with a hard smack of flesh that made the watching soldiers wince. Without pausing, Ciro broke the grip on his shoulders and took an outside line, narrowly avoiding the big Gaul's horny feet as they swept towards his ankles. Ciro slid past him and tried to leap away, but Artorath spun and held him before he was clear.

Their legs entwined as each man fought to throw the other. Artorath twisted out of Ciro's hands and very nearly threw him over his hip, the move spoilt by Ciro dropping into a low crouch and then launching himself, trying to take Artorath off his feet. Against such a big opponent, it only made Artorath stagger and automatically he crossed his forearms and pressed them against Ciro's throat, heaving backwards.

It might have been the end, if Ciro's heel hadn't blocked his step, so that Artorath fell like a tree, crashing into the earth with Ciro on top of him. Before the Romans could begin to cheer, the twined figures exploded into an even faster struggle, breaking and taking grips and using the slightest purchase to apply holds on joints that would have broken in smaller men.

Artorath used his powerful hands to lock Ciro's throat again and Ciro found his little finger and snapped it with a jerk. Though he growled, Artorath maintained the grip and Ciro was growing purple as he found another finger and sent that the way of the first. Only then did the big man let go, holding the injured hand.

Ciro came to his feet first, bouncing lightly. The big Gaul rose more slowly, with anger showing for the first time.

'Should we stop it?' Domitius asked. No one answered.

Artorath launched a hard kick that missed, stamping the ground as Ciro sidestepped and grabbed Artorath around the waist. He failed completely to lift the big man. Artorath managed to lock Ciro's wrist, but his broken fingers lost their hold and he bellowed in Ciro's ear as the Roman chopped his foot into Artorath's knee and brought him down on his head. The Gaul lay stunned, his great chest heaving. Ciro nodded to him and helped him to his feet.

Brutus watched with fascination as Artorath grudgingly opened his belt pouch to give back one of the coins he had won. Ciro waved it away and clapped him on the shoulder.

'You next, Brutus?' Domitius asked slyly. 'His fingers are broken, you know.'

'I would, of course, but it wouldn't be fair to hurt him further,' Brutus replied. 'Take him to Cabera and have that hand splinted.'

He tried to mime the action for Artorath, who shrugged. He'd had worse and there was still more silver in his belt than when he'd started. He was surprised to see open cheerfulness on the faces of the soldiers around the ring, even those he had beaten. One of them brought him an amphora of wine and broke the wax seal. Another patted him on the back before walking away. Mhorbaine was right, he thought. They really were a strange people.

The stars were incredibly sharp in the summer sky. Though Venus had set, Julius could see the tiny red disc of Mars and he saluted it with his cup before holding it out for Mhorbaine to fill. The rest of the Gauls had retired long before and even the watered wine had helped to relax the wariest of them towards the end of the feast. Julius had spoken to many of the men, learning their names and the locations of their tribes. He owed a debt to Mhorbaine for the introductions and felt a pleasant, drunken regard for the Gaul as they sat together.

The camp was silent around them. Somewhere an owl screamed and Julius jumped. He eyed the cup of wine and tried to remember when he had stopped adding water to it.

'This is a beautiful land,' he said.

Mhorbaine glanced at him. Though he had not drunk anywhere near as much as the others, he copied their sluggish movements with a rare skill.

'Is that why you want it?' Mhorbaine asked, holding his breath for an answer.

Julius did not seem to notice the tension in the man who

sat on the damp ground at his side and simply waved his cup at the stars, slopping the red liquid over the rim.

'What does any man want? If you had my legions, wouldn't you dream of ruling this place?'

Mhorbaine nodded to himself. The wind had changed in Gaul and he had no regrets about doing what he had to, to preserve his people.

'If I had your legions, I would make myself a king. I would call myself Mhorix, or Mhorbainrix, perhaps,' he said.

Julius looked blearily at him, blinking. 'Rix?'

'It means king,' Mhorbaine told him.

Julius was silent in thought and Mhorbaine filled their cups again, sipping at his own.

'But even a king needs strong allies, Julius. Your men fight well on foot, but you have only a handful of cavalry, whereas my warriors were born in the saddle. You need the Aedui, but how can I be sure you will not turn on us? How can I trust you?'

Julius turned to face him.

'I am a man of my word, Gaul. If I call you friend, it will last all my life. If the Aedui fight with me, their enemies will be mine, their friends will be my friends.'

'We have many enemies, but there is one in particular that threatens my people.'

Julius snorted and the heat of the wine filled his veins. 'Give me his name and he is a dead man,' he said.

'His name is Ariovistus, ruler of the Suebi and their vassal tribes. They are of Germanic blood, Julius, with cold skin, a plague of ruthless horsemen who live for battle. They raid further south each year. Those who resisted them at first were destroyed, their lands taken as right of conquest.'

Mhorbaine leaned closer, his voice urgent. 'But you broke the back of the Helvetii, Julius. With my riders, your legions will feast on his white warriors, and all the tribes of Gaul will look to you.'

Julius stared at the stars above, silent for a long time.

'I may be worse than Ariovistus, my friend,' he whispered.

Mhorbaine's eyes were black in the night as he forced a smile onto his hard face. Though he left omens to his druids, he feared for his people now that such a man had entered Gaul. Mhorbaine had offered his cavalry to bind the legions to his people. To keep the Aedui safe.

'Perhaps you will be; we will know in time. If you march against him, you must bring him to battle before winter, Julius. After the first snow, the year is over for warriors.'

'Can your winter be so terrible?'

Mhorbaine smiled mirthlessly. 'Nothing I can say will prepare you, my friend. We call the first moon "Dumannios" – the darkest depths. And it gets colder after that. You will see, when it comes, especially if you travel further north, as you must to defeat my enemies.'

'I will have your cavalry to command?' Julius said.

Mhorbaine looked him in the eye.

'If we are allies,' he said softly.

'Then let us make it so.'

To Mhorbaine's astonishment, Julius drew a dagger from his belt and gashed his right palm. He held out the blade.

'Bind it in blood, Mhorbaine, or it is not bound at all.'

Mhorbaine took the blade and cut his own palm, allowing Julius to take the wounded hand in a firm grip. He felt the sting of it and wondered what would come of the bargain. With his cup, Julius gestured to the red planet above them.

'I swear under the eye of Mars that the Aedui are named friends. I swear it as consul and general.' Julius let the hands fall apart and refilled their cups from the amphora he cradled in his lap.

'There, it is done,' he said. Mhorbaine shuddered and this time, drank deeply against the cold.

CHAPTER TWENTY-SIX

෨෧෨෧෨෧

Pompey leaned on the white marble balcony of the temple to Jupiter, the vast space of the forum stretching away below him. From the top of the Capitol, he could gaze on the heart of the city and what he saw displeased him immensely.

Crassus showed nothing of his private amusement as he too looked over the swelling crowds. He kept his silence as Pompey muttered angrily to himself, turning at intervals to point out some newly infuriating aspect of the scene.

'There, Crassus. Can you see them? The bastards!' Pompey cried, pointing.

Crassus looked past the quivering finger to where a long line of men in black togas wound their way from one side of the forum towards the senate house, pausing at intervals to burn incense. Over the wind, Crassus thought he could hear the sound of the dirge that accompanied their steps and it was all he could do not to laugh as Pompey stiffened at the wailing notes.

'What are they *thinking* to be mocking me in this way?' Pompey shouted, purpling with rage. 'The whole city to see them in their mourners' cloths. By the gods, they will love to see it. And what will we have as a result? I swear, Crassus, the people will use the Senate's disobedience as an excuse for riots tonight. I will be forced to declare another curfew and again I will be accused of ruling without them.'

Crassus cleared his throat delicately, taking care to choose his words. Below, the long line of senators paused in sequence as incense billowed out of golden censers against the breeze.

'You knew they could rebel against our agreement, Pompey. You told me yourself that they were growing fractious,' he said.

'Yes, but I did not expect such a public display of disorder, for all the trouble they have been giving me in the Curia. That fool Suetonius is behind part of it, I know. He courts that trader Clodius as if he were something better than the gang leader he really is. I wish you had broken him properly, Crassus. You should see the way they discuss and scrutinise my legislation. As if any of them have been senators for more than the blink of an eye. It is insufferable! At times, they make me want to take the powers they accuse me of. Then we would see something. If I were made Dictator, even for six months, I could root out the dissenters and remove this . . . this . . .' words failed him as he swept an arm at the forum below. The line of senators were nearing the Curia building and Crassus could hear the crowd cheering their stand against Pompey.

Crassus had no sympathy for his colleague. Pompey lacked the subtlety to massage his opponents, preferring to use his authority to batter the Senate into obedience. Privately, Crassus agreed with many of the other senators that Pompey already acted as Dictator over a city that was quickly losing patience with his autocratic style.

In the distance, the procession reached the steps up to the Curia and Crassus saw them pause. They played a perilous game in angering Pompey in such a way. Their mocking funeral for the death of the Republic was intended as a public warning, but the last embers of democracy could indeed be crushed if Pompey lost all restraint as a result of it. Certainly, if riots ensued, Pompey would be within his rights to clamp down on the city and, once pushed so far, Dictatorship was not such a great leap for him. If he declared himself in that position, Crassus knew only a war would wrest it from his hands.

'If you can see past your anger for a moment,' Crassus began gently, 'you must realise that they do not want to force you further than you have already gone. Is it too much to re-establish the elections you have stopped? You have your creatures now as tribunes of the people. Could you not allow the voting again on future positions? That would take some of the sting out of the demonstrations against you, and at least gain you time.'

Pompey didn't answer. The two men watched the senators disappear inside the Curia and the distant bronze doors swing closed behind them. The excited crowds remained, milling and shouting under the grim eyes of Pompey's soldiers. Though the funeral procession had ended, the younger citizens especially had been infected by the display and were reluctant to leave. Pompey hoped his centurions would have the sense not to be too harsh with them. With Rome in that mood, a riot could spring from the slightest spark.

At last, Pompey spoke, his voice bitter.

'They blocked me at every turn, Crassus. Even when I had the whole Senate with me, the whoreson tribunes stood up and vetoed my legislation. They set themselves against me. Why should I not put my own men into their positions? At least now I don't have my work ruined for some petty point or whim.'

Crassus looked at his colleague, noting the changes in him over the previous year. Dark pouches had swollen under his eyes and he looked exhausted. It had not been an easy period and with the citizens testing the strength of their leaders, Crassus was pleased enough to be free of the constant wrangling. Pompey had aged under the responsibility and Crassus wondered if he secretly regretted the bargain he had struck. Julius had Gaul, Crassus his fleet of ships and his precious legion. Pompey had the struggle of his life, begun on the first day in Senate when he had forced through a bill with Julius' proxy.

The Senate had borne the change in power well enough at first, but then the factions had begun to form and with new men like the merchants Clodius and Milo entering the Senate, it had become a dangerous game for all of them. Rumours had spread that Bibilus had been killed or mutilated and twice the Senate had demanded he be shown alive to them and made to explain his absence. Pompey had allowed them to send letters to the consul, but Julius' word had been good. Bibilus had not come and visitors to his house found it barred and dark.

After two debates had come close to violence, Pompey had his soldiers stand guard over the sessions, ignoring the protests of the senators. Now they paraded their dissatisfaction in front of the people, making the dispute public. Though Crassus found Pompey's fury amusing, he worried for what would come of it.

'No man rules Rome alone, my friend,' Crassus murmured.

Pompey glanced sharply at him.

'Show me the laws I have broken! My tribunes are appointed rather than elected. They were never meant to bring the work of the Senate to a complete halt and now they do not.'

'The balance in the system has been altered, Pompey. It is not a minor change you have brought about. The tribunes were the voice of the mob. You risk a great deal in altering that. And the Senate are discovering new teeth if they act together against you,' Crassus replied.

Pompey's shoulders slumped in weariness, but Crassus felt no sympathy. The man went at politics as if every problem could be met head-on. He was a fine general but a poor leader of a city, and the last one to know that truth was apparently Pompey himself. The very fact that he had asked to meet Crassus privately was proof of the problems Pompey faced, even though he would not ask outright for advice.

'They *were* meant to limit the power of the Senate, Pompey. Perhaps they were wrong to block you so completely, but replacing them has earned you nothing but anger in the city.'

Pompey flushed again and Crassus continued quickly, trying to make him understand. 'If you restore their posts to the vote, you will regain a great deal of the ground you have lost,' he urged. 'The factions will believe they have won a victory and fall apart. You should not let them grow any stronger. By Jupiter himself, you should not. You have made your point. Let it be known now that you care as much as they for the traditions of Rome. The laws you passed cannot be undone, after all.'

'Let those sneering dogs back in to veto me?' Pompey snapped.

Crassus shrugged. 'Those, or whoever else the citizens elect. If it is the same men, you may have a difficult time of it for a while, but this is not an easy city to rule. Our people are fed on a diet of democracy from childhood. At times, I think they have dangerously high expectations. They do not like to see their representatives taken from them.'

'I will think about it,' Pompey said reluctantly, looking away across the forum.

Crassus doubted he fully understood the danger. As far as Pompey was concerned, the resistance in the Senate was a passing thing, not the kernel that could lead to open rebellion.

'I know you will make the right decision,' Crassus said.

*   *   *

Julius rubbed his face wearily. How long had he slept, an hour? He couldn't remember exactly when he had passed out, but he thought the sky had been growing light. The colours seemed to have been washed out of the province and Mark Antony's voice had taken on a whining tone Julius had not noticed before. While half the legions were bleary-eyed and pale, Mark Antony looked as if he was ready for a parade and Julius was convinced he felt a moral superiority over those who had indulged the night before. The general's lips pursed as he listened to Julius' report of the agreement with Mhorbaine.

'I wish you had consulted me, before you pledged your support,' Mark Antony said, barely hiding his irritation at what he had heard.

'From what Mhorbaine said, this Ariovistus would be trouble for us at some point. Better to deal with him now, before he is so deeply rooted we'd never be able to throw him back over the Rhine. We do need allies, Mark Antony. The Aedui have promised three thousand of their cavalry at my disposal.'

Mark Antony struggled with his temper for a moment.

'Yes, they will promise us anything, sir. I will not believe it until I see them. I warned you Mhorbaine is a clever leader, but it looks as if he has somehow managed to set the two most powerful armies in Gaul at each other's throats. No doubt Ariovistus has pledged friendship as well, with the Aedui profiting from a war that could break both of his enemies.'

'I've seen nothing in Gaul that could stand against us,' Julius said dismissively.

'You have not seen the Germanic tribes. They live for war, keeping a professional class in the field at all times, supported by the rest of their people. And in any case, Ariovistus is . . .' Mark Antony sighed. 'Ariovistus cannot be touched. He is already a friend of Rome, named so ten years ago. If you take the field against him, the Senate could well remove your command.'

307

Julius turned and gripped the larger man by the shoulders.

'Do you not think this is something I should have been told?' he demanded.

Mark Antony looked back at him, flushing.

'I did not think you would make such a promise to Mhorbaine, sir. You barely even know the man! How could I possibly have foretold that you would pledge the legions nearly three hundred miles across the country?'

Julius dropped his hands from his general and stood back.

'Ariovistus is a ruthless invader, Mark Antony. My only allies have asked me to help them. I'll tell you honestly that I do not care if Mhorbaine hopes to see us broken against each other or not. I do not care if Ariovistus is twice the warrior you tell me. Why do you *think* I brought my legions to Gaul? Have you seen this land? I could drop a handful of seeds anywhere and see corn spring up before I could turn round. There are forests enough to build fleets, herds of cattle so great they could never be counted. And beyond Gaul? I want to see it all. Three hundred miles is just a step of the way I have in mind. We are not here for a summer, General. We are here to stay, just as soon as I have cut the path for the rest to follow.'

Mark Antony listened in astonishment.

'But Ariovistus is one of ours! You can't just . . .'

Julius nodded, holding up a hand. Mark Antony fell silent.

'It will take a month to build a road from here to the plain for the ballistae and onagers. I do not intend to go to war without them again. I will send a messenger to this Ariovistus asking for a meeting. I will address him with the respect due to a friend of my city. Will you be satisfied then?'

Mark Antony sagged with relief.

'Of course, sir. I hope you are not offended at my words. I was thinking of your position at home.'

'I understand. Perhaps you could send a messenger to me to receive the letter,' Julius replied, smiling.

Mark Antony nodded and left the room. Julius turned to Adàn, who had listened to the conversation with an open mouth.

'What are you gaping at?' Julius snapped, instantly regretting the words. His head throbbed and his stomach felt as if it had been squeezed dry by vomiting in the night. A vague memory came of staggering out to the bath-house in the dark and losing great gushes of dark fluid into the gutters there. Only yellow bile remained, but still it churned and surged up his throat.

Adàn chose his words carefully.

'It must have been this way for my country, once. Romans deciding the future for us, as if we had no say at all in the matter.'

Julius began a sharp reply, then thought better of it.

'Do you think the men of Carthage wept over their conquests? And how do you think your people decided the fate of those they found when they came to Spain? These Celts came from some foreign land. Do you think your ancestors troubled themselves over the original inhabitants? Perhaps even they were invaders from some distant past. Do not think your people are better than mine, Adàn.'

Julius gripped the bridge of his nose, closing his eyes against the throbbing headache.

'I wish I had a clear head to tell you what I mean. It is more than just the strength that matters. Carthage was strong, but beating them changed the world. Greece was once the greatest power, but when they weakened, we came and made them ours. Gods, I drank too much wine for an argument this early.'

Adàn did not interrupt. He sensed that Julius was on the edge of something important and he strained forward in his chair to hear. Julius' voice had a hypnotic quality, almost a whisper.

'Countries are taken in blood. Women are raped, men killed,

every horror you can imagine occurs a thousand times over, but then it ends and the victors settle the land. They farm and build cities and make laws. The people thrive, Adàn, whether you like it or not. Then there is justice and rule of law. Those who prey on their neighbours are executed, cut out from the rest. They have to be, because even conquerors grow old and value peace. The blood of the invaders is mingled with the people on the land until a hundred years later they are not Celt or Carthaginian, or even Roman. They are like . . . wine and water, impossible to separate. It begins in battle, but they are raised by each wave, Adàn. I tell you if I ever find a country that has not been tempered in fire, I will show you savages where we have built cities.'

'You believe this?' Adàn asked.

Julius opened his eyes, the dark pupils gleaming.

'I do not believe in a sword, Adàn, because I can see it. It is just the truth. Rome is more than iron swords and harder men. I will bring them up, kicking and screaming. Gaul will suffer under my hand, but I will make them greater than they can imagine by the time I'm done.'

The messenger sent by Mark Antony arrived at the door, clearing his throat softly to draw their attention. Both men snapped out of the reverie and Julius groaned, holding his head.

'Find me a cold cloth and see if Cabera has any of his powders for pain,' he told the young man. As he turned back, he saw Adàn's expression was grim.

'It is a strange view, General,' the young Spaniard ventured. 'I can see why you would think such a thing, with an army poised to rush over Gaul. But it will be little comfort to the families that lose their men in the days to come.'

Julius felt anger spike in him as the headache throbbed.

'Do you think they are weaving flowers for each other while we sit here? The tribes are at each other's throats, boy. At forty

310

years old, Mhorbaine's one of the tribal ancients. Think of that! Disease and war take them before they go grey. They may hate us, but they hate each other a great deal more. Now, let us leave this for another time. I have a letter to dictate for this Ariovistus. We will ask this "Friend of Rome" to go quietly back from the lands he has conquered and leave Gaul behind him.'

'Do you think he will?' Adàn asked.

Julius did not answer, but gestured for Adàn to take up his writing tablet and began to dictate the letter to the King of the Suebi.

Clearing the forests for the new road out to the plain took longer than Julius had hoped. Though the legions worked full days in the summer heat, each massive oak had to be cut down and then dragged out by teams of axemen and oxen. Cabera had begun to train some of the legion boys as assistants to deal with the broken bones and wounds that were the inevitable result of such labour. Two months passed agonizingly slowly before the first stone could be laid, but by the end of the fourth, the flat stones stretched almost forty miles, wide and strong enough to take the great catapults and siege machines without a tremor. New quarries had been dug in the hills and granite posts marked the miles from Rome, spreading the shadow further than it had reached before.

Julius gathered his council in the hall of the Roman buildings, Mhorbaine and Artorath sitting with them as his favoured allies. He looked round at them all, resting his gaze at last on Adàn, who was looking strangely at him. The young Spaniard had translated the messages that had flown between Ariovistus and the Roman province and, of all of them, he knew what Julius was about to say. Julius wondered if there had ever been a time when he was as innocent as the young Spaniard. If there had been, it was too far back to remember.

Ariovistus had not been an easy man to reach. The first two messengers had been sent back with the briefest of replies, disdaining any further interest in Julius or his legions. Mark Antony had managed to impress Julius with the need to walk carefully around the king, but the wording was dismissive and infuriating. At the end of the first month, Julius was waiting only for the road to be finished before taking his legions out to crush Ariovistus, friend of Rome or not. Yet he needed to be seen to have made every attempt to settle the issue peacefully. He knew Adàn was not the only one of his men sending letters back to Rome. Pompey would have spies keeping him well informed and the last thing Julius wanted was to have Rome declare him an enemy of the state for his actions. Such a thing was far from impossible with Pompey at the head of the Senate. No doubt the man had the senators trained to perfection and a single vote could remove Julius' authority at a stroke.

The weeks had passed slowly enough, with the days filled with meeting the tribal leaders, promising them whatever they wanted if they would allow passage through their lands and provide supplies for the army as they marched. Brutus had taken to the language with a flair that surprised them both and already he was able to take part in the negotiations, though his efforts reduced the Gauls to tears of laughter on occasion.

Adàn looked away as Julius smiled at him. The longer he spent in the company of the Roman leader, the more confused he felt. At times, when Julius tried to put him at his ease, Adàn could feel the immense personal charm and understand why others followed him. Then there were moments when he could not believe the utter callousness of the generals as they decided the fate of millions in their councils. He could never decide if Julius was as ruthless as men like Renius, or whether he truly believed bringing Rome to Gaul was a better path for the tribes than any they could have found on their own. It did matter to the young man. If he thought Julius believed his own words about the glories of civilisation, Adàn could justify the respect he felt for him. If it was all a game, or a mask for conquest, then Adàn had made the biggest mistake of his life in leaving Spain to follow him.

'Ariovistus has scorned my messengers once again,' Julius said to his generals. They exchanged glances. 'Though Mark Antony has expressed a desire for me to uphold the title of friend conferred on him, I cannot ignore the arrogance of this king. The scouts have reported a large army gathering on his borders for further conquest and I have agreed to safeguard Aedui lands with our legions.'

Julius flickered a glance at Mark Antony, who kept his eyes on the long table.

'Mhorbaine's cavalry will accompany the extraordinarii, for which I thank him,' Julius continued. Mhorbaine inclined his head with a wry smile.

'As this Ariovistus has given service to Rome in the past, I will continue to send my messengers as we march. He will have every chance to meet me and create a peaceful resolution. I have informed the Senate of my actions and await a reply, though it may not come before we leave.'

As they watched, Julius unrolled a map of the thinnest calf-skin vellum. He placed lead weights at the corners and the men rose from their chairs to look at the land he revealed to them.

'The scouts have marked the hills for us, gentlemen. The region is named Alsatia, three hundred miles to the north and west.'

'It borders the Helvetii land,' Brutus murmured, poring over the map Mhorbaine had given them. It was little better than a set of painted regions, without detail, but none of the Romans in the room had seen even that part of Gaul and were fascinated.

'If we do not send the Suebi back over the Rhine, the Helvetii will not survive the next summer,' Julius replied. 'After that, Ariovistus may look further south to our own province. It is our duty to establish the Rhine as the natural border for Gaul. We will resist any attempt to cross it, no matter what the source. If necessary, I will bridge it and lead punishment raids deep into their own land. This Ariovistus has become arrogant, gentlemen. The Senate have let him run loose for far too long.'

He ignored Mark Antony's wince at his words.

'Now let us prepare the marching order. Though I can hope for peace, we must prepare for war.'

CHAPTER TWENTY-SEVEN

༄ཚ༄ཚ༄ཚ

After the rush to meet and turn the Helvetii, the more formal
march along the new road was almost restful for the legion
veterans. Though the days were still heavy with heat, the trees
had begun their turn, already tinged with a thousand shades
of red and brown. Crows lifted from the forests as they passed
through, their voices harsh with warning. On the empty plains,
it was easy for the legionaries to imagine they were the only
men for a thousand miles.

Julius kept the Tenth and extraordinarii at the front. The
Aedui riders were given into the care of Domitius and Octavian
and began to learn the discipline Julius required of his allies.
Though he had been grateful to Mhorbaine for the added
force, he had made it clear that they had to learn to follow
orders and structure themselves in the Roman fashion. The
extraordinarii had a busy time with the Gaulish riders, who
seemed individualists to a man and not at all used to any form
of organised attack.

The great war machines accompanied the march, strapped down and safe while they were on the move, but with their expert teams close to them. Each of the heavy ballistae had a personal name cut into the great blocks of beech and each legion preferred to use its own, loyally certain that they could throw further and more accurately than any of the others. The scorpion bows looked little more than cart-loads of spars and iron before assembly. The heavy arms took three men to reset after each shot, but the bolt could punch through a horse and kill another behind it. They were valued weapons and the legionaries who came close would often reach out to touch the metal for luck.

The six legions stretched for ten miles on the road to the Helvetii plain, though that halved as Julius ordered a deeper formation over open ground. As near as he was to Aedui land, he did not yet fear an attack, but he was painfully aware of the exposed column and the vast array of equipment and baggage that accompanied them. There were weak links in the chain from the province, but at the first sign of danger, the legions could re-form into wide protective squares, proof against anything he had seen thus far in Gaul. Julius knew he had the men and generals he needed. If he failed, the disgrace would be his alone.

Mhorbaine had resisted the temptation to join them against his enemy. Though he had been torn, no leader of the Aedui could spend so long away from his people without usurpers rushing to take his place. Julius had bidden him farewell from the very edge of the Roman province, with the shining legions in a vast line behind him, standing with the tension of hunting hounds.

Mhorbaine had cast his eyes over the still ranks waiting for their general and shaken his head at their discipline. His own warriors would have been milling around aimlessly before a march and he found the Romans both depressing and frightening in comparison. As Julius turned away from him, Mhorbaine had called out the question he'd been turning over in his mind ever since he saw the strength of the force being sent against Ariovistus.

'Who guards your land while you are gone?' he called.

Julius turned back to him, his dark eyes boring into the Gaul.

'You do, Mhorbaine. But there will be no need for guards.'

Mhorbaine had looked askance at the Roman general in his polished armour.

'There are many tribes who would be willing to take advantage of your absence, my friend. The Helvetii may return, and the Allobroges would steal anything they can lift.'

He watched as Julius pulled his full-face helmet over his head, the iron features making him look like a statue come to life. His breastplate shone with oil and his brown arms were strong and scarred with a pattern of white lines against the darker skin.

'They know we will return, Mhorbaine,' Julius had said, smiling beneath the mask.

After the first mile, the iron helmet had come off, when the sweat pouring into his eyes began to sting and blur his vision. For all her best intentions, Alexandria had never walked a hundred miles in armour, no matter how well designed.

When they came across a town, Julius accepted grain or meat as tribute. There was never enough food to become complacent and he fretted at the guards he had to leave behind to keep the supplies coming from Mhorbaine. Using the legion night camps as way-stations, the first links to the north were laid down. Later would come more permanent roads and the merchants of Rome would reach further and further into the country, bringing anything they could sell. Given two or three years, he knew the roads would be manned by forts and guard-posts. Those who had no land in Rome would come then to mark out new farms and start afresh, and fortunes would be made.

It was a heady dream for Julius, though on that first march to Ariovistus his legions were never more than ten meals from starvation, a margin as desperately important as any other factor of their strength. Julius felt as if his force was being bled as he gave orders for mixed groups of cavalry and velites to keep the ground clear for the lifeline behind. He stretched his supply line as thinly as he dared, but Gaul was too vast to keep a thread right back to the Aedui and he vowed to find other allies when he had dealt with Ariovistus.

There were times when the land itself seemed to impede them. The ground was covered in heavy mounds of grass that shifted and turned underfoot, slowing the legions still further. It was a good day when they were twenty miles from the previous camp.

When his scouts reported riders spying on the legions, Julius had thrown aside his lists and tallies with relief. The first sightings had been little more than glimpses of armed men, but the legions tautened subtly at the news. The soldiers oiled their blades with extra care each night and there were fewer names on the discipline lists. He ordered the fastest of the extraordinarii out to search, but they lost their quarries in the woods and valleys, one of the best geldings breaking his leg at full gallop and killing his rider.

Julius was convinced the spies were from Ariovistus, but he was still surprised when a lone rider appeared as the legions paused to eat their noon meal. The man trotted his mount from an arrowhead of trees on a sharp slope of granite in the line of march, causing a flurry of signals and warning horns. At the sound, the extraordinarii left their food untouched and ran to their horses, leaping into their saddles.

'Wait!' Julius called to them, holding up a hand. 'Let him come to us.'

The legions formed ranks in a terrible silence, every eye focused on the rider who approached them with no sign of fear. Julius unwrapped his telescope and fixed the lenses, studying the man. What he saw made him frown, but he said nothing to those around him.

The stranger dismounted as he reached the first ranks of the Tenth. Briefly, he looked around him and then nodded to himself as he saw Julius in his armour and the array of flags and extraordinarii around him. As their eyes met, Julius struggled not to show the discomfort he felt. He could hear his legionaries murmuring nervously and one or two of them made protective signs with their hands at the rider's unearthly appearance.

He was dressed in leather armour over rough cloth, his lower legs bare. Round iron plates capped his shoulders, making him seem even more massive than he already was. He was tall, though Ciro topped his height by inches and Artorath would have dwarfed him. It was his face and skull that made the Romans glance uneasily at each other as he passed.

He looked like no race of men Julius had ever seen, with such a line of bone above his eyes that they seemed to peer out from constant shadow. His skull was shaved bare except for a long tail of hair at the joint of his neck that swung behind him as he walked, weighed down with dark metal ornaments wound into its length. The skull itself was heavily deformed, with a second ridge above the first.

'Do you understand me? What is your name and tribe?' Julius asked.

The warrior studied him without replying and Julius shook himself mentally, suddenly aware that the man must know the effect he had. Indeed, Ariovistus had probably chosen him for that reason.

319

'I am Redulf of the Suebi. I learned your words when my king fought for you and was named friend for life,' the man replied.

It was eerie to hear Latin from such a demonic-looking individual, but Julius nodded, relieved not to have to depend on the interpreters Mhorbaine had provided.

'You are from Ariovistus then?' Julius said.

'I have said it,' the man replied.

Julius felt a prickle of irritation. The man was as arrogant as his master.

'Say what you have been told then, boy,' Julius replied. 'I will not suffer a delay from you.'

The man stiffened at the taunt and Julius saw a slow flush spread along the bony ridges of his brow. Was it a deformity of birth, or the result of some strange ceremony amongst the men across the Rhine? Julius beckoned a messenger to him, murmuring that Cabera should be brought up to the front of the column. As the messenger darted away, the warrior spoke, his voice pitched to carry.

'King Ariovistus will meet you by the rock known as the Hand in the north. I am to say he will not allow your walking soldiers to accompany you. He will come with his riding men only and will allow the same for you. Those are his terms.'

'Where is this rock?' Julius asked, narrowing his eyes in thought.

'Three days' march north. Fingers of rock crown the peak. You will know it. He will wait for you there.'

'And if I choose to ignore the terms?' Julius said.

The warrior shrugged. 'Then he will not be there and will consider himself betrayed. You may expect war from us until one of our armies is broken.'

His sneer as he looked around at the Roman officers made his view of such an outcome perfectly clear. Redulf glanced at Cabera as he arrived, moving slowly on a stick and the

messenger's arm. The old healer was haggard from the privations of the march, but still his blue eyes looked with fascination at the warrior's unusual skull.

'Tell your master I will meet him where you say, Redulf,'
Julius said. 'I will honour the friendship my city has given him
and meet him in peace at the rock you named. Run back now
and tell him all you have seen and heard.'

Redulf glared at this dismissal, but contented himself with
another sneer at the Roman ranks before striding back to his
horse. Julius saw that Brutus had brought the extraordinarii
up to form a wide avenue down which the man was forced to
ride. He looked neither left nor right as he passed their ranks
and dwindled quickly into the distance of the north.

Brutus cantered up and dismounted.

'By Mars, he was a strange one,' Brutus said. He noticed one
of the Tenth near him making a protective sign with his fingers.
He frowned, considering the effect on the more superstitious
men under his command.

'Cabera? You saw him,' Julius said. 'Was it a birth deformity?'

Cabera looked into the distance after the rider.

'I have never seen one that was so regular, as if it had been
made deliberately. I don't know, General. Perhaps if I could
examine him more closely, I could be sure. I will think on it.'

'I suppose this Ariovistus isn't asking for peace and saving
us the trouble of dealing with his ugly men?' Brutus asked
Julius.

'Not yet. Now that we're close to him, he has suddenly
decided he will meet me, after all. Strange how Roman legions
can influence a man's mind,' Julius replied. His smile faded as
he thought of the rest of the king's message.

'He wants me to take cavalry alone to the meeting place,
Brutus.'

'What? I hope you refused. I will not leave you in the hands
of our Gaulish riders, Julius. Never in this life. You must not

321

give him the chance to trap you, friend of Rome or not.' Brutus looked appalled at the idea, but then Julius spoke again.

'Rome watches us, Brutus. Mark Antony was right about that. Ariovistus must be treated with respect.'

'Mhorbaine said his people lived in the saddle,' Brutus replied. 'Did you see the way that ugly bastard rode? If they're all like him, you won't want to be caught in the open with just the Aedui and a handful of extraordinarii.'

'Oh, I don't think I will be,' Julius said, a slow smile stealing across his face. 'Summon the Aedui to me, Brutus.'

'What are you going to do?' Brutus asked, thrown by the sudden change in his general's demeanour.

Julius grinned like a boy. 'I am going to mount the Tenth on horseback, Brutus. Three thousand of my veterans and the extraordinarii should be enough to clip his wings, don't you think?'

Pompey finished his address to the Senate and asked for speakers before the vote to come. Though there was a brittle tension in the three hundred men of the Curia, at least the threat of violence had diminished from their debates, if not the streets outside. At the thought, Pompey glanced over to where Clodius sat, a shaven-headed bull of a man who had been born in the gutters of the city and had risen simply by being more ruthless than any of his competitors. With Crassus' stranglehold over trade, Clodius should have found himself a quiet retirement, but instead had cut his losses and stood for election to the Senate. Pompey shuddered as he considered the brutal, flat features. Some of the things he had heard were surely exaggerated, he told himself. If they were true, it would have meant another city hidden beneath Rome, one perhaps that Clodius already ruled. The bullish figure was to be seen at every session of the Senate and when he was baulked, gangs of raptores would rampage through the city, disappearing into the maze of alleys whenever the legion guards came after them. Clodius was cunning enough to denounce the gangs in public, throwing his hands up in amazement whenever their violence coincided with some check to his ambition.

Restoring the tribune posts to the vote had removed one pillar of Clodius' popular support. After the disgraceful funeral procession two months before, Pompey had followed Crassus' advice. To his pleasure, only one of the original holders of the post had been brought back into the Senate. The fickle public had voted in a stranger for the second and though Pompey's enemies courted him outrageously, he had not yet declared any particular loyalties. It was just possible that Clodius had no hand in the man's election, though Pompey doubted it. The man was not above threatening families to achieve his aims and Pompey had already witnessed one vote where decent men had turned against him for no clear reason. They had not even met his eyes as they stood with Clodius, and Pompey had barely been able to restrain his rage in the face of the merchant's cold triumph. As a result of that, the free corn issued to the citizens now took a fifth of the entire revenue of the city and thousands more flooded in each month for the entitlement. Pompey knew Clodius found his most brutal supporters from amongst those rootless scavengers who came to the city. He could not prove it, but he thought a heavy tithe of that grain never reached the hungriest mouths, instead going into that darker Rome where Clodius and men like him bought lives as easily as they sold grain.

Pompey motioned for Suetonius to speak and sat down as the young Roman rose and cleared his throat. Nothing of his dislike showed on Pompey's face, though he despised a man who would apparently follow any dog for scraps. Suetonius had grown in confidence as Clodius showered him with praise and funds. He spoke well enough to hold the attention of the

Senate and his association with Clodius had given him a vicarious status he relished.

'Senators, Tribunes,' Suetonius began, 'I am no friend to Caesar, as many of you know.' He allowed himself a small smile at the chuckle from the benches. 'We have all heard of his victory against the Helvetii in Gaul, a most worthy battle that had the citizens cheering in the markets. Yet the matter of his debts is not a minor concern. I have the estimate here.'

Suetonius made a show of checking a paper, though he knew the figures by heart.

'To Herminius, he owes just under a million sesterces. The other lenders together, another million, two hundred thousand. These are not small sums, gentlemen. Without these funds, the men who advanced them in good faith may well be forced into poverty. They have the right to appeal to us when Caesar shows no sign or inclination to return to the city. The law of Twelve Tables is quite clear on the matter of debt and we should not support a general who scorns the statutes in this way. I urge the Senate to demand his return to clear his slate with the city. Failing that, perhaps an assurance from Pompey that the term in Gaul has some clear end, so that those who struggle in the wake of these debts can look forward to settlement on an agreed date. I will vote in favour of recalling Caesar.'

He sat down and Pompey was about to motion to the next speaker when he saw the new tribune had risen.

'Have you anything to add, Polonus?' Pompey said, smiling at the man.

'Only that this seems a small stick with which to beat a successful general,' Polonus replied. 'As I understand the matter, these debts are personal to Caesar, despite his use of them to supply and outfit his soldiers. When he returns to the city, his creditors can lay hands on him for the sums and if he cannot pay, the penalties are harsh. Until then, I do not see a role for the Senate in demanding his return into the hands of coarse moneylenders.'

A murmur of approval sounded from the senators and Pompey stifled a smile. Large numbers of them had debts and Suetonius would have to be a genius to make them call back a general to satisfy the grubby urging of men like Herminius. Pompey was pleased Polonus had spoken against the vote. Perhaps he was not in Clodius' pay after all. Pompey caught the tribune's eye and inclined his head as the next speaker rose, barely listening to the speech by some minor son of the nobilitas.

Pompey knew there were many who described his dismissal and restoration of the tribunes as a masterful stroke. The older members especially looked to him for leadership and strength to face the new players of the game. Many of them had come to him in private, but in the Senate their fear made them weak. There were not many who dared to risk the enmity of one like Clodius. Even for Pompey, the thought of Clodius becoming consul one day was enough to make sweat break out on his skin.

As the young senator droned through his speech, Pompey's gaze drifted to another of the new men, Titus Milo. Like Clodius before him, he had come to the Senate when his merchant ventures were lost. Perhaps because of that shared background, the pair appeared to dislike each other intensely. Milo was red-faced from drink and fat where Clodius was solid. Both men could be as coarse as the worst gutter whore. Pompey wondered privately if they could be set at each other's throats. It would be a neat solution to the problem.

The vote was taken quickly and for once Pompey's supporters did not waver. Clodius had not spoken and Pompey knew it was likely he had indulged Suetonius without pledging his full support. There would be no sudden reports of gangs rampaging through the markets that night. Clodius caught Pompey's thoughtful gaze on him and nodded his massive head as one equal to another. Pompey returned the gesture out of habit, though his mind seethed with some of the ugliest rumours. It was said that Clodius employed bodyguards who used rape as a casual tool of persuasion when they were on his business. It was just another of the tales circulating like flies about the man. Pompey gritted his teeth as he saw the secret gleam of amusement in Clodius' eyes. In that moment, he envied Julius in Gaul. For all the hardships of a campaign, his battles would be simpler and cleaner than those Pompey faced.

CHAPTER TWENTY-EIGHT

Brutus roared angry orders out to the Tenth as they trotted their Gaulish ponies towards the distant mass of horsemen at the foot of the crag of rock called the Hand. While he understood Julius' desire to have the veterans of the Tenth with him, they rode like wayward children. Above a walking pace, horses drifted into each other and on anything but the smoothest ground, the red-faced soldiers were thrown off, suffering the humiliation of being forced to run alongside until they could heave themselves back into the saddles.

As if that wasn't enough, Brutus seethed inwardly at Mark Antony being given control of the legions waiting behind them. He could accept the fact that Julius wanted Brutus and Octavian with him to control the extraordinarii, but Mark Antony had not earned the right to be Julius' second-in-command. Brutus was in a savage temper as he wheeled his mount to respond to a commotion behind him.

'Gather up your reins, by Mars, or I will have you whipped!'

he shouted to an unfortunate, milling group of triarii. In their heavy armour, they sat their horses like clanking sacks of corn and Brutus rolled his eyes as another leaned too far forward and slipped from sight under his pony's legs with a crash.

It was no way to approach a possible battle. The Tenth were used to the rhythms of foot soldiers and the sweating, swearing men around him had nothing of the calm he was used to.

Octavian cantered past him, using his powerful gelding to force a wobbling rank of ponies back into line. The two men exchanged glances as they passed and Octavian grinned, clearly amused by the situation. Brutus gave no answering smile, instead cursing the Tenth under his breath as two horses somehow became joined together ahead of him, their riders heaving at the reins until the tortured ponies panicked and bolted. Brutus caught them with a quick dart, holding on until the legionaries had regained control. They could not be expected to have the casual balance of thousands of hours of training and he only hoped Julius would have the sense to call a halt long before Ariovistus could see their lack of skill. For men born in the saddle, there could be no deception.

Before they had set off, Julius had come to him. He had seen Brutus' coldness and spoke to reassure him.

'I must have you with me, Brutus,' he had said. 'The extraordinarii are the only competent riders I have and they are used to your orders.'

Julius had stood close to him then, unwilling to be overheard.

'And if I am forced to fight, I do not want Mark Antony at my side. He thinks too much of this Ariovistus and his friendship with Rome.'

Brutus had nodded, though the words did not go far to appease his sense of betrayal. The post was owed.

The outriders saw the Hand and reported back before noon. As the Tenth neared the crag, Brutus could see thousands of horsemen in perfect ranks ahead. They had chosen a place for the meeting where cavalry were hampered by steep defiles on either side. The rock they called the Hand formed the highest point to the east, with the western side choked with dense forest. Brutus wondered if Ariovistus had men hidden in the dark oaks. He knew he would have placed them there and hoped the legions were not heading into a trap. One thing was certain, if it came to a retreat against those German riders, the Tenth would have to accomplish it on foot or be destroyed.

The cornicens sounded a dismount, a signal of two tones they had agreed on before leaving the camp. With relief, Brutus saw the Tenth lose their awkwardness as they touched the ground.

Only the extraordinarii stayed in the saddle to guard the flanks. The Tenth walked their ponies forward in grim bad humour. Brutus continued to harry them, calling out to the centurions to keep order as they advanced towards the meeting place and the King of the Germanic Suebi. The tension grew as they marched closer to the enemy and Brutus could see the details of the men they faced. He saw Ariovistus for the first time as the king rode out with three others and halted two hundred feet from his front line. Julius went forward to meet him with Domitius and Octavian, the tension visible in their stiff backs.

Brutus took a last look at the ranks of the Tenth.

'Be ready!' he called as he trotted out to join his general.

The noise of four thousand nervous horses dwindled behind them as he joined Domitius and Octavian, all three resplendent in their silver armour. Julius wore the full-face helmet and when he turned in the saddle to acknowledge Julius, Brutus saw the effect of the cold features that stared back at him.

'Now let's see what this little king has to say to me,' Julius' voice came from beneath the iron mouth.

The four men kicked their horses into a canter in perfect formation as they moved across the broken ground.

*   *   *

Julius recognised Redulf at Ariovistus' right shoulder and saw with astonishment that the other two warriors with the king were as strangely deformed as the messenger. One of them was shaven bald, but the other had a crown of black hair that did nothing to disguise the strange double ridge, as if some great fist had gripped his skull and squeezed it. They were all bearded and fierce-looking, clearly chosen for strength. All were adorned with gold and silver, making Julius pleased he had his sword tourney finalists as his honour guard. The perfect sets of silver armour outshone the Suebi warriors and Julius knew that, man for man, his companions would be more deadly.

Ariovistus himself did not have the ridged brow of the warriors at his side. His face was dominated by dark eyebrows and an untrimmed beard that covered most of his face, leaving only the cheeks and forehead clear. His skin was pale and the eyes that glowered at Julius were as blue as Cabera's. The king remained perfectly still as Julius rode up and halted without saluting.

The silence held as Julius and the king regarded each other, neither willing to be the first to speak. Brutus looked behind them to the ranks of horses and still further to where a greater force marked the southern tip of the lands Ariovistus had taken, fifteen miles down from the wide Rhine river. In the distance, Brutus could see two fortified camps that could have been twins of the Roman style. The mass of Suebi riders were not in formal array, but Brutus could see they had cleared the ground and could leap into a charge at short notice. He began to sweat as he saw the long spears they carried. Every man of the Roman infantry knew horses would not charge a shield wall any more than they could be forced to run into a tree. As long as the legions could hold their squares, they could advance through the forces of Ariovistus without real danger. The theory was little comfort in the face of so many of the pale, bearded warriors.

Julius lost patience under the calm scrutiny of the king.

'I have come to you as you asked, friend of my city,' he began. 'Though this is not your land, I have ridden to it and honoured your terms. Now I tell you that you must remove your armies across the natural barrier of the Rhine. Remove them immediately and there will be no war between us.'

'This is Roman friendship?' Ariovistus snarled suddenly, his voice a bass boom that startled them. 'I fought against your enemies ten years ago and the title was given to me, but for what purpose? So that I can be turned away from lands I have rightfully won as it suits you?' His teeth were deeply yellow in his beard and his eyes glinted under the heavy brows.

'It was not the right to take whatever lands you wanted,' Julius retorted. 'You have your home across the river and that is enough. I tell you, Rome will not allow you to have Gaul, or any part of it.'

'Rome is far away, General. You are all that represents your city in this place and you have never known the fury of my white soldiers. How do you dare to speak to me in this way? I rode in Gaul when you were no more than a child! What lands I have won are mine by right of conquest, by more ancient law than yours. They are mine because I have shown the strength to hold them, Roman!'

The angry rumble caused Julius' horse to shy nervously and Julius reached down to pat the gelding's neck. He controlled his temper to reply.

'I am here because you were named friend, Ariovistus. I honour you for my city, but I tell you again, you will cross the Rhine and leave the lands of Rome and Roman allies. If you live by right of conquest, then I will destroy your armies by the same right!'

Julius felt Brutus shift uncomfortably in the saddle on his right shoulder. The meeting was not going as he had intended, but the arrogance of Ariovistus nettled him.

'And what are you doing, Caesar? By what right do you take the lands of the tribes from them? Were they given to you by your Greek gods perhaps?' Ariovistus sneered as he raised his hands and gestured at the verdant countryside around them.

'You had answer enough when I sent back your messengers with empty hands,' he went on. 'I want nothing from you or your city. Go on your way and leave me in peace, or you will not live. I have fought for these lands and paid the blood price. You have done nothing but send a pack of Helvetii scavengers back to their homeland. Do you think that gives you the right to deal with me as an equal? I am a king, Roman, and kings are not troubled by men like you. I do not fear your legions, particularly those riders behind you, who cannot even keep their mounts still.'

Julius resisted the urge to look behind him, though he could see the perfect ranks of the Suebi and knew there would be nothing like such a calm order in his own lines. Under his mask, he flushed, relieved that it could not be seen.

'I *am* Rome,' Julius said. 'In my person you address the Senate and the people. You insult my city and all the countries under our rule. When you . . .'

Something whirred over their heads from the Suebi lines and Ariovistus cursed. Julius looked up to see a dozen long shafts arc towards his precious Tenth and turned savagely to Ariovistus.

'*This* is your discipline?' he snapped.

Ariovistus looked as furious as he was himself and Julius knew he had not ordered the attack. Both armies stirred restlessly and another single arrow looped over them.

'My men are eager for war, Caesar. They live to bathe in blood,' Ariovistus growled at him. He looked over his shoulder at his men.

'Go back to them and we will come for you,' Julius said, his voice hollow with finality under the mask. Ariovistus faced

332

him and in his eyes Julius saw a glittering fear. It didn't match anything he had seen so far and Julius wondered at the reason.

Before the king could answer, another flight of arrows whined overhead and Julius wheeled his horse away crying 'Ha!' to force a gallop back to his lines. Brutus, Domitius and Octavian went with him, pounding over the ground. Behind them, Ariovistus too dug in his heels and his men sent up a great cheer as they saw him return to them.

Julius issued a flurry of orders as he came back to the Tenth. The fastest of the extraordinarii galloped south to Mark Antony with instructions to make all speed in support. Others were sent into the forest to the west, to scout for hidden archers or a surprise force. The Gaulish ponies were taken to the rear and the Tenth were free at last of their distraction. They formed a huge defensive square, with shields overlapping against a cavalry charge. Spears were readied and arrows fitted to the sinew bowstrings. The front rank waited patiently to repel the first charge.

It did not come. To Julius' surprise, Ariovistus vanished deep within the mass of horsemen and suddenly they began to retreat in perfect order. Some of the Tenth shouted and jeered at them, but the scouts were not back from the woods to the west and Julius was not about to risk an advance without knowing who lurked in those green depths.

Ariovistus took his men out of spear and then arrow range before halting once more. Though there were clearly hot-headed youngsters in the Suebi lines, they showed their discipline in the retreat, with sections of them covering others as they moved back.

'What's his game?' Brutus muttered at Julius' side. 'While he delays, he must know our legions are coming up behind us.'

'He may mean to draw us in. I don't like the look of those woods,' Julius replied.

As he spoke, the first of his scouts galloped back to the Roman lines.

'Nothing, sir,' the man panted as he came close and saluted. 'No tracks or old fires and no sign of any force in hiding.'

Julius nodded, suddenly remembering the last time he had taken a scout's report without corroborating it.

Two more of his riders came out of the trees and reported before Julius was satisfied and baffled by the situation. Ariovistus had acted as if he were about to launch a wild charge, but his men stood with stolid indifference, unmoved by the beckoning gestures of the Tenth front line.

Julius tapped his fingers irritably on his saddle. Had they trapped the ground perhaps? It seemed unlikely. Spiked pits would be more of a hindrance to their own army while they outnumbered the single Roman legion.

'Shall we wait for Mark Antony?' Brutus asked.

Julius calculated the time it would take for the legions to reach his position and let out a sharp breath of frustration. It would be hours before they were there to support him.

'Yes. There is something here I do not understand. Their forces are swift and together they outnumber us perhaps two to our one. Ariovistus should attack unless he was bluffing, though I can't see how he could have been. I will not risk the lives of my Tenth on a trap until we are supported.'

The soldiers who heard this exchanged pleased glances, though Julius didn't see it as he stared towards the enemy. A commander who looked after his men was a valuable one, as far as they were concerned.

The horsemen of the Suebi stood silently a thousand paces from the Tenth and a fly buzzed around Julius' face as he looked over their lines.

'Stand ready, gentlemen. For now, we wait.'

*　　*　　*

By the time the vast column of legions had joined the Tenth, Ariovistus too had summoned his main force. At the best estimate of the scouts who dared the darts and arrows of the enemy horsemen, there must have been sixty thousand of the Suebi warriors. Each rider brought a running soldier, keeping up a terrific pace as one hand gripped the mane of the horse he ran alongside. Julius was reminded of the Spartans running to battle in the same way and hoped he would not face opponents of a similar calibre. Brutus had made a wry remark about the battle of Thermopylae, remembered from their tutors years before, but the Spartan king had been able to defend a narrow pass in mountains, whereas Julius could be flanked or even surrounded by such a mobile force. A better model was the battle of Cannae, he thought, where the Romans had been annihilated, though he did not voice the worry aloud.

Two hours after noon, Julius had his sixteen scorpion bows set up and pointing towards the enemy. They were perfect defensive weapons against a charge, but were so poorly manoeuvrable that they fell behind an advance after the first shots.

'I have never known a battle like this, Brutus, but they have waited too long now. Have Octavian protect our flanks with the extraordinarii. The rest is up to us.'

He chopped his hand down and all along the lines, cornicens blew their long horns in a single note that matched no order. The sound was intended merely to frighten the enemy and Julius saw a restless shifting amongst the Suebi as they reacted to it. Moments later, the scorpions fired and bolts as long as a man blurred across the distance between them, faster than could be seen or avoided. Horses in the front lines were spitted, the great bolts continuing on to kill indiscriminately behind them. As the scorpion teams worked feverishly to reload, Julius signalled the advance and with the Tenth at their head, the legions began their loping run towards the enemy, spears ready in their hands. Though they moved quickly, no man left his position and if the Suebi charged them, they could form impregnable squares with barely a check to their pace.

With the perfection of discipline, the legions spread out as soon as they were through the pinch between the forest and the Hand. Brutus commanded the Third on the right flank and Mark Antony took the left.

As they came into range for archers, the men readied their shields, but without warning the Suebi lines began to move away once more, faster by far than the Roman advance. Thousands of warriors cantered clear and re-formed half a mile distant.

It was not too far, though Julius feared being drawn out onto the green fields. Ahead of him, he could see the first of the Suebi camps struggling to close its gates. Hundreds of cart drivers were in a panic as they tried to get in. Julius shook his head in amazement that Ariovistus had abandoned them.

Bericus detached to the west to handle the stockade and another of the Ariminum legions moved smoothly up to the front to take the place of that five thousand. They swept past the stockade as Bericus took the people there without fuss or bloodshed. Julius saw their arms raised in panic as he passed them, but the rest of the Suebi were once again on the move, the solid formations becoming liquid as they broke apart to reform another half mile distant.

Julius signalled the halt and the legions crashed to a panting stop. Brutus came galloping in from the right wing.

'Let me take the extraordinarii. I can stop them long enough for you to bring up the rest,' he said, glaring at the enemy in the distance.

'No, I won't risk the only good horsemen I have,' Julius said, casting an eye over the whooping, ragged-looking Aedui, over-joyed to be reunited with their ponies. 'We are deep in his lands now. I want a hostile camp set up around the stockade as a base. I am not going to exhaust the men by charging all over Gaul after him. I want the legions behind camp walls and gates before nightfall. Have the ballistae readied when the carts come up behind us. Some hot food as well. I don't know about you, but I'm starving.'

Julius looked over at the black mass of horsemen of the Suebi and shook his head.

'Ariovistus is no fool. There has to be a reason for this cowardice. When the camps are ready, summon my council to me.'

CHAPTER TWENTY-NINE

෪෨෪෨෪෨

Building fortified camps under the very noses of the enemy was a new experience for the six legions. Every man who could be spared dug the outer trenches, throwing the loose earth up into great ramparts, shifting many tons of earth to the height of three men. The extraordinarii patrolled the perimeter and twice during the long afternoon, small groups had ridden hard at them, sending javelins flying before racing back to their own lines. It had been no more than young men showing their courage, but Julius could make nothing of Ariovistus' plans. His warriors seemed eager enough, but still the main army kept their distance, watching as the Romans raised earthworks and felled trees. Julius had smelt spices on the breeze as the day wore on and knew the Suebi were busy preparing food for their own men as he was about to do for his.

By the early evening, the huge camps were finished and the legions marched inside gates as solid as anything in Gaul. The legion carpenters were old hands at turning heavy trunks into shaped beams and the earthen ramparts were spiked solidly enough to resist the most determined attack. Julius could sense a mood of optimism amongst his men. The sight of a retreating enemy had raised their morale enormously and he hoped it would continue.

He gathered his council in the generals' tent inside the walls after a hot meal had been prepared and eaten. The Aedui horses had munched their way through a good part of his grain supply, but there could be no grazing outside with the Suebi so close. As night fell, Julius waited for Brutus to come and join the others. Lamps were lit and the first night watch went on duty without their shields, climbing wooden steps to the ramparts to scan the darkness for an attack.

Julius looked around at his council with a quiet satisfaction. Octavian had grown into a fine leader of men and Ciro too had justified his promotion to the position of centurion. Publius Crassus was a fearless commander and Julius would be sorry when he was sent back to lead his father's legion. Renius continued to train the men in gladius technique and Julius never hesitated in promoting those he recommended. If Renius said they were able to lead, they were. Domitius was capable of commanding a full legion and the men loved the silver armour he now wore constantly. At that time, in that place, they were in their prime and Julius was proud of them all.

As Brutus joined them, Cabera brought out a ball of clay he had wrapped in damp cloth. It shone in the lamplight as he massaged the brown ball into a semblance of a face, pinching out a nose and poking eyes with his fingernails.

'If ropes were placed in this way, you could alter the shape of the skull,' he said, winding a piece of cord around the little head and tightening it with a stick that he twisted until the clay began to bulge. When he had created a heavy ridge above the eyes, he repeated the process above it, until a copy of the odd Suebi features stared back at them.

339

'But the skull would break, surely?' Octavian said, wincing at the image.

Cabera shook his head. 'For a man, yes, but for a newborn child, when the skull is still soft, such a binding would produce the ridges. No demons, these men, for all the gossip in camp. They are brutal, though. I have never heard of a race that could mistreat their young in such a way. The first year, perhaps two, of their lives must be spent in agony, with these things pressing against their bones. I doubt they are ever fully free of pain. If I am right, it would mean they mark their warrior castes almost from birth.'

'You must show it around the camps, if they are talking, Cabera,' Julius said, fascinated by the contorted head. 'The Suebi need no other advantages with their numbers and our men are superstitious.'

A commotion outside the tent brought the council to their feet in an instant. The guards who were stationed there snapped muffled words at someone and then the unmistakable sounds of a scuffle could be heard. Brutus strode to the flap and flung it back.

Two of the Gaulish slaves taken by the Suebi were writhing on the ground.

'Sorry, sir,' one guard said quickly as he saluted Brutus. 'Consul Caesar said he should not be disturbed and these two ignored my warning.'

'You did well,' Brutus replied. He reached down and helped one of the Gauls to his feet. 'What was so important?' he asked.

The man glared at the guard before speaking, but Brutus didn't understand a word of the torrent that came in reply. Raising his eyebrows, Brutus exchanged glances with the guard.

'I don't suppose he understood your warning, either. Adàn? Would you come and translate for me, please?'

With Adàn there, the man spoke even faster. By then, his

340

companion had risen to his feet and stood sullenly rubbing his stomach.

'Are you going to stand out here all night?' Julius said, coming out to them.

'I think you're going to want to hear this, sir,' Adàn said.

'It explains why we couldn't bring them to battle, at least,' Julius said. 'If this Ariovistus is fool enough to listen to his priests, we can only benefit from it. I make it three days until the new moon. If he won't fight us till then, we can push him right back to the Rhine and hammer him against it.'

Julius' mood of worry and anger had disappeared at the news brought by the Gaulish slaves. His riders had rejoiced to find some of their own people amongst the rest and the crucial piece of information explained a great deal of the Suebi king's behaviour.

Julius listened as Adàn translated the man's torrent of words for his benefit. Ariovistus had been told he would die if he fought before the new moon. It meant the angry meeting had been a bluff of sorts, and Julius had called it when he ordered the Tenth into battle formation. Julius remembered the glimpse of fear he had seen in the king's eyes and understood it at last. It was a weakness in a leader to allow his priests so much sway over his army, Julius was certain. The Greeks had been crippled by their reliance on oracles. Even Roman generals had been known to delay and lose positions if the entrails of birds or fish showed disaster waiting to fall. Julius refused to bring such men to his battlefields, convinced they did more harm than good.

Julius had his rough map of the area held with lead weights on the table. He pointed to the black line that marked the winding Rhine to the north, less than fifteen miles away. Even with the heavy carts of the baggage train, it was a distance they could cross easily before the new moon and he blessed the gods for delivering Aedui slaves into his hands.

'We will break camp an hour before dawn, gentlemen,' Julius told his generals. 'I want the ballistae, onagers and scorpions with us as far as the ground will allow. If they fall behind, they are to be brought up slowly for the final battle. Octavian will command the extraordinarii, Mark Antony will take my right flank. Bericus on the left and all the scorpions to be brought to the front of any halt. The Tenth and Third Gallica will hold the centre. The men are to have a good breakfast tomorrow and fill their waterskins from the casks. Let them all know what we have learned tonight. It will give them heart. Make sure each man has his spears and weapons in good order.'

He paused as Mark Antony filled his cup, the Roman flushed with pleasure at the position he had been given. Mark Antony had heard about the arrogance of Ariovistus at the meeting and accepted that the friendship with Rome was at an end. No doubt Caesar's enemies would make much of it in the Senate, but that was a problem for another day.

Crassus sighed as Servilia's slave girl massaged the knotted muscles of his neck and shoulders. The frozen fruit he had eaten lay cold in his stomach and after he had been fully relaxed on the table, the luxury of a hot pool awaited him, steaming in the open night. Across from him, Servilia lay along a padded couch, looking up at the stars. Though there was no moon to light the heavens, the sky was clear and she could see the tiny red disc of Mars above the line of the tiled roof that surrounded the open courtyard. The hot pool gleamed under the light of lamps and heavy moths fluttered into the flames, crackling as they died.

'This place is worth every coin,' Crassus murmured, wincing slightly as the slave girl worked a painful point between his shoulder blades.

'I knew you would appreciate it,' Servilia replied, smiling with real pleasure. 'So few who come to my house have an eye for the beautiful things, but what are we without them?'

Her gaze fell on the freshly painted plaster of the new wing of her town house. Crassus had secured the land and she had paid a full market rate for it, without resentment. Anything else would have meant a shift of their relationship and she liked and honoured the old man who lay so comfortably under the strong fingers of her Nubian girl.

'Are you not going to press me for information then?' he asked without opening his eyes. 'Am I no longer useful to you?'

Servilia chuckled, sitting up.

'Old father, be silent if that is what you want. My house is yours for as long as you need it. There is no obligation.'

'Ah, the worst kind,' he replied, smiling to himself. 'What is it you want to know?'

'These new men in the Senate, Clodius and now Titus Milo, the owner of the meat market. Are they dangerous?' she said. Though she spoke lightly, Crassus knew her full attention was on the answer.

'Very much so,' he replied. 'I would not like to enter the Senate when they are there.'

Servilia snorted. 'You don't fool me with your sudden devotion to trade, old man. I doubt there is a word spoken there that doesn't find its way back to you.'

She smiled sweetly at him then and he opened his eyes and winked at her before shifting under the hands of the slave to guide her to a new place. Servilia shook her head at his games.

'How is your new legion shaping?' she asked.

'Well enough, my dear. When my son, Publius, returns from Gaul, I may find a use for them. If I survive the current unrest.'

'Is it that bad?' she asked.

Crassus propped himself up on his elbows, his expression becoming serious.

'It is. These new men sway the mob of Rome and recruit more and more to their gangs each day. The streets are no longer safe even for members of the Senate, Servilia. We must be thankful that Milo occupies so much of Clodius' time. If either one of them should destroy the other, the victor would be free to wreak havoc in the city. As it is, each man is the check on his colleague, at least for the moment. I have heard they consider parts of the city their own, so that the followers of Clodius may not cross certain streets without a beating, even in the day. Most of Rome cannot see the struggle, but it is there nonetheless. I have seen the bodies in the Tiber.'

'And Pompey? Does he not see the threat?'

Crassus shrugged. 'What can he do against their code of silence? The raptores fear their masters more than anything Pompey can do to them. He at least will not attack their families after they are dead. When a trial is considered, the witnesses disappear or become unable to remember. It is a shameful thing to see, Servilia. It is as if a great sickness has come into the city and I do not see how it can be cut out.' He sighed in distaste.

'The senate house is the core of it and I spoke the truth when I said I was glad my business takes me away from it. Clodius and Milo meet openly to sniff and taunt each other before their animals terrorize the city at night. The Senate do not have the will to control them. All the little men have fallen in with one or the other and Pompey has less support than he realises. He cannot match their bribes, nor their threats. At times, I wish Julius would come back. He would not see Rome descend into chaos while he had life in him.'

Servilia looked up at the bright evening star, trying to hide her interest. When she glanced at Crassus, she saw his eyes were open, studying her. There was little the old man didn't know or guess.

'Have you heard from Julius?' she asked at last.

'I have. He offers me trade concessions with the new lands in Gaul, though I think he paints a prettier picture than the full truth to tempt me in. Mind you, if half of what he says is true, I would be a fool to miss the opportunity.'

'I saw the notices around the city,' Servilia said softly, thinking of Julius. 'How many will respond?'

'With Clodius and Milo making life a misery with their struggle, I would think there will be thousands crossing the Alps in the spring. Land for the taking: who can resist such an offer? Slaves and trade for every man with enough energy to make the trip. If I were younger and poor, I might consider his offer myself. Of course, I am ready to provide the stores and supplies to anyone who wants to go to his fabulous new provinces.'

Servilia laughed. 'Always the merchant?'

'A merchant prince, Servilia. Julius used the term in one of his letters and I rather like it.' He waved away the slave girl and sat up on the long bench.

'He is more useful than he knows, is Julius. When the city looks too long inward to its own affairs, we create men like Clodius and Milo, who care nothing for the greater events of the world. The reports Julius pays to be read on every street corner raise the spirits of the lowest tanner or dyer in the markets.' He chuckled. 'Pompey knows it, though he hates to see Julius so successful. He is forced to fight for him in the Senate whenever Suetonius objects to some little breach of the laws. Such a bitter draught for that man to swallow, but without Julius and his conquests, Rome would become a stagnant pool, with all the fish eating each other out of desperation.'

'And you, Crassus? What does the future hold for you?'

Crassus rose from the table and lowered himself into the warm bath set in the floor, oblivious of his nudity.

'I find that old age is the perfect balm for raging ambition, Servilia. My dreams are all for my son.' His eyes twinkled in the starlight and she did not believe him.

'Will you join me?' he asked.

As an answer, Servilia stood and undid the single clasp that held the cool material to her. She was naked underneath and Crassus smiled at the unveiling.

'How you do love drama, my dear,' he said with amusement.

Julius swore as the Roman squares faltered. After two days of pursuit, he had forced the Suebi to face them only a few miles short of the Rhine. He knew he should have expected the attack, but when it came, the reversal had been so sudden that the armies clashed before the Roman legions could even untie their spears.

The warriors of Ariovistus were every bit as brutal as they had expected. They gave no ground unless it was over the corpses of their men and the cavalry swirled like smoke around the battlefield, with charges forming the instant the Romans broke their squares to attack.

'Mark Antony! Support the left!' Julius bellowed, glimpsing the general in the heaving mass. There was no sign of his order having been heard over the clash of arms.

The battlefield was in chaos and, for the first time, he began to fear a defeat. Every Suebi rider ran with another man hanging on the horse's mane and that speed of movement was making it almost impossible to counter them. Julius saw with horror that two of the Ariminum legions were close to being overwhelmed on the left flank and there was no sign of a supporting force arriving to help them. He could no longer see Mark Antony and Brutus was embroiled in the fighting, too far away to help. Julius tore a shield from a legionary's grasp and raced on foot across the battlefield.

The clash of arms and dying men grew in intensity as he neared them. Julius could feel the fear amongst his own legionaries and he began to call them by name. The chain of command seemed to have been broken in the attack and Julius was forced to gather optios and centurions to him to give his orders.

'Join the Twelfth and Fifth together. Double the square!' he told them, watching as they began to create order from the milling ranks around him. His extraordinarii were off on the flanks holding the Suebi from surrounding them. Where was Mark Antony? Julius craned around him, but could see no sign of him in the press.

Under Julius' constant barrage of orders, the two legions joined together and then wheeled to fight back to back as the Suebi crumbled the edges of their squares, picking men off with sudden flights of darts and stones. Again and again, the horses galloped at the legions only to halt in the face of the unbroken shield walls. The legionaries charged forward as the riders tried to turn and the carnage was horrific.

With the Rhine behind them, the Suebi had nowhere to run and Julius knew panic when he saw the front ranks of his beloved Tenth being smashed down by spears thrown at the gallop. The shields saved many and they rose in a daze, brought back to their position by their friends around them.

Still the legions forced themselves onward. The great ballistae and onagers were brought up and tore red ribbons in the enemy. The Tenth roared as Julius rejoined them, fighting all the harder under his watchful eye.

Julius saw the left and right flanks were holding. Brutus controlled the right, and the extraordinarii and Aedui cavalry had blunted the Suebi's attacks with wild courage. He advanced the centre and the Suebi were forced to fall back by the sheer ferocity of the legion formations.

Julius saw with pride that his officers knew their business, even without orders. When the foot soldiers of the Suebi rushed them, they widened their line to bring as many swords as possible into the attack. When the cavalry charged, they clashed into squares and fought on. The ballistae and onagers launched again and again until they were too far behind to risk their missiles falling on the Roman troops.

Julius saw Ariovistus gather his bodyguard around him, a thousand of the very best of the Suebi. Each one stood a head taller than the Romans and was marked with the strange ridges that frightened the legionaries. They charged the Tenth in the centre and Julius saw the square formed just too late to prevent the armoured warriors from reaching them.

The centre buckled and then, with a roar, the Tenth fought back like maniacs in a blood rage. Julius remembered how they had been created from the deaths of those who had faltered and he smiled with a vicious pleasure. The Tenth were his and they would not be turned. They would never run.

He surged forward with the soldiers around him, calling out for the flanks to form horns to compress the enemy. Julius caught a glimpse of the dark horses of the Aedui coming from the left and isolating a block of the Suebi from the main force. The Tenth climbed over bodies to reach the enemy. The ground was red and shining as they built speed into a charge and Ariovistus was forced to ride back from the front before the roaring Tenth and Third could reach him.

The whole of the Roman lines saw the king retreat and they responded, raising their heads. Julius exulted. The Rhine was less than a mile distant and he could see the shining water. He called his cornicens to him and ordered spears to be thrown, watching as the mass of missiles hampered any attempt by Ariovistus to re-form. A gap opened between the armies and Julius urged them all forward, calling to the men he knew. As he mentioned their names, they stood a little straighter and forgot their weariness under his gaze.

'Bring up the ballistae and scorpions!' he ordered and his messengers weaved their way back to help the sweating teams over the rough ground.

Without an apparent signal, the entire mass of the Suebi formed another charge and thundered down towards the Roman lines. Spears plucked some of them from their saddles and killed mounts that fouled those behind. Julius knew it was their last charge and his men moved into tight squares before he could order it.

The long Roman shields were overlapped and the men behind braced themselves to take an impact, their swords ready. Not one part of the Roman lines fell back from the terrifying sight of the horses coming at them. When it faltered, the legions tore them apart.

The army of Ariovistus began to be compressed against the river. Without the extraordinarii and the Aedui, Julius knew they could have overwhelmed the Romans, but though they hammered the flanks again and again, the legions continued their advance, killing anything that faced them.

The banks of the Rhine seethed with men and horses as they risked their lives to cross against the current. The great river was almost a hundred yards wide and those without mounts to cling to were swept away and drowned. Julius could see tiny fishing boats crammed with desperate men and watched as one of them overturned, the dark bobbing heads of the Suebi disappearing under the water.

On the left flank, a thousand of the enemy threw down their arms and surrendered to the Ariminum legions they had failed to break. Julius pushed on with his Tenth until they were standing on the banks of the river, looking at the mass of drowning men that choked the water from his side right to the deepest centre. Those of the Tenth who had been able to salvage or keep their spears threw them at the men in the water and Julius saw many struck in that way, slipping beneath the surface with no more than a single cry.

On the far bank, Julius saw a boat make it into the shallows and watched as the figure of Ariovistus climbed out and collapsed onto his knees for a moment.

'Ciro!' Julius called. His voice echoed as the name went back into the ranks of the Tenth, producing the powerful figure of the legionary, still panting with the strain of the battle. Julius handed him a single spear and pointed to the figure on the far bank.

'Can you reach him?'

Ciro hefted the spear in his hand. The soldiers around him stood back to give him room as he stared across the wide river.

'Quickly, before he rises,' Julius snapped.

Ciro took five steps back and then ran forward, heaving the spear into the air. The men of the Tenth watched it in fascination as it rose high into the sun and then fell.

Ariovistus stood to face the Romans on the far bank and never saw it. The spear hammered him off his feet, puncturing his leather armour over the stomach. The king flailed limply as the survivors of his bodyguard dragged him into the trees.

After a moment of awed silence, the legions cheered themselves hoarse. Ciro raised a single arm to them in salute and grinned as Julius clapped him on the back.

'A hero's throw, Ciro. By the gods, I have never seen a finer. Hercules himself could not have done better.' Julius roared his triumph with the others then and felt the exultation that comes from victory, when the blood seemed to rush like fire through the veins and tired muscles surged with fresh strength.

'My glorious Tenth!' Julius shouted to them. 'My brothers! Is there anything you cannot achieve? You, Belinus, I saw you strike down three of the warriors in the line. You, Regulus, you gathered in your century when poor Decidas fell. You will do him honour when you wear his plume.'

One by one, he called the names of the men who were with him, praising their courage. He had missed nothing of the day's fighting and they stood tall as his gaze swept the faces of his men. The other legions came closer to hear him and he could feel their pride and pleasure. He raised his voice to carry as far as it could.

'What can we not achieve, after this?' They cheered the words. 'We are the sons of Rome and I tell you this land will be ours! Every man who has fought for me will have land and gold and slaves to work it for him. You will be the new nobilitas of Rome and drink wine good enough to make you weep. I swear it before you all, on my honour. I swear it as consul. I swear it as Rome in Gaul.'

Julius reached down into the churned mud of the river bank, mixed with the blood of the Suebi. He grasped a handful and held it up to the assembled men.

'You see this clay? This bloody clay I hold? I say it is yours. It belongs to my city as much as the chariot races or the markets. Take it, hold it in your hands. Can you not feel it?'

He watched with wild pleasure as the legions copied his action, joking and laughing as they did so. They grinned at him as they held up their pieces of the land and Julius squeezed his fist closed, so that the clay dripped from between his fingers.

'I may never go home,' he whispered. 'This is my time. This is my path.'

CHAPTER THIRTY

꧁ꕥꕥ꧂

Tabbic and Alexandria wrapped their cloaks tight against the cold as they approached the locked door of the shop. The streets were rimed with dirty ice, making every step a danger. Alexandria held on to Tabbic's arm to help steady them both. Her two guards made their habitual inspection of the area as Tabbic pushed his key into the lock and swore under his breath when it jammed. All around them, the workers of Rome went to their jobs and shops and one or two nodded stiffly to Alexandria as they passed, miserable in the biting wind.

'Lock's frozen,' Tabbic said, pulling out the key and thumping his fist against the ornate door plate.

Alexandria rubbed her arms while she waited, knowing better than to offer advice. Tabbic may have been an irritable old man, but he had made the lock himself and if anyone could open it, he could. While she tried to ignore the wind, Tabbic reached for his jewellery tools and used a tiny pick to clear the ice. When that failed, he tried a few drops of oil and pressed one hand after another against the metal in an attempt to warm the mechanism, blowing on his fingers as they froze on contact.

'There she goes,' he said as the lock clicked at last and the door swung open to reveal the dark recesses of the workshop.

Alexandria's teeth chattered and her hands shook. It would be some time before she was warm enough to attempt any fine work and as usual she wished Tabbic would employ a slave to come in early and light the forge for them. He wouldn't hear of it. He had never owned slaves and had been irritated at Alexandria's suggestion, saying she of all people should know better.

If that hadn't been enough, it was even possible that the slave would be provided by one of the gangs and all their precious stock would disappear into the coffers of Clodius or Milo. The same reason prevented them from hiring a night guard, and Alexandria was thankful every morning when they found the shop untouched. For all Tabbic's traps and locks, they had been lucky so far. At least it wouldn't be long before they completed the purchase of a spacious new place in an area less troubled by the raptores. Tabbic had agreed to that at last, if only to fill the large orders that were the backbone of their business.

Tabbic hurried over to light the forge and Alexandria shut the door securely against the wind, unclenching her stiff fingers in something like ecstasy.

'We'll be going then, mistress,' Teddus said.

As always after the morning walk to the shop, his leg was barely holding him and Alexandria shook her head. Teddus never changed from one morning to the next and though she had never sent him straight back into the cold, he still gave her the opportunity.

'Not until you have something hot inside you,' she said firmly.

He was a good man, though his son might as well have been

353

mute for all the interest he took in those he guarded with his father. In the mornings, he was particularly sullen.

They could all hear the welcome crackle of the spills and wood chippings in the furnace as Tabbic nursed it into life. With the great iron block to warm them, the shop needed no other fire. Alexandria broke the ice on a water bucket she had filled the day before and poured it into the old iron kettle Tabbic had made in that same forge. The routine was comforting and the three men with her began to relax as the room tempera-ture eased above freezing.

Alexandria was startled when the door opened behind them.

'Come back later,' she called, then fell silent as three hard-looking men entered the confined space and carefully shut the door behind them.

'I hope we won't have to,' the first said.

He was a typical product of the back alleys of Rome. Too cunning to be interested in the legions and too vicious for any sort of normal work. Alexandria realised she could smell him, an unwashed stale reek that made her want to take a step back. The man grinned at her, revealing dark yellow teeth in shriv-elled gums. He didn't have to go on for her to know he was one of the raptores who clustered under Clodius or Milo. The shop owners in the area told terrible tales of their threats and violence and Alexandria found herself hoping Teddus would not provoke them. The leering menace of the men made her face the truth that her guard was just too old for his sort of work.

'We're closed,' Tabbic said behind her.

Alexandria heard a faint clink as he picked up some sort of tool. She didn't look round, but the eyes of the intruders fastened on him. The leader snorted contemptuously.

'Not to us, old man. Unless you want to be closed to everyone else,' he said.

Alexandria hated him for his knowing arrogance. He built

and made nothing, but still seemed to think he had the right to enter the shops and homes of hard-working people and make them afraid.

'What do you want?' Tabbic asked.

The leader of the three scratched his neck and examined what he found there before cracking something dark between his nails.

'I want your tithe, old man. This street isn't safe unless you pay your tithe. Eighty sesterces a month and nothing will happen. No one will be beaten as they walk home. Nothing valuable will be burnt.' He paused and winked at Alexandria. 'No one will be dragged into an alleyway and raped. We'll keep you safe.'

'You filth!' Tabbic shouted. 'How dare you come into my shop with your threats? Get out now, or I will call the guards. Take your grinning friends with you!'

The three men looked bored at the outburst.

'Come on, old man,' the first said, rolling his massive shoulders. 'See what I'll give you if you don't put that hammer down. Or perhaps the lad? I'll do him here in front of you, if you want. Either way, I'm not leaving until I have your first month's payment. Clodius don't like those who make a fuss and this street is his now. Better just to pay what you owe and be left in peace.' He chuckled and the sound made Alexandria shudder. 'The trick is not to think of it as your money. It's just another city tax.'

'I pay my taxes!' Tabbic roared. He waved a heavy hammer in the man's direction, making him flinch. The other two behind him shuffled in closer and Alexandria could see knives in their belts.

Teddus drew his short gladius in one sweeping movement and the atmosphere in the shop changed. All three of the men produced their knives, but Teddus held the sword with a wrist stronger than his lame leg. Alexandria could see the irritation in the leader's face. None of them looked round as Teddus' son drew his own dagger and held it. The younger man was nothing like the threat of his father and the leader of the raptores knew it. More importantly, he knew he would either have to kill the swordsman or leave.

'I won't warn you, whoreson. Get out,' Teddus said slowly, looking the leader in the eye.

The leader of the raptores lunged his head forward and back in a sudden spasm like a fighting cock. Teddus moved, but the man guffawed, his coarse laughter filling the shop.

'Bit slow, aren't you? I could take you here, but why should I bother when it's so much easier to wait for you in the dark?' He ignored Teddus then and looked back at Tabbic, still standing with his hammer raised to one shoulder.

'Eighty sesterces on the first of each month. First payment by the end of today. It's just business, you old fool. Will I take it with me now, or shall I come back for you one at a time?'

Once again, he winked at Alexandria and she recoiled from the knowledge in that glance.

'No. I'll pay you. Then when you're gone, I'll tell the guards and see you cut.'

Tabbic reached into his cloak and the chink of coins made the three men smile. The leader tutted aloud.

'No you won't,' he said. 'I have friends, me. Lots of friends who would be angry if I was taken out to the Campus and shown the butcher's knife. Your wife and children would be very sorry if my friends were angry about something like that.'

Deftly, he caught the thrown pouch of coins, counting them quickly before placing it inside his grubby tunic next to the skin. He chuckled at their expressions and spat a wad of dark phlegm onto the tiled floor.

'That's the way. I hope business is good, old man. I'll see you next month.'

The three of them opened the door, leaning into the wind

that came rushing into the shop. They left it open behind them and disappeared into the dark streets. Teddus walked over and shoved it closed, pulling down the locking bar. Tabbic did indeed look like an old man as he turned away from Alexandria, unable to meet her gaze. He was pale and shaking as he laid the hammer down on the bench and picked up his long brush. He began to sweep the clean floor in slow strokes.

'What are we going to do?' Alexandria demanded.

For a long time, Tabbic remained silent until she wanted to shout the question at him and break the stillness.

'What can we do?' he said at last. 'I won't risk my family for anything.'

'We can shut the shop until the new place is ready. It's halfway across the city, Tabbic. In a better area. It will be different there.'

Despair and weariness showed in Tabbic's face.

'No. That bastard didn't say anything about whether the shop was open or closed. He'll still want his money if we don't sell a single piece.'

'Just for a month, then. Until we close up and get out,' she said, wanting to see some spark of life break his stunned misery.

Tabbic hated thieves. Handing over coins he had worked days for hurt him more deeply than a physical pain. His hands shook with reaction as he changed his grip on the broom. Then he looked up at her.

'There is nowhere else, girl. Don't you know that? I'm just surprised they haven't been to us earlier. You remember little Geranas?'

Alexandria nodded. The man had been a jeweller longer even than Tabbic and produced beautiful work in gold.

'They used a hammer on his right hand when he wouldn't pay. Can you believe that? He can't earn with the mess they made of him, but they don't care about that. They just want the story to spread, so men like me will just meekly give up what we worked so hard for.' He stopped then, tightening his grip on the broom until it snapped loudly.

'Better lay out your tools, Alexandria. We have three pieces to finish today.'

His voice was hard and flat and Tabbic made no move to continue the morning routine as the shop was readied for customers.

'I have friends, Tabbic,' Alexandria said. 'Julius and Brutus may be away, but Crassus knows me. I can try to bring pressure on them. It must be better than doing nothing.'

Tabbic's grim expression didn't change. 'You do that. It can't hurt,' he said.

Teddus sighed, sheathing his sword at last.

'I'm sorry,' he muttered.

Tabbic heard him. 'Don't be. That cocky bastard didn't like the look of you, for all his words.'

'Why did you pay him then?' Alexandria asked him.

Tabbic snorted. 'Because your man would have killed him and they'd have come back to burn us out. They can't let even one of us win, girl, or the rest stop paying.'

He turned to Teddus and clapped his big hand on the man's shoulder, ignoring his embarrassment.

'You did well enough, though I'd find a man to replace your son, you understand me? You need a killer for your kind of work. Now I'll give you a hot drink against the cold and a bite to eat before you go on your way, but I want you here in plenty of time tonight, understand?'

'I'll be here,' Teddus promised, glancing at his son's flushed face.

Tabbic looked him in the eye and nodded, satisfied.

'You're a good man,' he said. 'I just wish courage was all it took.'

*   *   *

358

Brutus examined the cracked glass of the water clock. Even with fur gloves, his fingers were numb with cold. All he wanted was to go back to his barracks and wrap himself up like a hibernating bear. Yet the routines of the legions had to continue. Though the cold ate into the men worse than anything they had ever known, the legion watches had to be marked by the three-hour trickle of water from one glass bowl into another. Brutus swore softly to himself as his touch removed a piece of the glass, which fell with a thud into the snow. He rubbed the growth of beard that covered his face. Julius had seen the benefit of suspending shaving in the cold months, but Brutus found the moisture of his breath would crust into ice after only an hour outside.

'The shelters aren't working. We'll have to light fires under them. Just enough to keep the water from freezing. You have my permission to take a few billets of wood from the supply for each one. The sentries can keep it going during their watch. They'll be glad of the heat, I should think. Have the smiths make you an iron sheath to protect the glass and wood from the flames, or you'll boil half of it away.'

'I will, sir. Thank you,' the tesserarius replied, relieved he was not to be criticised. Privately, Brutus thought the man was an idiot not to have thought of it and the result was the destruction of the only way the Tenth had to fix the length of a watch.

The soldiers of Rome had finally understood why the tribes did not go to war in winter. The first snow had fallen heavily enough to break the roof of the barracks, turning the snug bunks into a chaos of wind and ice. The following day had seen the drifts made deeper and after a month Brutus could barely remember what it felt like to be warm. Though they lit huge fires below the walls each night, the heat reached only a few feet, blown away on the endless wind. He had seen ice floes the size of carts on the Rhine and sometimes the snow fell so heavily as to make a shifting crust from one bank to

359

the other. He wondered if the river would freeze solid before spring.

They seemed to spend their entire day in darkness. Julius had kept the men working as long as he could, but frozen hands slipped and a rash of injuries forced Julius to suspend the building as he came to terms with the winter at last.

Brutus passed on through the camp, his feet skidding painfully on the iced ruts left by the baggage trains. Denied grazing, they had been forced to slaughter most of the oxen, unable to afford the grain from the legion supplies. At least the meat stayed fresh, Brutus thought grimly. His glance strayed to the pile of carcasses under a dusting of snow. The meat was as hard as stone, like everything else in the country.

Brutus climbed the earthen wall of the camp and peered out into the greyness. Soft flakes touched him on the cheek and did not melt against his cold skin. He could see nothing out there but the stumps of the first trees they had felled and dragged back to be burnt for warmth.

The forest had at least protected them from the wind while it lasted. They knew now that they should have kept the closest trees to be cut last, but nothing the Romans had ever seen could have prepared them for the ferocity of that first winter. It was a killing cold.

Brutus knew many of the men were not well supplied with warm clothing. Those who had been given oxhides greased them daily, but they still became like iron. The going rate for a pair of fur gloves was more than a month's pay and that was rising as every hare and fox for a hundred miles was killed and brought in by the trappers.

At least the legions had been paid at last. Julius had captured enough silver and gold from Ariovistus to issue three months of back salary to each man. In Rome, it would have run through their fingers on whores and wine, but here there was little to do with it but gamble and many of the men had been returned to poverty only a few days after their share had been handed out. The more responsible ones sent part of their pay back to relatives and dependants in Rome.

Brutus envied those who had been sent back across the Alps to Ariminum before the passes had closed. It was a gesture that had pleased the men, though Brutus had known it was made out of necessity. In such a harsh winter, just staying alive was difficult enough. The warriors of the Suebi who had survived the battle could not be guarded for so many dark months. Better to sell them as gladiators and house guards, splitting them apart and retraining them. With the tradition that the proceeds of fighting slaves went to the legionaries, the Suebi would bring at least a gold coin to each man who had fought them.

The wind gusted harder along the wall and Brutus began to count to five hundred in his head, forcing himself to stay at least that long. Those who had to stand a watch up there were in a world of grey misery and they needed to see him bear it with them.

He pulled his cloak closer around his chest, wincing with each breath that bit at his throat until he wished it was as numb as the rest of him. Cabera had warned him about the danger and he wore two pairs of woollen socks under his sandals, though they seemed to make no difference at all. Eighteen men had lost toes or fingers since the first snow and without Cabera it would have been more. All those had been in the first few weeks, before the men learned to respect the cold. Brutus had seen one of the shrivelled black lumps clipped off with a hoof tool and the strangest thing had been the passive look on the legionary's face. Even with jaws of iron snipping through his bone, he had felt no pain.

The closest legionary was like a statue and as Brutus shuf-fled closer to him, he saw that the man's eyes were closed, his face pale and bruised-looking under a straggling beard. The penalty for falling asleep on watch was death, but Brutus clapped the man on his back in a greeting, pretending not to notice the spasm of fear as the eyes snapped open, immediately narrowing against the wind.

'Where are your gloves, lad?' Brutus asked, seeing the cramped blue fingers as the soldier pulled them out from his tunic and stood to attention.

'I lost them, sir,' he replied.

Brutus nodded. No doubt the man was as good a gambler as he was a sentry.

'You'll lose your hands too if you don't keep warm. Take mine. I have another pair.' Brutus watched as the young legionary tried to pull them on. He couldn't do it and after a brief struggle, one of them fell. Brutus picked it up and worked them over the man's frozen fingers. He hoped it was not too late. On impulse, he undid the clasp of his fur-lined cloak and wrapped it around the young soldier, trying not to wince as the wind seemed to bite every part of his exposed body, despite the under-layers. His teeth began to chatter and Brutus bit down hard to quieten them.

'Please, sir, I can't take your cloak,' the sentry said.

'It'll keep you warm enough to finish your watch, lad. Then you might choose to give it to the next one up in your place. I'll leave that to you.'

'I will, sir. Thank you.'

Brutus watched as the first tinges of colour began to return to the soldier's cheeks before he was satisfied. For some reason, he felt surprisingly cheerful as he made his way down. The fact that he had completed his tour of the camp was part of it, of course. A hot beef stew and a bed warmed with heated bricks would help him bear the loss of his only cloak and gloves. He hoped he would be as cheerful the next night when he had to walk the camp without them.

*   *   *

362

Julius pulled an iron poker from the fire and plunged it into two cups of wine. Shredded cloves sizzled on the surface and steam curled upwards as he placed the iron back into the flames and offered a cup to Mhorbaine.

Looking around him, Julius could almost believe in the permanence of the new buildings. Even in the short time before the first snows of winter, his legions had extended the road from the Roman province in the south to within almost five miles of the new camps. The trees they had felled became the structures of new barracks and Julius had been pleased with their progress until the winter struck in a single night and the following morning, a sentry had been found frozen to death on the wall. Their quarry work had been abandoned and the pace of their lives had changed as all attempts to make a permanent link to the south were turned into a more basic struggle for survival.

Even in the midst of it, Julius had used the time. The Aedui were old hands at dealing with the bitter winters and he employed them as messengers to as many tribes as they knew. At the last count, Julius had made alliances with nine of them and claimed the lands of three more in easy reach of the country vacated by Ariovistus. How much of it would hold when the winter finally ended, he did not know. If they fulfilled their promises, he would have enough volunteers to form two new legions in the spring. No doubt many of the smaller tribes had agreed only to learn the skills that had destroyed the Helvetii and the Suebi, but Julius had planned with Mark Antony how to seed the legions with his most trusted men. He had done it with those Cato sent to protect his son. He had even made legionaries out of the mercenaries under Catiline. Whether they knew it or not, the Gauls who came to him would become as solidly of Rome as Ciro or Julius himself.

He worried more about those tribes who would not respond to his summons. The Belgae had blinded the Aedui messenger and then led his horse within a short distance of the Roman camps, letting the animal find its own way back to food and warmth. The Nervii had refused to meet his man and three other tribes had followed their lead.

Julius could hardly wait for the spring. The moment of exultation he had experienced as Ariovistus was struck down did not repeat itself, but still he felt a confidence that could hardly be explained. Gaul would be his.

'The tribes you mention have never fought together, Julius. It is easier to imagine the Aedui standing back to back with the Arverni than any of those becoming brothers.' Mhorbaine sipped at his hot wine and leaned closer to the fire, relaxing.

'Perhaps,' Julius admitted, 'but my men have barely made a mark on most of Gaul. There are still tribes who haven't even heard of us and how can they accept the rule of those they have never seen?'

'You cannot fight them all, Julius. Even your legions could not do that,' Mhorbaine replied.

Julius snorted. 'Do not be so sure, my friend. My legions could murder Alexander himself if he stood against them, but with this winter I cannot see where I should take them next. Further to the north? The west? Should I seek out the more powerful tribes and beat them one by one? I almost hope they will fight together, Mhorbaine. If I can break the strongest of them, the others will accept our right to the land.'

'You have already doubled the holdings of Rome,' Mhorbaine reminded him.

Julius stared into the flames, gesturing with his cup at the unseen cold outside.

'I cannot sit and wait for them to come to me. At any moment, I could be recalled to Rome. Another man could be appointed in my place.' He caught himself before continuing, as he noted Mhorbaine's bright interest. For all the man had been a valuable ally, Julius had let the wine spill too many words from him.

The last letter from Crassus before the winter closed the passes over the Alps had been troubling. Pompey was losing control of the city and Julius had been furious at the weakness of the Senate. He almost wished Pompey would declare a Dictatorship to end the tyranny of men like Clodius and Milo. They were just names to him, but Crassus took the threat seriously enough to confide his fear and Julius knew the old man was not one to jump at shadows. At one point, Julius had even considered returning to Rome to bolster Pompey in the Senate, but the winter of Gaul had put an end to that. It was appalling to think that while he won new lands, the city he loved was falling into corruption and violence. He had long accepted that the conquest of a country had to come in blood, but that vision had no place in his own home and the very thought of it made him rage.

'There is so much to do!' he said to Mhorbaine, reaching again for the poker in the flames. 'All I can do is torment myself with plans and letters I cannot even send. I thought you said spring would have come by now? Where is the thaw you promised me?'

Mhorbaine shrugged.

'Soon,' he said, as he had so many times before.

CHAPTER THIRTY-ONE

⧢⧢⧢⧢⧢

When spring came, more than seven thousand families choked
the roads north of Rome. Out of the teeming streets of the
city, the exodus started to claim the new land that Julius promised. Those who feared the strength of Clodius and Milo took
to the wide roads to start a new life away from the crime and
dirt of the city, selling everything they owned to buy tools and
grain and oxen to pull their carts. It was a perilous journey,
with more than three hundred miles to the foothills of the Alps
and unknown dangers beyond.

The legions Julius had taken from Ariminum had stripped
the north of patrolling soldiers, stretching the protection of
Rome to breaking point. Though the roadside inns and forts
were still manned, long stretches in between were plagued by
thieves and many of the families were attacked and left by the
road in despair. Some were picked up by those who took pity
on them, while others were left to beg for a few coins or starve.
Those who could afford to hire guards were better off, and

they kept their heads down when they passed the wailing, crying people who had gone before them, standing in the spring rain with hands outstretched.

In special sessions of the Senate, Pompey read out the reports of Julius' victories as he received them. It was a bitter-sweet role he had found for himself and he could only shake his head at the irony of supporting Caesar as a way of controlling the new men of the Senate. Crassus had made him see that the victories in Gaul were all that kept the city from erupting in sheer panic as Clodius and Milo fought for supremacy in their secret, bloody battles. Despite the real power they had gained and the influence they wielded as brutally as a club, they had done nothing for Rome but feed on her. Neither Clodius nor Milo ever missed one of the reports. They had been formed in the gutters and the back-alleys of the city, but they thrilled to the details of battles in their name like any other citizen.

At first, Pompey had been prepared to declare a Dictatorship to control them. Freed from the restraints of the law, he could have had both men executed without a trial. Crassus had advised against such a final step. If they were killed, Crassus said, others would take their place and Pompey, perhaps Rome herself, would not survive. The Hydra of the Roman mob would grow new heads and whoever replaced them would know better than to walk in the open and attend the Senate. Crassus had spoken for hours to his old colleague and Pompey had seen the wisdom of his suggestions. Instead of resistance, he had gone out of his way to flatter and reward the men. He had sponsored Clodius for the position of chief magistrate and thrown a great dinner in his honour. Together, they had chosen candidates for the consular elections, lesser men who would do nothing to alter the fragile state of truce. It was a delicate balance that Pompey had found, knowing Clodius had chosen it in part to aid him against Milo as their own struggle continued.

Pompey considered the men as he read the latest report on the rostrum in front of him. In raising one, he had earned the enmity of the other and there was nothing but hatred in the eyes of Milo when he met them. Yet Clodius now spoke his name with pride of association and as spring had turned to summer, Pompey had even visited the man's home in the city and been flattered and courted in his turn. It was a dangerous game, but better than scattering the pieces and trying for Dictator. As things stood, it would mean civil war and he was not at all sure he would emerge the victor by the end.

As Pompey cleared his throat to speak, he inclined his head to Clodius and saw the man's pleasure at even the slightest mark of respect. That was what Crassus had seen in the newcomers to the Senate. Though they were savage, they craved the respectability of office and since Pompey had begun his new course, not one of his clients had suffered at the hands of Clodius' bullies. When Pompey had announced his desire to refurbish the racetrack, it was Clodius who had come to him with the offer of unlimited funds. Pompey had raised a statue to him in gratitude, praising his generosity in the Senate. Milo had responded with an offer to rebuild the Via Appia and Pompey had masked his delight at the man's transparency, allowing him to place his name on the Porta Capena where that road entered the city from the south. For the first time in more than a year, he felt that he had control of the city once again in his hands as the two men directed their energies more subtly, each as hungry as the other for recognition and acceptance. The new consuls were made aware of their precarious position and did nothing without first checking with their masters. It was stalemate and the private battles went on.

Pompey read the list of tribes Julius had smashed in the first battles of the spring, taking pleasure in the riveted stillness of the Senate. They listened with awe to the numbers of slaves that had been sent back over the Alps. The Remi had become vassals. The Nervii had been destroyed almost to the last man. The Belgae had been forced to give up their arms and surrender. The Atuatuci had been confined to a single walled town and then stormed. Fifty-three thousand had been sold back to the slave markets of Rome from that last tribe alone.

Pompey read Julius' reports and even he could barely comprehend the hidden strife that lay behind the simple lines. Julius did nothing to sell his victories to the Senate, but the dry tone was all the more impressive for what it did not say. Pompey read it through to the concluding remarks, where Caesar commended the report to the Senate and estimated the yearly revenues in tax from the lands he had taken. Not a sound could be heard in the Curia as Pompey reached the last line.

"'I declare that Gaul has been pacified and will now submit to the lawful rule of Rome.'"

The Senate rose to their feet and cheered themselves hoarse in a spontaneous display and Pompey had to raise his hand to quieten them.

When they had managed to restrain themselves, Pompey spoke, his voice filling the chamber.

'Our gods have granted us new lands, Senators. We must prove that we are worthy to rule them. As we brought peace to Spain, so shall we bring it to that wilder land. Our citizens will build roads and raise crops there to feed our cities. They will be heard in distant courts that take their authority from us. We will bring Rome to them not because of the strength of our legions, but because we are right and because we are just and because we are beloved of the gods.'

'Pacified? You told them Gaul was pacified?' Brutus said in amazement. 'There are places in Gaul where they haven't even heard of us! What were you thinking?'

Julius frowned. 'You would prefer I said "still dangerous, but

369

almost pacified"? Hardly the most inspiring words to bring our settlers over the Alps, Brutus.'

'I would have stopped short of "almost pacified" as well. It's more truthful to say that these savages nearly did for us all on more occasions than I care to think of. That they fought each other for generations until they found a common enemy in Rome and now we've stuck our hands into the worst wasps' nest I have ever seen. That would have been more truthful, at least.'

'All *right*, Brutus. It is done and that's the end of it. I know the situation as well as you and those tribes who have never seen a Roman soldier will see us soon enough as we build our roads across the country. If the Senate see me as the conqueror of Gaul, there will be no more talk of recalling me or forcing me to pay my debts. They can count the gold I send back to them and use the slaves to lower the price of wheat and corn. I will be free to run right through to the sea and beyond, even. This is my path, Brutus; can't you see I've found it? This is what I was born for. All I ask is another few years, five perhaps, and Gaul *will* be pacified. You say they have never heard of us? Well then, I will take lands that Rome does not even know exists! I will see a temple to Jupiter rise above their towns like a cliff of marble. I will bring our civilization, our science, our art to these people who live in such squalor. I will take our legions right up to where the lands meet the sea and over it. Who knows what lies beyond the far coasts? We don't even have maps of the countries there, Brutus. Just legends from the Greeks about foggy islands on the very edge of the world. Does it not fire your imagination?'

Brutus looked at his friend without answering, unsure if any response was really expected. He had seen Julius in this mood before and at times it could still touch him. At that moment, however, he was beginning to worry that Julius would not contemplate an end to their battles of conquest. Even the veterans compared their young commander to Alexander and Mark Antony did so shamelessly. When the handsome Roman had made the reference in the council, Brutus had expected Julius to scorn it for the clumsy flattery it was, but he had only smiled and gripped Mark Antony by the shoulder, refilling his cup with wine.

The plain of the Helvetii had been enclosed, the vast swathes of land sliced into farms for the settlers from Rome. Julius had been rash with his promises and, just to fulfil them, he had to stay in the field. Simply to pay his legions in silver, he was forced to sack towns and fight not for glory but to fill the coffers and send the tithe back to the senators. Brutus could see no end to it and, alone amongst Julius' council, he had begun to doubt the purpose of the war they fought. As a Roman, he could accept the destruction that was the herald of peace, but if it was all to satisfy Julius' desire for power, he could not take joy in it.

Julius never wavered. Though the coalition of the Belgae had pressed them cruelly in the spring, the legions had taken on some of their commander's confidence and the tribes were swept away without mercy. It was as if they were all touched by fate and could not lose. At times, even Brutus was infected by it and could cheer the man who raised his sword to them, his iron-faced helmet glittering like some malevolent god. But he knew the man beneath it and he knew him too well to walk quietly around him as the legionaries did. Though they won their victories with strength and speed, they saw Julius as the one responsible for all of it. While he lived, they knew they could not be beaten.

Brutus sighed to himself. Perhaps they were right. The whole of eastern Gaul was under the control of the legions and the roads were being built over hundreds of miles. Rome was growing out of the ground there and Julius was the bloody seed for the change. He looked at his friend and saw the fierce pride. Apart from the thinning hair and his scars, he was much the same man he had always known. Yet the soldiers said he was blessed by the gods. His presence on the battlefield was worth an extra cohort at least as they strove to fight well for him and Brutus felt ashamed of his own small grievances and the kernel of dislike that he fought to deny.

Publius Crassus had been given the command of two legions to travel to the north and Julius' current mood was owed to the fact that the senator's son had brought about the complete surrender of the tribes there. They had their path to the sea and, though Brutus had argued against it, he knew nothing would prevent Julius taking his precious legions to the coast. He dreamed of Alexander and the edge of the world.

Julius' council entered the long room of the fortified camp. They too had changed in their time in Gaul, Brutus noted. Octavian and Publius Crassus had lost the last traces of their youth in the years of campaign. Both men bore scars and had survived, now stronger. Ciro commanded his cohort with a devotion to Julius that reminded Brutus of a faithful hound. While Brutus could still discuss his doubts with Domitius or Renius, he had found Ciro would leave any room where he found the slightest hint of criticism. Both Romans regarded the other with dislike, forcibly masked for Julius' sake.

How we pretend for him, Brutus thought to himself. While Julius was there, they all acted the part of brothers, leaving their professional disagreements outside. It was almost as if they couldn't bear to see him disappointed in them.

Julius waited for the wine to be poured and laid his notes down on the table. He had already memorised the reports and would not need to refer to them again. Even as Brutus was submerged in his misgivings, he felt himself sit a little straighter under that blue gaze and saw the others respond in like fashion.

At the end of the day, we are all his dogs, Brutus thought, reaching for his cup.

'Your treaty with the Veneti has failed, Crassus,' Julius told the young Roman.

The senator's son shook his head in disbelief and Julius spoke to relieve his distress.

'I did not expect it to last. They are too strong by sea to feel bound by us and the treaty was only to hold them until we could reach the north-west. I will need control of that coast if I am ever to cross the sea.' Julius looked into the distance as he contemplated the future, then shook himself free of it. 'They have taken prisoners from the cohort you left and are demanding the release of their hostages in exchange. We must destroy them at sea if we are to bring them back to the nego- tiating table. I suspect they think that Rome fights only on the land, but there are a few of us who know better.'

He paused to let them chuckle and met Ciro's eyes with a smile.

'I have engaged shipwrights and carpenters to build a new port and ships. Pompey will provide crews to sail through the Pillars of Hercules and beat round Spain to meet us in the north. It suits my plans well enough in any case and we cannot let their oath-breaking go unanswered. Mhorbaine tells me the other tribes are restless and watch any challenge like hawks to see if we cannot respond.'

'How long before the ships are built, though?' Renius asked.

'They will be ready by next spring, if I can find funds to pay for them. I have written to request the Senate take on the burden of paying for our new legions. Crassus has assured me he will make the loan if the Senate fail us, but there is every reason to suppose they are pleased with our progress here. Perhaps too, the winter will not be so hard this year and we can make our preparations in the dark months.'

Julius drummed his fingers on the table.

'I have a single report from a scout on the Rhine. More of the Germanic tribes have crossed into our land and must be repulsed. I have sent five of the Aedui to confirm the sightings and bring a fresh estimate of their numbers. I will engage them before they come too far into our own land. Once they have been beaten, I plan to cross the river and pursue them as I should have done with the Suebi. I cannot allow the wild tribes over the river to attack our flanks whenever they smell a hint of weakness. I will make them a reply they will not forget in a generation and seal the Rhine behind me when I return.'

He looked around the table as they digested the news.

'We must move quickly to crush each threat as it appears. Just one more at this time and we would be stretched from one end of Gaul to another. I will take my Tenth and the Third Gallica under Brutus to the Rhine. One of the new Gaul legions will accompany us in the rear. There will be no conflict of loyalty against such an enemy. Mhorbaine has agreed to have his cavalry travel with me once again. The rest of you will act independently in my name.

'Crassus, I expect you to return to the north-west and destroy the land forces of the Veneti. Burn their ships, or at least force them off the coast and prevent them landing for supplies. Domitius, you will take the Fourth Gallica with him in support. Mark Antony, you will remain here with your legion. The Twelfth and Fifth Ariminum will stay with you. You will be my centre and I expect you not to lose any of the lands we have won while I am away. Use caution, but strike if the need arises.

'The last task is an easy one, Bericus. Your Ariminum legion has earned a rest and I need a good man to oversee the new settlers coming over the Alps. The Senate will be sending four praetors to govern the new provinces and they will need to be shown the realities of our situation here.'

Bericus groaned and rolled his eyes, making Julius laugh. The thought of having to play nursemaid to thousands of green Roman settlers was hardly an ideal appointment, but

Bericus was a sound administrator and Julius had spoken the truth when he said the legion had earned a period away from the pace of constant battle they had endured.

Julius continued to give out his orders and positions until each man there knew his lines of supply and the extent of his authority. He smiled when they replied with wit and he answered every query with the complete knowledge they had come to expect from him. The legionaries claimed that he knew the name of every man under his command and whether that was true or not, Julius had mastered every aspect of the legion life. He was never at a loss or unable to provide a quick answer to any question put to him and it all went further to establish the confidence of the men.

Brutus looked again around the table and found nothing but determination in those who were given tasks that meant hardship, pain and perhaps death for some or all of them. As Julius spread out his maps and began to move to the more detailed matters of terrain and supply, Brutus watched him, barely hearing the words. How many of the men in that room would see Rome again, he wondered. As Julius traced the line of the Rhine with his finger and told them his assessments, Brutus could not imagine a time when the man he followed could ever be made to stop.

CHAPTER THIRTY-TWO

⟨⟨⟨⟨⟨

On the first autumn day of Julius' fourth year in Gaul, Pompey and Crassus walked together through the forum, deep in conversation. Around them, the great open space at the centre of the city was filled with thousands of citizens and slaves. Orators addressed those who could be persuaded to listen and their voices carried over the heads of the crowd on a hundred different subjects. Slaves from wealthy houses hurried through, carrying packages and scrolls for their masters. It had become fashionable to dress house slaves in bright colours and many wore bright blue or gold tunics, a myriad of shades that wove through the darker reds and browns of workers and merchants. Armed guards made stately progress across the forum, each group surrounding their employer at the centre. It was the bustling, hurried heart of the city and neither Pompey nor Crassus noticed the subtle differences in the mood of the crowd around them.

The first Pompey knew of the trouble to come was a rough

shove as one of his legionaries was knocked into him. Sheer astonishment made Pompey forget his instincts for survival and he stopped. The crowd was thickening even as he hesitated and the faces were ugly with intent. Crassus recovered faster and pulled Pompey towards the senate house. If there was to be yet another riot, it was best to get clear as quickly as possible and send the guards out to restore order.

The space around the senators was filled with pushing, jeering men. A stone flew over their heads and struck someone else in the crowd. Pompey saw one of his lictors brought down with a blow from a length of wood and felt a moment of panic before he gathered his courage. He drew a dagger from his belt and held it blade-down so that it could be used to stab or slash. When one of the crowd pressed too close, he opened the man's cheek without hesitation, seeing him fall back with a cry.

'Guards! To me!' Pompey roared.

The crowd bayed at him and he saw three burly men force one of his legionaries to the ground, stabbing at him over and over as they were lost to view. A woman screamed nearby and Pompey heard his call taken up by the horror-struck citizens beyond the men who were attacking him. Milo's men, he was certain. He should have expected it after their leader's isolation in Senate, but Pompey had only a handful of soldiers and lictors with him and they would not be enough. He used his dagger again and saw Crassus lash out a fist, snapping the nose of an attacker.

The lictors were armed with a ceremonial axe and rods for scourging. Once they had freed them from the bindings, the hatchets were fearsome weapons in a crowd and they literally cut a path for Pompey and Crassus towards the senate house. Yet their numbers dwindled as knives were jabbed into them and the circle of safety around the two senators shrank until there was almost no room for them to move in the press.

Pompey knew hope and despair in the same moment when

he heard horns sounding across the forum. His legion had turned out for him, but it would be too late. Fingers yanked cruelly at his toga and he sliced his dagger into them, sawing in a frenzy until they fell away. Crassus was knocked from his feet by another stone and Pompey dragged him up and onward, holding him close as the older man gathered his wits. There was blood on his mouth.

The noise hammered at them and then changed slightly. New faces appeared in even greater numbers and Pompey saw them cut down the ones who struggled to reach him. Knots of bellowing men separated from the mass, fighting not as legionaries, but with cleavers and meathooks and stones held in their hands. Pompey saw one man's face smashed into pulp by repeated blows before he fell.

All forward movement ceased and though Pompey could see the steps of the senate house only a short distance away, it was too far. He jabbed his dagger into everything he could reach in a fury and didn't know he was shouting in a mindless rage.

The press of bodies lightened without warning and Pompey saw the bloody knives of raptores held almost in salute as they backed away. Crushed bodies and screaming, wounded men lay all about them, but they did not attack. Pompey beckoned, holding his dagger ready, the blade parallel to his forearm. Sweat poured from him and he watched in astonishment as the men pulled back to form a pathway to the steps of the senate house. He darted a glance in that direction and considered how far he would get if he ran, then decided against it. He would not show them his back.

In that moment, he saw the uniforms of his legions battering through the press and Clodius standing there, panting. The mob leader seemed terribly solid compared to the others. Though he was not a tall man, he was tremendously strong and the crowd gave ground instinctively around him, as wolves will look away from the most brutal of the pack. His shaven head gleamed with sweat in the morning sun. Pompey could only stare.

'They've scattered, Pompey, the ones who lived,' Clodius said. 'Call off your soldiers.' His right hand was wet with blood and the blade he carried had snapped off close to the hilt.

Pompey turned as an officer of his legion raised his sword to cut Clodius down.

'Hold!' Pompey cried, understanding at last. 'These are allies.'

Clodius nodded at that and Pompey heard the order repeated as the legion gathered around him, forming a fighting square. Clodius began to be pushed away, but Pompey took his arm.

'Do I need to guess who is behind this attack?' he asked.

Clodius shrugged his massive shoulders.

'He is already in the senate building. There will be no link back to him, you can be sure. Milo is cunning enough to keep his hands clean.' As if in irony, Clodius threw down his broken knife and wiped his bloody fists on the hem of his robe.

'You had men ready?' Pompey asked, hating the constant suspicion that was part of his life.

Clodius narrowed his eyes at the implication. 'No. I never set foot in the forum without fifty of my lads. They were enough to reach you in time. I knew nothing until it started.'

'Then we owe our lives to your quick thinking,' Pompey said. He heard a whimper cut off nearby and spun round. 'Are there any left alive to be questioned?'

Clodius looked at him. 'Not now. There are no names given in that sort of work. Believe me, I know.'

Pompey nodded, trying to ignore the inner voice that wondered if Clodius had staged the whole thing. It was an unpleasant thought, but he owed a debt to the man that would bind him for years. To many men in the Senate, such a debt would be worth the deaths of a few of their servants and Clodius was known to be ruthless in every part of his life. Pompey met

Crassus' eyes and guessed the old man was thinking along similar lines. Very slightly, Crassus lifted his shoulders and let them drop and Pompey looked back to the man who had saved them. There was no way of knowing and probably never would be.

Pompey realised he was still gripping his dagger and uncurled his fingers painfully from the hilt. He felt old next to the bull-like strength of Clodius. While part of him wanted to wash the blood from his skin and soak in a hot bath somewhere private and above all, safe, he knew more was expected from him. Hundreds of men stood within earshot and before nightfall the whole grisly incident would be the talking point of every shop and tavern in the city.

'I am late for the Senate, gentlemen,' he said, his voice growing in strength. 'Clean away the blood before I return. The corn taxes won't be delayed for any man.'

It wasn't much in the way of wit, but Clodius chuckled.

With Crassus at his shoulder, Pompey walked along the avenue of Clodius' men and many bowed their heads respectfully as they passed.

The Tenth withdrew in panic, their orderly lines dissolving into the chaos of a complete rout. Thousands of the Senones cavalry pursued them, breaking off from the main battle where the Ariminum legions fought solidly and held the line.

The fortified camp from the night before was less than a mile away and the retreating Tenth covered it at great speed, Julius with them. The extraordinarii protected the rear from the wild assaults by the Senones and not a man was lost as they reached the heavy gates of the fort and rushed inside.

The Senones were proving to be difficult adversaries. Julius had lost large numbers of the Third Gallica in an ambush from woodland and others since then. The tribe had learned not to

offer a direct battle against the legions. Instead, they skir-
mished and moved away, using their cavalry to harass the
Roman forces without ever allowing themselves to be caught
where they could be crushed.

The extraordinarii followed the men of the Tenth under the
gates of the fort and closed them behind. It was a humiliating
position, but the fort had been designed for exactly that
purpose. As well as giving protection for the night, it allowed
the legions to retreat to a strong position. The Senones riders
whooped and yelled as they rode round the huge banked walls,
though they were careful to keep out of range. Twice before,
Julius had been forced to bring back his entire force within the
walls and the Senones hooted as they brought it about again.

Their king rode with them and long banners waved from
spears set into his saddle. Julius watched from the wall as the
Senones' leader brandished his sword at the men in the fort,
mocking them. Julius showed his teeth.

'Now, Brutus!' he called down.

The Senones could not see into the camp and their cheering
continued unabated. Over the thunder of their own hooves,
they did not hear the extraordinarii as they gathered at the far
end and kicked their mounts into a gallop across the wide
camp, straight at the wall near the gate.

As they gathered speed, fifty men of the Tenth used lengths
of wood to break down the loose blocks that made up the wall.
It fell away just as Julius had designed it to do, leaving an open
space wide enough for five horses to ride abreast.

The extraordinarii came out like arrows, straight at the king.
Before his riders could react, he was surrounded and dragged
from his horse. They wheeled in the face of the enemy and
galloped back inside the gap in the walls, with the king yelling
across Brutus' saddle.

Julius opened the gates and the Tenth marched out in
triumph. The panic and fear they had pretended had vanished

and they hit the milling Senones with a roar. The Tenth hammered them with spears and swords and forced the Gauls further and further away from the fort and their captured king. Behind them, the hole in the wall was filled with carts that had been left for that purpose and Julius leapt into his saddle to race after them, glancing back to see the fort made secure once more.

It had taken a moonless night to construct the false wall, but it could not have worked better. The King of the Senones had been crucial to their attacks, a man able to answer every stratagem with speed and intelligence. Removing him from the battle was a vital step in beating the tribe.

Julius cantered to the front line of the Tenth and saw their pleasure at his presence. The Ariminum legions were holding their position as they had been told and now the Tenth could strike the rear of the Senones, smashing them between the two forces.

From the first instant of the Tenth reaching their lines, Julius could feel the difference in the shifting mass of riders and foot soldiers. They had relied too much on their king, and without him they were already close to panic.

Though they tried to detach in units as their king had ordered on previous days, the core of discipline had vanished. Instead of an orderly retreat for tactical advantage, two charges fouled each other as they tried to organise themselves. The Tenth smashed them down from their saddles and moved on. Rider-less horses ran screaming around the battlefield and the Senones were crushed, hundreds of them throwing down their arms and surrendering as the news of the king's capture spread.

Three miles away lay their largest town and Julius marched the Tenth towards it as soon as the warriors were disarmed and bound as slaves. The price for them would swell his coffers still further and the town was known to be wealthy. After he paid his share to the Senate, he still hoped to have enough to increase his fleet and finally be able to cross the grim channel between Gaul and the islands. They had captured nine ships from the Veneti, but he would need another twenty galleys to take more than a scouting force to sea. One more year to build them and then he would take his best men to lands no Roman had ever seen before.

As the Tenth marched towards the Senones' stronghold, Julius laughed aloud with the excitement of such a prospect, even as his mind filled with the thousand details of supply and administration that his men required to take the field. He was to meet with a delegation from three tribes along the coast in two days and expected them to bring tribute and a new treaty. With the Veneti fleet sunk or run aground, that whole part of the north had surrendered to him and now that the Senones had been removed from the equation, a full half of Gaul was his. There were no tribes who hadn't heard of the legions by then. Gaul was buzzing with the news of his conquests and he rarely saw a day when their leaders didn't travel to his camps and wait for his signature on a treaty. Adàn was kept busy and had been forced to take on three other scribes to handle the endless copying and translation.

Julius wondered what to do with the king he had captured. If he was left alive, Julius thought him capable of leading a rebellion in the years to come. The king's own ability prevented mercy and Julius decided his fate without regret.

As the Senones' town came into view, Julius looked with pleasure on it, already imagining the temples within. It was known that the Senones showed their love of the gods with coins and jewellery, forming rooms of treasure over many years. After the legion smiths had melted the precious metal down into bars and struck new coins, Julius would strip anything of value from every house and public building. He would leave the people alive and under the protection of the legions, but he needed their wealth to go on.

A cold wind touched him from across the plain and Julius shivered at the first chill of another winter. He narrowed his eyes as he looked east, imagining the Alps and the distance that he would have to cross. For the first time, he would not be spending the cold months in Gaul. Instead, he would travel to Ariminum for a meeting to decide the future.

The letter from Crassus crackled against his skin as he rode and Julius hoped he could still trust the promises of the old man. It was not the time to be recalled, with Gaul opening up before him. The islands over the sea haunted his dreams. There were still some who said they did not exist, but Julius had stood on the coastal cliffs and seen them shimmering whitely in the distance.

The Senones' town surrendered and the gates were thrown open. Julius rode in under the arches, his mind already on Ariminum and the future.

CHAPTER THIRTY-THREE

꩜꩜꩜

The legion guards on Ariminum's walls were well protected against the cold. As night fell, they pulled heavy cloaks over their armour and wrapped their faces in strips of cloth so that only a thin slit was left.

Fires were lit in braziers all along the stone crest and the legionaries were allowed to huddle around them. Most of them were new recruits, brought up from the towns in the south to replace those fighting for Caesar in Gaul. They showed their youth in the muttered wisecracks and the illicit flask of spirits that made them gasp and choke and clap each other on the back.

The city of Ariminum was a working town and there were few lights in the windows as the winter night darkened. Before dawn, the streets would fill again with carts and produce for the ships. The tradesmen would grab a few hot mouthfuls for a bronze coin on their way to another day and the legionaries on the walls would be relieved.

Against the backdrop of the silent city, one of the guards looked up and peered into the darkness.

'Thought I heard horses out there,' he said.

Two more left the warmth of their brazier to stand by him. They listened in perfect silence and just before they turned away, they heard something. Noise seemed to carry further in the strange stillness that comes from frozen ground.

The youngest guard narrowed his eyes and moved his head back and forth. There was nothing but gloom outside the walls, yet he could have sworn the darkness shifted whenever he set his eyes on it.

The shadows coalesced into sharper shapes and the young legionary stiffened, pointing.

'There! Riders . . . can't tell how many.'

The others lacked his keen eyesight and could only stare where he pointed.

'Are they ours?' one of them said, hiding his fear. His mind was filled with the image of barbarian tribesmen storming their city walls and the cold seemed to intensify as he shuddered.

'I can't tell. Should we fetch Old Snapper?'

The question made the three young soldiers pause. The possibility of raiders was one thing, but rousing their centurion for a false alarm was simply asking for trouble.

Teras was the eldest of them. He had no more experience than the others, having joined up later in life after failing to make his way as a merchant. Yet they looked to him as they had learned to do in matters of money and young women. He didn't know a great deal about either, but affected an air of worldly wisdom that had impressed the younger recruits.

While they hesitated, the force of riders came closer and the metallic noise of harness was mingled with the steady tread of marching men. The night wind snapped at long pennants that rippled unpleasantly as the dark figures advanced towards the gate.

'All right, go and get him,' Teras said, biting his lip in worry.

'Approaching the gate!' a voice shouted below them. The guards stood to stiff attention as they had been trained.

'We're closed. Come back in the morning,' one of the other sentries called, his companions stifling laughter.

There was one who should have been searched for drink before coming on watch, Teras thought bitterly. He could have hit the young fool in frustration, but the words had been spoken. Teras closed his eyes as he waited through a pregnant silence below.

'I will find whoever said that and kick his backside into bloody tatters,' the same voice replied, halfway between amusement and anger. 'Now open the gate.'

Teras turned to the men on the locking bar below. There were times when he wished he'd stayed a merchant, despite losing more money than he'd ever earned.

'Open it,' he said. The young men below looked up with worried expressions.

'Shouldn't we wait for ...'

'Oh, just open it. It's cold and they are Romans. If they were barbarians, do you really think they would be waiting for us to finish our argument?'

By the end, his voice had risen to a shout and the anger seemed to get through to them as nothing else could. The heavy locking bars were heaved away and the gate pulled smartly open.

Brutus rode through first and dismounted, handing the reins of his horse to the nearest guard.

'Right. Now where's that cheeky bastard on the wall?'

Teras saw another rider come through the gate, as heavily muffled as the guards above. He was an imposing figure nonetheless and Teras could see how the men behind him waited patiently for him to move through the gate. An officer; Teras could spot them a mile away.

'We don't have time,' the man said clearly. 'I'm late enough as it is.'

With a quick nod, Brutus threw a leg over his horse and heaved himself back into the saddle. The officer didn't wait for him, but kicked in his heels and trotted on through the dark streets, the rest following without a word.

Teras counted a full century by the time Snapper came climbing up to the wall beside him. The gate was securely fastened once again and the young guards resumed their positions, not daring to catch their centurion's eye.

Snapper was a veteran and if you believed all the stories the men told about him, he had been part of every major battle since the days of Carthage. Despite the fact that it would have made him centuries old, he would talk of those times as if he had been there personally, with a clear implication that only his presence had saved the Republic from invaders, poor discipline and, possibly, pestilence. Whatever the truth was, he was scarred, bad-tempered and deeply resentful of being given green recruits to turn into something approaching legionaries.

'You, you and . . . you,' the old soldier said grimly, pointing last to Teras. 'I don't know what you think you were doing tonight, but tomorrow you will be digging out the shithouse on Famena road. That I do know.'

Without another word, Snapper stomped down the slippery steps, still swearing under his breath. Teras could smell the sweetness of the alcohol on his breath for some time after he had gone.

The young legionary who had called out to Brutus shuffled over as Teras resumed his post by the brazier, warming his hands. He opened his mouth to say something.

'Don't,' Teras said grimly. 'Or I'll kill you myself.'

*　　　*　　　*

388

Julius found the meeting place without too much difficulty. The cryptic message from Crassus had asked him to remember where they had once planned the defeat of Spartacus. Though Julius had not seen Ariminum for a decade, the city was simply laid out and the house was the only one showing a light in an empty street near the docks. He had tried for secrecy as far as possible, leaving Gaul without warning to fly ahead of informers and making the best speed he could with a century of the Tenth. They had covered the first sixty miles in a little over ten hours and not once had the men complained or asked to rest longer than the short stops for food and water. When he was sure that even the fleetest of spies must be behind them, Julius had allowed a slower pace over the Alp passes and, in truth, they could not have gone much faster in the bitter cold and thin air. By the time they had completed their descent, Julius was certain that anyone who followed would have to wait until spring.

Julius left Brutus with the century to block the road. He strode up to the doorway he remembered from the old campaign and knocked on the timbers, pulling his cloak tightly around himself against the cold.

A man he did not know opened it and Julius wondered if he was the owner of the house.

'Yes?' the man said, looking blankly at Julius.

'Gaul,' Julius replied and the man stood back for him to enter.

Julius could hear the crackle and snap of a large wood fire before he entered the room. Pompey and Crassus rose to greet him and Julius felt a wave of affection for both of them as he clasped hands. They too seemed to feel it and the smiles were genuine.

'It's been a long time, my friend. Did you bring my son?' Crassus said.

'As you asked me to, yes. Shall I have him brought in?'

Julius watched Crassus struggle for a moment before replying.

'No, not until we have spoken,' he said reluctantly. 'There's food on the table and hot wine by the fire. Come and sit down and warm yourself.'

With a stab of guilt, Julius thought of his men shivering in the night outside. Crassus had asked for privacy for their meeting, but they would still need to find food and shelter before morning. He wondered how many men could be packed into the rambling Ariminum house or whether they would end up sleeping in stables.

'Have you been in the city for long?' Julius asked. Both men shook their heads.

'Just a few days,' Crassus replied. 'Much longer and I would have had to return to Rome. I'm glad you came.'

'How could I not after that mysterious note? Passwords and night marches across the north. All very exciting.' Julius smiled at the older men. 'In truth, I am glad to be here rather than in Gaul in winter. You have no idea how bitter it is in the dark months.'

The two former consuls exchanged glances and Julius saw that much of the friction between them had eased over time. He waited patiently for them to broach the reason for the meeting, though now he was actually with them, neither man seemed sure how to begin. Julius chewed on a piece of cold lamb as he waited.

'You remember our agreement?' Pompey said at last.

Julius nodded. 'Of course. You have both honoured it as I have.'

Pompey grunted agreement. 'But time has moved on. We must review the terms,' he said.

'I assumed as much,' Julius replied. 'There are new consuls now and you are wondering if there is still profit to be had from me. Tell me what you need.'

Crassus gave out a dry chuckle.

'Always so direct, Julius. Very well. The Senate has changed a great deal in the years you have been away.'

'I know it,' Julius replied and Crassus smiled.

'Yes, I'm sure you have your own sources. There is talk of recalling you from Gaul, you know. Your attacks over the Rhine did you no favours with the senators. The Germanic tribes were never part of your orders and Pompey was hard-pressed to protect you.'

Julius shrugged. 'Then you have my thanks. I considered it necessary to hold the Rhine border there.'

Pompey leaned forward on his chair and warmed his hands against the flames.

'You know how fickle they are, Julius. One year they are cheering you and the next calling for your head. It has always been that way.'

'Will you be able to prevent the recall?' Julius asked, holding himself absolutely still. Much depended on the answer.

'That is why we are here, Julius,' Pompey replied. 'You want to have your time in Gaul extended and I can give you that.'

'There was no talk of limits when I first set off,' Julius reminded him.

Pompey frowned. 'But now the situation has changed. You are no longer consul and none of us can stand again for years to come. There are too many new men in the Senate who know you only as a general somewhere impossibly distant. They look for some end to your reports, Julius.'

Julius looked calmly at him without replying.

Pompey snorted. 'You left the north bare when you took the legions at Ariminum. That cost you a great deal of support and we're hardly up to strength even now. Your debtors pursue you through the Senate. There is even talk of bringing a trial against you for killing Ariovistus. All of these things would require you to give up your command and return home.'

'So the price for me staying will be what? My daughter is already promised to you,' Julius said softly.

Pompey forced a smile onto his face and Julius could see how tired he was. Crassus spoke first.

'You understand, Julius. I am glad. For me, the price of my support is the return of my son to lead my legion. Pompey will secure a province for me and I will continue the education of my son there, now that you have trained him. He speaks well of you in his letters.'

'Where did you have in mind?' Julius asked with genuine interest.

'Syria. The Parthians are refusing to allow my ships to trade with them. The general of a legion can go where no mere merchant dares.'

'A merchant prince,' Julius murmured. Crassus grinned at him.

'Even he needs a good legion on occasion.'

Julius turned in his seat to look at Pompey.

'So Crassus has Syria to subdue for Rome. I give him his son to lead them. What could Pompey need from me? I have heard that Clodius and Milo create riots in the streets. Do you want my support? You would have it, Pompey. If you need me to vote for you as Dictator, I would return with my Tenth to deal with whatever may follow. On my word, I would. I still have friends there and I could carry it for you.'

Pompey smiled tightly at the younger man.

'I have missed your energy around the city, Julius. I really have. No, I have put shackles on Clodius and Milo is a spent force. Your reports are out of date. My needs are simpler.'

He glanced again at Crassus, and Julius wondered at the friendship that had sprung up between them. It was strange how much men changed over the years. Julius would never have believed they could be anything but reluctant allies at best, but they seemed as comfortable with each other as brothers. He wondered if Pompey had ever learned the truth of Crassus' involvement with Catiline. There were always secrets in Rome.

'I need gold, Julius,' Pompey said. 'Crassus tells me you have found great wealth in Gaul, much more than the city ever sees in taxes.'

Julius glanced at Crassus with interest, wondering how good his sources were in their estimates. Pompey continued, the words spilling out now that he had begun.

'My private income is not enough to rebuild the city, Julius. Parts have been damaged in rioting and the Senate does not have the funds. If you have, it would be used to finish the temples and houses we have begun.'

'Surely Crassus could advance you the money?' Julius asked.

Pompey flushed slightly. 'I told you, Crassus,' he snapped to his colleague. 'I will not come like a beggar . . .'

Crassus interrupted, laying a hand on Pompey's arm to soothe him.

'It is not a loan, Julius, but a gift that Pompey is asking.' He smiled wryly. 'I have never understood how money can be so uncomfortable a subject in so many quarters. It is simple enough. The senate treasury is not fat enough to supply the millions needed to rebuild parts of the city. Another aqueduct, temples, new streets. It all costs. Pompey does not wish to create new debts, even to me.'

Julius thought ruefully of the ships that waited on his payment. He suspected Pompey did not know the full content of the letter Crassus had sent him, but at least he had come prepared. Sometimes, Crassus' bluntness was a blessing.

'I have it,' he said. 'Though in return, I want the Tenth and Third added to the senate payroll. I cannot continue to fund their salaries out of my own purse.'

Pompey nodded. 'That is . . . acceptable,' he said.

Julius took another piece of cold meat from the table and ate it as he thought.

'I would need my orders confirmed in writing, of course. Another five years in Gaul, bound as solidly as you can make it. I do not want to have to renegotiate the terms next year.

Crassus, your son is ready for command. I am sorry to lose such a fine officer, but that was our agreement and I will hold to it. I wish you luck with your new province. Believe me when I say it is no easy task to cut new paths for Rome.'

Pompey said nothing, so with a smile Crassus spoke for him.

'And the gold, Julius?'

'Wait here,' Julius replied, standing.

He returned with Publius and Brutus, the three men struggling with a long cedar chest that had been bound with strips of iron. Both Pompey and Crassus stood as they entered the room and Crassus went to embrace his son. Julius opened the box and revealed enough fat yellow coins to impress even Crassus, so that he stepped away from his son and ran a hand over the gold.

'I have three more of these with me, gentlemen. More than three million sesterces by weight. Is it enough?'

Pompey too could not seem to look away from the precious metal.

'It is,' he said, his voice barely above a whisper.

'Then we have an agreement?' Julius said, looking from one to the other. Both senators nodded.

'Excellent. I will need rooms for my men tonight, here or in a tavern, if you can recommend a few places. They've earned the right to some hot food and a bath. I will return here at dawn to go through the details with you both.'

'There is something else that might interest you, Caesar,' Crassus said, his eyes twinkling. He glanced at Brutus as he spoke, then shrugged.

'A friend travelled up from Rome with us. I will show you the way.'

Julius raised an eyebrow, but Pompey too seemed to share some inner amusement as their eyes met.

'Lead on, then,' Julius said, following Crassus out into the colder corridors of the house.

Pompey was uncomfortable with the men Julius had brought into the room. Publius felt it and cleared his throat.

'I should bring in the rest of the gold, Consul, with your permission.'

'Thank you,' Pompey replied. He pulled a cloak from a peg on the door and went out with them into the night.

Crassus took a lamp from a wall bracket and led Julius down a long hall to the rear of the property.

'Who owns this house?' Julius asked, looking around at the richness of the furnishings.

'I do,' Crassus said. 'The owner fell into difficulties and I was able to acquire it at an excellent price.'

Julius knew that the owner would have been one of those who suffered under the monopoly of trade that had been Crassus' part of their original agreement. He was interested that the old man hadn't tried to have his licence extended, but the province Pompey had offered him would be enough to occupy his time. Julius hoped Crassus would have the sense to let his son make the decisions. Though he liked the old senator, the man was no sort of general, whereas his son could very well be a fine one.

'In here, Julius,' Crassus said, handing him the lamp.

Julius could see a childish delight on Crassus' wrinkled features that baffled him. He opened the door, closing it on the darkness behind.

Servilia had never looked more beautiful. Julius froze when he saw her and then fumbled for a place to hang the lamp, the simple process suddenly seeming difficult.

The room was warmed by a fire in a hearth big enough to stand in. No touch of the howling winter reached them and Julius drank in the lines of her as she watched him without speaking. She lay on a long couch and wore a dress of dark red cloth, like blood against her skin. He did not know what to say and only gazed in silence for a long time.

'Come here,' she said, holding out her hands to him. Silver bangles chimed on her wrist as she moved. He crossed the room and as he touched her hands, he folded into her embrace and they were kissing. There was no need for words.

Pompey regretted leaving the warmth of the house for the winter street but a nagging curiosity would not leave him. As the boxes of gold were heaved up and carried into the house, he walked along the line of silent soldiers, falling naturally into his role as an officer of Rome. They had stood to attention and saluted as soon as he appeared and now his inspection was natural, almost expected.

In truth, Pompey felt a responsibility for the Tenth. It had been his own order to merge Primigenia with a legion who had shamed themselves in battle and he had felt a proprietary interest when reading Julius' reports in the Senate. The Tenth had become Julius' most trusted men and it was no surprise to see them in the ranks Julius had chosen for the meeting.

Pompey spoke to one or two of them and they responded to his questions nervously, staring straight ahead. One or two were shivering, but they clenched their jaws as he passed, unwilling to show any weakness.

Pompey stopped in front of the centurion and congratulated him on the discipline of his men.

'What is your name?' he asked, though he knew it.

'Regulus, sir,' the man replied.

'I have had the pleasure of telling the Senate how well the Tenth have been doing in Gaul. Has it been difficult?'

'No, sir,' Regulus replied.

'I've heard it said that a legionary finds the waiting the hardest part of war,' Pompey said.

'It is no hardship, sir,' Regulus said.

'I am glad to hear that, Regulus. From what I have heard, you haven't had a chance for your swords to grow rusty. No doubt there will be more battles ahead.'

'We are always ready, sir,' Regulus said and Pompey moved on, speaking to another soldier a few places down the line.

Crassus came back into the warm room. His son was there waiting for him, and the old senator crossed to him, beaming.

'I have been so proud of you, lad. Julius mentioned your name twice in reports to the Senate,' Crassus said. 'You have done well in Gaul, as well as I could have wanted. Now are you ready to lead a legion for your father?'

'I am, sir,' Publius replied.

CHAPTER THIRTY-FOUR

๛๛๛๛๛

Julius woke long before dawn and lay in the warmth created by Servilia beside him. He had left her only once the night before to ask Crassus to bring his men in from the cold. While Crassus opened rooms and summoned food and blankets for the century, Julius had quietly closed the door once more and forgotten them.

Now, in the darkness, Julius could hear the snores of soldiers packed along every space of the house. No doubt the kitchens would be preparing breakfast for them and Julius knew he too should be rousing himself and planning the day. Yet there was a delicious lethargy in that warm dark and he stretched, feeling her cool skin against his arm as he moved. She stirred and murmured something he could not catch, enough to make him sit up on one elbow and look at her face.

Some women looked their best in the bright light of the sun, but Servilia was most beautiful in the evening or under the moon. Her face had nothing of the sharp hardness he had once seen. He could still picture her acid contempt when he had come striding into her home for their last meeting. It was a mystery to him how he could have engendered such apparent hatred and yet now have her in his bed, stirring like a dreaming cat. He might have held back after that first embrace in the firelight, but her eyes had been full of some strange grief and he had never been able to resist the tears of a beautiful woman. It stirred him as no smile or coquetry ever could.

He yawned in silence, the strain making his jaw crack. If only life were as simple as he wanted it to be. If he could dress and leave with nothing more than a final glance at her sleeping form, he would have a perfect memory of the woman he had loved for so long. It would have been enough to banish some of the pain she had caused him. He watched her smile in her sleep and his own expression lightened in response. He wondered if he was in her dreams and thought of some of the extraordinarily erotic sequences that plagued his sleep for the first few months in Gaul. He leaned closer to her ear and breathed his name into it, over and over, grinning to himself. Perhaps she could be made to dream of him.

He froze as she raised a hand to rub the ear without waking. The movement in the soft linen revealed her left breast and Julius found the image endearing and arousing at the same time. Though age had left its marks on her, as she lay there her breast was pale and perfect. Julius watched with fascination as the exposed nipple firmed and darkened and he considered waking her with the warmth of his mouth on it.

He sighed, lying back. When she woke, the world would intrude on them once again. Though Crassus would keep any secret, Brutus would have to be told his own mother was there in the north. Julius frowned in the darkness as he considered his friend's reaction to the news that Servilia once again shared his bed. Julius had seen Brutus' relief at the end of that relationship, punctuated with twin slaps in Rome. To see it rekindled could weigh heavily on him. He clasped his hands behind his head as he thought.

There could be no returning to Gaul until spring; he had always known that. Once the passes were blocked, nothing living could make the trip. At one point, Julius had considered travelling to Rome, but dismissed the idea. Unless he could be certain of making the journey without being recognised, he would be too much of a temptation for his enemies, with only a hundred men for protection. Rome was as unreachable as the passes over the Alps and Julius struggled with a feeling of claustrophobia at the thought of spending months in the dreary streets of Ariminum.

At least his letters would get through, he thought. And he could travel to the shipyards to oversee the fleet he had ordered. It seemed a vain hope to expect them to release the vessels without any more than his deposits, no matter what he promised. Yet without them, his plans for the sea crossing would be delayed, perhaps by as much as another year.

He sighed to himself. There were always battles to be fought in Gaul. Even when a tribe had paid tribute for two summers, they could plant their flags in the hard ground and declare war on the third. Without outright extermination, Julius was forced to face the fact that such rebellions could continue for his full term there. They were a hard people to put down.

His eyes were cold as he considered the tribes. They were nothing like the men and women he had known as a boy in Rome. They sang and laughed more easily, despite their short, hard lives. Julius still remembered his astonishment the first time he had sat with Mhorbaine listening to a storyteller weave an ancient tale for them. Perhaps something had been lost in Adàn's translation, but Julius had seen tears in the eyes of veteran warriors and at the conclusion of the story Mhorbaine had wept like a child, without a sign of embarrassment.

'What are you thinking?' Servilia said. 'You look so cruel, sitting there.'

Julius met her dark eyes and forced a smile onto his face.

'I was thinking of the songs of the Gauls.'

She pouted, pulling herself up on the cushion beside him. The fire was long dead and with a shiver she yanked the blankets to cover her shoulders, forming a nest of cloth from which she watched him.

'I travel three hundred miles and throw myself into a night of lascivious pleasure with you and you are still thinking of some grubby tribesmen? You amaze me.'

He chuckled and wrapped an arm around her, pulling the whole bundle close to his chest.

'I don't care why you came. I'm just glad you did,' he said.

This seemed to please her and she tilted her head to be kissed. Julius half-turned to respond and the scent of her perfume recalled all the passion and innocence of the past. It was almost too painful.

'I missed you,' she said. 'Very much. I wanted to see you again.'

Julius looked at her, struggling with his emotions. Part of him wanted to be angry with her. She had caused him so much grief that he had hated her for a long time, or told himself he had. Yet he had not hesitated after that first moment the night before. All his internal arguments and scabs had drifted away and again he felt as vulnerable as any other young fool.

'Am I an evening's entertainment to you, then?' he asked. 'You seemed to have no doubts when I left your house in Rome.'

'I *did* have doubts, even then. If I hadn't sent you away you would have grown tired of having an old woman in your bed. Don't interrupt, Julius. If I don't say it, I may not be able . . .'

He waited while she stared off into the darkness. One of her hands tightened slowly in the heavy cloth that covered them both.

'When you want a son, it cannot come from me, Julius, not any more.'

Julius hesitated before responding. 'You're sure?'

She sighed, raising her eyes. 'Yes, of course I'm sure. I was sure when you left Rome. Perhaps you are already thinking of children to carry on your line. You will turn to some young girl with wide hips to give you them and I will be thrown aside.'

'I have my daughter,' he reminded her.

'A son, Julius! Do you not want to have sons of your own to follow you? How often have I heard you speak of your own father? You would never be satisfied with a daughter who cannot set foot in the senate building. A daughter who cannot lead your legions for you.'

'That was why you left me?' he said, understanding. 'I can find a wife from any family in Rome to carry my blood. Nothing between us would change.'

Servilia shook her head in weariness. 'It would, Julius. It must. You would look at me with guilt for every hour we spent together. I couldn't bear to see it.'

'Then why are you here?' he demanded, suddenly angry. 'What has changed for you to come to me and set everything on its head once again?'

'Nothing has changed. There are days when I do not think of you at all and others when you are constantly in my thoughts. When Crassus told me he was coming to this meeting, I joined him. Perhaps I should not have done. By your side, the future is miserable for me.'

'I don't understand you at all, you know,' Julius said softly, touching her face. 'I do not care about sons, Servilia. If there is a time when I do, I will marry some daughter of a senator for that reason. If you are mine, I will love no other.'

She closed her eyes and in the first light of dawn, he could see tears spilling down her cheeks.

'I should not have come,' she whispered. 'I should have left you alone.'

'I was alone,' he said, gathering her in, 'but now you are here with me.'

402

The winter sun had risen when Julius found Brutus in the small courtyard of the house, deep in conversation with Crassus over the lodgings for the century of the Tenth. They had brought ten mounts from Gaul and hobbled them in the yard the night before, with heavy blankets against the cold. Brutus had refilled their nosebags with grain and broken the thin sheet of ice that had formed on the water buckets. At the sound of footsteps, Brutus looked up.

'I would like a private word,' Julius said.

Crassus understood immediately and left them together. Brutus began to brush the shaggy winter coats of the horses in long strokes.

'Well?' he said.

'Your mother is here,' Julius said.

Brutus stopped his brushing and looked at him. His face tightened with sudden knowledge.

'To see me, or to see you?'

'Both, Brutus.'

'So you raise your fist to my mother and now she comes crawling back into your bed, is that it?'

Julius tensed with anger.

'Just *once*, think before you speak to me. I will not suffer your anger this time, Brutus, I swear it. One more word in that tone and I will have you hanged in this courtyard. I'll pull the rope myself.'

Brutus turned to face him and Julius saw he was unarmed. He was glad of it. He spoke with a terrible slowness, as if each word was forced out of him.

'You know, Julius, I have given you a great deal. Do you know how many battles I have won for you? I've been your sword all the years of my life and I have never been anything but loyal. But the first *moment* you feel a prick of anger, you threaten me with a rope?'

403

He leaned very close to Julius.

'You forget yourself. I've been there from the *beginning*. And what has it gained me? Do you praise my name as you do Mark Antony's? Do you give me the right flank when I risk my life for you? No, you come out here and treat me like your dog.'

Julius could only stare at the pale rage he saw. Brutus' mouth twisted in bitter mockery.

'Very well, Julius. You and she are none of my concern. She made that perfectly clear to me before. But I will not stay here to watch you spend the winter . . . renewing your relationship. Is that sweetly enough phrased for you?'

For a moment, Julius could not answer him. He wanted to find words to ease the pain in his friend, but after his threats they would have been worthless. In the end, he set his jaw and retreated behind coldness.

'I will not keep you, if you want to go,' he said.

Brutus shook his head. 'No, it would be unpleasant for the pair of you having me as a witness. I will travel down to Rome until spring. There is nothing holding me here.'

'If that is what you want,' Julius said.

Brutus did not reply, simply nodding and turning back to his brushing. Julius stood in painful silence, knowing he should speak. Brutus muttered softly to his horse, easing the bit into its mouth. As he mounted, he looked down at the man he revered above all others.

'How will it end this time, do you think? Will you hit her?' he said.

'It is not your concern,' Julius replied.

'I don't like to see her treated as one of your conquests, Julius. When will you be satisfied, I wonder? Even Gaul is not enough for you, with another twenty ships being built. Campaigns are meant to end, Julius, or did no one ever tell you that? Legions are meant to come home when the war is over, not find another one and another.'

'Go to Rome,' Julius replied. 'Rest the winter. Just remember that I will need you in spring.'

Brutus unrolled a fur cloak and tied it tight around his shoulders before mounting. He had enough gold in his pouch to buy food on the journey south and he wanted to leave. Yet when he gathered the reins in his hands and looked down at the miserable face of his friend, he knew he could not dig in his heels and leave him there without speaking again.

'I'll be here,' he said.

Crassus and Pompey travelled back to Rome the following morning, leaving Julius the full run of the house. Within a week, he had settled into a routine of writing letters and reports in the morning with Adàn and spending the rest of the day with Servilia. He travelled with her to the shipyards in the west and for those weeks it was as if they were a newly married couple. Julius blessed the fact that she had come to him. After the exhaustion of his campaigns in Gaul, it was a pure joy to visit the theatres in a Roman city and listen to his own language in every mouth of the markets. It made him yearn to see Rome again, but even in Ariminum he had to be careful. If the moneylenders of his city found that he was back in the country, they would demand a settlement and he had very little left to tide his men over the winter.

Julius knew his one advantage lay in the fact that men like Herminius wanted their money more than his blood. If he were taken and brought back to the city, they would end up with nothing. Even so, his men wore cloaks over their distinctive armour in public and Julius avoided the houses of those who might have known him.

He revelled in Servilia and their lovemaking was like water in a desert. He could not quench his thirst and the scent of her was on his skin and in his lungs at all times. As the winter began to ease and the days lengthened, the thought of parting from her was almost a physical pain. At times, Julius thought of taking her with him, or arranging visits to the new lands he was taking for Rome. Thousands of other settlers were already farming stretches of the virgin soil and he could promise at least some comfort.

It was just a dream and they both knew it, even as they fantasised about establishing a small house for her in the Roman provinces. Servilia could no more leave the city than the Senate could. It was part of her: away from it, she was lost.

Through her, Julius learned how far Clodius and Milo had come in their domination of the poorer areas. He hoped Pompey's confidence was not misplaced and wrote to him again pledging support if Pompey wanted to force a vote for Dictatorship. Though Julius knew he could never fully trust the man, there were few others with the strength and ability to control their tempestuous city and the offer was genuine. Having Pompey as Dictator was far preferable to anarchy.

By the time the winter frosts had begun to lessen, Julius was already tired of the pale imitation of Rome that was Ariminum. He hungered for the mountain snows to clear, though the end of winter brought a secret guilt and fear. Each day that passed brought him closer to the point when he would either see his oldest friend return, or know he would have to cross the mountains without him.

CHAPTER THIRTY-FIVE

⚲⚲⚲⚲⚲

Brutus had shed his cloak for the last stage of the ride south to Rome. Though the air was still sharp, it had nothing like the bite of Gaul and the exertion of riding kept him warm. His original mount had been left far behind at the first legion post on the Via Flaminia. He had paid to have the gelding looked after and would collect the horse as his final change on his return. The system had allowed him a remount every thirty miles and he had made the journey in only seven days.

After his first joy at walking through the city gate, everything had soured as soon as he took in his surroundings. Rome looked the same in many ways, but his soldier's instincts had brought an immediate prickling alarm. Alexandria's letters should have prepared him for the changes, but she had not managed to convey the sense of raw panic that hung in the air. Half the men he passed were armed in some way or another. It was something a trained eye could spot at a glance. They walked differently with a concealed blade and Brutus could feel a tension he had never before experienced on the streets of his home. No one lingered or talked on street corners. It was almost a city under siege and unconsciously he copied the crowds as he hurried to Alexandria's shop.

He knew a moment of fear when he found it boarded up and empty. Passers-by heard him calling, but not one of them dared to meet his eyes. Even the beggars were missing from the streets and Brutus stood still as he considered the implications. The city was terrified. He had seen it before amongst those who knew a war was coming.

Even knocking on the doors of the other shops in the road was worrying. The owners looked sick with nervousness at the sight of him and three of them only stared blankly as he tried to ask where Tabbic had gone. The fourth was a butcher who held a heavy cleaver defensively the whole time Brutus was in his shop. The iron blade seemed to give him a confidence the others lacked and he directed Brutus to an area many streets away. Brutus left him still holding the weapon.

Out in the road, the feeling intensified again. When he had been in Greece, the veterans talked of an 'itch' that told them trouble was coming. Brutus felt it tickle him as he marched through the thin crowds. By the time he reached the address, he was almost certain he should get Alexandria out of the city before it exploded. Whatever was coming, he did not want her in the middle of it.

The new shop was much larger and occupied two full floors of a well-kept tenement. Brutus raised his hand to knock and saw the door was open. He narrowed his eyes then and drew his gladius silently. He'd rather look a fool than go unprepared into a dangerous situation and by that point he was jumping at shadows.

The interior was five times the size of the little shop Tabbic had owned before. Brutus edged inside, his gaze fastening on the figures at the far end. Alexandria and Tabbic were there, with two other men. Facing them were four others, of a type he had seen too often in the streets outside. None of them had seen him and Brutus forced himself to walk slowly towards the group, passing the huge new forge that lurked against the wall and threw heat at him as he passed. Its crackle hid the slight noise of his sandals on the stone floor and he was very close when one of the men stepped forward and pushed Alexandria down.

With a shout, Brutus raced forward and the four men spun to face him. Two carried knives and two had swords like his own, but he did not pause in his rush. Alexandria shouted wildly at him and only the desperation in her voice made him hold his first blow.

'No, Brutus! Don't!' she cried.

The men who threatened her were professionals, he saw. They moved aside so as not to be exposed to blades from behind as they faced him. Brutus lowered his sword and stepped into their range as if he had nothing to fear.

'What goes on here?' he demanded, glaring at the man who had pushed her.

'None of your concern, boy,' one of them said, jerking his sword in Brutus' direction to make him flinch. Brutus regarded him impassively.

'You really haven't the first idea who you are speaking to, have you?' he said, grinning nastily. His sword tip cut small circles in the air as he held it lazily at his side. The tiny movement seemed to draw the gazes of the other men, but the one who had spoken held his eyes, not daring to look away. There was something terrible in the way Brutus stood so casually before their blades and his confidence intimidated all of them.

'Who are they, Ria?' Brutus said, without looking at her.

'Collectors for Clodius,' she replied as she stood up. 'They are demanding more money than we have. More than we earn. But you mustn't kill them.'

409

Brutus frowned. 'Why not? No one would miss them.'

One of the raptores answered him. 'Because that pretty girl wouldn't like what our friends would do to her, boy. So put your sword . . .'

Brutus cut the man's throat and stood without expression as he collapsed, watching the others. Though he was only inches from their blades, not one of them dared to move.

'Anyone else want to make threats?' he said.

They stared wide-eyed at him and they could all hear the ghastly choking sounds coming from the floor. No one looked down.

'Oh gods, no,' he heard Alexandria whisper.

Brutus ignored her, waiting for one of the men to break the stillness that held them. He had seen Renius intimidate groups before, but there were always fools. He watched as the men shuffled backwards away from him until they were out of range of his gladius. Brutus took a sharp step towards them.

'No little taunts now, lads. No calling out as you go. Just leave. I'll find you if I have to.'

The men exchanged glances, but none of them broke the silence as they walked past the forges to the street door. The last to pass through closed it quietly behind him.

Alexandria was pale with anger and fear.

'That's it then,' she said. 'You don't know what you've done. They'll come back with more and burn this place down. Gods, Brutus, did you not hear what I said?'

'I heard, but I'm here now,' he replied, wiping his sword on the cooling body at his feet.

'For how long? We have to live with them when you've gone back to your legions, don't you realise that?'

Brutus felt a flare of anger start in him. He'd had just about enough of being criticised from Julius.

'I should have just watched, then? Yes? I'm not who you think I am if you expect me just to stand there while they threaten you.'

410

'He's right, Alexandria,' Tabbic broke in, nodding to Brutus. 'There's no taking it back now, but Clodius won't just forget us, or you. We'll have to sleep in the workshop for the next few nights. Will you stay with us?'

Brutus eyed Alexandria. It wasn't exactly the homecoming he had imagined on his ride south, but then he shrugged.

'Of course. It will save me rent, at least. Now, am I going to get a welcoming kiss or not? Not from you, Tabbic, obviously.'

'First, get rid of that body,' Alexandria said.

She had begun to shake with reaction and Tabbic placed a kettle on the forge to make her a hot drink. Brutus sighed and took hold of the corpse by its ankles, dragging it over the stone flags.

When he was out of earshot, Teddus leaned close to Alexandria.

'I've never seen anything that fast,' he said.

She looked at him, accepting the cup of hot spiced wine from Tabbic's hands.

'He won Caesar's tournament; remember it?'

Teddus whistled softly to himself.

'The silver armour? I can believe it. I won a bit on him myself. Will you be wanting me to stay tonight? It could be a long one when Clodius finds out about his man.'

'Can you stay?' Alexandria asked.

The old soldier looked away, embarrassed.

'Of course I can,' he said gruffly. 'I'll fetch my son as well, with your permission.' He cleared his throat to cover his discomfort. 'If they send men for us tonight, we could do with someone up on the roof as a lookout. He'll be no trouble up there.'

Tabbic looked at the pair of them and nodded as he came to a decision.

'I'm going to take my wife and children to her sister's house for a few days. Then I'll drop in on the old street and see if I can't bring a couple of stout lads back for tonight. They might

411

relish the chance to hit back for once, you never know. Lock the door behind me when I've gone.'

Clodius' men came in force in the dark, with torches to burn the shop to the ground. Teddus' son clattered down the back stairs to shout a warning and Brutus swore aloud. He had retrieved his silver armour from the last posting house by the city walls and now fastened the buckles and ties on the chest-plate as he readied himself. He looked around at the motley group that had assembled by Tabbic's forges. The jeweller had brought four young men back from the shops along the old road. They carried good blades, though Brutus doubted they could do much more than hack wildly with them. In the last hour before darkness had fallen, he had taught them the value of a repeated lunge and had them practise until their stiff muscles had loosened. Their eyes shone in the lamplight as they watched the silver-armoured warrior stand before them.

'We'll have to go out and meet them if they've come to burn. This place is wood-framed and we'd better have water buckets ready in case they get through. If there are enough of them, it could be . . . difficult. Who's coming?'

The four lads Tabbic had brought raised their new swords in response and Tabbic nodded. Teddus raised his hand with them, but Brutus shook his head.

'Not you. One more won't make a difference outside, but if they get past us, someone has to be here for Alexandria. I don't want her alone.'

Brutus looked at her then and his face tightened with disapproval. She had refused to go with Tabbic's wife and children and now he feared for her.

'If they come, Teddus will hold them while you get to the back stairs, all right? His son will guide you down to the alleys and you may get clear. That's if you are still staying? This is no place for you if they come in a mob. I've seen what can happen.'

His warning frightened her, but she raised her chin in defiance. 'This shop is mine. I won't run.'

Brutus glared at her, caught between admiration and anger. He tossed a small dagger at her and watched as she snatched it neatly from the air and checked the blade. Her skin was pale as milk in the gloom.

'If they come past us, you'll have to,' he said gently. 'I don't want to be worrying about what they'll do to you.'

Before she could reply, the shouting rose in the street outside and Brutus sighed. He drew his gladius and rolled his neck to loosen the muscles.

'Right then, lads. On your feet. Do what I tell you and you'll have a memory to cherish. Panic and your mothers wear black. Is that clear?'

Tabbic chuckled and the other men nodded mutely, in awe of the silver general. Without waiting for them, Brutus strode across the echoing floor and flung the door open. Orange flickers reflected in the metal he wore as he went out.

Brutus swallowed dryly as he saw how many men had been sent to make an example of them. The approaching crowd staggered to a stop as he came out and stood before them, his five men forming a single rank at his sides. It was one thing to terrify shop owners in the backstreets, quite another to attack fully armed soldiers. Every man in the crowd recognised the silver armour Brutus wore and their shouts and laughter died away to nothing. Brutus could hear the crackling of their torches as they watched him, their eyes catching the dim orange light and shining like a pack of dogs.

Renius had said once that one strong man could handle a mob, if he took the initiative and kept it. He had also admitted

413

that the most successful bluff could be called when a crowd could hide behind their numbers. No man seriously expected to die when he was surrounded by his friends and that confidence could lead to a rush against swords that no single one of them would have dared. Brutus hoped they had not been drinking. He took a deep breath.

'This is an unlawful assembly,' Brutus bellowed. 'I am the General of the Third Gallica and I tell you to go back to your homes and families. I have bowmen on the roof. Do not shame yourselves attacking old men and women in this place.'

In that moment, he wished Julius were with him. Julius would have found the words to turn them back. No doubt they would have ended up carrying him through the streets and joining a new legion. The thought made Brutus smile despite the tension and those who saw it hesitated. Some of them squinted up into the darkness, but could see nothing after the flare of the torches. In truth, there was nothing to see. If Brutus had been given another couple of days, he might have found a few good men to put up on the overhanging roof, but as it was, only Teddus' son watched them and he was unarmed.

A sudden crash made every man jump or swear and Brutus tensed to be rushed. He saw a tile had been dislodged from the roof, shattering amongst the crowd. No one had been injured, but Brutus saw more faces look up and saw them talk nervously amongst themselves. He wondered if it had been deliberate, or whether the young man would follow the tile shortly afterwards and thump down on the crowd like the clumsy sod he was.

'You should get out of our way!' a man shouted from back in the mass. A growl from the crowd agreed with him.

Brutus sneered. 'I'm a soldier of Rome, whoreson!' he bellowed. 'I didn't run from the slaves. I didn't run from the tribes in Gaul. What have you got that they didn't have?'

The crowd lacked a leader, Brutus could see. They milled

and shoved each other, but there was no one with the authority to force them onto the swords of the men in the road outside the shop.

'I'll tell you this much,' Brutus called out. 'You think you're protected, lads? When Caesar returns from Gaul, he'll find every one of the men who made threats against his friends. That is written in stone, lads. Every word of it. Some of you will be taking his pay already. They'll have lists of names for him and where to find them. Be sure of it. He'll go through you like a hot knife.'

In the darkness, it was difficult to be sure, but Brutus thought the crowd was thinning as those at the outskirts began to drift away. One of the torches was dropped by its bearer and picked up by another. No matter what hold Clodius had, Julius' name had been read on every street corner for years and it worked as a talisman on those who could slip into the night, unseen.

In only a short time, Brutus was left facing no more than fifteen men, no doubt the original ones that Clodius had sent to burn them out. None of those could retreat without being dragged from their beds the following morning. Brutus could see their faces shining with sweat as they saw the numbers dwindle around them.

Brutus spoke gently to them, knowing their desperation could only be pushed so far.

'If I were you, lads. I'd get out of the city for a while. Ariminum is quiet enough and there's always work on the docks for those who don't mind a bit of sweat.'

The core of men looked back angrily, undecided. It was still too many for Brutus to think he had a chance to win if they attacked. Their blades caught the light of the torches and there was no hint of weakness in the hard expressions they turned to him. He glanced at the men at his side and saw their tension. Only Teddus seemed calm.

'Not a word, lads,' Brutus murmured. 'Don't set anything off now.'

With a snort of disgust, one of the torchbearers threw his brand down onto the street and stalked away. Two more followed him and the others looked at each other in silent communication. In groups of twos and threes, they walked clear until there were only a few remaining in the street.

'If I were a vengeful man, I would be very tempted to cut you down, right now,' Brutus said to them. 'You can't stand here all night.'

One of them grimaced.

'Clodius won't let you get away with this, you know. He will raise hell in the morning.'

'Perhaps. I may have a chance to speak to him before he does. He may be reasonable.'

'You don't know him, do you?' the man said, grinning.

Brutus began to relax.

'Are you going to go home then? It's too cold to be standing out here.'

The man looked around at the last pair of his companions.

'I think I will,' he said. 'Was it true what you said?'

'Which part?' Brutus replied, thinking of his nonexistent archers.

'About being a friend of Caesar?'

'We're like brothers,' Brutus said easily.

'He's a good man for Rome. Some of us wouldn't mind seeing him come back. Those with families at least.'

'Gaul won't hold him for ever,' Brutus replied.

The man nodded and walked away into the dark with his friends.

CHAPTER THIRTY-SIX

ᕼᕼᕼᕼ

Brutus slept on the floor of the shop for a full week. The night after the failed attack, he visited Clodius' town house in the centre of the city, but found it better protected than a fortress and bristling with armed men. His sense of worry only deepened as the days crept by. It was as if the city were holding its breath.

Though Tabbic accepted his advice and kept his family away from the shop, Alexandria grew more and more irritable each day she was forced to spend sleeping on the hard floor. All her wealth was tied up in the new premises, from the walls and roof to the stocks of precious metals and the enormous forges. She would not leave it and Brutus could not return to the north while he felt she was in danger.

The young men who had stood with them against the collectors also stayed. Tabbic had offered them a salary as temporary guards, but they waved his coins away. They idolised the silver general who had called for their help and in return

Brutus spent a few hours each day teaching them how to use the swords they carried.

The tense crowds thinned around noon, when much of the city paused to eat. Brutus went out then with one or two of the young men, to gather food and information. At least they could always prepare a hot meal on the forges, but the usual gossip of the markets seemed to have been stifled. At best, Brutus could only pick up a few fragments here and there and he missed having his mother in the city. Without her, the details of the Senate meetings were unknown and Brutus felt an increasing frustration and blindness as the city wound tighter and tighter each night.

Though Pompey had returned to Rome, there seemed to be no order on the streets, especially after dark. More than once, Brutus and the others were woken from sleep by dim, muffled sounds of conflict. From the roof, they could see the distant glow of fires somewhere in the maze of backstreets and alleys. The armed gangs made no second attempt to attack the shop and Brutus worried that their masters were involved in a more serious struggle.

In the middle of the second week, the markets were full of the news that Clodius' raptores had attacked the house of the orator, Cicero, trying to trap him inside as they set it alight. The man escaped them, but there was no outcry against Clodius and to Brutus it was another sign that law in the city had broken down. His arguments with Alexandria became more heated and at last she agreed to leave and wait out the crisis at Julius' estate. Rome was fast becoming a battleground by night and the shop was not worth their lives. For one who had been a slave, though, the shop was the symbol of everything she had achieved and Alexandria wept bitterly at leaving it for the gangs.

Following her directions, Brutus risked a trip to Alexandria's house to pick up clothes and came back with Octavian's mother

Atia to add to those who huddled in the shop as darkness fell.

Each day became an agony of frustration for the young general. If he had been alone, it would have been simple enough to join Pompey's legion at their barracks. As it was, the crowd of people looking to him for safety seemed to grow each day. Tabbic's sister had brought her husband and children into the safety of the shop and joined Tabbic's three young daughters. The families of the young men had swelled their number still further and Brutus despaired at the thought of moving twenty-seven people through the violent city, even in daylight. When the Senate declared a general curfew at sunset, Brutus decided he could wait no longer. Only law-abiding citizens seemed to obey the edict of the Senate. The curfew had no effect on the roving gangs, and that same night the street next to the shop was set alight, with pitiful screams sounding in the darkness until they were consumed.

As the sullen city stirred the following morning, Brutus armed his group with anything that Tabbic could find, from swords and knives to simple iron bars.

'It's going to be a good hour through the streets and you could see things that will make you want to stop,' he said to them. He knew they looked to him to save them and he forced himself to remain cheerful in the face of that trust.

'No matter what happens, we do not stop, does everyone understand? If we are attacked, we cut and keep moving. Once we are through the gate, the estate is only a few hours away from the city. We'll be safe there until things have settled.'

He wore his silver armour, though it was now dulled with dirt and soot. One by one they nodded as he looked at them.

'The troubles will pass in a few days or weeks,' he said. 'I've seen worse, believe me.'

He thought of what Julius had told him about the civil war between Marius and Sulla and wished his friend were there. Though there were times when he hated him, there were few men he would rather have had at his back in a crisis. Only Renius would have been more of a comfort.

'Everyone ready?' Brutus asked them. He took a deep breath and opened the door to the street, peering out.

Rubbish and filth had piled up on the corners and wild dogs that were little better than skeletons growled and snapped at each other as they fought over morsels. The smell of smoke was in the air and Brutus could see a group of armed men lounging at a crossroads as if they were the owners of the city.

'Right. Move quickly now and follow me,' he said, his voice betraying his tension.

They walked out into the street and Brutus saw the group of men shift and stiffen as they were spotted. He cursed under his breath. One of the little girls began to cry and Tabbic's sister picked her up and shushed her as they walked on.

'Will they let us past?' Tabbic murmured at Brutus' shoulder.

'I don't know,' Brutus replied, watching the group. There were ten or twelve of them, all marked with soot smeared into their skin and hair. Most were red-eyed from their night's work and Brutus knew they would attack the slightest weakness.

The men drew blades and strolled across the open road to block their path. Brutus swore softly.

'Tabbic? If I go down, don't stop. Alexandria knows the estate as well as I do. They won't turn her away.'

As he spoke, Brutus lengthened his stride, drawing his gladius in one smooth sweep. He felt a rage in him that men such as these should threaten the innocents of his city. It struck at his most basic beliefs and he was spurred on by the wail of the children behind him.

The men scattered as Brutus took the head of the first, shouldering the body down and killing two more even as they turned to run. In moments, the rest of them were sprinting away, yelling in fear. Brutus let them go, turning back to the group that Tabbic and Alexandria were shepherding along, trying to stop the children from looking back at the bloody corpses Brutus had left in his wake.

'Jackals,' Brutus said shortly as he rejoined them. The children looked at him in terror and he realised his silver armour was splashed with blood. One of the youngest began to sob, pointing at him.

'Keep moving towards the gate!' he snapped, suddenly angry with them all. His place was with the legion of Rome, not shepherding frightened girls. He looked back and saw the men had gathered again, staring hungrily after him. They made no move in his direction and Brutus hawked and spat on the stones in disgust.

The streets were practically empty as they made their way to the gate. As far as possible, Brutus followed the main roads, but even there the signs of normal city life were missing. The great meat market owned by Milo was empty and desolate, with the wind whipping leaves and dust around their feet. They passed a whole row of gutted shops and houses and one of the young ones began screaming at the sight of a charred body caught in a doorway. Alexandria pressed her hand over the child's eyes until they were past and Brutus saw her hands were shaking.

'There's the gate,' Tabbic said to cheer them, but as he spoke, a mob of laughing, drunken men turned a corner into the road and froze as they saw Brutus. Like the group before them, they were filthy with ash and dirt from the fires they had started. Their eyes and teeth shone against their grimy skin as they scrabbled for weapons.

'Let us pass,' Brutus roared at them, frightening the children at his back.

The men only sneered as they took in his ragged followers. Their jeering was cut short as Brutus launched himself amongst them, spinning and cutting in a frenzy. His gladius had been forged by the greatest Spanish master of the blade and each of his blows sliced through their clothes and limbs, so that great gouts of blood sprang up around him. He did not hear himself screaming as he felt their blades slide off his armour.

A heavy blow stunned him down to one knee and Brutus growled like an animal and pushed himself up with renewed strength, jerking his gladius up into a man's chest from below. The blade ripped through ribs just as Brutus was sent staggering by a hatchet. It was aimed at his neck but cut into the silver armour, remaining wedged. He didn't feel any pain from his wounds and only dimly knew that Tabbic was there with the younger men. For once, he lost himself completely in the battle and made no defence in his lust for killing. Without the armour, he would not have survived, but Tabbic's voice came through his fury at last and Brutus paused to look at the carnage around him.

None of the raptores had survived. The stones of the road were covered in scattered limbs and bodies, each surrounded by dark spreading pools.

'All right, lad, it's over,' he heard Tabbic say, as if from a great distance. He felt the man's strong fingers press into his neck where the hatchet was lodged and Brutus' mind begin to clear. Blood streamed from his armour and as he looked down, he saw it pumping sluggishly from a deep wound in his thigh. He prodded the gash in a daze, wondering at the lack of pain.

Brutus motioned with his sword towards the gate. They were so close and the thought of stopping was unbearable. He saw Alexandria tear her skirt to bind his leg while he panted like a dog, waiting for breath to tell them to keep moving.

'I daren't take that axe out until I know how deeply you've been cut,' Tabbic said. 'Put your arm around my shoulder, lad. I'll take your sword.'

Brutus nodded, gulping rubbery spit.

'Don't stop,' he said weakly, staggering forward with them. One of the young men supported his other arm and together they moved under the shadow of the gate. It was unmanned. As the stones changed beneath their feet, a light snow began to fall on the silent group and the smell of smoke and blood was torn away by the breeze.

Clodius took a deep breath of the icy air, wondering at the sight of the forum around him. He had thrown everything into a last-ditch attempt to bring Milo down and the fighting had ripped through the centre of the city, spilling at last into the forum.

As the snow fell, more than three thousand men struggled in groups and pairs to kill each other. There were no tactics or manoeuvres and each man fought in constant terror of those around him, hardly knowing friend from enemy. As one of Clodius' men triumphed, he would be stabbed from behind or have his throat cut by another.

The snow fell harder and Clodius saw a bloody slush being churned up around the feet of his bodyguard as a group of Milo's gladiators tried to reach him. He found himself being forced back against the steps of a temple. He considered running into it, though he knew there would be no sanctuary from his enemies.

Were his men winning? It was impossible to tell. It had started well enough with Pompey's legion lured away to the east of the city to quell a false riot and a string of fires. Milo's men were spread all over the city and Clodius had struck at his house, smashing down the gates. He had not been there and the attack had faltered as Clodius searched for him, desperate to break the stalemate of power that had to end with the death of one or the other of them.

He could not say exactly when their silent war had erupted into open conflict. Each night had forced them closer and closer until suddenly he was fighting for his life in the forum, with snow swirling all around and the senate building over-looking them all.

Clodius turned his head as more men rushed in from a side street. He breathed in relief when he saw they were his own, led by one of his chosen officers. Like Milo's gladiators, they wore armour and cut through the struggling men to reach him.

Clodius spun to see three figures leaping at him with blades outstretched. He downed the first with a crushing blow from his sword, but the second shoved a dagger into his chest, making him gasp. He felt every inch of the metal, colder than the snow that lay so lightly on his skin. Clodius saw the man dragged off him, but the third attacker scrambled through and Clodius roared in agony as a knife entered his flesh over and over.

He sank onto one knee as his great strength gave out and still the man stabbed at him while Clodius' friends went berserk in fury and grief. At last they reached his attacker, but as they tore him away Clodius sank gently down into the bloody snow around him. He could see the senate steps as he died and in the distance he could hear the horns of Pompey's legion.

Milo fought a bitter retreat as the legion came smashing into the open space of the forum. Those who were too slow or entwined in their own struggles were cut down by the machine and Milo bawled for his men to get away before they were all destroyed. He had yelled with excitement when Clodius fell, but now he had to find a safe place to plan and regather his strength. There was nothing left to stand in his way if he could only survive the legion's charge. He skidded in the snow as he ran with the others, streaming in their hundreds like rats before the scythe.

Many of Clodius' men were caught before they could get clear and they too were forced into panicked flight as the legion destroyed everything in front of them. The forum emptied in all directions, the roads into it filling with running gangs, ignoring enemies in the face of a greater fear. The wounded screamed as they ran, but those that fell were cut to pieces as the line of legionaries rolled over them.

In only a short time, the vast space of the forum was empty, leaving the still, slumped figures of the dead, already being covered by a dusting of fine flakes. The wind howled along the temples. The legion officers conferred, snapping out orders to their units. Cohorts were dispatched to their posts around the city and more reports began to come in that the rioting had sprung up in the Esquiline valley. Pompey was there in full armour. He left a thousand men to control the centre of the city and took three cohorts north through the streets to enforce the broken curfew.

'Clear the streets,' he ordered. 'Get them back inside until we can control the gangs.' Behind him, new fires lit the grey sky and the snow still fell.

That night, the city erupted. Clodius' body had been carried into the temple of Minerva and thousands of men stormed the building, wild with grief and anger at the death of their master. The legionaries there were torn apart and fires were set all over the city as those who had followed Clodius hunted for Milo and his supporters. Pitched battles were fought in the streets against Pompey's men and twice the legionaries were forced to retreat as they were attacked on all sides and became lost in the maze of alleys. Some were trapped in buildings and burnt with them. Others were caught by large groups and over-whelmed by a savage mob. A city was no place for a legion to fight. Clodius' officers lured them in by making women scream and then dropped on them, stabbing mindlessly until they were dead or forced to run.

Pompey himself was forced back towards the senate house

by a mass of armed men. He broke them at last with a third shield charge, but there were always more. He thought that every man in Rome had armed himself and was on the streets and the numbers were simply overwhelming. He decided to retreat to the senate steps and use that building to coordinate his remaining forces, yet as he clattered back to the open space of the forum, his jaw dropped in horror at the sight of thousands of torches clustered around the building.

They had broken open the bronze doors and Clodius was being carried over their heads into the deeper darkness within. Pompey saw the senator's bloody corpse jerk and flop as they passed it up the steps.

The forum was full of armed men, shouting and roaring. Pompey hesitated. He had never run from anything in his life, and what he was witnessing was the end of everything he loved in Rome, yet he knew his men would be destroyed if he took them into the forum. Half the city seemed to be there.

Inside the dark senate house, Pompey saw the flicker of flames. Cheering men came out onto the snow-covered steps, howling as they waved their blades in the air. Grey smoke billowed out of the doorway and Pompey felt tears on his face, warm against his cold skin.

'My theatre. Re-form on my theatre,' he called to his waiting men.

They backed from the surging crowd around the Curia and finally Pompey turned away from the flames that crackled through the roof, shattering the marble with reports that echoed across the forum. It was a worse pain than he could have imagined seeing the capering figures against the flames. Only the darkness hid his men and he felt a raging frustration at being forced to retreat from the heart of his city. Only dawn would bring an end to it, he knew. The raptores had destroyed the rule of law and were drunk with their new power. But when the morning came, they would be dazed and exhausted, appalled at what they had done. Then he would bring order, and write it in iron and blood.

The weak morning light streamed in from the high windows of Pompey's theatre, illuminating the packed ranks of men he had summoned from all over the city. As well as the Senate themselves, Pompey had sent centuries of his legion to bring in the tribunes, the magistrates, the aediles, quaestors, praetors and every other rank of power in Rome. More than a thousand men sat on the wide rings around the central stage looking down on Pompey, and they were grim with fear and exhaustion. There were several faces missing from the ranks after the riots and not one of them failed to appreciate the seriousness of their position.

Pompey cleared his throat and rubbed briefly at the goose-bumps that had come up on his bare arms. The theatre was not heated and he could see their breath frost the air as they watched him in silence.

'Last night was the closest I have ever come to seeing the end of Rome,' he began.

They sat as still as statues to listen and Pompey saw determination in their expressions. All the petty rivalries had been forgotten in the face of the previous night's events and he knew they would give him anything to restore peace in the city before night fell once more.

'You have all heard that Clodius was killed in the fighting, his body burnt in the Curia, itself reduced to ashes. Much of the city has been destroyed by fire, and bodies choke every street and gutter. The city is in chaos, without food or water over great parts of it. By tonight, much of the population will be hungry and the violence could begin once more.'

He paused, but the silence was perfect.

'My soldiers captured Senator Milo at sunrise when he tried to escape the city. I intend to use the daylight hours to search

427

Rome for the rest in their chain of command, but trials would give their supporters time to regroup and rearm. I do not intend to give them another chance, gentlemen.' He took a deep breath. 'I have called you here to vote me the powers of Dictatorship. If I remain bound by our laws, I cannot answer for the peace of the city tonight or any other night. I ask that you stand to confirm my appointment.'

Almost as one, the thousand members of the ruling class stood. Some rose to their feet faster than others, but in the end Pompey nodded with fierce satisfaction and waved them back to their seats.

'I stand before you as Dictator. I now declare martial law throughout Rome. A new curfew will be enforced at sunset each evening and those caught on the streets will be executed immediately. My legion will cut out the leaders and torture will give us the names of the key men from the ranks of the street gangs. I declare this building to be the seat of government until the senate house is rebuilt. Food will be distributed from the forum and the north and south gates of the city each morning until the emergency is over.'

He looked round at the ranks of his people and smiled tightly. Now it would begin to hurt a little.

'Each of you will deliver a tithe of one hundred thousand sesterces or a tenth of your wealth, whichever is the greater. The senate treasury was looted and we need funds to put the city back on her feet. You will be repaid when the coffers are full once again, but until then it is a necessary measure.'

The first grumblings of disquiet went around the echoing chamber, but they were a tiny minority. The rest of them had been forced to look hard at the fragility of all they thought solid and would not baulk at paying for their safety. Pompey was sorry Crassus wasn't there. He would have stung the old man for a huge sum. Sending a begging letter would not have the force of a demand in person, but it could not be helped.

Pompey went on after a brief glance at his notes.

'I will recall a legion from Greece, but until they reach the city, we need every man who can use a gladius. Those of you who employ guards will leave numbers with the scribes as you leave. I must know how many men we can trust to take arms in the event of further rioting. My legion took heavy losses last night and those men must be replaced as a matter of priority if we are to crush the mob before it gains strength once more. I will execute the followers of Milo and Clodius without ceremony or public announcement.

'Tonight will be the most difficult, gentlemen. If we get through that, order will slowly be restored. Eventually, I will levy a tax on all citizens in Roman lands to rebuild the city.'

He still saw numb fear on many of the faces before him, but others showed the first glimmerings of hope at his words. He called for responses and many of them rose to query the details of the new administration. Pompey relaxed as he began to work his way through the questions. Already, the stunned look was fading from their faces as they fell into the routines of the old senate house. It gave him hope for them all.

CHAPTER THIRTY-SEVEN

ᗣᗣᗣᗣᗣ

Brutus eased himself down onto the stump of the old oak he had cut down with Tubruk, laying his stick next to him. In the green woods, it was easy to remember the old gladiator's smile as he had welcomed him home.

Wincing, Brutus stretched his leg out and scratched the purple line that ran from just above his knee almost to his groin. A similar line of stitching on his collarbone showed how close he had come to being killed in his frenzy. Both wounds had been dirty and he didn't remember much of the first week back at the estate. Clodia said he was lucky not to have lost it, but the lips of the gash had knitted at last, though the stitches itched abominably. Vague images of being bathed with wet cloths came back to him and he grimaced with embarrassment. Julia had grown into a young woman with more than a touch of her mother's beauty. He thought Alexandria must have taken her aside for a private word about his care. Certainly, there had been a few days when she hadn't come near him and when he saw her, her eyes had flashed like Cornelia's used to when she was angry. After that, only Alexandria had bathed away his sweat and grime.

Brutus smiled ruefully. Alexandria treated him as if he were a sick horse and rubbed him down with a rough detachment that left him glowing. It had been a relief to be finally strong enough to make his own way down to the bathing rooms and wash in privacy. She would have had the skin off him if he had dawdled in bed much longer.

It was peaceful in the woods. A bird sang in the trees nearby and in the meandering line of the path, his mind's eye could see two young boys sprinting through the bushes on their way to growing into men. Friendship had been a simple thing then, something he and Julius took for granted. Brutus remembered how they had pressed their bloody hands together as if the whole of life could be reduced to simple vows and actions. It was strange to look back on those days when so much had happened. There were times when he was proud of the man he had become and others when he would have given anything to be the boy again, with all his choices still before him. There were so many things he would change if he could.

They had been immortal in those long summers. They had known Tubruk would always be there to protect them and the future was simply a chance to carry on their friendship over years and other lands. Nothing would ever come between them, even if Rome herself should crumble.

Taking a knife from his belt, Brutus levered it under the first stitch and snapped the thread. With great care, he tugged the broken end through his skin, working his way down to the final knot. He was silent with concentration, though he was sweating by the time he finished and tossed the sticky cord away into the bushes. A thin trickle of blood worked its way down through the light hairs on his thigh and he wiped it into a smear with his thumb.

He stood slowly and felt light-headed and weak. He decided to leave the stitches on his neck alone for the time being, though they too itched abominably.

'I thought I'd find you here,' Julia said.

He turned to her and smiled at the awkward way she stood. He wondered how long she had been watching. How old was she, sixteen? Long-legged and beautiful. Alexandria would not be pleased to hear they had been talking in the woods together so he resolved not to tell her.

'I thought I'd try walking a little way. The leg is getting stronger, though it will be a while before I can trust it,' he said.

'When it's healed, you will go back to my father,' she said.

It was not a question, but he nodded. 'In a few weeks at most. The city is calm enough now Pompey is Dictator. We'll all be leaving you in peace then. This old place will be quiet again.'

'I don't mind it,' she said hurriedly. 'I like having people here, even the children.'

They shared a look of understanding and Brutus chuckled. Despite the best efforts of Tabbic and his sister, the young ones had been running wild around the estate after only a few days, enthralled by the woods and the river. Clodia had saved one from drowning on three occasions in the deep pool. It was strange how quickly the young had recovered from the nightmare of their trip out of the city. Brutus guessed that when they looked back on that strange year of their lives, they would not remember seeing men killed, or if they did, it would be nothing to their first ride on a horse around the yard, with Tabbic holding them in the saddle. Children were a strange breed.

Julia had inherited some of her mother's grace, he could see. Her hair was long and bound with a strip of cloth at the nape of her neck. She seemed to focus on his face with a peculiar intensity whenever he spoke, as if every word was valuable. He wondered what her childhood had been like, growing up on that estate. He had always had Julius, but apart from her tutors and Clodia, it must have been lonely for his daughter.

'Tell me about my father,' she said, coming closer.

Brutus felt an ache begin in his leg and before the muscles could spasm, he took his stick and levered himself back onto the stump. He looked into the rooms of memory and smiled.

'He and I used to climb this tree when we were young,' he said. 'Julius was convinced he could climb anything and he used to spend hours in the lower branches trying to work out a way of going higher. If I was with him, he could step into my cupped hands, but even then the next branch was too far to reach without jumping. He knew if he missed he'd come down on his head, perhaps bringing me with him.' He broke off to chuckle as the memories returned.

Julia came to sit next to him on the furthest edge of the wide stump. Even from there, he could smell the flower oil she used in bathing. He didn't know the bloom, but the scent reminded him of summer. He breathed deeply and just for a moment, he let his mind play with a picture of kissing the cool skin of her neck.

'Did he fall?' she said.

Brutus snorted. 'Twice. The second time, he pulled me out of the tree and I sprained my hand. He had a great bruise on the side of his face like he'd been slapped, but we still went up one last time and he reached that branch.' He sighed to himself. 'I don't think he ever climbed the old oak again. For him, there was nothing more to do.'

'I wish I had known you then,' she murmured and he looked at her, shaking his head.

'No you don't. We were a difficult pair, your father and I. The surprising thing is that we survived at all.'

'He's lucky to have you as a friend,' she said, blushing slightly.

Brutus thought suddenly of how Alexandria would view the

433

scene if she wandered into the woods. The girl was far too attractive for him to be playing the game of the dashing young soldier, back from the wars. In a moment or two, he'd be asking for her arm to steady him on the trip back to the house and stealing a kiss or two on the way. The scent of flowers filled his lungs and he took a grip on his wayward thoughts.

'I think I'll be getting back, Julia. You must be cold.'

Completely without his conscious control, his gaze swept over her neck and the swell of her breasts. He knew she had seen and was furious with himself. He looked away into the woods as he stood up.

'Are you coming in?' he said. 'It will be dark soon.'

'Your leg is bleeding again,' she said. 'It was too soon to take out the stitches.'

'No. I've seen enough wounds to judge. From now on, I'll walk or ride every day to build my strength.'

'I'll keep you company if you want me to,' she said. Her eyes were wide and dark and he cleared his throat to cover his hesitation.

'I don't think a pretty girl should . . .' Oh, wonderful. He stammered to a stop. 'I'll get by on my own, thank you.' He walked stiffly back down the path through the woods towards the house, cursing himself silently with all the energy he could muster.

Under the cold stars, Brutus walked his mare across the main yard towards the stables, panting slightly after his ride. He thought of Alexandria asleep in her room and frowned to himself. Nothing was as simple as he liked it to be, especially with the women in his life. If he'd wanted arguments and tense silences, he would have taken a wife. He smiled wryly at the thought, looking up at the moon and enjoying the silence. They had both suffered over the long, empty weeks at the estate, with nothing to do but heal and forget the ugliness of the riots. There were times when he itched to gallop, or fight, or take her to bed for an afternoon. His wound made him furious then. It didn't help that their lovemaking was limited by his inability to kneel and he hated to be weak.

He thought he loved her, in his way, but there were too many days when they would bicker over nothing until they were both sullen and hurt. He hated the long silences more than anything. Sometimes he wondered if they were only really in love when he was in another country.

The stable was warm, despite the chill of the night air and freezing stars. The light of the moon came through a high window, giving a pale gleam to the oak stalls. It was a peaceful place with only the dark shapes of the horses for company.

He was still sweating from the exertion of the ride and grimaced at how far he had fallen from peak condition during his illness. Just a couple of miles across country had brought him close to exhaustion.

The straw crackled behind him as he rubbed down the mare and he froze for a moment, wondering who else was up at that hour. He turned awkwardly to see Julia leaning against a post, her face pale in the dim light.

'Did you go far this time?' she murmured. She looked as if she had come from her bed, her hair loose on her shoulders. She had a soft sheet wrapped around her and he saw how it drew tightest over her breasts, wondering if she could see where his eyes lay.

'Just a few miles tonight. It's too cold for the old girl,' he said. The mare snorted gently and nudged him to continue with the brush.

'You will be leaving soon, though. I heard Tabbic talking. Pompey has beaten the gangs.'

'He has. He is a hard man, that one,' Brutus replied.

He could hear a tension in her voice that had not been there before. Whether it was the warm stables, or the smell of leather and straw, or simply her closeness, he found himself becoming aroused and thanked the gloom for hiding him from her sight. Without a word, he turned back to the mare and ran the brush down her flanks with long, sweeping strokes.

'My father promised me to him; did he tell you?' she said, suddenly, blurting out the words. Brutus stopped his brushing and looked at her.

'He didn't tell me.'

'Clodia says I should be pleased. He was not even a consul when they agreed the match, but now I shall be the wife of the Dictator.'

'It will take you away from here,' Brutus said softly.

'To what? To be painted by slaves each day and unable to ride? I've seen the women of the Senate. A pack of crows in fine dresses. And each night, I'll have an old man to press me down. My father is cruel.'

'He can be, yes,' Brutus replied. He would have liked to tell her of the grind of poverty he had seen in the city. She would never know hunger or fear as Pompey's wife. Julius had made a cold choice for his daughter, but there were worse lives to lead and it had given him Gaul. Brutus saw at once how the marriage would bind the houses and perhaps give Julius an heir. As much as he liked the girl, he saw how sheltered she must have been not to know the world as it really was.

'When do you go to him?' he asked.

She tossed her hair angrily.

'I would have gone already if my father were not away from the city. It's just a courtesy between them. The deal is already sealed and Pompey's messenger came with *such* pretty words and gifts. Enough gold and silver to choke me. You should have seen the slave's price they sent.'

'No, girl, you won't be a slave to him, not with your father's

436

blood in your veins. You'll wrap him around your fingers in no time at all. You'll see.'

She stepped closer and again he could smell the scent of dark flowers. As she reached out to him, he held her wrists, letting the brush fall into the straw.

'Now what would you be thinking?' he muttered, his voice hoarse. None of it seemed real and even in the dimness, he could see the pale lines of her neck against the shadows.

'I'm thinking I will not go to him a virgin,' she whispered, leaning in so that her lips brushed his throat. He could feel the panting warmth of her breath and nothing else mattered half as much.

'No,' he said, at last, 'you will not.'

Releasing her wrists, he took hold of the wrap she wore and pulled it gently apart, exposing her to the waist. Her breasts were pale and perfect in the dark, the nipples hard. He heard her breathe faster as he ran his hand down her back, feeling her shiver.

He kissed her then, until her mouth opened its heat for him. Without another word, he lifted her in his arms to a pile of straw and lowered her down onto it. His wounds were a distant ache he could barely feel as he pulled off his clothing. His own breath was harsh in his throat, but he made himself move slowly as he bent down over her and her soft mouth opened once again with a cry.

The group who gathered in the courtyard to go back to Rome were transformed from the dusty, terrified refugees who had knocked at the gates almost two months before. Clodia had told the children they could come out to see her any time they wished and one or two of them had to be forcibly prised away from her on the last morning. The old nurse adored her young charges and there were tears on both sides.

Tabbic had chafed at every day spent away from the city and barely had the patience to make his goodbyes now that the day had come. Alone of the group, he had made several trips back as soon as he had seen the walls of the city manned with Pompey's legion once more. The shop had survived the fires in the district. Though it had been looted, the vast forge that was the heart of their business had survived unscathed. Tabbic was already planning a new door and locks to replace the one that had been broken down and it was his reports of the new peace that had brought their time at the estate to an end. Pompey had been ruthless in destroying the leaders of the gangs, and by day at least, the city was beginning to look like herself again. There were rumours that Crassus had sent a huge sum to the Senate and hundreds of carpenters were busy rebuilding. It would be some time before the citizens would think of such luxuries as jewellery, but Tabbic would be ready for them. His small part of the work was his gift to the city, but it meant a great deal. Picking up his scattered tools was the first step in putting the horrors of the riots behind them.

Brutus had been tempted to rest his leg a little longer, but Alexandria had become increasingly cold with him over the previous days. He did not think she could know what had happened in the stable, but there were times when he caught her looking sideways at him, as if she wondered who he was. Without being sure how he knew, he was certain that if he stayed behind, it would be the last he saw of her.

As far south as they were, spring had come early and the trees were already beginning to bloom in the woods. No doubt Julius would be waiting impatiently for him in the north and reluctantly Brutus knew it was time to be on his way. He would return to the rough company of his legionaries, though somehow the thought of it did not fill him with enthusiasm as it used to. Brutus positioned the wooden block he needed to mount, glancing stealthily around the open yard as he gathered the reins. Julia was not there and he felt Alexandria's eyes on him as he looked for her.

A house slave opened the heavy gate and swung it wide so that they could see the track leading down to the main road into the city.

'There you are!' Clodia said. 'I thought you were going to miss them leaving.'

Julia came out of the house and went around to all of them to say goodbye and accept their thanks as mistress of the house. Brutus watched closely as she and Alexandria exchanged a few words, but both women smiled and he could see no tension between them. He relaxed slightly as Julia came to him and reacted naturally as she leaned forward to kiss him goodbye. He felt her tongue dart out against his lips for an instant, making him freeze in embarrassment. Her mouth tasted of honey.

'Come back,' she whispered as he shoved himself into the saddle, not daring to look at Alexandria. He could feel her eyes boring into the back of his head and knew his cheeks were flaming as he tried to pretend nothing had happened. Not a story for Julius, he was fairly certain.

The children called and waved in a chorus as they began their journey to the city. Clodia had prepared packages of meat in boiled peppers for all of them and one or two were already dipping greasy fingers into the cloth packages. Brutus cast one last glance at the estate he had known as a child and fixed it in his memory. When everything else in his life could twist out of all recognition, some things remained solid and gave him peace.

CHAPTER THIRTY-EIGHT

꩜꩜꩜

The torches flickered on the gold crown of the Arverni as the priest held it up to the warriors. In his other hand, he held a golden torc that shimmered and twisted as it wound around his fingers.

The priest had daubed his body with blood and earth in long smears that made him seem part of the shadows in the temple. His chest was bare and his beard smoothed with clay into rough white spikes that quivered as he spoke.

'The old king is dead, Arverni. His body will be burnt, though his name and deeds continue in our mouths for all our years. He was a man, Arverni. His cattle numbered in thousands and his sword arm was strong to the end. He spread his seed wide to bring his sons into the world and his wives tear their hair and skin in grief. We shall not see him again.'

The priest eyed the tribe who had packed themselves into the temple. It was a bitter night for him. For twenty years he had been the old king's friend and counsellor and shared his fear for the future when age and weakness had begun to steal his breath. Who amongst his sons had the strength to lead the tribe through such difficult times? The youngest, Brigh, was but a boy and the eldest was a blustering boaster, too weak where a king should be strong. Madoc would not be king.

The priest looked into the eyes of Cingeto as he stood there on the dark marble with his brothers. That one was warrior enough to lead them, but his temper was already famous amongst the Arverni. He had killed three men in duels before he reached his manhood day and the old priest would have given anything for a few more years to see who he would become.

The words had to be spoken, though the priest felt a coldness in his heart as he drew breath.

'Which of you will take the crown from my hand? Which of you has earned the right to lead the Arverni?'

The three brothers exchanged glances and Brigh smiled and shook his head.

'This is not for me,' he said and took a pace back.

Cingeto and Madoc turned their eyes on each other and the silence became oppressive.

'I am the eldest son,' Madoc said at last, the high colour of anger starting on his cheeks.

'Aye, but you're not the man we need now,' Cingeto murmured softly. 'Whoever takes the crown must prepare for war or see our tribe scattered.'

Madoc sneered. He was taller than his brother and he used his height to intimidate, looming over Cingeto.

'Do you see armies on our lands? You show me where they are. You *point* them out to me.' He spat the words at his brother, but Cingeto had heard them all before.

'They are coming. They have gone north, but they will come back into the heartlands soon enough. I have met their leader and he will not let us live out our lives. His taxmen have already robbed the Senones and sold thousands as slaves. They could

441

not stop him and now their women cry in the fields. He must be fought, my brother. You are not the man to do it.'

Madoc sneered at him. 'They were just Senones, brother. The Arverni are men. If they come to trouble us, we will ride them down.'

'Can you see no further than that?' Cingeto snapped. 'You are blind, as the Senones were blind. I will make the Arverni a torch in the dark to gather in the other tribes. I will lead them against these Romans until they are swept out of Gaul. We cannot stand alone any more.'

'You are too frightened of them to be a king, little brother,' Madoc said, showing his teeth.

Cingeto smashed a hand across Madoc's mouth and forced him back a step.

'I will *not* see my people destroyed by you. If you will not yield to me, then I will have the crown by challenge.'

Madoc ran his tongue over his lips, tasting blood. His eyes became hard.

'As you wish, little brother. Fire and the gods watching. It is right.'

Both men turned back to the priest and he nodded.

'Bring the irons. It will be decided in fire.'

He prayed the gods would give courage to the right man to lead the Arverni through the dark days ahead.

Julius panted as he led his horse through the high pass. The air was thinner there and though spring had come in the valleys, on the peaks the air hurt the lungs of even the fittest of them. Julius looked at Brutus ailing far below the century of the Tenth. He had lost much of his stamina in recovering from his wounds and there were times when Julius thought they would have to leave him to come on later. Yet he stayed doggedly on their trail, riding whenever the pass levelled.

442

When he had first seen the dusty horseman come into Ariminum, Julius' spirits had leapt to hear the latest news of the city. The cold formality of the report he received filled him with confusion. He had wanted to shake the man who limped into the house and spoke so distantly of his experiences. The old anger had washed over him as he listened, though he had not given way to it. Servilia had gone and the rift between them was his to mend.

Julius could recall a thousand times when he had used a few words, or a compliment, or even a nod to build the men around him. He felt only sadness when he realised his oldest friend needed the same harmless lies. It was one thing to clap a soldier on the back and see him stand a little taller. It was quite another to give up the honesty of his oldest friendship and Julius had not yet acted on his decision. After the initial report, they had hardly spoken.

Julius' thoughts turned to Regulus, who trudged at his side through the snow. He was one of those who formed the core of a legion. Some became little better than animals in the ranks of Rome, but men like Regulus never seemed to lose that last part of their humanity. They could show kindness to a woman or a child and then go to battle and fling away their lives for something more than themselves. There were senators who saw them only as killing tools, never men as they were, who could understand what Rome meant. The legionaries always used their votes in the elections when they had the chance. They wrote home and swore and pissed in the snow like any other and Julius understood how Marius had loved them.

It was not a responsibility to be borne lightly, leading such men. They looked to him for food and shelter, for order in their lives. Their respect was hard to win and could be lost in a single moment of cowardice or indecision. He would not have had it any other way.

'Shall we run, Regulus?' Julius said, between tearing breaths.

The centurion smiled stiffly. The habit of shaving had come back to them all in Ariminum and Julius saw the man's face was red and raw in the wind.

'Best not leave the horses behind, sir,' Regulus replied.

Julius clapped him on the back and took a moment to look around at the mountains. It was a deadly beauty that they passed through. The aching white of the high peaks shone in the sun, and behind, Brutus struggled on to keep them in sight.

Regulus saw Julius glance down the twisting path.

'Shall I go back to him, sir? The general's limp is getting worse.'

'Very well. Tell him I'll race him into Gaul. He'll understand.'

The long irons were heated in braziers until the tips were red. Madoc and Cingeto had stripped to the waist and now both men stood sweating on the floor of the temple. All the families were there to watch and neither of them showed the slightest fear as the priest checked the irons over and over until he was satisfied and the hairs on the back of his right hand shrivelled as he passed it over the basket of iron.

At last, the old priest turned to face the two brothers. Their chests were paler than their arms and faces, he saw. Madoc was heavy with muscle, the bull his father had once been. Cingeto was a more compact figure, though there was not a piece of spare flesh on him. The old priest drew himself up to address the silent families of the Arverni.

'A king must have strength, but he must also have determination. All men feel fear, but he must conquer it when the need is great.' He paused for a moment, savouring the words of the ritual. His old master had used a long stick to correct a faltering recital. He had hated him then, but now he used that same cane on the apprentices in the temple. The words were important.

'By right of blood, these men have chosen the trial of fire. One will take the crown and one will be banished from the lands of the Arverni. That is the law. Yet the man to lead us should have a mind as sharp as his sword. He should be cunning as well as brave. The gods grant that there is such a man before us today.'

Both brothers remained still as he spoke, preparing themselves for what was to come. The priest grasped the first of the irons and pulled it out. Even the dark end he held made his hand stiffen.

'To the elder goes the first,' he said, his eyes on the glowing tip.

Madoc reached out and took the length of iron. His eyes were bright with malice as he turned to Cingeto.

'Shall we see which one of us is blessed?' he whispered.

Cingeto did not reply, though sweat poured off him. Madoc brought the rod closer and closer to his brother's chest until the blond hairs began to sizzle, giving off a powerful smell. Then he laid it against his brother's skin and pressed it deeply into the flesh.

Cingeto's lungs emptied in a great heave of air. Every muscle in his body went rigid with the agony, but he did not cry out. Madoc ground the iron against him until the heat had faded and then his own face tightened as he put it back into the fire.

Cingeto looked down at the brown welt that had been raised on his skin. It leaked pale fluid as he took in a deep breath and steadied himself. Without a word, he drew another iron and Madoc began to breathe faster and faster.

Madoc grunted as the metal touched him and, in a fury, he grabbed for another from the brazier. The priest touched his hand in reproof and he dropped it to his side, his mouth opening and his breath coming harshly.

The trial of fire had begun.

*   *   *

445

At the end of the second day in the mountains, the rugged path began to tilt down to Gaul. Julius paused there, leaning against a rock. When he looked up, he could see the plateau of the high pass above them and was astonished that they had put it so far behind. They were all desperate for food and sleep, and Julius felt a strange clarity of vision, as if hunger and the wind had sharpened his senses. Below him, Gaul stretched with a darker green than he could have believed existed. His lungs felt huge inside his chest and he took great breaths for the sheer pleasure of being alive in such a place.

Brutus felt he had been trudging through the mountains all his life. His weak leg throbbed every time he put his weight on it and without the horse to lean on, he was sure he would have fallen long before. As the century rested, he and Regulus weaved their way through the column to the front. Julius heard some of his men cheer, calling out encouragement. He turned back to see them and smiled as the pair responded to the voices, forcing themselves on. The strength of the brotherhood between his soldiers never failed to fill him with pride. As Julius watched, Brutus and Regulus grinned at the hoots and calls, laughing together as Regulus muttered some reply.

Julius looked back at Gaul below them. Spread out before him, it looked deceptively peaceful, almost as if he could take a step and land right in the heart of it. He hoped that one day a traveller through the passes would look down on cities as great as Rome. Beyond it lay the sea that called to him and he pictured the fleet that would carry the Tenth and Third over it. The tribes would pay their gold in taxes and he would use it to see what lay over the dim white cliffs. He would take Rome to the edge of the world, where even Alexander had not been before him.

Brutus came to his side and Julius saw dark rings around his eyes. The climb had hurt his friend, but in his exhaustion he seemed to have lost some of the coldness he had brought back from Rome. As their eyes met, Julius motioned towards the country below.

'Have you ever seen anything more beautiful?'

Brutus took a water bottle from Regulus and tilted it back between cracked lips.

'Are we in a race or not?' he said. 'I'm not waiting for you.'

He staggered down the slope and Julius watched him with affection. Regulus hesitated by Julius' side, unsure whether he was to follow.

'Go on, stay with him,' Julius said. 'I'll follow you down.'

The smell of flesh and fire was strong in the temple. Both men were bleeding as their skin cracked open with each turn of the irons. Eleven times they had withstood the pain and Cingeto now swayed with his teeth showing whitely against his skin, ready for the twelfth. He watched his brother closely. The test was as much in the mind as in the body and each man knew it could only end when one refused to touch the other. As each burn was added, they both knew it meant they would face at least one more and the knowledge ate at them as their strength dwindled.

Madoc hesitated as he wrapped his fingers around the black iron. If he held it to his young brother, he would have to stand another on his own skin. He did not know if he could, though the desire to see Cingeto humbled was still strong in him.

The trial was a bitter test. Through the waves of pain, the only solace was the thought that in a moment their tormentor would feel the same. Determination and strength crumbled in the face of such torture and Cingeto felt hope leap in him as his brother continued to hesitate. Was it cruelty in him to be drawing out the moment, or had he lost his taste for the irons at last?

'Gods give me the strength for another,' he heard Madoc whisper and Cingeto almost cried out as the red-tipped metal came out from the flames once more. He saw Madoc raise it and closed his eyes in anticipation and fear. His whole body cringed from the contact and always there was the terror that he would not have the will to go on when the choice was his. The spirit chose the winner of the trial of fire, never the flesh, and now Cingeto understood as he could never have done without experiencing it.

A clang reverberated around the temple and Cingeto's eyes snapped open in astonishment. Madoc had thrown down the iron and now stood before him, pain twisting his face into lines of weariness.

'Enough, little brother,' Madoc said and almost fell.

Cingeto reached out to steady him and winced as his burns throbbed with the movement.

The priest smiled in joy as the two men turned to face him. He was already planning his addition to the history of the tribe. Eleven irons withstood by the princes of the Arverni! He could remember no more than nine and even the great Ailpein had stood only seven to become king three hundred years before. It was a good omen and he felt some of the dark worry ease from him.

'One to be king and one to be gone,' he said aloud, repeating it to the gathered families. He stepped forward to Cingeto and placed the band of gold on his brow and the torc around the straining sinews of his neck.

'No,' Cingeto said, looking at his brother. 'I will not lose you after tonight, my brother. Will you stay and fight them with me? I will need you.'

The priest gaped at them in horror. 'The law . . .' he began.

Cingeto held up a hand, struggling against pain that threatened to overwhelm him.

'I need you, Madoc. Will you follow me?'

His brother straightened, wincing as fresh blood wound trails down his chest.

'I will, my brother. I will.'

'Then we must summon the tribes.'

Julia walked to the base of the old senate house steps and shivered at the empty space that had been cleared beyond. The smell of smoke was still subtly in the air and it was easy to imagine the rioting coming even to this place. Already, the new building was being constructed and the noise of the crowds was accompanied by hammering and shouts from the workers.

Clodia fussed at her shoulder, nervous in the great forum.

'There, you've seen the damage and taken a risk you shouldn't have. The city is hardly safe for a young woman, even now.'

Julia looked at her with scorn. 'You can see the soldiers, can't you? Pompey has control now; Brutus said so. He's busy with his meetings and speeches. He's forgotten about me, perhaps.'

'You're talking nonsense, girl. You can't expect him to lurk at your window like a young man. Not in his position.'

'Still, if he hopes to bed me, he should show a little interest, don't you think?'

Clodia looked sharply around to see if anyone in the crowd was taking an interest in their conversation.

'It's not a fit subject! Your mother would be ashamed to hear you talk so brazenly,' she said, gripping Julia by the arm.

Julia winced and pulled her arm away, enjoying the chance to make the old woman uncomfortable.

'That's if he's not too old to find it. Do you think he might be?'

'Stop it, girl, or I'll slap that smile off your face,' Clodia hissed at her.

Julia shrugged, thinking deliciously of Brutus' skin against her. She knew better than to tell Clodia of the night in the stable, but her fear had been taken away with the first sharp

449

pain. Brutus had been gentle with her and she had found a private hunger Pompey would enjoy when he finally made her his wife.

A voice broke into her thoughts, making her start with guilt.

'Are you lost, ladies? You look quite abandoned, standing next to the old steps.'

Before Julia could answer, she saw Clodia dip and bow her head. The sudden servility from the old woman was enough to make her take a second look at the man who had addressed them. His toga marked him as one of the nobilitas, though he carried himself with a natural confidence that would have been enough on its own. His hair shone with oiled perfection, Julia noticed. He smiled at her appraisal, allowing his eyes to drop to her breasts for a brief moment.

'We are just moving on, sir,' Clodia said quickly. 'We have an appointment with friends.'

Julia frowned as her arm was taken in a firm grip once again.

'That is a pity,' the young man said, eyeing Julia's figure. Julia blushed then, suddenly aware that she had dressed quite simply for her visit.

'If your friends do not mind waiting, I do have a small house nearby where you could wash and eat. Walking in this city is tiring without a place to rest.'

As he spoke, the young man made a subtle gesture at his waist and Julia heard the distinct chime of coins. Clodia tried to pull her away, but she resisted, wanting to puncture the man's easy arrogance.

'You have not introduced yourself,' she said, widening her smile. He positively preened at the interest.

'Suetonius Prandus. I am a senator, my dear, but not every afternoon is spent in work.'

'I have ... heard of the name,' Julia said slowly, though it would not come to her. Suetonius nodded as if he had expected to be known. She did not see Clodia grow pale.

'Your future *husband* will be waiting for you, Julia,' Clodia said.

She was successful in moving her charge a few paces away, but Suetonius came with them, unwilling to let her go so easily. He put his hand over Clodia's to bring them all to a halt.

'We are having a conversation. There is no harm in that.' Once again, he jingled his coins and Julia almost laughed aloud at the sound.

'Are you offering to buy my attention, Suetonius?' she said.

He blinked at her bluntness. Playing the game, he winked.

'Would your husband not mind?' he said, leaning closer. Something about his cold eyes changed the mood in an instant and Julia frowned at him.

'Pompey is not yet my husband, Suetonius. Perhaps he would not mind if I spent the afternoon with you; what do you think?'

For a moment, Suetonius did not understand what she had said. Then a sick awareness stole over him and his face became ugly.

'I know your father, girl,' he muttered, almost to himself.

Julia raised her head slowly as the memory came back. 'I thought I knew the name! Oh yes, I know you.' Without warning, she began to laugh and Suetonius flushed with impotent anger. He dared not say a word to her.

'My father tells wonderful stories about you, Suetonius. You should hear them, you really should.' She turned to Clodia, ignoring her pleading eyes. 'He put you in a hole in the ground once, didn't he? I remember him telling Clodia. It was very amusing.'

Suetonius smiled stiffly.

'We were both very young. Good day to you both.'

'Are you leaving? I thought we were going to your house to eat.'

'Perhaps another time,' he replied. His eyes were bulging with anger as Julia stepped a little closer.

'Be careful as you go, Senator. Thieves will hear the coins you carry. I could myself.' She forced an earnest expression onto her face as he flushed in anger.

'You must give my regards to your mother, when you see her next,' he said suddenly, running his tongue over his lower lip. There was something deeply unpleasant in his gaze.

'She died,' Julia replied. She was beginning to wish she had never begun the conversation.

'Oh, *yes*. It was a terrible thing,' Suetonius said, but his words were made hollow by a flickering smile he could not control. With a stiff nod, he walked away across the forum, leaving them alone.

When she finally looked to Clodia, she raised her eyebrows. 'I think we annoyed him,' she said, her amusement returning.

'You are a danger to yourself,' Clodia snapped. 'The sooner you are Pompey's wife, the better. I only hope he knows enough to beat you when you need it.'

Julia reached over and took Clodia's face in her hand. 'He wouldn't dare. My father would skin him.'

Without warning, Clodia slapped her hard. Julia pressed her fingers against her cheek in astonishment. The old woman trembled, unrepentant.

'Life is harder than you realise, girl. It always was.'

The King of the Arverni closed the door of the hall with a heave against the wind, leaving a sudden pressure in his ears and a drift of snow on the floor at his feet.

He turned to the men who had gathered at his word, between them representing the most ancient tribes of Gaul. The Senones were there and the Cadurci, the Pictones, the Turoni, dozens of others. Some of them were vassals of Rome, others represented only a pitiful fraction of the power they had once known, their armies sold into slavery and their cattle stolen to feed the legions. Mhorbaine of the Aedui had refused his offer, but the others looked to him for leadership. Together, they could mass an army that would break the back of the Roman domination of their land and Cingeto hardly felt the winter cold as he considered their hawk-like expressions.

'Will you take my orders, in this?' he asked them, softly. He knew they would, or they would not have travelled in winter to come to him.

One by one, each man rose and pledged his support and his warriors. Though they may have had little love for the Arverni, the years of war had opened them to his arguments. Alone, they must fall, but under one leader, one High King, they could throw the invaders out of Gaul. Cingeto had taken that role for himself and, in their desperation, they had accepted him.

'For now, I tell you to wait and prepare. Forge your swords and armour. Lay in stocks of grain and salt a part of each bull you slaughter for the tribe. We will not make the mistakes of previous years and spend our strength in fruitless attacks. When we move, we move as one and only when the Romans are extended and weak. Then they will know Gaul is not to be stolen from its people. Tell your warriors they will march under the High King, joined as they were once joined a thousand years ago, when nothing in the world could stand against us. Our history tells us we were one people, horsemen of the mountains. Our language shows us the brotherhood and the way.'

He was a powerful figure standing before them. Not one of the kings dropped their gaze from his fierce expression. Madoc stood at his shoulder and the fact that he had allowed his younger brother to take their father's crown was not lost on any of them. Cingeto's words spoke to more ancient loyalties than those of tribe and they felt their pulses race at the thought of rejoining the old peoples.

'From this day, all tribal disputes are ended. Let no Gaul kill one of his people when we shall need every sword against the enemy. When there is dissent, use my name,' Cingeto said softly. 'Tell them Vercingetorix calls them to arms.'

CHAPTER THIRTY-NINE

෬෨෬෨෬

Julius stood with an arm wrapped around the high prow of the galley, filled with a restless impatience as the white coast grew before his eyes. He had learned from the disastrous experiences of the first expedition and this time, the year was young for the crossing. The fleet that churned the sea to foam around him with their long oars was a hundred times the size of his first and it had cost him every coin and favour he had accumulated in Gaul. He had stripped his defences for this blow across the water, but the white cliffs of the Britons had been his first failure and he could not allow a second.

It was hard not to remember the blood-red surf as his galleys had run ashore and been smashed. That first night when the blue-skinned tribes had attacked them in the water was burnt into his memory.

He gripped the wood more tightly as he remembered the way the Tenth had forced a landing through the roaring sea darkness. Too many had been left floating face-down, with the seabirds landing on their bodies as they bumped and rolled in the swell. No matter how he looked at it, those three weeks had been disastrous. It had rained every single day with a blinding force and cold. Those who had lived through the carnage of the landing had been closer to despair than he had ever seen them. For days, they had not known if any of the galleys had survived the storm. Though Julius had hidden his relief from the men, he had never been more thankful than when he saw his battered galleys limping in.

His legions had fought bravely against the blue-skinned tribes, though Julius had known even then that he would not stay without a fleet to supply him. He had accepted the surrender of Commius, their chief, but his thoughts had already been on the following spring.

The lessons of that harsh coast had been well learned. On every side, Julius could hear the shouts of shipmasters as they called the beat of the oars. The sea spray lashed him as the prow rose and fell and he leaned outwards, his gaze sweeping the coast for the painted warriors. This time, there would be no turning.

As far as he could see in any direction, his galleys were pulling through the waves. Hundreds of ships that he had begged and bought and hired to take five full legions back to the island. In stalls on the heaving decks were two thousand horses to sweep the painted tribes away.

With a chill that had more to do with memory than the cold, Julius saw the lines of warriors appear on the cliffs, but this time he scorned them. Let them watch as the greatest fleet the world had ever known came to their shores. Let them see.

The waves had none of the rage and power he had experienced the year before. In the height of summer, the swell was barely rocking the heavy galleys and Julius heard the cornicens signal all along the line. Boats were lowered and the Tenth led them in.

Julius leapt over the side into the surf and could hardly believe it was the same piece of coast. He saw the men drag the boats up the shingle, far beyond the reach of storms. All around him was the busy energy that he had known for years. Orders were called, packs and armour collected, as they formed a defensive perimeter and summoned in the next units with long bronze horns. Julius shivered as his wet cloak slapped against his skin. He walked up the beach and looked back to sea, showing his teeth. He hoped the painted Britons were observing the army that would cut through their land.

In moving so many men from boats to the shore, some injuries and errors were to be expected. One of the small craft overturned as its occupants tried to climb out and an optio had a foot crushed by its weight. More than a few packs and spears were dropped into the sea and had to be retrieved by their owners, urged on by swearing officers. With only one arm, Renius slipped as he climbed out of a boat, disappearing under the water despite the hands grabbing at him. He was dragged out still roaring in indignation. Despite the difficulties, landing so many without losing a life was a feat in itself and by the time the sun was dipping down towards the horizon, the Tenth had flagged the ground for the first hostile camp, barring the way down to the shore while they were still vulnerable.

They saw no further sign of the tribes who had defended their land so viciously the year before. After the initial sight-ings on the cliffs, the Britons had pulled back. Julius smiled at the thought of the consternation in their camps and villages and wondered what had become of Commius, the king of the southern hills. He could only imagine what it must have been like for Commius to see his legions for the first time and send his blue-skinned fighters down to the sea to throw them back. With a shudder, Julius remembered the huge dogs that fought with them and took a dozen wounds before they fell. Even they had not been enough to beat the veterans of Gaul.

Commius had surrendered when the legions had fought up the dunes and onto the fields beyond, crushing the blue warriors before them. The king had kept his dignity as he walked into the makeshift camp on the beach to offer his sword. The guards would have stopped him, but Julius had waved him in, his heart racing.

He remembered the awe he had felt at finally speaking to men who were barely myths in Rome. Yet for all their wild looks, Julius had found the tribesmen understood the simple Gaulish speech he had laboured to learn.

'Across the water, the fishermen call you the "Pretani", the painted ones,' Julius had said, slowly hefting the sword in his hand. 'What name do you have for them?'

The blue king had looked at his companions and shrugged. 'We don't think of them, much,' he had replied.

Julius chuckled at the memory. He hoped Commius had survived the year he had been away. With the beach secure, Brutus brought in his Third Gallica to support the Tenth and Mark Antony added to the numbers of Romans on the high ground, each cohort protecting the next as they moved inland in measured stages. By the time the first night fell, the galleys had retreated out to deep water where they could not be surprised and the legions were busy with the task of building forts.

After years in Gaul, they undertook the familiar work with calm efficiency. The extraordinarii swarmed at the edges of the positions, ready to give the alarm and hold off an attack until the squares could form. The walls of banked earth and felled trees went up with the ease of long practice and as the stars and moon moved to midnight, they were secure and ready for the day.

Julius summoned his council as the first hot food was being passed out to those who had worked so hard for it. He accepted a plate of vegetable stew and sniffed appreciatively for the benefit of the legionaries. They smiled as he tasted it and he passed through them, pausing to speak to any man that caught his eye.

Bericus had been left in Gaul, with only his legion and the irregulars to cover that vast territory. The Ariminum general was an experienced, solid soldier who would not risk those under his command, but Brutus had been appalled at the danger of leaving so few to hold Gaul while they were away. Julius had waited through his protests and then continued with his plans. Brutus had not been part of the first landing as the storm blew his galley far out to sea. He could not understand the need Julius felt to make the second a shattering blow. He had not seen the sea run red and seen the legionaries fall back from the blue-skinned warriors and their monstrous dogs.

This year, Julius vowed, the Britons would bend the knee to him or be crushed. He had the men and the ships. He had the season and the will. As he passed into the torch-lit interior of the command tent, he laid the bowl of food on a table to go cold. He could not eat with the tension that churned in him. Rome was as distant as a dream and there were moments when Julius could only shake his head in amazement at being so far from her. If only Marius or his father could have been there to share it with him. Marius would have understood his satisfaction. He had gone deep enough into Africa to know.

His council came in pairs or threes and Julius mastered his feelings to greet them formally. He ordered food brought to them and waited while they ate, clasping his hands behind his back as he looked out of the tent to the night sky. He had rough maps made after the first landing to point them north and the scouts who had drawn them would travel out to judge the strength of those they would face. Julius could hardly wait for the first light.

*   *   *

The news of the fleet had travelled swiftly. When the full might of the invasion had become apparent, Commius had torn up the plans he had made to defend the coast. There was no mistaking the intention of such a vast force and no chance whatsoever that the Trinovantes could stand against them. They pulled back to a string of hill forts twelve miles inland and Commius sent out messengers to all the tribes around him. He called the Cenimagni, and the Ancalites. He called the Segontiaci and the Bibroci and they came to him out of fear. No man alive had ever seen so large a gathering of their enemy and they knew how many of the Trinovantes had been killed the year before against a smaller number.

That first night was spent in argument as Commius tried to save their lives.

'You did not fight them last time!' he said to the leaders. 'Just a few thousand and they broke us. With the army they have brought now, we have no choice. We must bear them as we bear the winter. It is the only way to survive their passage.'

Commius saw the anger on the faces of the men before him. Beran of the Ancalites stood and Commius faced him with pale resignation, guessing at his words before they were spoken.

'The Catuvellauni say they will fight. They will accept any of us as sword brothers under their king. It's better than lying down to be taken one by one, at least.'

Commius sighed. He knew of the offer by the young king, Cassivellaunus, and it made him want to spit. None of the men there seemed to understand the level of danger from the army that had landed on their coast. There was no end to them and Commius doubted they could be hurled back into the sea even if every man in the land took arms against them. The King of the Catuvellauni was blinded by his own ambition to lead the tribes and Commius wanted no part of that foolishness. Cassivellaunus would learn in the only way possible, as Commius had before him. For the others, though, there was still hope.

'Let Cassivellaunus gather the tribes under his banners. It will not be enough, even with us. Tell me, Beran, how many men can you take away from your crops and herds to fight?'

Beran shifted uneasily at the question, but then shrugged.

'Twelve hundred, perhaps. Less if I keep back enough to protect the women.'

Under Commius' stern eye, each of them added to the numbers.

'Between us all then, we can gather *perhaps* eight thousand warriors. Cassivellaunus has three and the tribes around him can bring six more to war, if they all agree to follow him. Seventeen thousand, and against us my men counted as many as twenty-five, with thousands more on horseback.'

'I've known worse,' Beran said, with a smile.

Commius glared at him. 'No you haven't. I lost three thousand of my best against them on the beach and amongst the corn. They are hard men, my friends, but they cannot rule us from over the sea. No one has ever managed to do that. We must wait them out until the winter sends them back. They know by now what the storms can do to their ships.'

'It will be hard to ask my people to put away their swords,' Beran said. 'There will be many who want to join the Catuvellauni.'

'Then let them!' Commius shouted, losing his temper at last. 'Let anyone who wants to die, join up under Cassivellaunus and fight. They will be destroyed.' He rubbed angrily at the bridge of his nose. 'I must think of the Trinovantes first, no matter what you decide. There are few enough of us left now, but even if I had a host of men, I would wait and see how the Catuvellauni fared in the first battle. If their king is so hungry to lead us all, let him show he has the strength to do it.'

The men looked at each other, searching out agreement. The spirit of cooperation was an unusual experience, but nothing about the situation was normal since the fleet had been sighted that morning.

461

Beran spoke first.

'You are no coward, Commius. That is why I have listened to you. I will wait and see how Cassivellaunus fares in the first skirmishes. If he can make these new men bleed, I will join him to the end of it. I do not want to be standing by with my head bowed while they are killing my people. It would be too hard.'

'Harder still to see your temples smashed and ashes made of the Ancalites,' Commius snapped. He shook his head. 'Do whatever you think is right. The Trinovantes will not be part of it.' Without another word, Commius stormed out of the low room and left them alone.

Beran watched him go with a frown. 'Is he right?' he said.

The same question was in all their minds as Beran turned to them.

'Let the Catuvellauni meet them, with what men they can muster. I will have my scouts watching and if they say these "Romans" can be beaten, I will march.'

'The Bibroci will be with you,' their man said. The others added their voices and Beran smiled. He understood how the King of the Catuvellauni could want to gather the tribes under him. The men in the room could bring nearly eight thousand warriors to the field. What a sight that would be. Beran could hardly imagine so many men united together.

Julius came upon the hill forts of the Trinovantes twelve miles in from the coast. The sound and smell of the sea was far behind his marching columns and those legionaries who looked to the future murmured appreciatively as they passed through fields of corn and even cultivated vines that they stripped of the acid white grapes as they passed. Wild apples grew there and in the heat at the end of summer, Julius was pleased to see the land was worth taking. The coast had shown little of the promise of the fields beyond them, yet his eyes searched constantly for the dark scars of mines. Rome had been promised tin and gold from the Britons, and without it Julius knew the greed of the Senate would never be satisfied.

The legions stretched across miles of land, separated from each other by the heavy baggage trains. They had supplies for a month and tools and equipment to cross rivers and build bridges, even to construct a town. Julius had left nothing to chance in this second attempt at the white cliffs. He signalled the cornicens to blow the halt and watched as the vast columns responded, their formations shifting subtly at the edge of his vision as they moved from marching files to more defensive positions. Julius nodded to himself with satisfaction. This was how Rome should make war.

The hill forts stretched in a straggling line across the land, each one a solid construction of wood and stone that held the crest of sharply rising land. A river marked on his maps as the 'Sturr' ran below them and Julius sent out his water-carriers to begin the lengthy process of refilling the legion supplies. They were not yet in need, but Gaul had taught him never to spurn an opportunity to collect water or food. His maps ended at the river and for all he knew, it might be the last source of fresh water until they reached the Tamesis, the 'dark river' sixty miles from the coast. If it even existed.

Julius summoned Brutus and Octavian and detached a cohort of his veteran Tenth to approach the forts. As he gave his orders, Julius saw the powerful figure of Ciro march through the ranks to him. Julius grinned at the big man's worried expression and answered his question before it could be asked.

'Very well, Ciro. Join us,' he called.

Julius watched as relief flooded the features of the giant soldier. Ciro's loyalty could still touch him. The armour of the Tenth gleamed painfully as Julius looked them over and again he felt himself filled with a powerful excitement. At any moment, the armies of the Britons might appear to strike at them, but there was nothing out of place in the perfect ranks and files. The legions were ready and something of Julius' own confidence showed in their faces.

In the pure, clean air, Julius heard birds call far above him as he rode slowly up the slope to the largest of the forts. He began listing the defences and planning how to break them if the occupants would not surrender. The walls were well constructed and any attacking force would have to face a barrage of missiles from above as they stormed the gate. Julius imagined the dimensions of the battering ram that would be necessary to breach such heavy timbers and the answer did not please him. He saw dark heads outlined on the high walls and sat straighter in the saddle, aware that he was being observed and judged.

Inside the fort, there were shouts and horn notes blaring. Julius stiffened as the main gates were heaved open. The lines of triarii ahead of him drew their swords without an order as each one of them expected a charge to come screaming out at them. It was what Julius would have done had he been on the hill and he clenched his fists on the reins as the dark interior of the fort was revealed.

No warriors came surging out. Instead, a small group of men stood in its shadow and one of them raised an arm in greeting. Julius ordered the cohort to sheathe their swords to defuse some of the tension. Octavian moved his horse a pace ahead of Julius and looked back at his general.

'Let me take a fifty inside first, sir. If it's a trap, we'll make them show themselves.'

Julius looked at his younger relative with affection, seeing no sign of fear or hesitation in the man's calm eyes. If it was a trap, those who entered the fort first would be killed and Julius was pleased that one of his blood should show such bravery in front of the men.

'Very well, Octavian. Enter and hold the gate for me,' he replied, smiling.

Octavian snapped out orders to the front five ranks and they broke into a run up the last part of the hill. Julius watched the reactions of the Britons and was disappointed to see them stand their ground without a sign of fear.

Octavian kicked his mount into a canter to pass under the gate and Julius could see his armour shining in the main yard as he wheeled and rode back. By the time Julius had brought the rest of the cohort up, Octavian had dismounted and a quick exchange of glances was enough for Julius to grin. It had been an unnecessary caution, but Julius had learned about risk in Gaul. There were times when there was nothing else to do but charge and hope, but those were rare. Julius had found that the more he thought and planned, the fewer were those occasions when he had to depend on the sheer strength and discipline of his men.

Julius dismounted under the shadow line of the gate. The men who waited for him were mostly strangers, but he saw Commius there and embraced him. It was a purely formal gesture for the benefit of the warriors who watched in the fort. Perhaps both men knew that only the size of the Roman army forced the apparent friendship on them, but it did not matter.

'I'm glad to see you here, Commius,' Julius said. 'My scouts thought this was still the land of the Trinovantes, but were not sure.' He spoke quickly and fluently, making Commius raise his eyebrows in surprise. Julius smiled as if it were nothing and continued.

'Who are these others?'

Commius introduced the leaders of the tribes and Julius greeted them all, memorizing their names and faces and thoroughly enjoying their discomfort.

'You are welcome in Trinovantes land,' Commius said at last. 'If your men will wait, I will have food and drink brought. Will you step inside?'

Julius looked closely at the man and wondered if Octavian's suspicions could yet become reality. He sensed he was being tested and finally threw off his caution.

'Octavian, Brutus ... Ciro, with me. Show me the way, Commius, and leave the gates open, if you don't mind. It is too hot a day to shut out the breeze.'

Commius looked coldly at him and Julius smiled. The centurion Regulus was there and Julius spoke to him last before following the Britons inside.

'Wait a single watch for me to return. You know what must be done if I am not seen by then.'

Regulus nodded grimly and Julius saw the words were not wasted on Commius as his expression hardened.

The fort seemed larger than it had on the track up the hill. With the other Britons, Commius led the four Romans through the yard and Julius did not look up as he heard the shuffling feet of Trinovantes warriors craning to see them. He would not honour them by showing he heard, though Ciro bristled as he glanced at the upper levels.

Commius led them all into a long, low room constructed of heavy honey-coloured beams. Julius looked around him at the spears and swords that adorned the walls and knew he was in Commius' council chamber. A table and benches showed where Commius sat with his people and at the far end was a shrine and a thread of silver smoke that lifted past a stone face set in the wall.

Commius took his seat at the head of the table and Julius moved to the far end without a thought. It was natural enough for the Romans to take one side and the Britons the other, and when they were seated Julius waited patiently for Commius to speak. The sense of danger had lifted. Commius knew as well as anyone that the legions outside would trample the forts into ash and blood if Julius did not come out and Julius was sure the threat would prevent any attempt to hold or kill him. If it did not, he thought the Britons would be surprised at the savagery that would follow. Brutus and Octavian alone were so far from common swordsmen that their speed and skill seemed almost magical, while a single blow from Ciro could snap the neck of all but the strongest men.

Commius cleared his throat.

'The Trinovantes have not forgotten the alliance of last year. The Cenimagni, Ancalites, Bibroci and Segontiaci have agreed to respect that peace. Will you honour your word?'

'I will,' Julius replied. 'If these men will declare themselves my allies, I will not trouble them past the taking of hostages and a level of tribute. The other tribes will see they have nothing to fear from me if they are civilised. You will be my example to them.'

As he spoke, Julius glanced around the table, but the Britons gave nothing away. Commius looked relieved and Julius settled back into his seat for the negotiations.

When Julius finally came out again, the Britons gathered along the high walls of the fort to see him go, the tension clear on their pale faces. Regulus watched closely as his general raised an arm in salute. The cohort turned in place and began the march down the hill to the waiting legions. From that height, the extent of the invasion force could be seen and Regulus smiled at the thought of every battle going as easily.

As the cohort was absorbed back into the main body of men, Julius sent a rider to fetch Mark Antony to him. It took an hour for the general to arrive and Julius strode through the silent, waiting lines of soldiers to greet him.

'I am going north, but I cannot leave these forts at my back,' Julius said as Mark Antony dismounted and saluted. 'You will stay here with your legion and accept the hostages they send. You will not provoke them into battle, but if they arm, you will destroy them utterly. Do you understand my orders?'

Mark Antony glanced up at the forts that loomed over their

position. The breeze seemed to be increasing in strength and he shivered suddenly. It was not an easy task, but he could do no more than salute.

'I understand, sir.'

Mark Antony watched as the great legions of his homeland moved off with a tramp and thunder that shook the ground. The breeze continued to strengthen and dark clouds swept in from the west. By the time the first walls of the camp were going up, a driving rain had begun to turn the earth into heavy clay. As he saw his tent being assembled, Mark Antony wondered how long he would be left to guard the allies in their dry, warm forts.

That night, a summer storm struck the coast. Forty of the Roman galleys had their oars and masts torn out and were driven onto the cliffs and smashed. Many more lost their anchors and were driven out to sea, tossed and battered in the darkness. The sheer number of them made it a night of terror, with the desperate crews hanging out over the sides with poles to fend away the others before they were crushed.

Hundreds lost their lives in collision or drowning and as the wind softened once more just before dawn, it was a bedraggled fleet that limped its way back to the shingle beach. Those who had seen the bloody savagery of the first landings moaned in terror as they saw a dark crust of bodies and wood along the shore.

With dawn, the remaining officers began to restore order. Galleys were lashed together and the metal spars of siege machines were dropped as makeshift anchors to hold them. Scores of landing boats had been ripped overboard, but those that survived spent the morning travelling from ship to ship, sharing the supplies of fresh water and tools. The dark holds of three galleys were filled with the wounded and their cries could be heard over the wind.

When they had eaten and the Roman captains had discussed the position, some voted for an immediate return to Gaul. Those who knew Julius well refused to listen to the idea and would not put a single oar in water until they had his orders. In the face of their resistance, messengers for Julius were sent ashore and the fleet waited.

Mark Antony received them first as they came inland. The great force of the gales had been lost a few miles from the coast and he had experienced no more than a bad storm, though flickering lightning had woken him from sleep more than once. He read the damage reports in dawning horror, before he mastered his spinning thoughts. Julius had not foreseen another storm to damage the fleet, but if he had been there, he would have given the same order. The galleys could not be left exposed to be hammered into driftwood over the course of the campaign.

Mark Antony opened his mouth to order a return to Gaul, but the thought of Julius' fury prevented the words.

'I have five thousand men here,' he said, an idea forming. 'With ropes and teams, we could bring the galleys in one by one and build an inland port for them. I hardly felt the storm, but we would not need to go so far from the coast. Half a mile and a wall to protect them would keep the fleet safe and ready for when Caesar returns.'

The messengers looked blankly at him.

'Sir, there are hundreds of ships. Even if we brought the slave crews out as labour, it would take months to move so many.'

Mark Antony smiled tightly.

'The slave crews will be responsible for their own ships. We have ropes and men to do it. I would think two weeks would be enough and after that, the storms can blow as they will.'

The Roman general ushered the seamen out of his tent and summoned his officers. He could not help but wonder if anyone had ever attempted such a thing before. He had never heard of it, though any port had one or two hulks out of water. Surely this was just an extension of the same task? With that thought, his doubts faded away as he lost himself in calculation. By the time his officers were ready to be briefed, Mark Antony had a string of orders for them.

CHAPTER FORTY

〰〰〰〰

The resemblance to the Gauls was striking as Julius ordered his legions into the attack. The British tribes of the interior did not affect the blue skin, but they shared some of the ancient names Julius had first heard in Gaul. His scouts had reported a tribe calling themselves the Belgae in the west, perhaps from the very same line he had destroyed across the sea.

A long crest of hills formed a ridge over the land that the legions climbed in the face of arrows and spears. The Roman shields were proof against them and the advance was inexorable. The legions had sweated to pull the heavy ballistae up the hills, but they had proved their worth as the Britons tried to hold the plateau and were taught respect for the great machines. They had nothing to match the sheer power of the scorpion bows and their charges were shattered in disarray as the legions moved on to the slopes beyond. Julius had known that part of their advantage lay in speed across open land and the tribes gathered under Cassivellaunus fell back as each position was taken and the Roman lines moved on.

Despite the resistance, Julius could not escape the suspicion that the tribes were drawing them in to a place of their choosing. All he could do was maintain the pace, always on the edge of routing them. He had the extraordinarii harry the retreating enemy in darting raids under Octavian and Brutus. The ground the legions walked was littered with spent spears and arrows, but few had found flesh and the advance did not falter during the long days.

Twice on the second morning, they were attacked in the flank by men left behind by the main British force. The maniples had not panicked as they held them back and the extraordinarii had charged them down as they had been trained, smashing through the desperate tribesmen at full speed.

At night, Julius had the cornicens sound for camps to be built and the baggage trains brought up food and water for the men. The nights were harder as the tribes kept up a din of shouting that made sleep almost impossible. The extraordinarii rode shifts around the camps to repel attacks and more of them fell in darkness from unseen arrows than at any other time. Yet even in that hostile land, the routines continued. The metalworkers repaired weapons and shields and the doctors did their best with those who had taken wounds. Julius was thankful for those Cabera had trained, though he missed the presence of his old friend. The illness that had struck him after healing Domitius was a terrible thing, a thief that stole away his mind in subtle stages. Cabera had not been well enough to make the second crossing and Julius only hoped he would live long enough to see them all return.

Julius had thought at first that he would crush the tribes against the river as he had done years before with the Suebi, against the Rhine. But the King of the Catuvellauni had fired the bridges before the legions could reach them and then spent the days reinforcing his army with warriors from all the surrounding regions.

Under heavy arrow fire from the opposite bank, Julius had sent scouts to find a place for fording, but only one looked suitable for the legions and even then, he was forced to leave behind the heavy weapons that had crushed the first attacks of the Britons and begun their long retreat.

Reluctantly, Julius arranged his ballistae, onagers and scorpion bows all along the bank to cover the attack. It occurred to him then that the best of tactics could be defeated by difficult terrain. His legions formed a column as wide as the flags his scouts had jammed in the soft mud of the Tamesis, marking the drop into deeper water. There could be no subterfuge in such a place. A barrage from the ballistae set the range across the river and gave the legions a clear landing ground of almost a hundred feet. After that, the head of the column would be engulfed by the Britons. The tribesmen had all the advantages and Julius knew that would be the turning point in the battle. If his men stalled on the opposite bank, the rest of the legions would not be able to cross. Everything they had gained from the coast could be wasted.

There was something eerie in preparing for war with the enemy so close yet unable to do more than watch. Julius could hear his officers bark out orders as the lines and files formed and in the distance he could hear echoes of similar shouts. He looked over the dark Tamesis and sent runners to his generals as he noted different aspects of the ground and the formations of the Britons. They looked confident enough as they hooted at the Romans and Julius saw a group of them bare their buttocks and slap them in his direction, to the general merriment of their friends.

He understood their confidence and felt nervous sweat drip into his eyes as he gave orders. The legions would be vulnerable to bow fire and spears as they crossed the river and the death toll would be high. Julius had sent scouts up and down the Tamesis to look for other fords he could use to land flanking forces, but if they existed, they were too far away to make it worthwhile. Even the best generals were forced on occasion to rely on the skill and sheer ferocity of the men they led.

Julius would not be amongst the first to cross. Octavian had volunteered to lead the extraordinarii over, with the Tenth close behind. The young Roman would be lucky to survive the charge, but Julius had given way to him, knowing it had to be his choice. The Tenth would smash their way in behind the cavalry and establish a clear area for the others to follow on their heels. Julius would come in with the Third Gallica and Brutus, with Domitius following them over.

The sun was clear in the sky as Julius pulled on his full-face helmet, turning the cold iron features towards the Catuvellauni. He raised his sword and some of them saw the gesture, beckoning him on.

Julius looked at Octavian, who watched him, waiting for the signal. The extraordinarii were grim and their spatha blades glittered as they held their position. By the time they reached the opposite bank they would be at full gallop and Julius felt a moment of breathless anticipation as they waited to bring death to the Britons.

In silence, Julius dropped his arm and the cornicens blared out all over the vast column. Julius heard Octavian roar and the extraordinarii surged forward into the shallow water in a mass, faster and faster. The horses churned the water into froth as the Roman cavalry lowered their swords over their mount's heads and leaned forward, ready for the first kills. Arrows and spears punched into them and horses and men screamed, staining the water red as their bodies slipped into the current. The Britons roared and came on.

It called for precision, but every man on the heavy ballistae was ready. As the Britons surged forward to meet the extraordinarii, Julius signalled the teams and a last load of iron and stone flew over the heads of the galloping Romans, smashing the first impetuous ranks into rags.

Great holes appeared in the mass of the enemy and Octavian aimed his horse for one, the gelding staggering slightly as he reached dry ground. His mount was blowing heavily and he was drenched in freezing water. He heard the bellow of the Tenth as they charged across the ford behind him and he knew the Roman gods were watching the sons of their city, even so far away.

There was no room for thought in that first charge. Octavian and Brutus had chosen the extraordinarii for their skills with horse and sword and they formed an arrowhead without a single order being called, striking against the Britons and carving a path deep into their ranks.

The Tenth could not use their spears with their own cavalry so close ahead, but they were the veterans of Gaul and Germany and whoever stood to face them was cut down. The Britons fell back in disarray before the combined attack and their main advantage was lost with incredible speed as the Tenth widened their line with the perfection of a dance and the spaces they created filled with legions coming over. The squares formed on the flanks and the extraordinarii moved amongst them, their speed and agility protecting them from the spears and swords of the Catuvellauni.

Julius heard horns wail out over the enemy's heads and they fell back and to the flanks, opening a wide avenue in their midst. Through it, Julius could see a cloud of dust and then a wall of horses and chariots galloping at suicidal speed. The Roman cornicens sounded the order to close up and the squares halted, the men within locking shields and setting themselves in the alien soil to hold the position.

The chariots were manned by two warriors and Julius marvelled at the skill of the spearmen who balanced so precariously at high speed while their companions held the reins of the charging horses. At the last moment, the spears were launched and Julius saw legionaries killed by a wave of the shafts, thrown with enough power to punch through even the Roman shields.

Octavian saw the carnage that resulted and shouted new orders. They disengaged from the flanks and cut across the line of the chariots before they could throw again or turn. The Britons rushed in amongst them and Julius saw horses and men gutted and cut down, blood spraying amongst them. The Tenth and Third pushed forward and closed the centre, over-whelming the chariot men as they fought with roaring desperation. Some of the Britons' horses panicked and Julius saw more than one knock legionaries to the ground as empty char-iots were dragged through the field behind their wide-eyed mounts.

'The extraordinarii are clear!' Julius heard Brutus shout to him and he nodded, ordering spears. It was not the most discip-lined of attacks. Many of the Romans had lost their weapons in the fighting, but still a few thousand of the dark shafts went up and added to the chaos of the Catuvellauni as they tried to re-form.

Julius looked back and saw that two of his legions were still in the river, simply unable to go further against the press of their own men. He signalled an advance and the Tenth responded with the discipline he had come to expect, locking shields and forcing a way through and over the enemy.

The Roman line widened as the extraordinarii fell back to protect the flanks. Their insane first charge had thinned their numbers, but Julius cheered as he saw Octavian was still there. His young relative was covered in gore and his face looked swollen and black with a spreading bruise, but he was snap-ping out orders and his men took up the new formation with something of their old polish.

On the open land, the Roman legions were unstoppable. Time and again, the Catuvellauni charged their lines and were thrown back. Julius marched over clumps of bodies that marked each failed attempt. Twice more, the Tenth and Third held charges by the vicious chariots and then a different note sounded amongst the enemy horns and the Catuvellauni began to retreat, a gap opening between the armies for the first time since the river.

The Roman cornicens blew for double time and the legions broke into a jog, their officers haranguing the men to keep formation. The wounded Britons were run down almost immediately and the exhausted stragglers fell to Roman swords even as they screamed. Julius saw two men supporting a third until they were forced to drop him almost at the feet of the pursuing Tenth. All three were trampled and stabbed for their courage.

As the sun moved, Julius jogged with the others, panting. If the King of the Catuvellauni thought they could outrun his legions, he would learn. Julius saw nothing but determination in the ranks about him and he felt the same pride. The legions would run them into the ground.

Even then, Julius checked the land for ambush, though he doubted the possibility. Cassivellaunus had seen his best hope was to hold the Romans at the river and would have thrown everything he had into those first assaults. However, Julius had fought too many battles to allow a surprise and his extraordinarii harried the enemy up ahead, while smaller groups peeled away to scout.

It was almost with disappointment that Julius heard a falling, mournful note from the enemy horns. Julius guessed at its meaning even before he saw the first Britons throw down their weapons in disgust. The rest followed.

Julius had no need to give the orders to accept the surrender. His men were experienced enough and he barely took notice as the Tenth moved amongst them, forcing them to sit and collecting weapons to enforce the peace. Not a single warrior was killed after the initial surrender and Julius was satisfied.

He looked around him and saw houses clustered together less than a mile ahead. The legions were on the very edge of the towns around the Tamesis river and Cassivellauni had surrendered in sight of his people before the running battle brought them into the streets. It was an honourable decision and Julius greeted the man without rancour as he was brought to him.

Cassivellaunus was a black-haired, fleshy-faced young man who wore a pale robe belted around his waist and a long cloak over heavy shoulders. His eyes were bitter as Julius met them, but he sank down onto one knee and bowed his head before rising, the fresh mud spattering his woollen clothes.

Julius removed his helmet, enjoying the freshness of the breeze on his skin. 'As commander of the forces of Rome, I accept your surrender,' he said formally. 'There will be no more killing. Your men will be held prisoner until we have negotiated hostages and tribute. As of this moment, you may consider yourself a vassal of Rome.'

Cassivellaunus looked quizzically at him as he heard the words. The king looked over the Roman lines and saw their organisation. Despite a running fight of almost two miles, the formations were sharp and he knew he had made the right decision. It had cost him a great deal. As he looked at the Roman in his dirty armour, with blood-smeared sandals and three days' growth of beard on his chin, Cassivellaunus could only shake his head in disbelief. He had lost the land his father gave him.

CHAPTER FORTY-ONE

Vercingetorix planted his spear in the ground before the gates of Avaricum and rammed a Roman head on the point. Leaving his grisly trophy behind him, he rode in through the gates to where the tribal leaders had gathered in his name.

The walled town in the centre of Gaul had a population of forty thousand and most of those had come out onto the streets to point and stare at the High King. Vercingetorix rode through them without looking left or right, his thoughts on the campaign ahead.

He dismounted in the central courtyard and strode through shadowed cloisters into the main hall of government. As he entered, they rose to cheer him and Vercingetorix looked around at the faces of the Gallic leaders, his expression cold. With a stiff nod of acknowledgement, he walked to the centre and waited for silence.

'A bare five thousand men stand between us and our land. Caesar has left to attack the painted people as once he came to Gaul. This is the time for which we have planned so patiently.' He waited through the storm of talk and cheers that echoed round the chamber. 'We will give them a warm homecoming by the winter, I promise you that. We will take them by stealth and by the dozen or the hundred at a time. Our cavalry will attack their foraging parties and we will starve them from Gaul.'

They roared at the idea, as he had expected, but still his eyes were cold as he readied himself to tell them the price they must pay.

'The legions have only one weakness, my friends, and that is in their lines of supply. Who in this room hasn't lost friends and brothers against them? On an open plain, we would fare no better than the Helvetii did years ago. All our armies together could not break them in the open.'

The silence was oppressive as the leaders waited for their High King to continue.

'But they cannot fight without food, and to deny them forage we must burn every crop and village in Gaul. We must uproot our people from Caesar's path and leave him nothing but a smoking wasteland to feed his Roman mouths. When they are weak with hunger, I will bring my men into fortresses like the one at Gergovia and they can see how many lives they lose against those walls.'

He glared round at the men of Gaul, hoping that they would have the strength to follow this most terrible path.

'We can win. We can break them in this way, but it will be hard. Our people will be frightened at being forced off their land. When they cry out, you will tell them they once rode three thousand miles to reach here. We are still one people, for those who can see it. The land of Gaul must rise. The Celts must rise and remember the old blood that calls them.'

They stood in silence for him and beat their swords and knives together in a clashing noise that filled the space and shook the foundations. Vercingetorix held his arms up for quiet and it was a long time coming. His people stood with eager expressions and they believed in him.

'Tomorrow, you will begin to move your tribes to the far south, leaving only those who are thirsty for war. Take your grain stores with you, for my riders will burn anything they find. Gaul will be ours again. I speak not as one of the Arverni, but from the line of the old kings. They watch over us now and they will bring us victory.'

The clash of metal began again and became deafening as Vercingetorix walked out in the shadowed cloisters to rejoin his army. He trotted his horse back through the streets and ducked his head unconsciously as he passed under the Avaricum gates.

When he reached his horsemen, he sat high in the saddle and gazed fondly at the flags of Gaul. Dozens of tribes were represented in ten thousand riders and truly, he felt one with the old blood.

'It is a good day to ride,' he told his brother Madoc.

'It is, my King,' Madoc replied. Together they heeled their horses into a gallop, streaming across the plain.

Julius sat on a hill with his cloak on the damp ground under him. A light rain was falling and through it they could see the galleys he had ordered sent round the coast to find where the dark river poured into the sea. With their shallow draught, they had been able to come all the way in to the ford and anchored just before it. Brutus and Renius sat with him, watching supplies being unloaded by teams of the Tenth and Third.

'Did you know the captains found a bay further down the coast?' Julius said aloud. He sighed. 'If I had known of it, the storms that took so many of my ships would have battered in vain. Protected by cliffs and deep water with a sloping shore for the boats. We will know for the future, now that we have found it, at least.' He ran a hand through his wet hair and shook droplets from the end of his nose.

'They call this summer? I swear I haven't seen the sun in a month.'

'It makes me homesick for Rome,' Brutus answered slowly. 'Just to imagine olive trees in the sun and the temples of the forum. I cannot believe how far away from all that we've come.'

'Pompey will be there, rebuilding,' Julius said, his eyes hardening. 'The senate house where I stood with Marius is no more than memory. When we see Rome, Brutus, it will not be the same.'

They sat in silence while each of them considered the truth of the words. It had been years since Julius had seen his city, but somehow he had always expected it to be there unchanged for when he returned, as if everything else in life was held in glass until he was ready to make it move once more. It was a child's dream.

'You will go back, then?' Brutus said. 'I had begun to think you would have us all grow old out here.'

Renius smiled without speaking.

'I will, Brutus,' Julius said. 'I have done what I came for and a single legion will be enough to hold the Britons. Perhaps when I am an old man and Gaul is as peaceful as Spain, I will return here to carry the war to the north.'

He shivered suddenly and told himself it was the cold. It was strangely peaceful watching the efforts of the galley crews below while they were far above them. The hills around the Tamesis were gentle slopes and if it hadn't been for the constant drizzle, it might have felt like a distant world of strife that could not come close to the men on the hill. It was easy to dream.

'There are times when I want it all to end, Brutus,' Julius

said. 'I miss your mother. I miss my daughter as well. I have been at war as long as I can remember and the thought of returning to my estate to tend the hives and sit in the sun is a terrible temptation.'

Renius chuckled. 'One you successfully resist each year,' he said.

Julius glanced sharply at the one-armed gladiator. 'I am in the flower of my youth, Renius. If I accomplish nothing else in life, then Gaul will be my mark on the world.'

As he spoke, he touched a hand unconsciously to his head, feeling the receding hairline. War aged a man more than just the passing of years, he thought. Where once he had felt as if he could never grow old, now his joints ached in the damp and morning brought a stiffness that took longer and longer to pass each year. He saw Brutus had noticed the gesture and frowned.

'It has been a privilege to serve with you both, you know,' Renius said suddenly. 'Have I ever told you? I would not have been anywhere else but with you.'

Both of the younger men looked at the scarred figure who sat hunched forward on his cloak.

'You are growing maudlin in your old age,' Brutus said with a smile. 'You need to feel the sun on your face again.'

'Perhaps,' Renius said, pulling a piece of grass between his fingers. 'I have fought for Rome all of my life and she still stands. I've done my part.'

'Do you want to go home?' Julius asked him. 'You can walk down this hill to the galleys and have them take you back, my friend. I will not refuse you.'

Renius looked down to the bustling crowd on the river and his eyes were filled with yearning. He shrugged then and forced a smile.

'One more year, perhaps,' he said.

'There's a messenger coming,' Brutus said suddenly, breaking in on their thoughts. All three turned to look at the tiny figure on horseback who lunged up the hill towards them.

'It must be bad news for him to seek me here,' Julius said, rising to his feet. In that moment, his contemplative mood was broken and the other two sensed the change in him like a sudden shift in the wind.

Their damp cloaks were crumpled and all three men felt the weariness of constant war and problems, watching the lone rider with a sort of dread.

'What is it?' Julius demanded as soon as the man was close enough to hear.

The messenger became clumsy under their scrutiny, dismounting and saluting in a tangle.

'I have come from Gaul, General,' he said.

Julius' heart sank. 'From Bericus? What is your message?'

'Sir, the tribes are rebelling.'

Julius swore. 'The tribes rebel every year. How many this time?'

The messenger looked nervously at the officers.

'I think . . . General Bericus said all of them, sir.'

Julius looked blankly at the man before nodding in resignation.

'Then I must return. Ride to the galleys below and tell them not to leave until I am with them. Have General Domitius send riders to the coast to Mark Antony. The fleet must be put to sea to cross to Gaul before the winter storms begin.'

Julius stood in the rain and watched the rider make his way down to the river and the galley crews.

'So it is to be war once more,' he said. 'I wonder if Gaul will ever see the peace of Rome in my lifetime.' He looked tired at the burden and Brutus' heart went out to his old friend.

'You'll beat them. You always do.'

'With winter coming?' Julius said bitterly. 'There are hard months ahead, my friend. Perhaps harder than any we have

484

known.' With appalling effort, he controlled himself until the face he turned to them was a mask.

'Cassivellaunus must not know. His hostages are already on board the galleys, his son amongst them. Take the legions back to the coast, Brutus. I will go by sea and have the fleet waiting for you there.' He paused and his mouth tightened in anger.

'I will do more than beat them, Brutus. I will raze them from the face of the earth.'

Renius looked at the man he had trained and was filled with sorrow. He had no chance to rest and each year of war stole a little more of his kindness away from him. Renius gazed south, imagining the shores of Gaul. They would regret having unleashed Caesar amongst them.

CHAPTER FORTY-TWO

❦❦❦❦❦

The Gaul irregulars counted almost all the tribes amongst their ranks. Many of them had fought for the legions for five years or more and they acted and thought as Romans. Their pay was in the same silver and their armour and swords came from the forges of the regular legions.

When Bericus sent three thousand of them out to protect a shipment of grain, there were few that could have seen the subtle differences between their ranks and that of any other Roman force. Even the officers were from the tribes, after so long in the field. Though Julius had salted them with his best men in the beginning, war and promotion had altered the structure. They hardly noticed.

The convoy of wheat had come from Spain at Bericus' order and had to be protected as it wound its way down from the northern ports. It was enough to feed the towns and villages that had stayed loyal. Enough to keep them alive through the winter while Vercingetorix burned anything he could find.

The irregulars marched south in perfect order at the pace of the slowest cart. Their scouts were out for miles around them to warn of an attack. Every man there knew that the grain would be a threat to the rebellion as it gathered force in the heartlands and hands rarely strayed from their swords. They ate cold meat on the move from their own dwindling rations and stopped only barely in time to build a hostile camp each night.

When it came, the attack was like nothing they could have expected. On a wide plain, a dark line of horsemen came thundering towards them. The scouts galloped in even as the column was reacting, shifting the heavy carts into a defensive circle and preparing their spears and bows. Every eye was fixed in fear on the enemy as the sheer size of their cavalry became apparent. There were thousands of them riding through the mud and grass towards the carts. The weak sun reflected on their weapons and many of the Gauls began to pray to old gods, forgotten for years.

Marwen had been a soldier for Rome ever since he had exchanged hunger for the silver coins four years before. As he saw the size of the force against them, he knew he would not survive it and experienced the bitter irony of being killed by his own people. He cared nothing for politics. When the Romans had come to his village and offered him a place with them, he had taken their bounty and given it to his wife and children before walking out to fight for Rome. It had been better than watching them starve.

Promotion had been a wonder, when it came. He had been part of the battles against the Senones and had ridden out with Brutus to steal their king from the very heart of them. That had been a day.

Lost in bitter memory, he did not at first notice the faces of the men as they turned to him, looking for orders. When he saw them, he shrugged.

'This is where we earn our pay, lads,' he said softly.

He could feel the ground shake under his feet as the riders stormed towards them. The defensive ranks were solid around the carts. The spears had been jammed into the mud to repel the charge and there was nothing else to do but wait for the first acceleration of blood. Marwen hated the waiting and almost welcomed it to crush the fear that wormed in his stomach.

Horns sounded and the line of charging horses heaved to a halt just out of range. Marwen frowned as he saw one man dismount and walk over the soft ground towards them. He knew who it was even before he could be sure of the yellow hair and the fine gold torc the man wore to battle. Vercingetorix.

Marwen watched in disbelief as the king walked closer.

'Be still,' he ordered his men, suddenly worried that one of his archers would loose a shaft. His blood coursed through him and Marwen breathed faster as the king approached. It was an act of suicidal bravery and many of the men muttered in admiration as they readied their blades to cut him to pieces.

Vercingetorix came right up to them, meeting Marwen's eyes as he noted the cloak and helmet of his rank. It may have been imagination, but seeing him there, so close, with his great sword sheathed on his hip, was something glorious.

'Speak your piece,' Marwen said.

The king's eyes flashed and the yellow beard split as he grinned. He saw Marwen's hand tighten on his gladius.

'Would you kill your king?' Vercingetorix said.

Marwen let his hand drop in confusion. He looked into the calm eyes of the man who faced him with such courage and shivered.

'No. I would not,' he said.

'Then follow me,' Vercingetorix said.

Marwen glanced right and left at the men he commanded and saw them nod. He looked back at Vercingetorix and without breaking his gaze, went slowly down to kneel in the mud. As if in a dream, he felt the king's hand on his shoulder.

'What is your name?'

Marwen hesitated. The words of his rank and unit caught in his throat.

'I am Marwen Ridderin, of the Nervii,' he said, at last.

'The Nervii are with me. Gaul is with me. On your feet.'

Marwen rose and found his hands were shaking. He heard Vercingetorix speak again through the tumult of his thoughts.

'Now burn the grain in those carts,' the king said.

'There are some Romans amongst us. We are not all from Gaul,' Marwen said suddenly.

The king's pale eyes turned to him. 'Do you want to let them live?'

Marwen's face hardened. 'It would be right,' he said, raising his head in defiance.

Vercingetorix smiled and clapped him on the shoulder. 'Then let them go, Nervii. Take their swords and shields and let them go.'

As the Gaul irregulars marched behind their king, the horsemen raised their swords in salute and cheered them. Behind, the wagons of precious grain were hidden in crackling flames.

As Julius landed in the sheltered bay of Portus Itius on the coast of Gaul, he could see vast brown spires of smoke in the distance. Even the air tasted of battle and he felt a great anger at the thought of another rebellion against him.

He had not wasted a moment of the crossing and was already busy with orders and plans that had to be implemented before the winter closed the mountains. Getting news back to Rome of his second assault against the Britons would be a race against time, but he needed the goodwill it would bring on the streets of the city. There would be no senate tithe that year, when he needed every coin to smash the tribes under Vercingetorix. The name was on the mouths of the lowest workers and Julius could barely remember the angry young man who had stormed out of his first meeting with the chieftains, eight years before. Not so young any more, either of them. Cingeto had grown into a king and Julius knew he could not allow him to live. They had both walked a long path since the beginning and the years had been filled with blood and war.

As Julius climbed up onto the quayside, he was already deep in conversation with Brutus, breaking off to dictate to Adàn at his shoulder. Fast-riding extraordinarii had been sent to summon Bericus and as soon as he arrived, Julius would gather his council and plan the campaign. A glance at the brown smoke on the horizon was enough to firm his resolve. This was his land and he would not falter if every man in Gaul took arms against him.

The returning legions occupied the port and built their camps out of routine, though there was a tangible tension and weariness in the ranks. They too had fought for years with Julius and more than a few were sickened at the thought of another year of war, or even longer. Even the hardest of them wondered when it would all end and they would be allowed to reap the rewards they had been promised.

On the third day, Julius gathered his council at the coastal fortress they had built, part of a chain that one day would dominate the coast of Gaul.

Domitius came in first, wearing the silver armour he had won. Dark bristle covered his cheeks and his armour had lost much of its shine. The breastplate especially was a battered testament to the wars he had fought for Julius. Without a word, he grasped Julius' hand and forearm in the legionary grip before taking his place.

Mark Antony embraced his general as they met. Julius had

reason to be pleased with him when he saw the tallies of their treasury. The sums of gold and silver in the reserve were vast, though they were dropping day by day as the cities and towns of Gaul waited to see if the rebellion would succeed. Already, the food supply was critical and Julius was grateful to Mark Antony for taking that part of his burden. The thousands of legionaries had to be fed and watered before they could fight and already it was clear that Vercingetorix was trying to cut their supplies. The burning plumes of smoke had all been farms and when the extraordinarii galloped out to them, they found them empty and deserted. Julius felt a grudging admiration for the ruthlessness of the new king. Vercingetorix had made a choice that would also kill the villages and towns that remained loyal to the legions. Thousands of his own people would die for their allegiance and more if the legions could not end it quickly. It was a high cost, but starvation would wither the Roman legions as surely as swords.

Julius had chosen a room that looked over the sea for their gathering and birds wheeled and screeched outside on the grey rocks. He greeted each man with real pleasure as they came in. Bericus had taken a wound in the first engagement with Vercingetorix and had his shoulder and chest bandaged. Though the Ariminum general looked tired, he could not help but respond to Julius' smile as he showed him a seat and brought a cup of wine for his good hand. Octavian came in with Brutus and Renius, in the middle of a discussion of tactics for the cavalry. All three greeted Julius and made him smile at their confidence. They seemed not to share his own doubts and worries, but then they were used to having him there to solve them. He had no one.

As they gathered, Julius felt himself lifted by their mood. The years of war had not broken his friends. When they spoke of the latest rebellion it was with anger and resilience rather than defeat. They had all invested years in the hostile land and every man there was angry to see their future threatened. Though they talked amongst themselves, each man watched Julius for some sign he was about to begin. He was the core of them. When he was absent, it was as if the purest part of their drive and energy had been taken. He bound men together who would not have suffered each other's company in any other circumstances. Such a bond, in fact, that they did not even think of it as they settled and he faced them. He was simply there and they were slightly more alive than before.

Cabera was brought in last by two men of the Tenth who acted as his attendants. Julius strode over to him as soon as the old healer was settled and took his frail hands in his own. He spoke too quietly for the others to hear above the noise of the gulls and wind.

'Further than any other man in Rome, Cabera. I have been off the edge of the world. Did you see me here, so long ago?'

Cabera didn't seem to hear him at first and Julius was sad at the changes age had wrought in him. Guilt too tugged at his conscience. It was at Julius' request that Cabera had healed Domitius' shattered knee and that act of will had been too much for his ageing frame. He had not been strong since that day. At last the eyes lifted and the dry, cracked mouth twitched upwards at the edges.

'You are here because you choose to be, Gaius,' the old man said. His voice was little louder than an escaping breath and Julius leaned closer to his lips. 'I have never seen you in this terribly cold room.' Cabera paused then, and the muscles of his neck jumped in spasm as he took a deeper breath.

'Did I tell you I saw you killed by Sulla?' he whispered.

'Sulla is long dead, Cabera,' Julius said.

Cabera nodded. 'I know it, but I saw you murdered in his house and again in the cells of a pirate ship. I have seen you fall so often I am sometimes surprised to see you so strong

492

and alive. I do not understand the visions, Julius. They have caused me more pain than I have ever imagined.'

Julius saw with swelling grief that there were tears in the old man's eyes. Cabera noticed his expression and chuckled dryly, a clicking sound that went on and on. Though Cabera's left arm lay useless in his lap, he reached up with the other and brought Julius even closer.

'I would not change a day of it, the things I have seen. You understand? I haven't long and it will be a relief. But I regret nothing of what has happened since I stepped into your home so long ago.'

'I would not have survived without you, old man. You can't leave me now,' Julius murmured, his own eyes filling with tears and memory.

Cabera snorted and rubbed his face with his fingers.

'Some choices are denied us, Gaius Julius. Some paths cannot be avoided. You too will pass the river in the end. I have seen it in more ways than I can tell you.'

'What did you see?' Julius said, aching to know, yet gripped by a numbing fear. For an instant, he thought Cabera had not heard him, the old man was so still.

'Who is to know where your choices will take you?' The voice continued its sibilance. 'Yet I have not seen you old, my friend, and once I saw you fall to knives in darkness in the first days of spring. On the Ides of March, I saw you fall, in Rome.'

'Then I will never be in my city on that day,' Julius replied. 'I swear it to you, if it will give you peace.'

Cabera raised his head and looked past Julius to where the shrieking gulls fought and struggled over some scrap of food.

'Some things are better not to know, Julius, I think. Nothing is clear to me any more. Did I tell you of the knives?'

Gently, Julius laid the old man's hands together on his lap and arranged the cushions so he could sit upright.

'You did, Cabera. You saved me again,' he said. With infinite tenderness, Julius lifted the old man up on the cushions to make him comfortable.

'I am glad of that,' Cabera said, closing his eyes.

Julius heard a long breath coming from him and the frail figure became utterly still. Julius gave a muffled cry as he saw the life go out of him and reached out to touch his cheek. The silence seemed to go on a long time, but the chest was still and would not move again.

'Good bye, old friend,' Julius said.

He heard a scrape of wood as Renius and Brutus came to stand with him and the years fell away so that it was two boys and their tutor standing there, seeing a man hold a bow without a tremor in his arms.

Julius heard the other members of his council stand as they realised what had happened. He turned red-rimmed eyes to them and they could not bear to meet the pain they saw in his face.

'Will you join me in the prayers for the dead, gentlemen? Our war will wait another day.'

As the gulls shrieked in the wind outside, the low murmur of their voices filled the cold room. At the end, there was silence and Julius breathed a last few words as he looked at the shrunken body of the old man.

'And now I am adrift,' he said, so quietly that only Brutus at his side could hear.

CHAPTER FORTY-THREE

It was dark in the tent and Adàn had only a single tallow candle to give him enough light to write. He sat in perfect silence and watched as Caesar sprawled on a bench with his arm out-stretched to be bandaged. There was blood on the first layers and the strip of cloth itself was dirty, having been taken from a corpse. Julius grunted as the doctor made a knot and pulled it tight. For a moment, his eyes opened with the pain and Adàn saw they were dim with exhaustion.

The doctor gathered his sack of equipment and left, letting a blast of air into the stuffy interior that made the candle flicker. Adàn looked over the words he had recorded and wished Julius would sleep. They were all hungry, but the winter had burnt flesh from the commander as much as any of the men. His skin was tinged with yellow and tight across his skull and Adàn saw dark hollows underneath his eyes that gave him a look of death.

Adàn thought Julius had slid into sleep and began to gather

his scrolls to steal away without waking him. He froze as Julius scratched at the sweat stains of his tunic and then rubbed his face. Adàn shook his head slowly at the changes in the man since he had first known him. Gaul had taken more than it had given.

'Where did I finish?' Julius said, without opening his eyes. His voice was a croak that made Adàn shiver in the gloom.

'Avaricum. The doctor came in as I was writing about the final day.'

'Ah yes. Are you ready to go on?'

'If you wish it, sir. It might be better if I left you to get some rest,' Adàn said.

Julius did not respond past scratching his unshaven chin.

'Avaricum came soon after the murder of three cohorts under Bericus. Are you writing this?'

'I am,' Adàn whispered. To his surprise, he felt the sting of tears begin as Julius forced himself on and the Spaniard could not explain them.

'We built a ramp up to the walls and stormed the town. I could not hold the men back after what they had seen. I didn't try to hold them.' Julius paused and Adàn could hear his breath as a harsh susurration above the noise of the legions outside.

'Eight hundred survived us, Adàn. Record the truth for me. Out of forty thousand men, women and children, only eight hundred lived when we were finished. We burned the town around them and stripped what grain they had left in their stores. Even then, you could count the ribs on the soldiers with me. Vercingetorix had moved on, of course, and every town we came to was destroyed. He drove the cattle before him and left us nothing but birds and wild hares to trap. To feed forty thousand men, Adàn. Without the stores of Avaricum, we would have been finished.

'We routed them over and over whenever we caught them in the open, but all the tribes of Gaul had joined him and he

496

outnumbered us every time. Bericus was killed in the third month, or the fourth, I cannot remember. His own irregulars caught him in an ambush. We did not find his body.'

Julius lapsed into silence as he remembered how Bericus had refused to believe that the men he had trained would kill him. He had been a decent man and he paid with his life for that belief.

'Vercingetorix moved on south to Gergovia and the hill forts there and I could not break those walls.'

Adàn looked up at the silence and saw Julius' mouth twist in anger. Still, he lay back with his eyes closed and the croaking voice seemed to come from deep within.

'We lost eight hundred men at Gergovia and as spring came I saw my soldiers eat green corn until they vomited. Still, we destroyed the armies who dared to take the field against us. Brutus and Octavian did well against the banners there, but the numbers, Adàn ... Every tribe we have called friends has risen against us and there are times ... no. Strike that out, my doubts are not to be written.

'We could not starve him out in Gergovia and our own men were weakening. I was forced to move west to gather supplies and still we could barely find enough to stave off death. Vercingetorix sent his generals against us and we fought all the way while he raced ahead by night. I have marched a thousand miles this last year, Adàn. I have seen death walking with me.'

'But now you have trapped him in Alesia,' Adàn said softly.

Julius struggled to sit up and leaned over his knees, his head sagging.

'The greatest hill fort I have ever seen in Gaul. A city on four hills, Adàn. Yes, I have him trapped. We starve on the outside while he waits for us all to die.'

'Grain and meat are coming in from the south now. The worst is over,' Adàn said.

Julius shrugged so lightly it could have been a breath.

'Perhaps. Write this for me. We have built trenches and fortifications for eighteen miles around Alesia. We have thrown up three great hills from the earthworks, so massive as to allow us to build watchtowers on them. Vercingetorix cannot leave as long as we remain here – and we will remain. Our prisoners talk of him as king of all the Gauls and until he is dead or captured, they will continue to rebel. We have cut them down in thousands and they will still come each spring until their king is dead. Let them know in Rome, Adàn. Let them understand what we are doing here.'

The tent flap opened and Brutus was there in the darkness, glancing over at Adàn as he saw the light of the tiny flame.

'Julius?' he said.

'I am here,' came the voice, barely a whisper.

'You must come out once more. The scouts are back and they say an army of Gauls is coming to relieve the forts.'

Julius looked at him with red-rimmed eyes that seemed more dead than alive. He stood and swayed from exhaustion and Brutus stepped in to help him pull on the armour and scarlet cloak that the men needed to see.

'So those men who escaped the fort were to bring an army back,' Julius murmured as Brutus began to lace the chestplate to the strips of iron around his neck. Both men were dirty and stank with sweat and Adàn was struck by the tenderness as Brutus took a rag and wiped the armour down with it, handing Julius his sword from where it lay propped and forgotten against a pole. Without a word, Adàn took the red cloak from its peg and helped Brutus drape it around the shoulders. It could have been his imagination, but in the armour he thought Julius stood a little straighter, sheer will forcing some of the weariness from his face.

'Summon the council, Brutus, and bring the scouts to me. We shall fight on both sides if need be, to put an end to this king.'

'And then we shall go home?' Brutus said.

'If we live, my friend. Then we shall go home at last.'

The Roman generals who came to the central camp at the foot of Alesia showed the marks of the wars they had fought. Drinking water had been rationed as well as food and not one of them had enough to shave or wash the grime of months in the field from their faces. They sank onto the benches and sat listlessly, too tired to talk. The scorched earth and months of war since returning from Britain had hurt them all and now this last blow had brought them to the edge of despair.

'Generals, you have heard from the scouts and there is little more for me to tell you,' Julius said. He had taken a pouch of precious water from a guard and upended it into his mouth to take away the dust from his throat.

'The men are eating at last, though supplies are thin and of poor quality. Without the sacrifices of our settlers, we would have even less. Now the Gauls have gathered all the tribes against us and even the Aedui cavalry have vanished to join them. Mhorbaine has betrayed me at the last.'

Julius paused and rubbed a hand over his features.

'If the scouts are right, we have little chance of surviving the battle. If you ask it of me, I will try for an honourable surrender and save the lives of our legions. Vercingetorix has shown he is no fool. We would be allowed to travel back to the Alps with our settlers. Such a victory would establish him in his role of High King and I think he would accept. Is this what you want?'

'No, it isn't,' Domitius said. 'The men would not accept it from us, and not from you. Let them come, Caesar. We will destroy them again.'

'He speaks for me,' Renius added and the others nodded. Brutus and Mark Antony joined the voices and Octavian rose to his feet. Despite their tired faces, there was determination there still. Julius smiled at their loyalty.

'Then we will stand or fall at Alesia, gentlemen. I am proud to have known you all. If this is where the gods say it ends, then let it be so. We will fight to the last.'

Julius scratched the bristles on his face and smiled ruefully.

'Perhaps we should use a little of the drinking water to look like Romans for tomorrow. Bring me my maps. We will make plans to humble the tribes one more time.'

Vercingetorix stood at the high walls of Alesia, looking out over the plain. He had rushed up to the windswept heights at the first reports from his watchmen and he gripped the crumbling stone fiercely as he saw a mass of torches moving towards them.

'Is it Madoc?' Brigh asked eagerly.

The king looked at his youngest brother and held his shoulder in a sudden burst of affection.

'Who else would it be? He has brought the armies of Gaul to sweep them away.' With a glance around him, he leaned his head close. 'The princes of the Arverni are hard men to defeat, are we not?'

Brigh grinned at him.

'I had begun to lose hope. There's not more than a month of food left . . .'

'Tell the men to eat well tonight then. Tomorrow we will see the Romans broken and then we will cut our way out past their forts and walls and reclaim Gaul from them. We will see no more of these legions for a generation.'

'And you will be king?' Brigh asked.

Vercingetorix laughed.

'I *am* king, little brother. King of a greater nation. Now the tribes remember the call of blood, there is nothing in the world to hold us down. Dawn will end it and then we will be free.'

The first grey light revealed a camp of Gaulish horsemen that stretched for three miles across the land. As the legions awoke, they heard a dim and tinny cheering from the great linked forts of Alesia as the inhabitants saw those who had come to relieve them.

The morning was cold, despite the promise of summer. The food that had been brought in from the Roman province at the foot of the Alps was prepared and handed out on tin plates, the first hot meal in days for many of the men. With the Gauls arrayed before them, they ate without joy and the plates emptied too quickly. Many of the men licked them clean for the last scrap of sustenance.

The Roman fortifications around Alesia were high enough to give the Gauls pause as they considered the best manner of attack. The walls reached twenty feet and were manned by forty thousand of the best foot soldiers in the world. It was no easy task, even with the colossal numbers Madoc had assembled.

Madoc did not know himself how many were with him, just that he had never seen such an army gathered in one place. Even then, he was cautious, as Vercingetorix had told him to be when he escaped from Alesia to summon the tribes.

'Remember the Helvetii,' Vercingetorix had said.

Even when vastly outnumbered, the Romans had beaten every army sent against them and those who still lived were veterans and survivors, the ones hardest to kill. Madoc wished his brother were out there to direct the horsemen. He could feel the scrutiny and hope of the defenders in the Alesia forts and it intimidated him. He knew by then that his brother was a better king than he would have been. Madoc alone could not

501

have bound the tribes together, more closely than they had known for a thousand years. Old disputes had been forgotten and in the end they had all sent their best men to aid the High King and break the back of the Roman occupation.

Now it all depended on his word and tens of thousands waited on him as the sun rose.

Julius climbed a hill to address the men he had fought with for nine years in Gaul. He knew hundreds by name and as he reached the crest and steadied himself against the base of the watchtower, he saw familiar faces waiting for him to speak. Did they know how weary he was? He had shared the privations of the march and the battles across Gaul. They had seen him push himself further than any of them, going without sleep for days at a time until there was nothing left in him but an iron will that kept him on his feet.

'I will not ask you to fight for Rome!' he roared out to them. 'What does Rome know of us here? What does the Senate under-stand of what we are? The merchants in their houses, the slaves, the builders and the whores have not been with us in our battles. When I think of Rome, I cannot think of them, so far away. My brothers are those I see before me.'

The words came easily in front of the legions. He knew them all and a thin cheer began as they gazed up at the scarlet-cloaked figure. He could not have explained the bond to a stranger, but that had never been necessary. They knew him for what he was. They had seen him injured with them and exhausted after a march. Each man there had a memory of when he had spoken to them that they treasured more than the silver coins they were paid.

'I will not ask you to fight this last time for Rome. I will ask it for me,' he said and they lifted their heads higher to hear him, the cheering swelling in the ranks.

'Who dares to call themselves Rome while we live? The city is just stone and marble without us. We are its blood and its life. We are its purpose.' Julius swept a hand out to the massed hordes of the Gaulish army.

'What an honour it is to have so many come against us! *They* know our strength, my legions. They know we are unbreakable in spirit. I tell you, if I could change places and be out there, I would be afraid of what I see before me. I would be terrified. For they are not us. Alexander would be proud to walk with you as I do. He would be proud to see your swords raised in his name.' He looked down at the crowd and saw Renius there, staring at him.

'When our hearts and arms are tired, we go on,' Julius roared at them. 'When our stomachs are empty and our mouths dry, we *go on*.'

He paused again and smiled down at them.

'Now, gentlemen, we are professionals. Shall we cut these bastard amateurs to pieces?'

They clashed their swords and shields together and every throat bellowed their approval.

'Man the walls! They are coming!' Brutus shouted and the legions ran to their positions. They stood straight as Julius climbed down and walked amongst them, proud of them all.

Madoc felt a touch of fear as he saw the full extent of the Roman lines around Alesia. When he had escaped only a month before, the first trenches were being dug into the clay and now the walls were solid and manned with soldiers.

'Light torches to burn their gates and towers!' he ordered, seeing the lines of light spring up amongst the tribes. The crackle of flames was the sound of war and he felt his heart race faster in response. Still he worried as he looked over the vast fortifications that crouched on the land and waited for them. The speed of the Gaulish horses would be wasted against such a barrier. If the Romans could not be tempted out, Madoc knew each step would be bloody.

'Spears ready!' he called down the line. He felt thousands of eyes on him as he drew his long sword and pointed it at the Roman forces. His beloved Arverni were ready on the right flank and he knew they would follow his orders. He wished he could be as sure of the others in the heat of battle. As soon as they began to die, Madoc feared they would lose what little discipline he had been able to impose.

He raised his fist and brought it down in a sharp movement, kicking his horse into a gallop to lead them in. Behind him came a thunder that drowned out all other sound and then the Gauls roared. The horses flew towards the walls and every hand held a spear ready to throw.

'Ballistae ready! Onagers, scorpions ready! Wait for the horns!' Brutus shouted left and right. They had not been idle in the dark hours and now every war machine they possessed was facing outwards to smash the greater enemy. Every eye on the walls watched as the horde galloped towards them and their faces were bright with anticipation.

Huge logs soaked in oil were lit and gave off a choking smoke that did nothing to dampen the enthusiasm of those who were ready to smash them down onto the heads of the Gauls.

Brutus nodded as he gauged the range and tapped the nearest cornicen on the shoulder. The man took a deep breath and the long note sounded, almost swallowed in the release of hundreds of massive oak arms slamming into their rests. Stone and iron flew through the air with a whining sound and the Romans showed their teeth as they waited for the first touch of death.

*　　*　　*

Madoc saw the launch and for a moment he shut his eyes and prayed. He heard the cracks and thumps of missiles all around him and dwindling screams that he left behind. When he opened his eyes, he was amazed to find himself alive and whooped aloud for the sheer pleasure of it. Gaps had been broken open amongst the tribes, but they closed as the distance to the legions shortened and now their blood was up.

The Gauls released their spears with all the fury of men who had survived the Roman machines. They arched up and over the walls and before they could land, Madoc had reached the wide pits that ran along the edge of the Roman walls. Thirty thousand of his best men vaulted from their saddles and began to scramble up, digging their swords into the earth to climb over the spikes meant to hinder them.

Madoc saw the legionaries above in a glimpse as he climbed and without warning the earth gave way and he dropped down at the base. He shouted in anger and began the climb again, but he heard the crackle of flames and saw a group of Romans lever something massive over the edge and drop it towards him. He tried to leap away, but it hammered him down in a splinter of bone and blackness.

From the walls, Julius watched as the first attack was sent reeling. He ordered the war machines to fire again and again, using logs and stones that broke the legs of horses as they rolled amongst them. The gates in the walls were burning, but it did not matter. He did not intend to wait for them to fall.

All along the miles of fortifications, the Roman legionaries were battering those who reached them, using shields and swords in a frenzy. The bodies began to pile at the foot of the wall and Julius hesitated. He knew his soldiers could not fight at such a pace for long, weak as they were. Yet the Gauls seemed intent on a direct assault, throwing their lives away on Roman iron.

The vast bulk of the horsemen had not even been able to reach the Roman lines through their own people and Julius feared that if he sent the legions out, they would be engulfed. His face hardened as he made the decision.

'Octavian. Take the extraordinarii against them. My Tenth and Third will be behind you, just as we were against the Britons.'

Their eyes met for an instant and Octavian saluted.

Ropes were attached to the gates to pull them inwards, once the great iron bars had been removed. The wood was burning well by then and when the gates fell the rush of air made the flames leap. The extraordinarii galloped through the fire to smash the enemy, their hooves clattering on the gates as they passed over. They vanished into the smoke and the Tenth and Third poured out after them.

Julius saw teams beat out the flames and heave the gates back into position before the Gauls could take advantage of the breach. It was a dangerous time. If the extraordinarii could not force the Gauls back, those legions ready to charge out and support them would not be able to move. Julius squinted through the smoke, following a legion eagle as it pounded through the boiling mass of tribesmen. He saw it fall and be dragged up by an unknown soldier. The Twelfth Ariminum were ready to go out, and Julius did not know what they would find.

He glanced up at the forts of Alesia and the men he had permanently watching for them to attempt an attack. How many could he leave as the reserve? If Vercingetorix broke out, Julius was sure his legions would falter at last, hammered on two sides. It must not be allowed to happen.

Renius caught his eye as the distinctive figure hovered near him with a shield ready to hold over Julius' head. Julius smiled briefly, allowing him to stay. The gladiator looked pale and old, but his eyes scanned the field ceaselessly to protect his general.

Julius saw a clear space appear on the bloody ground, covered in feebly moving bodies and the dead. Some of them were Roman, but the vast majority were the speared and crushed enemy. A huge arc was opening in the press as the Tenth heaved them back and walked over flesh with a barrier of their shields. Julius saw the last spear throws disappear into the Gauls and he judged it was time.

'Twelfth and Eighth in support!' he called. 'Bring down the gates!' Once more the ropes were yanked taut and ten thousand more rushed out to replenish those who had gone before.

The war engines were silent then, as the legions carved their way through the Gauls. The tight squares were engulfed and lost to view, then appeared like stones in a flood, still surviving, still solid as they disappeared again.

With four legions in the field, Julius sent one more to follow them, keeping barely enough men to hold the walls and watch the forts at their backs. The cornicens stood waiting at Julius' shoulder and he glanced at them, his eyes hard.

'On my word, sound the recall.'

He gripped the edge of his cloak with his free hand and twisted it. It was hard to see what was going on, but he heard Roman voices shout orders and all along the walls the Gauls were falling back to meet the threat that had come out to take them on. Julius made himself wait.

'Now blow the horns. Quickly!' he snapped at last, looking out onto the battlefield as the long notes wailed over it. The legions had gone far and fought on all sides, but they would not allow a rout, he knew. The squares would retreat step by ordered step against the horsemen, killing all the time.

The Gauls moved like bitter liquid in swirls of screaming, dying men as the legions fought their way back. Julius shouted wildly as he saw the eagles appear once more. He raised his arm and it trembled. The gates came down and he saw the legions stream in and rush back to the walls to shout defiance at the enemy.

The Gauls surged forward and Julius looked to the teams of ballistae men, waiting with desperate impatience. The whole of the Gaulish army was rushing in then and the moment was perfect, but he dared not order them to fire without knowing his legions were safely back.

He barely saw the launch of spears, but Renius did. As Julius turned away, Renius threw up the shield and held it against the numbing impact of the whining heads. He grunted and Julius turned to acknowledge the act, his face going slack as he saw the bloody ruin of Renius' neck.

'Clear! All clear, sir!' his cornicen shouted.

Julius could only stare as Renius fell.

'Sir, we must fire now!' the cornicen said.

Barely hearing him, Julius dropped his arm and the great ballistae crashed their response. Tons of stone and iron sliced through the horsemen of Gaul once more, cutting great swathes of empty space on the field. The tribes were too closely packed to avoid the barrage and thousands were mown down, never to rise again.

A powerful silence swelled as the tribes pulled back out of range. Dimly Julius heard his men cheering as they saw the numbers of dead left behind on the field. He went to Renius' side and closed the staring eyes with his fingers. He had no more grief left in him. To his horror, his hands began to shake and he tasted metal in his mouth.

Octavian trotted through the legionaries to look up to where Julius knelt, chilled in sweat.

'One more, sir? We're ready.'

Julius looked dazed. He could not have a fit in front of them all, he could not. He struggled to deny what was happening. The fits had been quiet in him for years. He would not *allow* it. With a wrench of will, he stood swaying, forcing himself to focus. He pulled off his helmet and tried to breathe deeply, but the ache in his skull built and bright lights flashed. Octavian winced as he saw the glazed eyes.

508

'The legions still stand, General. They are ready to take the battle to them once more, if you wish it.'

Julius opened his mouth to speak, but could not. He crumpled to the ground and Octavian leapt from his saddle, scrambling up to hold him. He barely noticed the body of Renius at his side and shouted to the cornicen to fetch Brutus.

Brutus came at a scrambling run, paling as he understood.

'Get him out of sight, quickly,' he snapped to Octavian. 'The command tent is empty. Take his legs before the men see.' They lifted the twitching figure that had been lightened by the months of starvation and war, dragging him into the shadowed interior of the command post.

'What are we going to do?' Octavian said.

Brutus pulled the metal helmet from Julius' rigid fingers and lifted it.

'Strip him. Too many men saw us take him in. They must see him come out.'

The men cheered as Brutus strode into the weak sun, wearing the full helmet and armour of his friend. Behind him, Julius lay naked on a bench, with Octavian holding a rope of twisted tunic between his teeth as he writhed and shuddered.

Brutus ran to the wall to assess the state of the enemy and saw they were still reeling from the second smashing attack of the ballistae. In the darkness of the tent, it had seemed longer. He saw the legions look to him, waiting for orders and knew a moment of the purest panic. He had not been alone in command since setting foot in Gaul. Julius had always been there.

Behind the mask, Brutus looked out desperately. He could think of no stratagem but the simplest of all. Open the gates and kill everything that moved. Julius would not have done it, but Brutus could not watch from the wall as his men went out.

'Fetch me a horse!' he bellowed. 'Leave no reserve. We are going out to them.'

As the gates reopened, Brutus rode through, leading the legions. It was the only way he knew.

As the Gauls saw the full force of legions coming onto the field, they milled in chaotic fear, wary of being drawn in again to be crushed by the war engines. Their lines were in disarray without the leaders who had been killed in the first attacks.

Brutus saw many of the lesser tribes simply dig in their heels and ride from the battlefield.

'Better that you run!' he shouted wildly.

Around him, the extraordinarii forced their mounts into a gallop, their bloody weapons ready. The legions roared as they accelerated across the plain and when they crashed into the first lines, there was nothing to hold them.

CHAPTER FORTY-FOUR

∽∽∽∽∽

By nightfall, those Gauls who survived had left the field of battle, streaming back to their homes and tribal lands to carry news of the defeat. The Roman legions spent most of the night on the plain, stripping corpses and rounding up the best of the horses for their own use. In the darkness, the Romans separated into cohorts that roamed for miles around Alesia, killing wounded and collecting armour and swords from the dead. As another dawn approached, they returned to the main fortifications and turned their baleful gazes on the silent forts.

Julius had not surfaced from tortured dreams before sunset. The violence of the fit had racked his wasted body and when it left him, he sank into a sleep that was close to death. Octavian waited with him in the tent, washing his flesh with a cloth and water.

When Brutus came back, spattered with blood and filth, he stood looking down on the pale figure for a long time. There were many scars on the skin and without the trappings of rank, there was something vulnerable about the wasted figure that lay there.

Brutus knelt at his side and removed the helmet.

'I have been your sword, my friend,' he whispered.

With infinite tenderness, he and Octavian exchanged the battered armour and clothing until, once again, Julius was covered. He did not wake, though when they lifted him, his eyes opened glassily for a moment.

When they stood back, the figure on the bench was the Roman general they knew. The skin was bruised and the hair was ragged until Octavian oiled it and tied it.

'Will he come back?' Octavian murmured.

'In his own time, he will,' Brutus replied. 'Let's leave him alone now.' He watched the faint rise and fall of Julius' chest and was satisfied.

'I'll stand guard. There will be some who want to see him,' Octavian said.

Brutus looked at him and shook his head.

'No, lad. You go and see to your men. That honour is mine.'

Octavian left him as he took position outside the tent, a still figure in the darkness.

Brutus had not sent the demand for surrender to Vercingetorix. Even in the armour and helmet, he knew Adàn would not be fooled for a moment and that honour belonged to Julius. As the moon rose, Brutus remained on guard at the tent, sending away those who came to congratulate. After the first few, the word spread and he was left alone.

In the privacy of the silent dark, Brutus wept for Renius. He had seen the body and ignored it while he and Octavian were heaving Julius' body into the tent. It was almost as if some part of him had recorded every detail of the scene to be recalled when the battle was over. Though he had only glanced at the old gladiator, he could see his cold corpse as if it was daylight when he shut his eyes.

It did not seem possible that Renius could not be alive. The man had been the closest thing Brutus had had to a father in his life and not to have him there brought a pain that forced tears out of him.

'You rest now, you old bastard,' he muttered, smiling and weeping at the same time. To live for so long only to die from a spear was obscene, though Brutus knew Renius would have accepted that as he accepted every other trial in his life. Octavian had told him how he had held the shield for Julius and Brutus knew the old gladiator would consider it a fair price.

A noise from the tent told him Julius had woken at last before the tent flap was thrown back.

'Brutus?' Julius asked, squinting into the darkness.

'I am here,' Brutus replied. 'I took your helmet and led them out. They thought I was you.'

He felt Julius' hand on his shoulder and fresh tears wound down the dirt of his face.

'Did we beat them?' Julius asked.

'We broke their back. The men are waiting for you to demand a surrender from their king. It's the last thing to do and then we're finished.'

'Renius fell at the last. He held a shield over me,' Julius said.

'I know, I saw him.' Neither man needed to say more. They had both known him when they were little more than boys and some griefs are cheapened by words.

'You led them?' Julius said. Though his voice was strengthening, he still seemed confused.

'No, Julius. They followed you.'

At dawn, Julius sent a messenger up to Vercingetorix and waited for the response he knew must come. Every man and

513

woman in Alesia would have heard of the slaughter of Avaricum. They would be terrified of the grim soldiers who stared up at the fortress. Julius had offered to spare them all if Vercingetorix surrendered by noon, but as the sun rose, there was no response.

Mark Antony and Octavian were with him. There was nothing to do but wait and, one by one, those who had been there from the beginning came to stand at his side. The missing faces hardly seemed worth the price, at times. Bericus, Cabera, Renius, too many more. Julius drank the wine he was offered without tasting it and wondered if Vercingetorix would fight to the bitter end.

The legions were never silent when the killing was done. Each man had his particular friends to boast with and, in truth, there were many stories of bravery. Many more could not answer their names at the dawn muster and the pale bodies that were brought in were testimony to the struggle they had fought together. Julius heard a cry of agony as a soldier recognised one of the corpses and knelt, weeping until others in his century took him away to get him drunk.

Renius' death had hurt them all. The men who had fought with the old gladiator had bound his neck in cloth torn from a tunic and laid him out with his sword. From Julius to the lowest-ranking legionary, they had suffered through bouts of his temper and training, but now that he had gone, the men came in silent grief to touch his hand and pray for his soul.

With his dead laid out in the cold sun, Julius looked up at the walls of Alesia and thought through ways of burning them out of their stronghold. He could not just sit idle with Gaul in his hands at last.

There could be no more rebellions. Over the days to come, the word of the defeat would be taken to every tiny village and town across the vast country.

'Here he comes,' Mark Antony said, interrupting Julius' thoughts.

They all stood as one, straining to see the king as he descended the steep path to where the legions waited. He was a lonely figure.

Vercingetorix had changed from the angry young warrior Julius remembered so long before. He rode a grey horse and wore full armour that gleamed in the first light. Julius was suddenly aware of his own grime and reached to detach his cloak, then let his hand fall. He owed the king no special honour.

Cingeto's blond hair was bound and plaited in heavy cords to his shoulders. His beard was full and shone with oil, covering the gold links he wore at his throat. He rode easily, carrying an ornate shield and a great sword that rested on his thigh. The legions waited in silence for this man who had caused them so much grief and pain. Something about his stately descent kept them quiet, allowing him this last moment of dignity.

Julius walked to meet the king with Brutus and Mark Antony at his sides. As he strode to the foot of the road, the rest of his generals fell in behind and still no one spoke.

Vercingetorix looked down at the Roman and was staggered at the differences since their first meeting, almost a decade before. His youth had been left on the fields of Gaul and only the cold, dark eyes looked the same. With a last glance up at the forts of Alesia, Vercingetorix dismounted and lifted his shield and sword in his arms. He dropped them at Julius' feet and stood back, holding the Roman's eyes for a long moment.

'You will spare the rest?' he asked.

'I gave you my word,' Julius replied.

Vercingetorix nodded, his last worry vanishing. Then he knelt in the mud and bowed his head.

'Bring chains,' Julius said and the silence was shattered as the legions banged their swords and shields together in a cacophony that drowned out all other sound.

CHAPTER FORTY-FIVE

❧❧❧❧❧

As winter came again, Julius took four of his legions across the Alps to base themselves around Ariminum. He brought five hundred chests of gold with him on carts, enough to pay the tithe to the Senate a hundred times over. His men marched with coins in their pouches, and good food and rest had restored much of their polish and strength. Gaul was quiet at last and new roads stretched across the fertile land from one coast to another. Though Vercingetorix had burnt a thousand Roman farms, the land was taken up by new families before the end of summer and still they came, lured by the promise of crops and peace.

A bare three thousand of the Tenth had survived the battles in Gaul and Julius had awarded land and slaves to each man under his command. He had given them gold and roots and he knew they were his, as Marius had once explained to him. They did not fight for Rome, or the Senate. They fought for their general.

He would not hear of a single one of them spending a night out in the open and every house in Ariminum was suddenly home to two or three of the soldiers, packing the town with life and coins. Prices went up almost overnight and by the end of the first month there, the last of the wine ran dry, right across the port city.

Brutus had come with the Third Gallica and set about drinking himself to oblivion as soon as he was free and alone in the city. Losing Renius had hit him hard and Julius heard continual reports of his friend involved in a different brawl each night. Julius listened to the innkeepers who brought their complaints and paid their bills without a murmur of protest. In the end, he sent Regulus to prevent Brutus killing someone in a drunken rage and then heard reports of the two of them roaring around the town together, causing even more damage than Brutus alone.

For the first time since Spain, Julius did not know what the next year would hold for him. A million men had died in Gaul to serve his ambition and another million had been sold to Roman quarries and farms, from Africa to Greece. He had more gold than he had ever seen and he had crossed the sea to beat the Britons. He had expected to feel joy in his triumph. He had equalled Alexander and found a new world beyond the maps. He had taken more land in a decade than Rome had managed in a century. When he was a boy, if he could have seen Vercingetorix kneel, he would have gloried in it, seeing only the achievement. But he would not have known how much he would miss the dead. He had dreamed of statues and his name being spoken in the Senate. Now that those things were real, he scorned them. Even victory was empty because it meant the struggle was at an end. There were too many regrets.

Julius had taken Crassus' house in the centre of the city and at night he thought he could still smell the perfume Servilia wore. He did not send for her to come to him, though he was lonely. Somehow the thought that she would break him out of his depression was too much to bear. He cherished the dark days of winter as reflections of himself and embraced the black moods as old friends. He did not want to pick up the reins of his life and go on. In the privacy of Crassus' home, he could waste the days in idleness, spending afternoons watching the dark skies and writing his books.

The reports he had written for the city of his birth had become something more for him. Each memory was somehow constrained as he wrote it down. The ink could not express the fear and pain and despair and that was right. It eased his mind to write each part of the years in Gaul and then put it aside for Adàn to copy out.

Mark Antony joined him at the house at the end of the first week. He set to work removing dustsheets from the furniture and making sure Julius ate at least one good meal a day. Julius tolerated the attention with reasonably good grace. Ciro and Octavian came to the house a few days later and the Romans set to work making it as clean as a legion galley. They cleaned out the clutter of papers in the main rooms and brought a bustle to the house that Julius found harder and harder to dislike. Though he had enjoyed the isolation at first, he was used to having his officers around him and only raised his eyes in mock indignation when Domitius turned up to take a room and the following night Regulus brought Brutus in over his shoulder. Lamps were lit all around the house and when Julius went down to the kitchens, he found three local women hard at work there making bread. Julius accepted their presence without a word.

The wine shipments from Gaul arrived by ship and were seized upon thirstily by the citizens. Mark Antony secured a private barrel and in a night where they managed to forget the barriers of rank, they drank themselves unconscious to finish

518

it in one session, lying where they fell. In the morning, Julius laughed aloud for the first time in weeks as his friends staggered about and crashed, swearing, into the furniture.

With the passes closed, Gaul was as distant as the moon and ceased to trouble his dreams. Julius' thoughts turned to Rome and he wrote letters to everyone he knew in the city. It was strange to think of those he had not seen for years. Servilia would be there and the new senate house must have been completed. Rome would have a fresh face to cover her scars.

In the mornings, with his study door closed to the rest, Julius wrote to his daughter at length, trying to make a bridge to a woman he did not know. He had given permission for her to marry in his absence two years before, but he had heard nothing since. Whether she read them or not, it was balm to his conscience to do it and Brutus had urged him to try.

It was tempting to gather a few horses and go back to the city, but Julius was wary of the changes that could have occurred in his absence. Without consular immunity, he would be vulnerable to his enemies there. Even if the Senate had left him the rank of tribune, it would not save him from the charges of killing Ariovistus or exceeding his orders over the Rhine. Julius was owed more than one Triumph by the Senate, but he doubted Pompey would be pleased to see him lauded by the citizens. Marrying Julius' daughter should have been a rein on his temper, but Julius knew him too well to trust his goodwill, or his ambition.

The winter passed in slow comfort. They rarely talked of the battles they had fought, though when Brutus was drunk, he would arrange bread rolls on the table and demonstrate to Ciro what the Helvetii should have done.

When the winter solstice came, the legions celebrated with the city, lighting lamps on every house so that the promise of spring could be seen in the streets. Ariminum shone like a jewel in the darkness and the whorehouses ran double shifts all night. From that point on, the atmosphere changed subtly. With the longest night over, the reports of damage and brawls came with greater frequency to Julius' desk, until he was half tempted to send the lot of them out to the plains to camp in the barren fields. Slowly, he began to spend more and more of each day on the business of supply and pay, falling back into the routines that had sustained him all his adult life.

He missed Renius and Cabera more than he could believe. It had come as a surprise for Julius to realise that he was the oldest of the men who shared Crassus' house with him. Where the others seemed to expect him to provide order in their lives, he had no one, and the habits of war were too strong to lightly lay aside. Though he had known some of the men in the house for years, he was the commanding officer and there was always a slight reserve in their manner around him. At times, Julius found the busy house strangely lonely, but the coming of spring went some way to complete the restoration of his goodwill. He took to riding around the outskirts of the city with Brutus and Octavian, building up their fitness. Ciro watched him closely whenever they were together, smiling as touches of the old Julius were visible, however briefly. Time healed what did not show and though there were dark days still, all the men felt the rise of spring in their blood.

The bundle of letters that came on a bright dawn looked like any other. Julius paid the carrier and shuffled them into piles. He recognised Servilia's handwriting on one for her son and was pleased to find another for himself towards the bottom. His mood was one of pleasant anticipation as he took his letter into the front room of the house and lit a fire, shivering as he broke the seal and opened it.

As Julius read, he rose from his seat and stood in the full glare of the rising sun. He read the letter from Servilia three times before he began to believe it and then he sank back, letting the letter fall.

The merchant prince had fallen.

Crassus and his son had not survived the attacks of the Parthians in Syria. Most of the legion Julius had trained had fought clear, but Crassus had led a wild charge when he saw his son unhorsed and the enemy had cut him off from the rest of his men. The legionaries recovered their bodies and Pompey had declared a day of mourning for the old man.

Julius sat and stared out at the sun until the glare was too much for him and his eyes stung. All the old names were gone now and, for all his faults, Crassus had been a friend to him through the darkest days. Julius could read Servilia's own grief in the neat lines as she described the tragedy, but Julius could not think of her. He rose and began to pace the room.

As well as the personal feelings of loss, Julius was forced to consider how Crassus' dying would change the balance of power in Rome. He did not like the conclusions he drew. Pompey would suffer least. As Dictator, he was above the law and the triumvirate and would miss only Crassus' wealth. Julius wondered who would inherit the old man's fortune now that Publius was dead with him, but it hardly mattered. Far more important was the fact that Pompey no longer needed to have a successful general in the field. He might well view such a man as a threat.

As Julius thought through the implications, his expression became bleak. If Crassus had lived, some new compromise could have been hammered out between them, but that hope had died in Parthia. After all, Julius knew if he had found himself in Pompey's position, he would have been quick to clear the field of anyone who could be a danger. As Crassus had once told him, politics was a bloody business.

With a sudden dart, he stepped over to the table and opened the rest of the letters, looking only at the first lines of each

521

until he froze, and took a deep breath. Pompey had written to him and Julius felt fury surge as he read the pompous orders. There was not even a mention of Crassus in the lines and Julius threw the letter down in disgust as he began to pace once again. Though he knew he should have expected no more from the Dictator, it was still a shock to read his future in the lines.

The door to the room slammed open and Brutus entered, holding his own sheaf of letters.

'Have you heard?' Brutus said.

Julius nodded, plans forming in his mind.

'Send men out to collect the legions, Brutus. They've grown fat and slow over the winter and I want them out of the city by noon tomorrow to begin manoeuvres.'

Brutus gaped at him.

'Are we heading back to Gaul, then? What about Crassus? I don't think . . .'

'Did you hear me?' Julius roared at him. 'Half our men are near useless with their whores and wine. Tell Mark Antony we are leaving. Have him start at the docks and round them up.'

Brutus stood very still. Questions came to his lips and he throttled them, his discipline forcing a salute. He left and Julius could hear his voice rousing the others in the house.

Julius thought again of the letter from Pompey and the betrayal. No sign of the years they had known each other had been present in the words. It was a formal order to return to Rome – alone. To return to the one man in the world who might fear him enough to kill him.

Julius felt light-headed and weak as he considered the implications. Pompey had no rivals except one and Julius didn't trust his promise of safe passage for a moment. Yet to disobey would launch a fight to the death that could very well destroy the city and everything Rome had won over centuries.

He shook his head to clear it. The city was stifling him and he longed for the breezes of the plains. There he could think and plan his answer. He would gather the men on the banks of the Rubicon river and pray for the wisdom to make the right choice.

Regulus stood alone in the little courtyard of Crassus' home, looking at the letter in his hands. An unknown hand had written the words on the parchment, but there could only have been one author. Just two words sat like spiders in the centre of the blank page and yet he read them over and over, his face tight and hard.

Take him, it said.

Regulus remembered how he and Pompey had spoken the last time they had been in Ariminum. He had not wavered then, but that was before he had been to Britain with Julius and seen him fight at Avaricum, Gergovia, Alesia. The last most of all. Regulus had seen Julius lead legions past the point when any other would have fallen and been destroyed. He had known then that he followed a greater man than Pompey and now he held an order to kill the general.

It would be easy, he knew. Julius trusted him completely after so many years together and Regulus thought there was friendship there between them. Julius would let him come close and then it would be just another life to add to those Regulus had taken for Rome. Just one more order to obey as he had obeyed so many thousands before.

The dawn breeze chilled the skin of the centurion as he tore the letter into halves, then quarters, not stopping until the shreds lifted in the wind and flew. It was the first order he had ever disobeyed and it brought him peace.

CHAPTER FORTY-SIX

Pompey leaned against the columns of the temple to Jupiter and looked over the moonlit city below the Capitol. Dictator. He shook his head and smiled in the darkness at the thought.

The city was quiet and already it was hard to imagine the gangs and rioting that had once seemed like the end of the world. Pompey looked over to the new senate house and remembered the flames and screams in the night. In a few years, Clodius and Milo would be all but forgotten in the city, but Rome went on and she was his alone.

The Senate had extended his Dictatorship without the slightest pressure from him. They would do it again, he was sure, for as long as he wanted. They had seen the need for a strong hand to cut through all the laws with which they had bound themselves. Sometimes it was necessary, just to make the city work.

Part of Pompey wished Crassus had lived to see what he had made out of the chaos. The strength of grief Pompey had felt when he heard of his death had surprised him. They had known each other for the best part of thirty years, through war and peace, and Pompey missed the old man's company. He supposed it was possible to grow used to anything.

He had seen so many fall in his life. There were times when he could not believe that he was the one to have survived the turbulent years, where men like Marius and Sulla, Cato and Crassus had all gone over the river. Yet he was still there and there was more than one race in life. Sometimes, the only way to triumph was to survive while others died. That too could be a skill.

A feather of breeze made Pompey shiver and consider going back to his home to rest. His thoughts turned to Julius then and the letters he had sent north. Would Regulus take the decision out of his hands? Pompey wished it could be so. The part of him that held his honour felt ashamed at what he had ordered and still contemplated. He thought of Julius' daughter, heavy with new life inside her. She had a hard edge that had brought her through the pressure of being wife to the most powerful man in Rome. Still, he could not share his plans with one of Caesar's blood. She had done her duty well and fulfilled an old agreement he had made with her father. There was nothing more he needed from her.

There could be no sharing of power, now that he understood it. Julius would either be killed in the north, or he would obey his orders and the result would be the same.

Pompey sighed at the thought and shook his head with genuine regret. Caesar could not be allowed to live, or one day he would come into the Senate and the years of blood would begin again.

'I will not allow it,' Pompey whispered into the breeze and there was no one to hear him.

*   *   *

525

Julius sat on the banks of the Rubicon and looked south. He wished Cabera or Renius were there to advise him, but the decision was his alone in the end, as so many others before it. His legions stretched away into the night around him and he could hear the sentries walk their routes in the darkness, calling out the passwords that meant routine and safety.

The moon was bright under a clear spring sky and Julius smiled as he looked over the men who sat with him. Ciro was there at his shoulder and Brutus and Mark Antony sat on the other side, looking over the bright thread of the river. Octavian stood nearby with Regulus, and Domitius lay on his back and looked up at the stars. It was easy to imagine Renius there and Cabera with him. Somehow, in imagination, they were the men he remembered, before illness and injury had taken them. Publius Crassus and his father had gone, and Bericus, too. His own father and Tubruk; Cornelia. Death had followed them all and brought them down one by one.

'If I take the legions south, it will be civil war,' Julius said softly. 'My poor battered city will see more blood. How many would die this year, for me?'

They were silent for a long time and Julius knew they could barely imagine the crime of attacking their own city. He hardly dared to give voice to it himself. Sulla had done it and was despised in memory. There was no way back for any of them after such an act.

'You said Pompey promised safe passage,' Mark Antony said at last.

Brutus snorted. 'Our Dictator has no honour, Julius. Remember that. He had Salomin beaten half to death in the tournament and where was honour then? He isn't fit to walk where Marius walked. If you go alone, he will never let you leave. He'll have you under the knife as soon as you step through the gates. You know it as well as any of us.'

'What choice do you have, though?' Mark Antony said. 'A

civil war against our own people? Would the men even follow us?'

'Yes,' Ciro's bass growl sounded out of the darkness. 'We would.'

None of them knew how to respond to the big man and a strained silence fell. They could all hear the river whisper over the stones and the voices of their men around them. Dawn was near and Julius was no closer to knowing what he would do.

'I have been at war for as long as I can remember,' Julius said softly. 'Sometimes I ask myself what it has been for if I stop here. What did I waste the lives of my friends for if I go meekly to my death?'

'It may not *be* death!' Mark Antony said. 'You say you know the man, but he promised . . .'

'No,' Regulus interrupted. He took a step closer to Julius as Mark Antony looked up at him. 'No, Pompey will not let you live. I know.'

Julius saw the strained features of the centurion in the moonlight and he rose to his feet.

'How?' he asked.

'Because I was his man and you were not meant to leave Ariminum. I had his order to kill you.'

All of them came to their feet and Brutus put himself solidly between Regulus and Julius.

'You *bastard*. What are you talking about?' Brutus demanded, his hand resting on his sword hilt.

Regulus didn't look at him, instead holding Julius' gaze.

'I could not obey the order,' he said.

Julius nodded. 'There are some that should not be obeyed, my friend. I'm glad you realised that. Sit down, Brutus. If he was going to kill me, do you think he would have told us all first? Sit down!'

Reluctantly, they settled back onto the grass, though Brutus glared at Regulus, still unsure of him.

'Pompey has only one legion guarding Rome,' Domitius said speculatively. Julius glanced at him and Domitius shrugged. 'I mean, it could be done if we moved too quickly for him to reinforce. We could be at the walls in a week if we pushed the pace. With four veteran legions against him, he couldn't hold the city for even a day.'

Mark Antony looked appalled at this and Domitius chuckled as he saw his expression. There was already more light as dawn approached and they looked at each other guardedly as Domitius continued, raising his hands.

'It could be done, that's all. One gamble for the whole pot. One throw for Rome.'

'You think you could kill legionaries?' Julius asked him.

Domitius rubbed his face and looked away.

'I'm saying it might not come to that. Our soldiers have been hardened in Gaul and we know what they can do. I don't think Pompey has anything to match us.'

Brutus looked at the man he had followed from childhood. He had swallowed more bitterness in their years than he would ever have believed and as they sat together, he did not know if Julius even understood what he had been given. His pride, his honour, his youth. Everything. He knew Julius better than any of them and he saw the glitter in his friend's eyes as he contemplated another war. How many of them would survive his ambition, he wondered. The others looked so trusting, it made Brutus want to close his eyes rather than be sickened. Yet despite it all, he knew Julius could bring him with a word.

Domitius cleared his throat.

'It's your choice, Julius. If you want us to go back to Gaul and lose ourselves, I'm with you. The gods know we'd never be found in some of the places we've seen. But if you want to go to Rome and risk it all one last time, I'm still with you.'

'One last throw?' Julius said and he made it a question for all of them.

One by one, they nodded, until only Brutus remained. Julius raised his eyebrows and smiled gently.

'I can't do it without you, Brutus. You know that.'

'One last throw, then,' Brutus whispered, before looking away.

As the sun rose, the veteran legions of Gaul crossed the Rubicon and marched on Rome.

HISTORICAL NOTE

⟋⟍⟋⟍⟋⟍

As with the previous two books, I think an explanatory note can be useful, especially when the history is sometimes more surprising than the fiction.

I have mentioned Alexander the Great throughout the book as a hero for Julius. Certainly the Greek king's life would have been well known to all educated Romans, complementing their interest in that culture. Though the setting was Cadiz rather than a deserted Spanish village, the first century biographer Suetonius provides the detail of Caesar sighing in frustration at the foot of Alexander's statue. At the age of thirty-one, Julius had achieved nothing in comparison. He could not have known that his greatest victories would come after that point.

Apart from his wives, Julius is reported as having had a number of prominent mistresses, though Suetonius said Servilia was the one he loved most of all. Julius did buy her a pearl valued at one and a half million denarii. Perhaps one of the reasons he invaded Britain may have been to find more of them.

He was quaestor in Spain before he returned as praetor, which I have not gone into for reasons of pace. He was a busier man than any writer can hope to cover and even a condensed version fills these books to bursting point.

He did stage a gladiatorial combat in solid silver armour and ran huge debts pursuing public fame. It is true that at one point he had to physically leave the city to avoid his creditors. He became consul with Bibilus and chased his colleague out of the forum after a disagreement. In Bibilus' absence, it became something of a joke in Rome to say a document was signed by Julius and Caesar.

As a minor point, the Falernian wine Julius poured into his family tomb was so expensive that a cup of it cost a week's salary for a legionary. Unfortunately, the grapes grew on Mount Vesuvius, by Pompeii and in AD 79, the taste was lost forever.

The Catiline conspiracy was as important in its day as the Gunpowder Plot in England. The conspiracy was betrayed when one of them confided in a mistress who reported what she had heard. Julius was named, probably falsely, as one of the conspirators, as was Crassus. Both men survived the upheaval without stains on their characters. Catiline left the city to take command of the rebel army while his friends were to help create chaos and rioting in the city. Part of the evidence against them showed that a Gallic tribe had been approached for warriors. After a heated debate as to their fate, the lesser conspirators were ritually strangled. Catiline was killed in the field.

The conquests of Gaul and Britain comprise most of the second part of this book. I have followed the main events that began with the migration of the Helvetii and the defeat of Ariovistus. It is worth mentioning that Julius Caesar himself is sometimes the only extant source for the details of this campaign, but he records mistakes and disasters as faithfully as his victories. For example, he tells quite candidly how a mistaken report made him retreat from his own men, believing them to be the enemy. In his commentaries, he puts the number of the Helvetii and allied tribes as 386,000. Only 110,000 were sent home. Against them, he had six legions and auxiliaries – 35,000 at most.

His battles were rarely a simple test of strength. He formed alliances with lesser tribes and then came to their aid. He fought by night if necessary, on all terrains, flanking, bribing and outmanoeuvring his enemies. When Ariovistus demanded only cavalry at their meeting, Julius ordered the foot soldiers of the Tenth to mount, which must have been a sight to see.

I did worry that the sheer distances he covered must have been exaggerated until my cousin took part in a sixty-mile trek. She and her husband completed it in twenty-four hours, but soldiers from a Ghurka regiment completed it in nine hours, fifty seven minutes. Two and a third marathons, non-stop. One must be careful in this modern age where pensioners seem able to ski down Everest, but I think the legions of Gaul could have matched that pace, and like the Ghurkas, have been able to fight at the end.

It was not such a great stretch to suppose that Adàn might have understood the language of the Gauls, or even the dialect of the Britons, to some extent. The original Celts came across Europe from an unknown place of origin – possibly the Caucasus mountains. They settled Spain, France, Britain and Germany. England only became predominantly Romano-Saxon much later and of course maintains much of that difference into modern times.

It is difficult to imagine Julius' view of the world. He was a prolific reader and would have known Strabo's works. He knew Alexander had travelled east and Gaul was a great deal closer.

He would have heard of Britain from the Greeks, after Pytheas travelled there three centuries before: perhaps the world's first genuine tourist. While we have lost Pytheas' books, there is no reason why they should not have been available then. Julius would have heard of pearls, tin and gold to lure him over from Gaul. Geographically, he thought that Britain was due east of Spain rather than to the north, with Ireland in between. It could even have been a continent as big as Africa, for all he could be sure on that first landing.

His first invasion of Britain in 55 BC was disastrous. Storms smashed his ships and ferocious resistance from blue-skinned tribes and vicious dogs was almost his undoing. The Tenth literally had to fight their way through the surf. He stayed only three weeks and the following year brought eight hundred ships back, this time forcing his way through to the Thames. Despite this vast fleet, he had stretched himself too far and would not return a third time. As far as we know, they never paid the tribute they promised.

Vercingetorix would hold a similar place in history and legend as King Arthur if he had managed to win his great battle against Julius. Napoleon III did erect a statue to him in later times, recognising his achievement and place in history. He united the tribes and saw that scorching the earth and starving the legions was the only way to defeat them. Even his great host was eventually broken by the legions. The High King of Gaul was taken in chains to Rome and executed.

The exact details of the triumvirate with Crassus and Pompey are not known. Certainly the arrangement benefited all three men and Julius' term in Gaul went on for many years after his consular year had ended. Interestingly, when Pompey sent the order for him to return alone after Gaul, Julius had very nearly completed the ten-year hiatus the law demanded between seeking a consul's post. If Julius had secured a second term at that point, he would have been untouchable, which Pompey must have feared.

Clodius and Milo are not fictional characters. Both men were part of the chaos that almost destroyed Rome while Julius was in Gaul. Street gangs, riots and murder became all too common and when Clodius was finally killed, his supporters did indeed cremate him in the senate house, burning it to the ground in the process. Pompey was elected sole consul with a mandate to establish order in the city. Even then, the triumvirate agreement might have held if Crassus had not been killed fighting the Parthians with his son. With the news of that death, there was only one man in the world who could have challenged Pompey for power.

Finally, I have made one or two claims in the book that may annoy historians. It is debatable whether the Romans had steel or not, though it is possible to give a harder sheath to soft iron by beating it in charcoal. Steel, after all, is only iron with a fractionally higher carbon content. I do not think this was beyond them.

I did worry that having Artorath, a Gaul, described as close to seven feet tall would be too much for some, but Sir Bevil Grenville (1596-1643) had a bodyguard named Anthony Payne who was seven feet, four inches tall. I dare say he could have put Artorath over his shoulder.

There are hundreds more little facts that I could put in here, if there were space. If I have changed history in the book, I hope it has been deliberate rather than simple error. I have certainly tried to be as accurate as I could be. For those who would like to go further than these few pages, I can recommend *Caesar's Legion* by Stephen Dando-Collins which was fascinating, and also *The Complete Roman Army* by Adrian Goldsworthy, or anything else by that author. *The Twelve Caesars* by Suetonius should be required reading in every school. My version is the translation by Robert Graves and apparently which one of the Emperors you like the most is quite revealing about your own character. Lastly, for those who want more of Julius, you could not do better than to read Christian Meier's book *Caesar*.

Conn Iggulden